"I'll give the canine t **There was determin**

"And I'll speak to Flora and Margaret and see if they can work something out so you won't have to work with one particular dog."

Cass gave him an earnest look. "I'll do what I can to make that work. I really do appreciate you letting me cry on your shoulder."

To his astonishment, Cass placed a hand on his shoulder and gave him a quick kiss on the cheek.

Pleasure zipped through him. When he saw Cass's shocked face seconds later with its charming pink cheeks, he was mesmerized. This tough woman appeared flustered. She shook slightly and he feared she might fall. Lyle reached for her.

Cass stood close enough that he could smell the fresh scent of her hair.

"I'm sorry," Cass murmured.

Lyle lowered his head to hear her words, bringing his lips closer to hers. He watched them, the soft full pads that looked so delicious.

"That was inappropriate. I shouldn't have done that." Cass glanced at him then away.

"I'm not," he said quietly. "I rather liked it."

The Holiday Rescue

Susan Carlisle & Annie O'Neil

Previously published as *Highland Doc's Christmas Rescue*
and *Making Christmas Special Again*

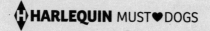

HARLEQUIN MUST❤DOGS

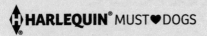 **HARLEQUIN**® MUST♥DOGS

Recycling programs
for this product may
not exist in your area.

ISBN-13: 978-1-335-23082-9

The Holiday Rescue

Copyright © 2020 by Harlequin Books S.A.

Highland Doc's Christmas Rescue
First published in 2019. This edition published in 2020.
Copyright © 2019 by Susan Carlisle

Making Christmas Special Again
First published in 2019. This edition published in 2020.
Copyright © 2019 by Annie O'Neil

This edition published by arrangement with Harlequin Books S.A.

For questions and comments about the quality of this book, please contact us at CustomerService@Harlequin.com.

Harlequin Enterprises ULC
22 Adelaide St. West, 40th Floor
Toronto, Ontario M5H 4E3, Canada
www.Harlequin.com

Printed in U.S.A.

CONTENTS

Susan Carlisle's love affair with books began in the sixth grade, when she made a bad grade in mathematics. Not allowed to watch TV until she'd brought the grade up, Susan filled her time with books. She turned her love of reading into a passion for writing, and now has over ten Harlequin Medical Romance novels published. She writes about hot, sexy docs and the strong women who captivate them. Visit susancarlisle.com.

Books by Susan Carlisle

Harlequin Medical Romance

First Response

Firefighter's Unexpected Fling

Pups that Make Miracles

Highland Doc's Christmas Rescue

Christmas in Manhattan

Christmas with the Best Man

Stolen Kisses with Her Boss
Redeeming the Rebel Doc
The Brooding Surgeon's Baby Bombshell
A Daddy Sent by Santa
Nurse to Forever Mom
The Sheikh Doc's Marriage Bargain

Visit the Author Profile page
at Harlequin.com for more titles.

HIGHLAND DOC'S
CHRISTMAS RESCUE

Susan Carlisle

To Dallas
I'm proud of the man you are,
and your father would be also.

Chapter 1

As the taxi rolled up the rise Cass Bellow looked out the window at the snow-blanketed Heatherglen Castle Clinic in northern Scotland. Why had she been sent here?

More than once she'd questioned her doctor's wisdom in transferring her to this private clinic for physical therapy. Weren't there plenty of other places in warmer climates? Particularly in her native US. Or, better yet, couldn't she have just gone home and handled what needed doing on her own? But, no, her doctor insisted she should be at Heatherglen. Had stated that he sent all his patients with extensive orthopedic injuries there. He declared the place was her best hope for a full recovery. Finally, at her argument, he'd bluntly told her that if she wanted him to sign off on her release she must complete her physical therapy at Heatherglen.

As the car came to a stop at the front door she studied the Norman architecture of the building with its smooth stone walls and slate roof. The place was huge, and breathtaking. There were more chimneys than Cass had a chance to count. This place was nothing like what she'd expected. Though it was early November, festive Christmas wreaths made of greenery and red bows already hung on the outside of the lower floor windows. They further darkened her mood.

When she had been given the search and rescue assignment assisting the military after an explosion in Eastern Europe, she had never dreamed she'd end up in traction in an army hospital on a base in Germany. Her shattered arm and leg had finally mended, but she needed physical therapy to regain complete use of them. Now she'd been sent to this far-flung, snowy place to do just that. All she really wanted was to be left alone.

She opened the cab door and wind blasted her. Despite the heat coming from the still running car, she shuddered. As Cass stepped out, one of the large wooden castle doors, decked with a huge Christmas wreath full of red berries, opened. A tall man, perhaps in his mid-thirties, with the wide shoulders of an athlete stepped out. With rust-colored hair and wearing a heavy tan cable sweater and dark brown pants, he looked like the epitome of what she thought a Scottish man should be. As he came down the few steps toward her, he smiled.

"Hello, you must be Ms. Cassandra Bellow. I'm Dr. Lyle Sinclair, the medical director here at Heatherglen. You may call me Lyle."

His thick Scottish brogue confirmed her earlier thoughts. Yet she was surprised by the way the sunny cheerfulness of his voice curled around her name, nudging at her icy emotions. Irritated, she pushed that odd notion away. This doctor was far too happy and personable for her taste. Her goal was to do what must be done with as little interaction with others as possible. She planned on nursing her wounds in private.

"Yes, that's me." To her satisfaction her flat, dry tone dropped the brightness of his smile a notch. If she could just get to her room and collapse she'd be happy. Her right side was burning from the ache in her arm and the agony of putting her full weight on her right leg.

"Flora McNeith, the physiotherapist whose care you'll be under, couldn't be here to greet you and asked that I get you settled in." Concern filled his face. "Do you need a wheelchair? Crutches?"

"No, I can walk on my own. Run, that's another

thing." She pulled at her jacket to stop the biting flow of air down her neck.

A light chuckle rolled out of his throat and over her nerve endings. "I understand. Then let's get inside out of this weather." He looked up at the sky. A snowflake landed on the dark red five o'clock shadow covering his cheek.

Cass averted her eyes and gave the cobblestone drive, cleared of snow, a searching look. It was farther than she wanted to walk, yet she wouldn't let on. The three steps up to the door looked even more daunting.

All she needed was fortitude to make the walk and climb those steps. She had plenty of that. Soft snowflakes continued to drift down as she took a deep breath and steeled herself to put one foot in front of the other. With another silent inhalation, she started toward the entrance. Dr. Sinclair walked beside her.

She managed the first two steps with no mishap but the toe of her short boot caught the edge of the last one. Grabbing at air, Cass finally found the fabric covering Dr. Sinclair's arm. She yelped with the effort to hold on. Being right-handed, she'd instinctively flailed out that arm and immediately regretted it. Pain shot through it, but not as sharp as it had been weeks earlier. She gritted her teeth, thrusting out her other arm to ease the fall.

Instead of tumbling onto the steps, her body

was brought against a hard wall of human torso. The doctor's arm circled her waist and held her steady. Her face smashed into thick yarn. A hint of pine and smoke filled her nose. For some reason it was reassuring.

"Steady on, I've got you." His deep burr was near her ear.

Cass quickly straightened, getting her feet under her even though pain rocked her. She refused to show it, having already embarrassed herself enough. Her lips tightened. "I'm fine. Thank you."

Glancing at him, she got the weirdest impression that the concern in his eyes had nothing to do with her physical injuries, as if he was able to see her true pain. That was a crazy idea. She shook that odd thought off and focused on where she was.

Taking a third fortifying breath, Cass stepped into the massive foyer.

No way was she going to let him see the effort it took to keep walking. She'd lived through much worse. She'd always been self-sufficient. Weakness wasn't in her vocabulary. As a young girl she had learned the power of being emotionally strong.

Still, that brief human contact had been nice.

There were two enormous cement urns filled with pine and berries on either side of the doors. Cass looked further to see the stone arched beams of the ceiling then on to a grand staircase. On the floor beside it lay a pile of pine wood. Here she was in this strange place for the holidays when all she wished for was home. She would get her arm and leg strong again as fast as she could, then return to America to grieve her loss in private.

"Are you sure you're okay?" The doctor stood too close as if he was afraid she might stumble again.

"I'm fine." The words sounded sharp and overly loud in the cavernous entrance hall. If she could just get to her room, she could nurse the excruciating throbbing in her arm and leg. She would be limping by then as well.

"On our way to your room, let me tell you where a few things are. This is Admissions." He waved a hand to indicate a room off the hall. "Louise, my administrative assistant, and I have our offices there. She's out this afternoon as well. You two can sort out the paperwork in the morning. I'm sure you're tired."

Cass was beyond tired. The effort it had taken her to travel from Germany to Fort William then the drive north had worn her out. She hadn't recovered anywhere near as much as she wanted to believe.

"Over here is the dining room." He walked across the hall and stood in a wide doorway.

Cass joined him. Despite her physical distress,

she loved his accent. It was soothing, for some reason.

The room he wanted her to see was long and wide with a dark barrel ceiling sculpted out of wood from which hung large, black iron chandeliers. A fireplace Cass could stand up in filled the wall on the far end with flags arranged overhead. The walls were partially covered in wainscoting. Above that were a few male portraits in impressive frames. A huge table, surrounded by imposing matching chairs, capable of seating at least twenty people, stood in the center of the room. An oriental rug in blue and red lay beneath it. The only thing out of place was a pile of greenery on the floor in one corner and a few boxes stacked beside it.

He must have noticed the direction of her gaze. "Pardon the mess. We're in the process of decorating for Christmas."

Cass pretended he hadn't spoken. Not even the holidays could heal her broken heart.

Dr. Sinclair was saying, "All meals are served here, unless there's a reason the resident is incapable of joining us. We dress for the evening meal. It's at seven."

"Dress? As in diamonds and tux?"

Chuckling, he shook his head. "No. More like no workout clothes allowed. The idea is for the residents to use their skills and have something positive to look forward to. We work on the principle that if you don't use it, you lose it."

She glanced at him. He really was quite handsome in a rugged way. "Like?"

"Fastening a button, passing a bowl or even manipulating a fork." He turned toward the central hall.

"I have no trouble with any of those so why must I attend?" She joined him.

"Because we want our residents to feel like they're part of our family, which they are," he said over his shoulder as he started down the hall.

She had zero interest in being sociable. All she wanted was time to herself to think about what she would do next, where she wanted her life to go. How she could get past the mass of emotions churning inside her. Could she continue working in search and rescue? Work with a new dog? Learn to trust another man?

Maybe she could just make sure she wasn't around when it was dinnertime. This place sounded more like a prison than a clinic. "Hey, do you mind telling me why I was sent here?"

That got his attention. "So you can regain your mobility."

"I know that. I mean why here in particular? Couldn't I have gone to a clinic in America? What makes this place so special?"

He shoved his hands into his pockets. "As I understand it, your orthopedic doctor believes this is the right clinic for you."

She stepped toward him, pinning him with a direct look. "What led him to believe this specific clinic was the right place for me to complete my physical therapy?"

Dr. Sinclair shifted his weight and raised his chin. "I'm not sure what you're looking for but our residents have an uncommonly high success rate of making as complete a recovery as possible, and by recovery I mean holistic recovery. Our state-of-the-art clinic features a peaceful atmosphere conducive to healing…" he waved a hand around, indicating the castle "…and our canine therapy has proved to be fundamental in facilitating that recovery as well. Does that reassure you?"

Canine therapy. Cass took a step back, her chest constricting. She couldn't deal with this right now. It was too soon after the loss of her dog and partner, Rufus. "I'm not interested in canine therapy."

Her German shepherd-wolfhound mix partner had been with her for four years. She'd had him since he was a puppy. She'd even gone to Germany to pick him up from the breeders. They had trained together at a search and rescue school in California. They'd understood each other, trusted one another.

Now he was gone. Despite him being an animal, the hurt of his loss was more acute than the pain of broken bones or her ex-boyfriend's assessment of her ability to maintain a relationship. She and Rufus had been all over the world together, crawling in and over disaster sites that others only saw on TV while drinking their morning coffee. As a team, they had been a part of tragedies that no one should ever see or experience. Gratitude and guilt filled her in equal measure.

She felt the doctor's keen observation and focused on his mild expression. He turned and started down an adjacent hall to the left, saying, "This way to the lift."

Cass glanced at the staircase in relief then followed, taking careful steps to ensure there wasn't a repeat performance of what had almost happened outside.

He looked over his shoulder. "As our residents improve, they use the stairs whenever possible."

Cass once more eyed the daunting set of wide steps made of gray marble. "And that's mandatory?"

Dr. Sinclair gave her a grin. "'Mandatory' is such an unfriendly word. Why don't we go with 'greatly encouraged'? It's part of the graduation program to be able to walk up and down the stairs, but we don't require that until you're ready."

Did her relief show on her face? "What makes you think I'm not ready?"

"Maybe the tight line of your lips that indicates

that little stumble outside hurt more than you wish to admit."

Cass grimaced inwardly. The man had an acute sense of awareness. Could he see that more than her body pained her? That her heart hurt? Cass hoped not. She was nowhere near ready to share her feelings. "I don't hurt."

"Liar." He gave her a flash of a smile. One she was sure made people want to confide in him, which she wasn't going to do. As if he knew what she was thinking, he said in a gentle manner, "You do know it isn't weakness to admit you're in pain or that you need help. That's what we're here for."

She'd had enough of this. All she wanted was to get to her room. "Who're you, the resident shrink?"

They walked out of the elevator and started down a wide hallway lined with portraits. A few decorations were already in place here and there. A red carpet runner muffled their steps.

"No, but as clinic administrator and emergency medical doctor I help develop the patients' therapy. All the doctors here work together to form patient plans. Recovery is as much mental as it is physical."

"So you think I have emotional issues?" Cass certainly did have them. She couldn't keep her job without a dog, and she wasn't sure she could handle having another one. To possibly lose another best friend would be too much, too painful. To get close enough that someone or something mattered was more than she wanted at this point.

Lyle's…wasn't that his name?…mouth quirked as he stopped to face her.

"Why, Ms. Bellow, in some ways I think everyone has issues. So don't go thinking you're special. Here we are." He pushed open a thick wooden door. "Your room belonged to the lady of the castle."

Cass couldn't deny it was a grand room. Its large canopy bed was hung with seafoam green curtains and covered with a matching spread. Beneath a bank of windows was a seating arrangement of a loveseat and two cushioned chairs. A chest, which she guessed held a TV, was nearby and on the opposite wall was a large fireplace with a fire already burning. The gleaming oak floor had a plush rug in the center of it. The festive fairy had been at work decorating in here as well. There was greenery along the mantle and groups of candles on tables. If she must be in this clinic, then she had won the lottery for the perfect room. She could hide out here in comfort.

"One of the staff should've put your luggage in here." He looked around. "There it is. Great." He pointed to the far side of the room where there was another door. "Through there is your bath. You'll find a hot tub, which I encourage you to use often. I'll leave you now to settle in. You don't have to be at dinner tonight. A tray of food will be sent up. Breakfast is between six and eight in the dining room. I'll let Flora know you've arrived. She may not have a chance to check in with you this evening, but you can expect to see her first thing in the morning. One of the staff will come and collect you at seven for breakfast. Is there anything you need before I go?"

Cass had slowly wandered around the room as he spoke. "I don't think so."

"If you have any questions, just pick up the phone. Somebody is on duty twenty-four hours a day. I hope your stay is a positive one."

Before he could say more a man appeared in the hallway behind him. "Lyle, you said to let you know when Andy Wallace arrived. The ambulance is at the back entrance. I'm on the way after the wheelchair now."

"Thanks Walter. I'll go down." Lyle turned to her. "See you around, Ms. Bellow."

Later that evening after dinner, Lyle bowed his head against the howling wind as he walked to his cottage. Seeing the once strong, always smiling Andy Wallace with sunken eyes and needing a wheelchair had made for a tough last few hours.

Andy was older than him. They had only been acquaintances growing up. Still, Lyle could remember Andy and Nick, Lyle's best friend

Charles's older brother, laughing and always into something. Now Andy was a shell of that person. After an IED had exploded under his Humvee in Afghanistan he was a patient in a clinic started in honor of Nick. The irony was sickening.

Ms. Bellow wore the same sad expression as Andy. That look implied the weight of the world lay on her slender shoulders. His staff had their work cut out for them with those two. He and Charles, the Laird of Heatherglen and a doctor as well, had discussed both patients but Lyle suspected there was more to Cassandra Bellow than was on paper. She didn't even try to hide her desire to be elsewhere.

That resolute and dejected air about Cass indicated a serious psychological injury, but she carried her issues like a backpack they were so obvious. Maybe being at Heatherglen would help her with not only her physical problems but with what was bothering her heart and soul as well.

He recognized that look in both his residents because he'd seen it in his own eyes every time he'd shaved while serving in the Royal Army Medical Corps. All the men in his family had been expected to make a career in the armed forces and he hadn't disappointed. As one of his father's two sons, Lyle himself had been encouraged, then expected, to join the army. The importance of serving had been drummed into him his entire life.

Yet medicine had pulled at him. To find a happy medium he'd combined the two.

Despite that compromise, he'd found the discipline and unwavering devotion of military life wasn't for him. He wanted to concentrate on caring for people in the way he loved best, personally. To his father's disappointment and ongoing puzzlement, Lyle had resigned his commission and returned home, remaining in the reserves.

His father still hadn't given up on the belief that Lyle would return to active duty someday soon. Every time they were together the subject came up. Now that his father's health was declining, the pressure had grown. If Lyle resumed active service, he could make his father's last few years happier, make him proud. But the exchange would be that Lyle would be miserable.

Charles had been in the process of setting up the clinic when Lyle had returned home from overseas. He'd asked Lyle if he would consider being the administrator, as well as run the emergency centre for the surrounding villages. Lyle had accepted and never looked back. He had found where he belonged. Still, his father's disappointment weighed on him.

The decision to return to the military hung there. Then there was his obligation to the clinic…

While he'd been in the Middle East that hopeless look he recognized in Cass's and Andy's eyes had grown in his own after receiving his "Dear John" letter from Freya. He had been caught in a net with no way out. Freya had called a halt to their relationship while he had been thousands of miles away, unable to talk to her face to face. For months the pain had been like a gnawing animal in his chest. It wasn't until he had returned and started work at the clinic that he could at last breathe and see the relationship for what it was.

Lyle continued along the snowy, muddy path toward his cottage. He knew this walk by heart. The moon was large tonight and he didn't need his torch. From experience he was sure his house-keeper had left a fire laid. The thought of lighting it and a warm drink kept him moving. Thankfully he had a full belly from the meal he'd shared with the residents before leaving the clinic. He wasn't required to dine at the castle, but Mrs. Renwick was a much better cook than he was. Since he didn't much enjoy eating alone, he ate most of his meals at the clinic. And just as he'd expected, the two newest residents hadn't been in attendance.

Going through some paperwork in his office the next morning, he allowed his thoughts to wander to Ms. Bellow. He had gone to Andy Wallace's room to make sure he was comfortable and had spoken to the overnight nursing staff about him. Yet despite his curiosity about Cass, Lyle hadn't searched her out. Because she wasn't under his direct care, he couldn't think of a reason to do so. Flora would have her case well in hand. Still, he felt compelled to see Cass.

She'd whetted his curiosity for some reason. Something about her sharp, self-assured tone and unwillingness to show her obvious pain made him want to understand what was going on behind those gloomy eyes. He'd felt her fragility when she had leaned against him. All bones and skin, as if she had lost weight. Being injured would have caused some of that but she was *too* thin. He felt the odd need to protect her, reassure her. Not that he would let that show. Still, just before lunch he couldn't stop himself from walking to the physical therapy department.

Lyle found Flora, with her dark head down, working at her desk. He knocked lightly on the door.

She looked up and smiled. "Hello, Lyle. What can I do for you?"

"I just wanted to check in on Cass Bellow. I haven't seen her today." He put his hands in his pockets.

"She was here for therapy this morning." Flora put down her pen. "She was ready to start when I arrived."

He leaned against the doorframe. "Great. When

we met yesterday, I was afraid she might be resistant."

Flora shook her head a little. "If there was a problem it was with her working too hard. She acted determined to be finished with her recovery well before the prescribed time. I had to remind her that she could hurt herself further if she pushed herself too hard."

"I'm sure that you'll see she takes it slowly and easily." Lyle took a step into the office. "By the way, did you tell her there's animal therapy as well? I got the impression it was a surprise to her when I mentioned it. I don't think she was told by her doctors in Germany that it's a central part of our program here."

Flora's eyes darkened with concern. "I did mention it but was called away before more was said."

"I'll speak to Esme. If Cass doesn't show up at the canine therapy center, then I'll talk to her."

Flora nodded. "Good."

"I told Cass the residents eat together, and she didn't look any happier about that."

Flora picked up the pen and tapped it on the desk once. "You and I have been at this long enough to know how to handle an uncooperative patient. We know physical issues often include adjusting to a new way of life." She lifted her shoulders and let them drop. "Why would Cass be any different?"

"Agreed. What about Andy Wallace? Have you had your session with him?"

"I'll see him this afternoon."

"Let me know how it goes. I don't think he's in any better frame of mind than Ms. Bellow."

Flora grinned. "We don't get all those great accolades for being the best therapy clinic for nothing."

"You have a point." He nodded his head at the door. "I'm on my way to get a sandwich for lunch. Care to join me?"

"Thanks, but I need to finish some paperwork for the boss."

Lyle chuckled. "And he appreciates your efforts. See you later." He left, walking to the dining room to pick up some food before returning to his office. Lyle planned to continue checking up on Cass and Andy for a few days until he was satisfied with their compliance, then he'd back away.

After lunch, Cass sat in her room by the fire, rubbing her thigh, glad therapy was over for the day. It had been grueling. Less from what she had been asked to do and more from her pushing herself. She had broken into a sweat and had clenched her teeth more than once not to cry out as pain had shot through her leg. Flora had warned her to slow down. It had been strenuous and stressful at best. Even her arm had resisted a couple of the exercises.

Making matters worse was the discovery Cass had made that she had stamina issues. The hospital stay in traction had taken a lot out of her. She'd always been fit, had worked out regularly with ease. Now she just felt frustrated. Regaining her strength wasn't going to happen fast enough.

That morning she'd been up and dressed by the time Melissa, a staff member, had knocked on her door. She had slept well the night before. Sleeping in the hospital hadn't been ideal. The peace and quiet of this country castle did have its appeal.

She had on some of the few clothes she habitually kept packed in her to-go bag. The knit sweatpants and T-shirt would have to do for workout clothes. When she and Rufus had caught the transport plane to Eastern Europe, nowhere in her plans had she thought to prepare for weeks of being in a hospital or being in a physical therapy clinic in Scotland in the winter.

Melissa had escorted Cass by elevator to the ground floor. There she had been led to the dining room.

"I'll return in a few minutes to show you to the physical therapy department," Melissa had said.

There hadn't been anyone else in the room. Cass had been thankful for that. She'd gone to the buffet and helped herself to a boiled egg and a slice of toast. She had just finished her second glass of orange juice when the woman returned.

"Flora's ready for you."

After placing her dishes on a tray, Cass followed Melissa down a long hall off the main one. They entered an area that looked like a gym where exercise equipment faced a bank of three large windows. In another corner of the spacious room were mats. Two high padded tables sat in the middle.

"You can have a seat on a table and I'll let Flora know you're here," she'd been told.

Cass scrambled up on the table with more effort than she liked.

A leggy, dark-haired woman wearing what looked like the latest fashion in exercise clothes soon joined her. Dressed in a hot pink jacket over a black top and leggings that came to mid-calf she made Cass feel extra-frumpy in her outfit. The woman even wore makeup.

She offered her hand, "Hi, I'm Flora McNeith. It's nice to meet you, Cass. I apologize that I wasn't here to meet you yesterday. I'm sure Lyle took good care of you."

"Who? Oh, yeah, the doctor."

She chuckled. "Most woman consider him more memorable than that. We should get started on your therapy."

Over the next hour Cass showed Flora the range of motion in her leg and arm. For the first thirty minutes they concentrated on her leg and the last half-hour on her arm. Flora applied a cold compress before working with either part of her body, then a warm one after.

When they were through Flora said, "I'm sending you to the whirlpool for half an hour. After lunch someone will show you to your afternoon therapy at the canine therapy center."

She didn't give Cass time to respond before she turned to another patient who had entered the room. Cass had no intention of going to the canine therapy center. She wasn't ready to be involved with a dog again, any dog. Wasn't sure she'd ever be ready. Why had her doctors in Germany insisted on sending her to this clinic when they knew her background? Maybe they had thought it would be what she needed since she had been a dog handler, but she wasn't emotionally ready. She would just make it clear, without explanation, that she wouldn't be going to the canine therapy center.

As she walked toward the door marked "Whirlpool" Cass groaned. She almost cried with pleasure as she slipped into the hot swirling water. Today she had taken the first step towards her complete discharge and regaining her life. The one that didn't include Rufus.

After her trip to PT she'd stopped by the dining room long enough to grab a sandwich, leaving the soup behind. With food eaten, a warm shower taken and clean clothes on, Cass now had a nap on her agenda. She would be perfectly happy spending the rest of the day in her room.

She woke with a start when there was a sharp knock on her door. "Coming." Cass opened it to find a staff member there. This time it was a young man.

"I'm here to show you the way to the canine therapy center."

"I'm sorry but I don't feel like going." What she really meant was she *wasn't* going.

The man studied her a moment as if he expected her to say more, then nodded. "I understand."

Cass settled back in the chair and looked into the fire. She knew her abilities and strengths. The wound of losing Rufus was too raw. Her emotions in general were stretched to snapping point. She couldn't cope with the thought of interacting with a dog even if it was supposed to speed up her recovery.

She loved her job, but could she ever return to it, ever get so involved with another animal that she risked reliving this almost unbearable suffering? What if it wasn't a dog? Could she ever open up enough to anyone again to take the chance of losing her heart?

Chapter 2

Lyle stood outside Cass's door. She had refused to go to her canine therapy appointment. From the information he'd received from Flora she'd been more than game to do the work in physical therapy. Why was she balking at the rest of the program?

It was important. He and his colleagues had been highly successful in using canine therapy in the recovery of their patients. Cass needed to participate. He had read in her paperwork that she'd worked as a dog handler for search and rescue. Certainly she wasn't afraid of dogs. If anything, he would have thought that she would be eager to meet her assigned dog.

Lyle rapped on the door twice.

He heard a voice call, "Just a minute." Then a few seconds later the door opened.

Cass was dressed in a T-shirt, a zip-up hoodie, jeans and socked feet. She only came as high as his shoulders. She pushed at her short blonde hair, her tone demanding as she said, "Yes?"

"I understand that you don't want to go to your canine therapy appointment." Frustration with her resistance made him sound sterner than he'd intended.

"You understand correctly." She stepped back into the room.

He moved to just inside the doorway. "It's part of the program here. Everyone's required to participate."

"Why?" She stood feet slightly apart as if preparing for a fight.

He lowered his voice. "Because we've found that people recover faster when part of their therapy involves a dog. It's almost crucial to full recuperation. Why don't you let me show you the way to the center?"

"No, thank you." She put her hand on the door.

His brow rose. Did she intend to close it on him? "Are you in pain? Do I need to speak to Flora?"

A look of something close to panic filled her eyes. "No, I'm just tired. I don't feel like it today."

He checked his watch. It was too late now for

her to go anyway. She had already wasted half her time. "Okay, that's understandable. Rest is good. Take the remainder of the afternoon off. I'll see you at dinner."

She made no comment as she closed the door.

Lyle had to back out into the hall to avoid having the door shut in his face. When was the last time he'd been thrown out of a room? He couldn't even remember one. People didn't treat him like that, yet Cass had effectively done so. He shook his head. She would be a tough nut to crack.

It was almost dark when Lyle started for home. Cass hadn't been at dinner. Neither had she ordered a tray. He had left his meal long enough to go to her room, determined he'd be less understanding this time. If she couldn't follow the clinic protocols, she would be transferred elsewhere.

There was no answer when he knocked on her door. He tried three times before he called her name. Finally, he opened the door a crack and listened for the shower running. Nothing. He called again then stuck his head in to look. Cass wasn't there. First thing in the morning he was going to confront her when she showed up for her PT session with Flora.

A short time later Lyle turned to go through the gate leading to his cottage when he saw a dark shadow of a person down the way. They were sitting on the fence. Who was it? He was acquainted with most people around here but didn't recognize this person. The locals knew better than to sit outside at this time of year. His conscience wouldn't allow him to go home without first checking on the stranger.

He didn't wish to scare whoever it was, so he approached slowly. Still, there was no movement. Were they so deep in their thoughts they didn't hear him walking up? He stepped closer. He still couldn't tell if it was a man or a woman. The person didn't move. He went nearer, close enough he could touch them. Just as he was about to, they turned and looked at him. *Cass!* He had assumed she was safely in the castle somewhere, if not already back in her room. He would have never thought she might wander out into the night and cold. What had possessed her to come outside?

All she wore was a thin jacket. Her hands were shoved into her pockets. She wasn't dressed adequately for this weather. She should have on a woolly hat and scarf and a thicker jacket. "What're you doing here?"

She looked away, toward the last of the dying light.

"Are you okay? It's much too cold to be sitting here."

"I had to get out. I've been cooped up in a hospital for weeks. I needed some fresh air." Her words were so soft he leaned forward to hear them.

Lyle glanced in the direction she was looking

and saw nothing that should hold her attention. He could only guess that her thoughts were so deep she had no idea what danger she was in. Could she even find her way back to the castle?

But first things first. "How long have you been out here?"

It took a moment before she answered, "I don't know."

Had frostbite started? He needed to get her out of the cold.

"Why're you here, Doctor?" Her voice sounded stronger.

That was encouraging. Much more like herself than her first few words. He pointed. "I live just down the lane there."

"Oh." Cass glanced over her shoulder then shrugged as if disinterested.

"I went to your room looking for you during dinner. I thought by now you would've come out of hiding and gone to your room for the night, prepared to ignore any knock on your door." He took a seat beside her.

This time she really looked at him. "What gave you that idea?"

"The expression on your face when I told you that you'd be expected for dinner in the dining room. I guessed you weren't planning to come. However, I didn't expect you to run outside to get away."

She pursed her lips and nodded. "Yeah, I don't think I'm gonna make those communal meals. And I'm not running away."

"We're not going to discuss that now. What we need to do is get you inside and warmed up." He stood.

Cass didn't move. Instead, her attention went to the sky once more. "Don't worry about me. I'm all right."

Lyle's brows drew together. He was sure she didn't appreciate the full effect of his reaction because of the dim lighting. "So you're knowledgeable enough about the area that you can get around without getting lost?"

Cass straightened and glared at him. "I work in search and rescue. I assure you I can manage to get myself back to the castle."

There was spunk in her voice. "That remains to be seen. You're obviously ignorant of the danger of being out in this weather without adequate clothing. I'm not taking any chances on losing one of our residents to exposure. Right now, you're going to the closest warm place and that's my cottage. When you're defrosted and dry, I'll walk you back to the castle."

It wasn't until that moment that Cass registered she was bone cold. How long had she been sitting here, staring off into space?

"Come with me. My cottage isn't far." He offered his large gloved hand, palm up.

She stared at it a moment. Was she acting crazy, like he already thought she was? Cass took his hand just long enough to slide off the wall. He turned and she trailed after him. They didn't go far before they entered a small clearing with a two-story stone cottage sitting in the middle. Trees surrounded it. A light over the door was on and another burned brightly in the window. Someone was expecting him.

"Is your wife going to mind you bringing a wayward patient home?"

"If I had one, she wouldn't mind." He walked to the door and opened it, then turned and waited for her to enter.

Cass stepped in, giving him room to follow. They stood in a small hallway. He waved a hand toward a room off to one side as he closed the door and began removing his coat. "Go on in and take off your shoes. They must be wet. I'll have the fire burning in a minute."

She entered what must be his living area. There was a small couch and a large leather chair situated close to the fireplace. The seat of the chair had a dip in it. It was obviously the doctor's favorite spot. A lamp and a stack of books sat on the floor beside it. A desk with papers strewn across it was against the wall with a window that faced the front lawn. Behind the desk stood a wooden chair. On the other side were shelves full of haphazardly placed books and a few framed pastoral scenes on the wall. The room had a very masculine feel to it. The man certainly owned his space. Cass found that comforting and reassuring in some odd way.

Lyle soon joined her, minus his outer clothing and shoes. He was in his socked feet, which made him seem even more approachable. "You don't have your shoes off yet? You need to get that jacket off as well. It looks like it's soaked through."

Cass started to remove a boot. "I can tell you spend a lot of time telling people what to do."

"You can thank my father and time in the army for that." He pulled a box of matches off the mantel, knelt and lit the fire. It soon came to life. "You really don't have any idea how long you've been outside?"

Cass considered pretending she hadn't heard the question. She'd gotten lost in her thoughts, her disappointment and grief, but the last thing she wanted to do was confess why she'd been out there. "No, I'm not sure."

He stood. "You really are going to have to be more careful around here. It's easy to wander somewhere you shouldn't. With or without snow."

Although she hadn't yet gotten her boot off, Cass removed her coat. It was heavier than usual.

He was right. She hadn't noticed how wet she had become.

The doctor reached for it and she allowed him to take it. Going to the desk, he hung it over the back of the chair, which he then pulled closer to the fire.

"Do you regularly bring patients home to sit by the fire?" She dropped one boot to the floor.

He grinned. It was a nice one. The kind that made her want to return it. "No. I'd have to say you're the first. But then I only do it for people sitting on my fence who are obviously about to freeze to death."

Shivering, Cass removed the other boot and let it drop beside the first one.

He pulled a colorful knit throw of orange, browns and tan off the back of the leather chair and draped it over her shoulders. She pulled the edges around her. Warmth filled her immediately. After letting it seep in, she removed her wet socks and spread them on the hearth. With a sigh, she stretched her ice-cold feet out toward the flames. Rubbing her stiff damaged leg, she got comfortable on the small sofa.

"I'll go and brew a pot for tea." Lyle started out of the room.

"The English and their tea," Cass murmured.

"I heard that. And I'm Scottish. Not English," he said with a clipped note.

Cass winced. She'd just been chastised. Her

mother would be displeased with Cass for being rude, no matter what the circumstances.

He looked over his shoulder. "I forget you're American. Would you prefer coffee? I think I have some in the back of the pantry." He waited, an expectant look on his face.

She mustered a slight smile. "No, tea is fine. You've already gone to a lot of trouble for me."

"No trouble." He left the room.

While listening to him moving around in another part of the house, Cass laid her head back against the cushion of the sofa and gazed into the flames. The feeling was returning to her feet. She wiggled them. This was nice. The most peaceful she had felt in weeks.

Lyle returned with a small tray. On it were two steaming mugs, a milk jug and a sugar bowl. "Do you take yours with sugar and milk?"

"I don't know. My coffee I like with both."

"Then let's try it that way." The doctor mixed the ingredients in and handed her a mug.

She wrapped her hands around it, letting the heat seep into her icy fingers.

He sank into his chair with his mug in his hand. The chair fit him perfectly. "How're you feeling now?"

"Much better. I had no idea how cold and wet I was."

Leaning forward, he rested his elbows on his

knees with the mug between his palms. "You really need thicker socks and boots. There's a good shop in the village for those."

"My sturdy boots were cut off and discarded when I was taken to the medical tent. I went straight from the tent to the hospital and from the hospital to here. When I can, I'll buy another pair. And maybe replace my cellphone." She had said more than she had intended.

His brows went up. "Medical tent? I had no idea. Do you mind telling me what happened?"

"It wasn't in my file?"

He pursed his lips and gave a noncommittal shake of his head. "Yes, but I'd like to hear it about it from you. I think you need to talk."

"Being a shrink again, Doc?"

"It's Lyle, and I was going more for being your friend." He leaned back, looking completely comfortable. "If you don't want to talk about it that's fine."

Now she was being put on the spot. If she didn't tell him something he would think she was a head case. "There's not much to tell. I was searching for a girl lost in the rubble of a building after a major explosion in Eastern Europe. It had been two days and there wasn't much hope. I found her alive but in the process a wall fell on me. So now you have it." Cass had been careful not to use the word *we*. She didn't want to talk about Rufus. She refused to break down in front of this stranger, no matter how nice he was.

"Wow, that's some story."

And he hadn't heard it all. Wouldn't ever as far as she was concerned. "Yeah, makes for a great party story."

He gave her a direct look. "I think it makes you a pretty impressive person. Your type of work can be both rewarding and very depressing."

He was right about that. His piercing empathy made her conscious of her vulnerability. She wasn't used to people seeing through what she said that clearly. The men she'd had relationships with certainly hadn't—including Jim, her latest disaster. Now she had scars on her body. How would men react to them?

Lyle put the mug down. "How're your hands and feet feeling now?"

Relieved he'd changed the subject, she answered, "Instead of being numb they feel like needles are being pushed into them."

"That's good. The feeling is returning."

Giving him a wry smile, she brought the mug to her lips again. The warmth flowed through her, matching the heat in the room. "So how come the administrator of the prestigious Heatherglen Castle Clinic is living way out here in the woods?"

Looking over the edge of the mug, he gave her an indulgent look. "In the daylight it's not that far out. This was the gamekeeper's cottage. When I returned from serving in the Middle East I needed a place to live. Turned out this came with the administrator's job."

"I don't see you as the military type." He didn't strike her as a squared shoulders, stand-at-attention kind of man. His smile was too quick, his manner too easygoing to fit into that strait-laced world.

"Aye. I was born and bred to it."

The words were flat, suggesting that hadn't been a completely good thing. There was more there but she didn't ask. It wasn't her business and she didn't like him prying into hers, so she wouldn't.

"You were overseas?"

"Aye, two tours in the Middle East."

"That couldn't have been much fun." She was sure that was an understatement.

A dark look came over his face. "It wasn't."

He must have seen stuff similar to what she had in her work. She would never have guessed they'd have anything in common. Cass didn't want to talk about the similarities in their backgrounds. Instead she would rather lock it away and not think about the past. Or the pain. "So you were raised around here?"

"Yes. In the village of Cluchlochry. My parents don't live far from here. Where're you from?"

His tone led her to believe he loved the area. "Indiana, but I live in Montana now."

He raised his eyebrows and nodded approvingly. "I've been there. Beautiful scenery."

"It is. That's my favorite thing about it. But even with all the snow, it's pretty around here as well."

"In the spring it's like living inside an emerald it's so green." Reverence made his Scottish accent more pronounced.

Did it do the same when he whispered in a woman's ear when he desired her? Heaven help her! *That* wasn't a thought she should be having. Where had that idea come from? She swallowed hard and wiggled her toes. Surely it was the fire making her skin so hot.

"Let me have a look at those. I want to make sure you don't have the beginnings of frostbite." He went down on one knee in front of her.

"Look at what?" Her mind had been in a completely different place. "Oh, my feet. I don't think that's necessary."

He gave her an odd look then patted his thigh. "But I do. Put your foot up here."

With reluctance she did as he requested. Lyle's leg was firm beneath her bare sole, his corduroy pants soft.

He cradled her heel gently in the palm of his hand. All his touches were functional and professional, yet a streak of response zipped through her. She pulled back and sat straighter, watching the top of his head with its light, curly red hair. Were those coils as soft as they looked? She almost reached out a hand. Almost…

"Wiggle your toes for me."

Her head jerked up. It took her a long second to comply.

His fingers traveled over her toes. She pulled back but he held her foot securely. He raised his head, a slight grin on his lips. "Ticklish." It was more a statement than question.

"A little." It sounded childish to admit.

Cass groaned inside.

"There's no sign of frostbite here. That's good." He placed that foot on the floor. "Let me see the other one."

Cass didn't even try to resist this time. He gave that foot the same attention as the other, but without tickling her. For some reason that disappointed her.

"Wiggle," he commanded.

She did.

"Good." He rose from the floor and moved to pick up one of her socks. "These are still damp. You really are going to have to get some thicker ones when you buy those boots if you plan to take walks. When the snow melts it can get very muddy. I'll get you some dry ones to wear back to the castle." He left the room.

It was past time for her to get back to the clinic but his place was so cozy, so comfortable. Too much Lyle's space. She shouldn't be having such a reaction to him. This wasn't the time to add more conflicting emotions to those she already had.

He soon returned and handed her a pair of thick, very masculine navy socks. She had no doubt these would keep her feet dry. He took his chair while she pulled them on. Immediately her feet were warmer."

"These feel great. Thank you. I'll have them laundered and returned as soon as possible."

He poked at the fire, making sure the screen was secure around it. "No hurry. I know where to find them if I need them."

Cass reached for her shoes. "I think it's time for me to be going. I've taken up enough of your evening."

Lyle didn't disagree with her. Instead he rose and went into the hallway. With her shoes now on, Cass reached for her damp coat.

"Wait. You need a dry coat as well." He had one in his hand, holding it open for her. She slipped her arms in and he settled the heavy jacket on her shoulders. There was that same smell she had caught when she'd first met him. The coat swallowed her whole but it was like being wrapped in his arms. Although that was an unsettling and unrealistic notion, it was nevertheless a reassuring one.

Lyle pulled on his own outdoor clothing while she waited. He studied her a moment. "You need a hat, scarf and some gloves as well." Disappearing upstairs, he returned with a handful of woolen items.

"I can't take these. Surely you need them." She offered them back to him.

He shook his head. "I have a drawer full. My mother knits these."

Cass ran her hand across them. The wool was so soft. "It feels wonderful."

"Try on the hat. It may not be tight enough, but it'll be better than nothing." He watched her expectantly.

Cass pulled the dark tan hat over her head, tucking in stray hair around her face. She still held the scarf. "I'll be all right without this."

"No, you won't." His stern look stopped her from further argument.

Cass wasn't used to having people tell her what to do. A bit irritated, she wrapped the scarf around her neck. It too smelled of pine and wood smoke, like him. Those scents would forever remind her of Lyle.

She forced that thought out of her head and focused on tucking the ends of the scarf inside her borrowed coat. "Your mother does a beautiful job."

"Thank you. What I can count on is that you'll stay warm in them. These gloves will be far too large but they will work for right now. You'll need to buy some of those as well. Now, come on, it's time we got you back to the castle."

She inhaled. There was that scent again. Yes, she needed to get out of here. Something about Lyle and his home made her wish for things better left alone.

Chapter 3

Lyle opened the door and the bitter cold embraced her. Cass pulled the scarf a little tighter around her neck, glad to have it. Lyle closed the door behind them, blocking out all but the porch light.

It was cold and darkness had taken over. As they walked further away from the house she could see the stars shining brightly. She paused in awe. It was beautiful.

Cass had been to many places in the world, but few compared to how amazing it was here with the moon and the stars…and the peace. In the distance there was a rise with what looked like the ruins of an old building on its crest. She pointed. "What's that place?"

"That's the old castle keep. The first laird of Heatherglen build it. It's a tumble of stones now but you can get a beautiful view of the valley, including the village, from up there. There's a path to it, but I don't recommend you go off on your own. The path can be a bit tricky in a number of places."

"Are you worried about me wandering away?"

He searched her face for a moment. "I'd like to hope not, but based on the facts I have so far, I feel like you might."

"I repeat, I was a member of a search and rescue team." One that was broken now. She no longer had a partner.

He pulled a flashlight out of his pocket and turned it on now that they were way from the cottage. "I understand that, but surely you've always had help."

She'd always had Rufus. Had relied on him to return them back home safely. Now she had no one. At this particular moment Lyle was fulfilling the role Rufus had had in her life. Still, she wasn't sure she could ever let herself truly rely or care for anybody, whether dog or human, ever again.

"Search and rescue is an interesting vocation. How did you get started in that?"

"When I was ten my younger brother got lost in the woods while my family was on a camping trip.

He was gone almost twenty-four hours. My parents and I were terrified we would never see him again. The search and rescue people saved the day. Later on in college I realized I wanted to help people like my family had been helped." She paused. Why was she telling this virtual stranger all of this? What about Lyle had her talking so much?

He matched his pace to her slower one. "You and your kind are special people. I worked with a few of you while I was in the army. Did you do your training there?"

"No. I didn't start that until after college. While I was in school I worked at the vet clinic at the university. I was there most weekends as a volunteer. Some of the dogs were retired search dogs. After working with them I had no doubt what I should be doing."

"It sounds like an exciting way to make a living." He sounded truly impressed.

Sometimes it could be too exciting. She had no interest in reliving the last few months of her life. "It can be, but it also has its downsides. It's awful to see people desperately searching for loved ones or learn that a family member can't be saved."

"I know what you mean. War can do devastating things to a body. Trying to piece it back together can be the stuff of nightmares." His sincerity convinced Cass he understood all too well.

In spite of her determined efforts to conceal her

private hell, she was feeling uncomfortably vulnerable yet again. "I'd rather not compare notes on what we've seen." Her last assignment was at the top of the list.

"You're right. Some things are better left in the past."

Cass couldn't agree more. She'd had enough issues generated in the recent past to last her a lifetime. She wobbled when she stepped into a snow-covered dip in the ground.

His hand nestled in her elbow. "How's that leg feeling?"

"Like a building fell on it and it had more PT than it liked."

"I bet it does. You're doing too much. A walk outside might have been over the top." He moved the torch so that it illuminated the snow in front of her.

"I'm handling it." She was, just barely though.

"I spoke to Flora and she said you might have overdone things today."

She pulled her arm from his hold. "Are you going around checking up on me?"

"That's part of my job." Nothing in Lyle's voice was apologetic.

Cass stepped as far away from him as the path would allow. "Well, I'll have you know I don't need a babysitter."

"I'll keep that in mind. I also understand you're

in a big hurry to leave us. You know, you can hurt people's feelings with that attitude."

When was the last time she had been teased? Her personality didn't make people do that often. "I'm not as interested in people's feelings as I am in getting my leg and arm well again. You do know I could've made it back by myself. All I had to do was come out the gate and follow the fence back."

"That may have been so, but I couldn't take the chance of you getting lost. It looks bad in the press for the clinic to lose a patient."

No matter how she tried to push him away, or how close she came to rudeness, he seemed to take it in stride. She had to appreciate his sense of humor and self-assurance. He had an ability to make her smile even when she didn't want to or feel like it.

A whimper from somewhere up ahead caught Cass's attention. Her senses went on full alert. She searched the ground for who or what was making the noise. Her reaction came from years of being vigilant at her job. Unable to see clearly in the small amount of light, she angled her head to listen. There it was again.

Lyle turned his flashlight toward a hedge nearby. The sound came again. It was animal, not human. This time Lyle stepped in the direction of it.

"Do you hear that?"

"Yes." She didn't move from her spot. The noises brought back painful memories. Like the ones Rufus had made just before he'd died.

"It's an animal in trouble." Lyle took small steps toward the shrubbery, making the light arc back and forth. The whimper came again, and he focused the beam in that spot. "It's a dog."

Cass's chest tightened. She couldn't deal with a dog right now. Even a stray.

"Hey, buddy, do you need some help?" Lyle asked in a tender, soothing tone. His shoulder moved as if he were reaching out a hand.

There was a growl.

Cass still remained rooted where she was. She couldn't make herself step forward.

"We can't leave it out here in the cold. It looks like it's starving." Lyle reached out his hand again.

Another growl.

Lyle spoke over his shoulder. "If I can get it to come to me I'll take it to the canine therapy center. Esme will check it out and see about it."

Cass forced herself to take a step closer. She looked over Lyle's back to where the light was directed. He reached forward once more.

The dog snarled, showing its teeth.

"It doesn't look like it's going to let me take it. I can't just leave it here. I'm afraid it'll freeze before morning."

Cass was shocked back to reality. The animal

was so obviously undernourished. It shook in the cold. Its big brown eyes had a pitiful, fearful look. Cass's heart lurched. She had to do something. Everything in her that made her vulnerable to getting hurt again reached out to this pathetic animal. She didn't want to care but couldn't help herself.

Lyle didn't understand Cass's standoffishness. After all, she had worked with a dog. He glanced back at her. She just stood there, staring at him and the dog. "I don't recognize it as anybody's around here. I know them as well as I know their owners."

Finally, Cass blinked and stepped forward, but there was little enthusiasm on her face. "Let me see if I can help." She went down on her knees, paying no attention to the wetness that must be seeping into her jeans. Removing a glove, she reached out her hand, letting the small scruffy dog smell her.

The dog slowly extended its nose. It obviously liked Cass far better than him. It crawled out from under the hedge and came to Cass. Just a puppy, it was small with muddy matted hair. One of its ears stood up while the other flopped. It had an oddly patterned coat, making it look of mixed breed. Cass lifted the dog to her chest.

Lyle stood. "It figures. I've always been far better with people than animals. It likes you."

Cass gave him a dry smile. When she struggled to stand he helped her.

"The canine therapy center is right down this way. Not far. Just behind the castle. It used to be the stables. It's just through the woods." He led them back to the path. "We'll take it there. Esme will see to it."

Cass didn't say anything as she came to stand beside him. As they walked she held the dog close but not overly so. Was she afraid of the dog? Or was there more going on? Lyle would have thought she'd be the first in on a rescue.

Soon they reached the center. The lights were still on. "Esme must be keeping another late night. I'm glad I didn't have to call and get her out in the weather again. She's the veterinarian. This therapy center/veterinary center is Esme's brainchild." He hurried ahead and held the door for Cass.

She moved in past him.

"Esme, it's Lyle," he called as the door closed behind him.

"Hey, be there in a sec," came Esme's voice from another room.

She soon appeared with a broad smile on her face. Her short blonde hair was disheveled, as if she had been running her hands through it. "What's going on?"

Lyle nodded toward Cass, who still held the dog. "We have a patient for you."

Esme looked at the dog then gave Cass a questioning look.

"Esme, this is Cass Bellow, one of our new residents. She hasn't made it down to meet the dogs yet, so you haven't met her."

"Welcome, Cass. So, who do you have there?" Esme reached for the dog.

It growled.

"Aw, I see you have that special touch," Esme said, speaking to Cass. "Bring it back here and I'll give it a look." Esme led them down a short hall into an examination room. "Put it on the table."

Cass did as she was told.

Esme went to touch the dog again and it rumbled a complaint deep in its chest.

"I'll give him something to ease his anxiety." Esme went to draw up a syringe of medicine.

"Apparently Cass has that special something with animals." Lyle looked at her, expecting to see a positive expression, but instead she appeared distraught. What was wrong?

Esme quickly and efficiently gave the dog an injection. It soon rested easily in Cass's arms. "You can put him on the table now. He shouldn't be any trouble."

Cass placed the dog on the metal table and backed away. "I think you have this now." She looked at him. "I can find my way back to the castle from here."

Cass was out the door before Lyle could stop her.

"She seemed in a hurry," Esme murmured as she started examining the dog.

Lyle agreed. That accompanied intense curiosity about the stricken look on Cass face as she'd fled.

The next evening Lyle entered the dining room. A number of the residents were already there and engrossed in conversation. Cass wasn't one of them. He hadn't seen her since the night before. The few times he had left his office during the day she hadn't been anywhere in sight. After her reaction to the dog he'd been very interested in how she was doing.

Everyone was seated at the table and the food was ready to serve when Cass entered the room. Relief washed through him. He had feared he was going to have to go and find her and he hadn't been looking forward to the conversation that would have taken place.

She was dressed in a simple white button-down shirt and jeans. On her feet were the same boots she'd worn the night before. Her hair was brushed back and it didn't look as if she had any makeup on. There was a fresh, simple air about Cass that appealed to him. Something he was completely unprepared for.

For too long he'd held onto Freya because she had been something safe and secure in a world he'd been unable to control. He had been too young, too unsure of life and couldn't see that before he'd gone overseas. Still, the way their relationship had ended had colored how he viewed potential partners. He was gun-shy, and he'd be the first to admit it. The next time he got involved with a woman he wanted it to be a mature, mutual lifelong commitment. That certainly couldn't be with a resident who would soon be gone and had her own life thousands of miles away. He needed to stop any kind of thoughts like the ones he was having now.

"We're glad to have you join us," he informed Cass as he stood and pulled out the chair next to him. Smiling, he added, "I was worried I might have to go out in the weather to hunt you down."

She gave the therapy dog belonging to the resident on the other side of her a long uncertain look before taking the offered seat. "It isn't because I didn't think about skipping out."

"I'm glad you changed your mind."

She gave him a direct look. "Hunger pangs changed it for me."

He nodded. "Whatever the reason, I'm glad you're here. Let me introduce you to everyone."

"You don't—" She didn't finish the sentence when those at the table turned to look at her.

"Everyone, this is Cass." Lyle then went round the table, giving each person's name. They either nodded or said hello to her as he went. She offered them all a tight smile.

The food was served family style out of large bowls and platters, passed around the table. Cass only took small amounts of a few items. At this rate she would never gain back the weight he suspected she had lost.

"I thought you might like to know that the puppy we found last night is doing well. Esme said he's fine except for being underweight. He should make a full recovery."

"That's good." She started picking at her meal.

Cass wasn't helping much with making conversation. Lyle made another effort. "She's going to ask around and see if anyone claims him."

"That's nice." Cass took a bite of food as if she loathed doing it.

Roger, the man sitting on the other side of her, asked her a question. Cass gave him a two-word answer. Apparently, she didn't want to carry on a conversation with anyone. But she needed to. If he had ever seen someone badly in need of interaction, it was Cass.

He tried another approach. "I see the residents and staff have been busy in here today. It looks festive."

Cass looked around as if she was seeing the room for the first time.

How could she not react to the greenery and red

bows hanging from the chandeliers, along with the large matching centerpiece of green boughs, velvet bows, and crimson balls? Or the mantel filled with decorations? In his experience it was the kind of stuff women loved.

Other than her hesitant look at the dog beside her, she appeared unaware of everything and everyone. He'd forced Cass into noticing him, but only for an all-too-brief moment. For some reason he wanted her to initiate an interaction with him. He wanted her to like him.

Lyle transferred his attention to Alice, who sat on his other side. Maybe giving Cass space would help open her up a bit. He and Alice carried on a lively conversation about the upcoming village Christmas market beginning this weekend. They went on to discuss some of the other events planned for the festive season, like the annual Christmas festival at the castle, and the live nativity in the village.

"I was told there would be a tree lighting in the village and a parade in a few weeks." Alice's eyes lit up with excitement.

"There is and they even include some of the dogs from the center."

He glanced at Cass a few times during the discussion and caught her listening. When she saw him looking, she focused on her food again. He decided to try to draw her into conversation once more. "Cass, do you like craft markets?"

Her head jerked up. "I…uh… I do."

"Then you'll want to be sure and catch the minibus into Cluchlochry on Saturday morning. The village has a pretty impressive one. Great place to buy Christmas presents."

"I'll think about it." She pushed back her chair. "Right now I need to go for a walk before it gets dark."

"Hey, before you go could I speak to you for a moment in private?"

Her expression said no. Yet she answered, "Okay, but just for a minute. I really want to walk."

"I promise not to take up too much of your time." He rose when she did and followed her into the hall. "Why don't we go to the lounge?" With a hand he directed her down the hall. She headed that way and he joined her. They turned a corner and entered another hall. At the first doorway, Lyle opened the door to the large room with numerous sitting areas. A fire roared in the fireplace in the center of the main wall. Windows filled the opposite side.

"Why don't we have a seat?"

"I'm starting to feel like I'm being brought into the principal's office. You could have gotten on to me about not going to canine therapy again today in the hall outside the dining room." Cass sat on the edge of a cushion of the closest sofa.

"I could have, but I'm more interested in finding out why you're so resistant to the idea of canine therapy. Especially since I know your job entailed working closely with a dog. I assume you at least like animals a bit. I noticed you were slow to help with the dog we found and left the center as quickly as you could. I read in your file that you lost your partner." He didn't miss the stricken look that flickered in her eyes. "Is that what the problem is? I'd like to help. The staff here would like to help."

Cass shot to her feet. "I don't want your help or anyone else's. If you want me to go to canine therapy, fine. I'll be there tomorrow."

"There you are." Charles walking toward them stopped anything further Cass might have said.

Lyle came to his feet. "Hi, Charles. I'd like you to meet Cassandra Bellow. She's one of our newest residents. Cass, this is Dr. Charles Ross-Wylde. Also the Laird of Heatherglen and Esme's brother."

Charles smiled at Cass. "It's nice to meet you. Please call me Charles."

"Hello. You have a lovely home…castle." Cass's words were tight and formal. She glanced toward the door.

Charles chuckled. "Thank you. You're American, aren't you?"

"I am."

"You must be the woman who works in search and rescue?" He gave her an earnest look. "Interesting job."

"It can be." Cass looked toward the door again. "Why don't I let you two talk?" She slipped away.

Lyle watched her go. He had no doubt Cass would keep her word about going to therapy. How much she would get out of it was another question. He'd just have to trust that the dog she was paired with would do what was needed to help her heal.

"Lyle."

He looked at Charles, who was grinning at him with twinkling eyes. "What?"

"You like her, don't you?"

"Why would you say that?" Lyle didn't want to discuss his confused reactions to Cass Bellow. Not even with his best friend Charles.

He laughed. "Because I called your name three times before you answered!"

Lyle wanted to groan. Now Charles would ask questions every time he saw him. "Did you have something important you wanted to talk to me about?"

Charles looked at him with a knowing smile on his lips. "It isn't as interesting as Ms. Bellow but we need to talk about Andy and his progress."

"Ah. Why don't we go to my office to do that?"

* * *

Cass was still stomping and swinging her arms in exasperation when she reached the main road after the long walk down the castle drive. How dared Lyle treat her as if she were a disobedient child? She was doing her physical therapy. Aware of what she needed, it wasn't canine therapy. But he wasn't going to give up.

She'd gone to dinner like he wanted, wasn't that enough? She would go to the canine therapy center tomorrow all right, but her participation in the therapy would be minimal and uncooperative. That should keep him off her case.

"Be strong," she said to the trees, and shoved her hands into her jacket pockets. When her brother had been lost, her mother and father had hugged her too tightly and had constantly reminded her they all had to remain strong. Afterwards Cass had used the mantra "Be strong" whenever she'd felt helpless. Even now, years later, she was using it to defy that feeling.

"Be strong!" she yelled to the sky.

She'd been strong when Jim had broken her heart, then soon after that when she'd learned that Rufus was gone. She'd been strong when the doctors had warned her she might never regain full use of her crushed arm and leg. She had been strong during the grueling hospital stay. During her agonizing physical therapy sessions here.

Only it didn't matter how strong she was. Nothing changed. She was alone with no one to lean on.

The sound of a vehicle coming up the road drew her attention. The driver was going too fast for the icy conditions. As it came around the curve the back end went one way and then the other. The skid landed the front end of the car in the stone wall between Cass and the road.

She hurried out the castle gate and over to the car with her heart pounding, ignoring the ache in her leg. The engine was still running even though the hood was crumpled. The hot air of the radiator hitting the cold air created stream, making it difficult to see.

Cass reached out to touch the side of the car with a shaking hand. She'd not done any rescue work or even given anyone medical attention since her last assignment. Now here she was faced with an accident without the support of her partner. Could she do it? Would she break down and cry? She inhaled deeply, bracing herself. "Stay strong."

She ran her hand down the side of the car to keep her bearings as she worked her way to the driver's door. Cass pulled it open. She could, would, get through this.

The driver groaned, his palm pressed to his forehead.

"Are you okay?" Her instinct and training

kicked in. "Don't move. You could have more injuries."

"I'm fine." His words were slurred.

She placed a hand on the man's shoulder. "I'm an EMT. I know what I'm talking about. More help will be here soon."

The man pulled his hand away from his head. Blood covered it.

"Don't move," she said firmly. "Keep your head back. I'm going to reach in and turn the engine off." She found the ignition key and turned it. The steam dissipated.

There was a moan from the back seat. She had someone else to check on. If she only had a cellphone to call for help. Hers had been damaged in her accident and she hadn't had time to replace it yet. Surely the driver had one. "Sir, do you have a phone? Tell me where it is, don't try to find it yourself."

The man gave her a weak yes and told her it was in his jacket pocket. Cass carefully reached inside his pocket and retrieved it.

Cass quickly dialed 999. When a person answered, Cass gave the call handler all the necessary information. She then stepped to the rear passenger door. Pulling it open, she found crumpled in the footwell a lady of around sixty. "You're going to be fine. I know you're in an uncomfortable position but try not to move."

The woman groaned, but Cass knew from the sound she was barely conscious. Using her fingers, Cass searched for a pulse in the woman's neck. She located one but it wasn't strong.

A voice she recognized as Lyle's said from behind her, "Don't move her. She may have concussion."

Cass said over her shoulder, "I've already told her that. And I've already called for help."

"I know. I must have called right after you."

She needed to get the man's bleeding under control. "Do you have any supplies?"

"No. I was on my way home when I heard the crash."

Cass stood. "You see about this woman and I'll look for a first-aid kit."

She worked her way to the front passenger door. Opening it, she searched the glove compartment for anything they could use. All she found was a stack of napkins. Those would have to do.

"Cass, we need to lay this lady down on the seat so I can examine her properly," Lyle said.

"Okay, take these napkins and have the man hold them to his head. I'll crawl in the back and help lift the woman up."

Lyle accepted the napkins and applied them to the man's head. "I need to get him to the clinic to stitch him up, but first we need to take care of this woman. She's lost consciousness."

Cass had been busy climbing into the backseat on her knees while he talked. Her leg rebelled at the position but she continued. She reached under the woman's arms and locked her hands across her chest. To Lyle she said, "Ready?"

"On three. One, two, three."

Cass pulled the woman against her chest. As the woman's back came up on the seat, Lyle grabbed her ankles and lifted. Soon they had her lying across the seat. She moaned and her eyelids flickered.

"Will you check her pulse and heart rate while I see if she has any internal injuries?" Lyle asked, as he started pressing on the woman's midsection.

"Her heart rate is steady but not very strong," Cass reported.

"Okay. So far I can't find any additional injuries." He continued to examine the woman.

A minibus pulled out of the castle gate and drew up alongside them.

"We need to get them both up to the clinic where I can give them a thorough evaluation." Lyle continued searching for problems.

Cass looked at the top of his head as he worked. "Shouldn't we wait on an ambulance?"

"That'll take too long. It has to come from Fort William. We're the emergency care for this area."

"Really?"

Now he met her look. "Rural area. That's how it is."

That made sense.

He was an impressive man to assume the responsibility for so many lives.

The staff member who had been driving the minibus joined them.

"Ron," Lyle said, "we need to get these people to the clinic ASAP. The man should be able to sit up front. We'll need the stretcher for the woman."

Ron nodded and headed back to the minibus.

Lyle backed out of the car. "Cass, would you please continue to monitor her while I have a look at the man?"

"Okay." Cass picked up the woman's wrist and placed two fingers on the inside. It took a second but she located a pulse. Still shallow but steady.

"I'm going to get this man into the minibus," Lyle called. "You good there?"

"Yes." Cass remained focused on the woman, trying not to think about her own recovering leg and arm as she began to worry about the injured woman being exposed to the cold. "Bring a blanket if you've got one."

"Will do." A few minutes later Lyle returned, pushing a gurney with Ron's help. "It's going to take all of us to get her loaded."

The two men positioned the gurney right outside the door.

Lyle handed her the blanket. Cass spread it over the woman. He tucked it around her legs. "Cass, if you'll support her head and shoulders while Ron and I get on either side of her and lift her out, I think we can make it work."

Cass wasn't looking forward to the pain she was sure would rocket through her leg and arm from the exertion. That didn't matter. Caring for the hurt woman was more important. Cass worked her hands under the woman's shoulder blades and supported her head with her upper arms. "Ready."

"Okay Ron. One, two, lift!"

Slowly the two men maneuvered the woman over the seat onto the gurney. Keeping the woman's upper body and neck as straight and stable as possible, Cass crawled across the seat and out the other door. By then electrifying pain was coursing through every nerve of her leg. Her arms and back were convulsing under the strain. When she tried to stand, her traumatized leg gave way. She grabbed the gurney. Though it wobbled on its wheels, she managed to balance on her other leg.

"Damn," Lyle swore as he reached for her. "I can't believe I got so caught up in what was happening I forgot you were a recovering patient. Sit down." He guided her to a seat of the vehicle. Giving her a stern look, Lyle ordered, "Stay there while we get this lady loaded."

Cass hated to admit it but she was relieved to sit. Her eyes were watering from intense pain. As she took a moment, emotions swamped her. Her loss of direction, missing Rufus, the fog of her future all came down on her. Sorrow tightened her chest.

Lyle gave her a concerned look. For a second Cass feared he would question her but instead he said, "Ron, let's get this woman strapped down and loaded." Mere moments later he returned to her. "It's your turn."

Clenching her jaw, she stood. No matter how sick and unsure she felt inside, Cass refused to let it show, even if she had to struggle to do it. She feared Lyle was too perceptive and had already guessed. Cass said with more confidence than she felt, "I can walk."

"Maybe so, but you aren't going down on my watch." He wrapped an arm around her waist and guided her to the back of the vehicle.

Hot awareness of his strong sturdy body zipped through Cass as Lyle held her tight. Unable to stop herself, she leaned against him. After hesitating a moment, she rested her arm around his middle back and hobbled to the minibus. She couldn't ignore the sensations simmering in her core any more than she could ignore her agonizing leg.

Lyle held her steady until she reached for the frame of the door. Cass was climbing into the minibus when she was lifted off her feet and placed gently on the floor. She looked over her shoulder. "Thanks."

"No problem. Have a seat and move down." Lyle wasted no words. He was all business.

She did as she was told, scooting down to the end of the small bench seat. Lyle joined her. Their bodies touched all the way along one side. Strangely she wanted to rest her head against his shoulder but she resisted the urge. She refused to show any more weakness. What would Lyle think of her if she had given in to that impulse?

Ron close the doors. They were soon moving. Lyle's attention remained on the woman on the gurney, which was locked to the floor with straps. She still hadn't regained consciousness. Lyle took her pulse as they rode. He gave Cass a nod.

From what Lyle had said, Cass assumed that they were headed to the castle. By the winding of the road she could tell she was right. After making a big circle, Ron backed the minibus to a stop. Seconds later he opened the door.

Lyle climbed out with one agile move. "You stay put," he told her. "I don't want you to fall. Someone will be out to get you." He didn't wait for her response before he and Ron unhooked the gurney and rolled the woman inside.

Cass forced herself not to shake. Memories of lying in the rubble of that building flooded back. The sound of her calling Rufus's name and him not answering. The waiting until someone could get to her. Panic rose when Lyle didn't come. Pain throbbed through her body. She needed to get out of here.

She searched the area she could see. It was a part of the castle she wasn't familiar with. The vehicle was backed up to a small loading dock with two double doors. Her impatience grew to be an almost living thing. She had to do something. What if Lyle needed her help? Just as she was about to rise, Ron came through the doors, leaving them swinging. He gave her a glance then hurried down the steps nearby. Her heart dipped. He must be going after the man up front.

With Ron and Lyle concentrating their energies on the injured people, it would be some time before someone would come to assist her. She decided she wasn't in so much pain that she couldn't get herself inside.

Giving her leg a rub, she pushed up off the bench, making sure she didn't use her right arm. It took effort. With a tight jaw she made it to her feet. She slowly moved out of the minibus, steadying herself by pressing her hand on the side of it. Just as she was stepping off, the doors swung open again and out came Melissa, pushing a wheelchair.

She positioned the wheelchair just outside the van doors and stepped inside. "Lyle sent me out for you. He said you wouldn't stay seated long. I guess he was right."

Cass didn't like Lyle thinking he knew her that

well, but she couldn't deny he was right. She took a step forward, trying to keep as much weight as possible off the leg. Cass couldn't deny the wheelchair was welcome.

"Here, let me help." Melissa supported Cass to the chair and assisted her into it.

With Cass secure, she pushed her inside. They entered a large emergency examination room complete with all the most up-to-date equipment. Cass was fascinated. She'd had no idea this area of the clinic existed. There were many facets to Dr. Sinclair and his "clinic".

Lyle stood beside the older lady, who still lay on the gurney. Thankfully she was now conscious and talking to him. Ron was busy cleaning the driver's head wound at an exam table nearby.

"What can I do to help?" Cass asked, putting her hands on the arm of the wheelchair, preparing to stand.

Lyle gave her a piercing look of reprimand. "Nothing. You've done enough. You need to take care of yourself."

"Surely you need some help." Cass looked from him to the man Ron was seeing to and back.

Another member of the nursing staff rushed in. Behind her came another.

"We have plenty of help. Melissa, please see that Cass gets to her room. I'll let Flora know what's happened. She may want to examine you. Melissa,

Cass actually might also benefit from some time in the hot tub." Lyle's attention returned to his patient.

Seconds later Cass was being wheeled out of the room. It didn't take Melissa long to get her up to her room and hot water running in the tub. Cass gratefully slipped into the whirling water, looking forward to the relief it would bring her leg and arm. She'd survived her first emergency without Rufus. It had been a sad moment but somehow an encouraging one. In a small way, Cass was moving forward.

Lyle was ready for some rest but he needed to check on Cass first. The ambulance from Fort William had arrived to take the injured woman to the hospital. Lyle had stitched the gash on the man's forehead and sent him home with family members. After a quick check on Cass he was headed for his cottage and bed. The adrenalin spike of handling an emergency had worn him out.

He knocked lightly on Cass's door in case she was already sleeping. After waiting a minute and getting no answer, he turned to leave. He would see her tomorrow.

The door opened a crack. "Yes?"

He could only see a sliver of her but it was enough to tell that her hair had been pushed back and her face was freshly scrubbed. She looked adorable and unsure at the same time.

What was it about her that captivated him? That pulled at him like no other woman he knew did. Was it her strength? Determination? Her vulnerability? He needed to solve the puzzle and move on. Cass wouldn't be here long and he wasn't going to waste his emotions on anyone he didn't intend to keep forever. He'd already gone down that road.

The dirty street behind him was graveled with disappointment and heartache. He had vowed the lane ahead would be paved with the love and loyalty of a woman who wanted him as much as he did her. A lifelong partner. The next time he fell in love, he would get it right.

He shoved that fantasy aside and concentrated on what he was there for. "How're you doing?"

"Better after a hot bath."

"Good. You were impressive out there, Cass. You stayed in control. I know you must have been in pain. You should have said something. More than that, I should've thought." Guilt filled him. "I'm sorry."

She opened the door wider. "Hey, I'm an EMT. I'm trained to help."

"True, but you're also a patient here. I should have remembered that." She looked cute in her T-shirt with her pink-tipped toes.

"I'm fine." For once her eyes weren't clouded with hidden feelings. In fact, there was a hint of a smile in them.

"I'm glad. Then I'll let you get some rest." He needed to go. Right now. He started down the hall.

"Hey, Lyle."

He almost kept going, but curiosity got the better of him.

"You were pretty impressive out there too."

He smiled. It felt good to have someone praise him, especially Cass. He was confident in his abilities, but it didn't hurt to have others notice. His father certainly hadn't. "Thanks. Sleep well, Cass."

Chapter 4

Cass's hand shook as she wrapped it around the handle of the glass door of the canine therapy center the next afternoon. She had said she'd keep her appointment and she would. But she wasn't looking forward to it.

The thought of having anything to do with a dog made her want to break down and cry. The pain of losing Rufus was still too raw. It might be silly for a grown professional woman to feel this way, but she didn't care. Rufus was gone. Some part of her clung to the irrational hope he would be waiting with his tail wagging when she returned home. No other dog could replace him.

She would do what she had to, then hurry to her room for a good cry.

When she jerked the door open the young man sitting behind the desk started. This was the same high-ceilinged room with the rough board walls where she and Lyle had brought the puppy a couple of nights before. He'd said it used to be the stables and she could now see that. The other night all that'd filled her mind was that she had a dog in her arms.

"Can I help you?" the man at the desk asked.

"I'm Cass Bellow. I'm a resident at the clinic."

He looked down as if checking a list, then back at her. "Oh, yes, we've been expecting you." As he got to his feet he added, "Come with me. Margaret assists with the canine therapy program. She's back here."

Cass forced her feet to move and followed him down a hall. It wasn't the same one Lyle and Esme had led her down to the examination room the other night. The man pushed through a swing door. Cass entered a room furnished with easy chairs.

A dark-haired woman was down on her heels next to a woman seated in an easy chair holding a small black dog of no pedigree. Cass recognized the woman in the chair from the dinner table at the clinic. Lyle had introduced them, but Cass didn't remember her name. Shame pricked her. She hadn't even tried.

"Margaret, this is Cass Bellow," the man announced.

The dark-haired woman looked at them, stood and came toward Cass with one hand outstretched. She smiled. "It's great to finally meet you."

Was that her subtle way of reprimanding her for not showing up for her earlier appointments? The temptation to run grew.

"I help Esme with the canine therapy here at Heatherglen," Margaret continued.

The man quietly left the way they had come in.

Staring at the small dog that was enjoying the woman's gentle pats, Cass's chest tightened. She wasn't ready for this. She had no interest in doing *anything* with a dog.

Margaret was saying, "I thought you might like to meet Muffin. He's a sweet little dog. He'll be your companion during your stay. Let me get him and you can get acquainted." She stepped through a side door.

Cass stood, knees shaking, in the middle of the room, looking everywhere but at the other woman. She didn't want any responsibility for a dog for the next month. Especially one named Muffin. Her breathing became shallow. Her mouth turned dry. She shifted from one foot to the other. The need to leave intensified. This was too much. A meltdown was building if she didn't get out of there. She wasn't ready, might not ever be. What if she became too attached to the ridiculous Muffin? She would be leaving soon. All this pain would be there again.

Without thought Cass bolted for the door and up the hall to the front room. She had to get out of there. Ignoring the man behind the desk calling her name, she shoved the door open and stumbled into the cold air. Sucking in a deep breath, she kept going, heading toward the castle. By way of a side door she'd found yesterday, she slipped inside unnoticed.

Instead of going to her room, where someone would surely look for her, she headed for the conservatory. While exploring she'd also found an alcove hidden behind some large palm plants and banana trees with only a small sofa. There she could lick her wounds in private.

Relief washed through her when she found the floral fabric-covered settee empty. She sat, pulling her legs up under her and wrapping the coat Lyle had loaned her tighter. When would the pain go away?

She had no idea how long she had been sitting there staring off into space when she heard, "Cass?"

Lyle.

She stiffened. How had he found her? It didn't matter. She had no intention of explaining herself. Why couldn't he just leave her alone? "Go away."

He just stood there.

Finally, she murmured, "How did you know where to find me?"

"I saw you come in here. When I had a call from the center I knew where to look."

Great. She'd believed she'd made her escape. Her focus remained on the green spots showing in the snow that was melting outside. "So now you're riding to the rescue."

Lyle came to sit beside her. "I'd just like to help. Be a friend. I was told you looked upset."

Maybe if she ignored him he would go away. Instead of him taking the hint to leave, he settled further back into the cushions, his big body almost touching hers. They remained like that for a while, neither saying anything.

"You're not leaving, are you?" Cass stared at the dust motes dancing in the sunbeam streaming through the glass.

"Not until I know you're okay." He stretched his legs out and crossed his ankles.

She huffed. "Let me assure you I'm not going to harm myself."

"I didn't think that but it's good to hear."

He settled back as though he was content to stay the rest of the day. As the silence between them grew so did her temper. She hissed, "What do I have to say to get you to leave?"

For a moment she thought he was ignoring her.

When he did reply, concern laced his voice. "I'd like to understand why you're determined to have no part in our canine therapy program, especially since you work with a dog all the time."

Could she tell him? Would he understand? Was that the only way to get him to leave her alone? If he knew, maybe he would see to it she didn't have to go to canine therapy.

She opened her mouth to tell him about Rufus but the words stuck in her throat. If she said it out loud, then it would make it true. She didn't want that. Couldn't live with that. She closed her eyes tight. Maybe if she said it really fast she could get it out. "Rufus, my partner, died. Now I don't know if I can be around a dog all the time."

The moisture she had been banking for days seeped out of her closed eyelids. She took a deep breath in an effort to stop the sob welling in her throat but it didn't work. Instead she doubled over in agony. As she tried to catch her breath Lyle ran his large hand across her back in a comforting stroke.

Then he cupped her shoulder and pulled her against his chest. She buried her face in his shirt, her fingers clutching his sides. All the emotions she had held in check since the day that wall had collapsed flowed freely. The pain deep within her consumed her. Rufus was gone. Life as she'd known it had gone with him.

Lyle held her close, rubbing her shoulders and back. "Let it all out," he whispered.

Cass did. All the raw feelings she'd held in check for weeks flowed, leaving her nothing but a heaving shell. She couldn't stop the pain, fear and sorrow from escaping.

Lyle continued holding her and murmuring soft reassuring words while she clung to him.

She had no idea how much time had passed when she woke with a start. Disorientated, she still had a sense of safety. Slowly it dawned on her she was still in Lyle's arms.

Embarrassment flooded her. Placing her palms on his chest, she pushed into a sitting position. Yet one of his hands remained on her back.

"I'm so sorry for that ugly scene," she heard herself saying. "I don't know why I fell apart like that. It isn't like me."

"I'd imagine it was because you needed to. You've been under a tremendous strain." He shifted, putting his hands on his thighs.

She missed the reassuring weight immediately. Lyle was right, there was a lot of stress and emotion involved in her profession. She should be able to handle it. But where Rufus was concerned she was lost. Cass wiped at his sweater. "I've made a mess of your clothes."

"I don't mind. I'm glad I was here to help." He sounded as if he meant it.

"So part of your job description is to have patients cry all over you?" Cass managed a weak smile.

He looked at her tenderly. "Not all patients. I have to say you're a special case."

Warmth gradually replaced the coldness running through her. Lyle was a nice man saying all the right things. For an instant she wished he wasn't a doctor speaking to a patient.

"I knew about you losing your dog, it was in your file. But I had no idea that going to canine therapy would be so difficult for you. You've had a tough time physically and…" he paused "…emotionally. Flora, Esme and I didn't recognize that. I'm sorry. Would you like to talk about what happened? I'm a good listener." His words were encouraging, not demanding.

Cass shook her head, both in response and to clear it.

He waited a few moments then asked, "When did you learn the details of what happened?"

"I realized the wall was falling but I had no idea…" She swallowed. Her throat was tight and dry. Inhaling, she fought through the final pang of denial. "I didn't find out Rufus didn't make it until I woke up in the hospital. When I asked about him, one of the nurses had to ask around for the information."

Lyle put his arm around her shoulders again

and gave her a supportive squeeze. "I'm sorry. It shouldn't have happened like that."

Cass continued to look at the windowsill. It was such a large one. Almost big enough to use as a seat. "No matter when I was told, or how, it wouldn't have made…the terrible truth any easier to hear."

"Maybe not, but at the very least the news should have been given to you in a sensitive manner." He sounded irritated on her behalf. "Will you tell me about your dog?"

She didn't want to, but he deserved to know why she'd just sobbed herself into an exhausted sleep all over him. "Rufus was more than my dog. He was my partner and best friend."

And her longest relationship. He been there more than once when a relationship with a man had ended. Those guys had either been intimidated by a woman who handled such an emotionally demanding job, or they didn't like her leaving for weeks at a time on the spur of the moment. For a couple of them her relationship with Rufus had been a bone of contention. They'd wanted all her attention and hadn't understood the uncanny connection between her and her canine partner. Now she had physical scars that they might find offensive, too.

Jim, the latest and the man she'd believed was

The One, had felt her job was too risky. It had been nice to have someone worry over her at first, but it had soon started to feel restrictive. Despite their breakup he'd been kind enough to call her while she'd been in the hospital, but it had soon turned into a conversation that was more about him telling her *I told you so* than about his real concern for her. There had been no sympathy on his part for Rufus. She'd thought at one time they might have a chance at a real life together. Sadly, she'd really cared for Jim but there was no hope of that after their conversation.

Lyle removed his arm. She wanted it back. It was comforting. "How long was this dog your partner?"

"Four years. He was two when I got him. We spent the first eight weeks in training. He was born in Germany. Most good rescue dogs are. The Germans are known for breeding them to be work dogs. In fact, most of his commands I gave in German." It felt better, and was easier, to talk about Rufus than she'd imagined.

"Interesting." Lyle waited.

She looked at him. His expectant expression suggested he was truly interested in what she was saying. Yet she couldn't imagine him actually caring.

"How did you train together?"

"Are you really interested?" What if he was just asking to keep her talking as part of her "therapy"? None of the men she had known before him had cared one way or another. Why would he be any different?

"Aye. I wouldn't have asked if I wasn't." His voice carried concern. It had been so long since she'd heard that in a man's voice, it struck a deep chord within her.

"I had to do a written test and have a physical. Then I had to have a home visit so the powers-that-be knew I could care for a working dog. An animal like Rufus can cost as much as ten thousand American dollars so handlers are vetted closely. That kind of money can't be wasted. Rufus had to have a physical as well, and learn obedience basics and detection, especially body odor recognition. It was pretty intense for both of us."

"A powerful bonding experience for you both."

Cass's chest tightened from the memories. They had indeed bonded. She had loved the dog, heart and soul. At least Lyle *seemed* to understand. "Though he was only four, he was getting old for a working dog. Rufus was going to have to retire soon. I had already put in the paperwork to take him after he was done."

"Going to canine therapy was almost like punishment for you. You should have said something." His distress was evident in his voice.

She looked away in horror. "And embarrass myself, like I did a few minutes ago?"

Lyle took hold of her hand. His was large, secure…comforting. "You haven't embarrassed yourself. It's okay to be human."

"Yeah, but blubbering all over you is a bit too human."

He leaned closer until his shoulder touched hers. "I didn't mind. I'm just sorry I kept pushing you into canine therapy."

"I figured you'd seen it in my file." She winced at how pitiful she sounded.

"Yeah, but that didn't mean I understood how close you were."

Great. He probably thought she had really gone off her rocker. "I don't know if I can handle being around a dog right now. I'll be leaving here in a few weeks and I, uh, just can't risk becoming attached to another one." What she wasn't telling him about was the heavy guilt she carried over the fact that Rufus had sacrificed himself to save her life. If he hadn't barked, she would have never looked up to see the wall starting to fall. Or that he'd jumped and pushed her out of the way. It had been a split second between her life and Rufus's death.

"I understand completely," Lyle said sincerely. "Would you consider an alternative kind of therapy, if we can come up with one? Maybe just helping out at the canine clinic. Not having a specific dog assigned to you."

She was doubtful it would work but she could try. At least he was trying to work with her. Somehow she had to get past this grief, rebuild her life emotionally and move on. Yet her heart protested with a fresh pang even as she said with caution, "That might work."

"If it doesn't, then we'll try something else." His sincere tone and expression convinced her he would at least listen if she complained. Lyle's comfort was the first she'd had since Rufus had died. She was going to hang onto it.

He let her hand go and shifted away. "Do you feel up to a bite to eat?"

"I don't want to go to the dining room."

"It's too late for that." He tilted his head toward the glass.

Cass was shocked to find it was dark. How long had they been sitting there? "I'm so sorry. I made you miss dinner."

"Not a problem. Mrs. Renwick will have left me something in the kitchen. Let's go see what we can find."

"I think I'll just go up to my room." She wanted to get away. Regain her composure.

"Nonsense. You must be hungry, and I could use the company while I eat."

She had kept Lyle from his hot meal. She owed him. "Okay, I can do that."

"Not the most excited acceptance I've been given to a dinner invitation, but I'll take it." He stood.

Cass liked his sense of humor. He seemed to take life as it came without too much angst. She lacked that ability. Her way of meeting life's challenges now consisted of worry, fear of failure and the guilty conviction she hadn't done enough to make a difference. She wanted to save everyone, give them what her family had received. The chances of achieving that desire were slim to none, but still it was her goal. Now she was just a mass of nerves, help to no one. Not even herself. Squaring her shoulders, she said, "I'll try to do better in the future."

He offered his hand. "That's what I like to hear. That old tough Cass. You had me worried there for a while."

Lyle still thought she was tough? She would have thought he would have seen her as the opposite after the last few hours. She took his hand just long enough to get to her feet. "How's that?"

He put his hands in his pockets and rocked back on his heels. "I don't handle crying females well."

"I'm sorry I made you uncomfortable." She couldn't meet his eyes.

"Hey, I'm glad I was here to help. Now, let's go and get some dinner." He started toward the hall and she joined him.

Lyle led the way to the kitchen. His heart went out to Cass. She was distraught over the loss of her dog. He knew well the empty hole loss could leave in your life. He had felt it intensely when Freya had left him. When he'd told Cass that he didn't handle women crying well, he hadn't been kidding. All he'd done was hold her.

The fact that he'd liked having her cry on his shoulder was a bit unnerving. What had begun as a professional obligation to check on a resident in crisis had ended in a very personal act of compassionate empathy. Was he drawn to her because he could sense her private suffering? Whatever it was, Cass held some sort of spell over him. One he didn't mind being captivated by.

Cass followed him quietly to the kitchen, seeming fine with doing so. They walked through the now silent dining room to the swing door beside the fireplace. He held it open for her as they entered the large commercial-style kitchen.

"Have a seat at the table." There was a small wooden one next to two corner windows in the large room. "I'll see what I can find in the fridge."

Her chair scraped over the tile floor as she took a seat.

Opening one of the doors of the very large fridge, Lyle announced with deliberate cheer, "Ah, we have roast beef and vegetable soup. How does a sandwich and a bowl of hot soup sound?"

"That's fine."

He glanced over his shoulder. "Again, I was looking for a little more enthusiasm."

A fake smile contorted her lips as she swung a fist overhead. "Great!"

He grinned. "That's more like it."

"Can I help?"

"Sure." He started pulling bowls and a platter off the shelves. When Cass reached him he handed her a few of them. She carried them to the table. Lyle followed with the rest. "You unwrap the containers while I get plates and things together." He searched cabinets and drawers for what they needed, making a couple of trips to the table to put everything down. She was halfway through removing the plastic wrap from the bowls when he said, "Now I'll warm up the soup if you'll make the sandwiches."

"All right."

He pushed the uncut loaf towards her. "I'd like two thick slices."

"Noted." She picked up a bread knife and start cutting.

Lyle ladled soup from its storage container into

a saucepan and turned on the stove. As he stirred, he watched Cass work.

Standing, she placed two slices of bread on a plate and buttered them. That done, she unwrapped the rest of the containers. Next she cut slices of roast beef, laying them on the bread. She finished with condiments and lettuce.

Cass's movements were concise and efficient. She had a no-nonsense way about her. Her blonde hair swung over her cheek and she pushed it back with impatience as if she had no time for things to get in her way. She cleaned up as she went. He got the distinct impression she took responsibility for herself and expected others to do the same for themselves. It must have been a rare event for her to let someone witness her raw emotions. Strangely, he was honored he had been the one there for her.

Lyle carried the steaming saucepan to the table and poured the soup into the bowls he'd found earlier, then returned the pan to the stove.

As he came to take his seat at the table Cass inhaled deeply. "That smells wonderful."

He grinned. "I can take credit for it being hot but not for how it smells."

She returned his smile and his heart made an extra thump. He filled the two tall glasses with milk. "Those sandwiches look good."

"I can take credit for how they look but not how they taste." Cass was trying to mimic his accent.

They both laughed as they settled onto their chairs.

She gave him a shy glance. "I don't do Scottish well, do I?"

"I'm going with it needs work." He looked at her over his sandwich just before he took a large bite. He appreciated the sparkle in her eyes that had replaced the earlier dull sadness.

They ate in silence for a few minutes before Cass let her spoon rest against the side of the bowl. "Do you know how the woman we helped is doing?"

He nodded. "I spoke to her doctor this morning. They kept her in overnight for observation, but she seems to be fine."

Cass lifted a spoonful of soup to her mouth. "I'm glad to hear it. How about the man?"

"He'll come in next week to have his stitches removed." Lyle took another bite of his sandwich.

"You really are a jack-of-all-trades, aren't you?" She appeared fascinated.

He rather liked that idea. In fact, he liked her. It had been too long since he'd let himself be drawn to a woman. It would be short-lived, of course, as Cass would be returning to the States soon, but why couldn't he enjoy her company while she was here? It would certainly make his Christmas more interesting. "I wouldn't exactly say that I'm Santa, spreading cheer, but I try to help out where I can."

They finished eating and Lyle started cleaning the table. "Even with my special powers I'd better do the washing-up if I don't want to get on the wrong side of Ms. Renwick."

"I'll help," Cass said in such a firm tone he didn't dare argue.

Together they covered the food and returned it to the refrigerator. His hand brushed hers as she handed him a bowl and he saw color bloom in her cheeks. Despite her tough exterior, her face couldn't conceal her attraction to him. Her gaze met his before she quickly returned to the table to pick up their plates.

Instead of joining him again, she went to the sink and turned on the water. Now she was trying to hide from him. With that in mind, he did his best as he finished clearing away to give Cass space while she washed up. He was aware enough of her to realize she was trying to avoid more contact between them. Was she attracted to him? Was she noticing his every move, as he did hers?

Cass turned toward him, her hip resting against the counter. "Didn't you say that Ms. Renwick leaves food for you?"

"She does, but that doesn't mean she isn't particular about how her kitchen is kept." Lyle stacked the bowls in the cabinet.

"So, if I'm not careful I'll end up on her wrong side?" Cass hung a dishcloth back just as it had been when they'd come into the kitchen.

"I wouldn't worry about it too much, she's really a softy at heart."

Despite his assurance, they stood at the door and gave the kitchen one last look before they exited the room.

"I don't think we've left anything out of place," Cass said as the door swung closed behind them. "My mother is just as particular about her kitchen."

"I'm sure Ms. Renwick will be pleased." That was the first time she'd revealed a personal detail without being asked. He was delighted she had begun to open up.

Cass led the way through the dining room and continued into the hall, where she stopped and turned. Her eyes flickered up to meet his gaze then down to the floor just as quickly. "Thanks for supper…and for, you know…" she glanced up at him in a self-conscious manner "…a while ago. My…uh, meltdown."

She looked so apologetic he crammed his hands into his pockets to keep himself from hugging her. "Not a problem."

"I'll give the canine therapy another try." There was determination in her words.

"And I'll speak to Flora and Margaret and see

if they can work something out so you won't have
to work with one particular dog."

Cass gave him an earnest look. "I'll do what I
can to make that work. I really do appreciate you
letting me cry on your shoulder."

To his complete astonishment, Cass placed a
hand on his shoulder, came up on her toes and
gave him a quick kiss on the cheek.

Pleasure zipped through him. When he saw
Cass's shocked face seconds later with its charming pink cheeks he was mesmerized. This tough
woman appeared flustered. Her eyes had gone
wide in surprise before she blinked a couple of
times and looked away. She shook slightly and he
feared she might fall. Lyle reached for her.

Cass stood close enough that he could smell the
fresh scent of her hair.

"I'm sorry," Cass murmured.

Lyle lowered his head to hear her words, bringing his lips closer to hers. He watched them, the
soft full pads that looked so delicious.

"That was inappropriate. I shouldn't have done
that." Cass glanced at him then away.

"I'm not," he said quietly. "I rather liked it."

Her eyelids fluttered closed, then her gaze met
his. They stood there watching each other for
precious moments. The tip of her tongue made a
flicker of an appearance. Lyle wanted a taste, just
a small one, of that glossy moistness on her bot-

tom lip. He lowered his head and placed his mouth over hers. Cass remained still in his hands. Lyle took the kiss deeper.

Cass returned it for a second before she slipped out of his hands and whispered, "Goodnight."

Lyle watched her walk away. Disappointment filled him. Everything in him wished he could stop her without frightening her. He wanted more than a chaste meeting of lips. It hadn't been nearly enough. He sought a full, no-holding-back kiss from Cass. There was an attraction between them he wanted to explore. It had been a long time since he'd experienced such a driving need to kiss a woman breathless.

Chapter 5

Cass walked to the canine center the next afternoon still astounded she had foolishly kissed Lyle. Making her embarrassment worse and her pleasure more, Lyle had actually looked pleased she had kissed him.

But she didn't do that sort of impulsive thing. Ever. She thought through her actions first. Never had she fallen apart like that in front of anyone. To do something so rash only showed how open the wound was that made up her life. Then there had been her crying jag. Until last night she had held it together despite all she'd been through. Talking about Rufus had broken her.

Lyle had been incredibly kind when she'd really needed someone. Beneath his attention she'd opened up like never before. He'd listened without judgement instead of running away. Lyle acted as if he cared, understood her loss.

Cass shook off that admission.

She'd kissed Lyle. What had she been thinking? She hadn't been, instead she had just reacted. It had been a stupid, careless move. Being here at the castle was about therapy and making a full recovery, not romance. Her heart couldn't handle those emotions right now. Even if it could, what did she imagine would come of it? Nothing, that was all that could happen.

As she entered the canine therapy center, Margaret greeted her at the door as if she had been waiting for her. Instead of taking her into the room where she had been the day before, Margaret escorted Cass into another one where the dogs were housed in pens with fenced runs. Cass shoved her shaking hands down into her coat pockets. She didn't want anyone to see that her hands were trembling.

Margaret stopped in front of the first cage. "The dogs on this side of the building are the ones we call the 'reimagined' dogs. They're working dogs that we get from all over the world. When they're too old we take in the ones we can, retrain them and give them new purpose. Esme also has a breeding program for specialized therapy dogs for epilepsy and diabetes patients. We train from puppy age until they are just over a year old. Those dogs are Labrador retrievers, Labradoodles and golden retrievers."

Cass nodded.

"Now, this is Oscar. He's a sweet dog and has been paired with Mr. Ellis."

"I've seen them together some." Cass recognized the small black and white, wire-haired dog, along with a number of others. They'd all been paired with patients at the clinic.

"And you should remember this one. He's the dog I understand that you and Lyle brought in the other night. We're calling him Dougal."

Cass nodded. Dougal suited the little dog. Rufus had already been named when Cass had got him, but his name had suited him too.

They moved to the next pen. The dogs were getting larger as they went.

"This is Morrow. He used to be a guide dog."

He was being "reimagined," much as Cass was working to do with her life. If she didn't return to search and rescue, what was she going to do? Could she accept a new partner and try again? A sick feeling welled up in her, but she forced it down with a clenched jaw. She'd already made a spectacle of herself in front of Lyle. She *would not* do the same in Margaret's presence.

Margaret kept moving down the aisle, introducing Cass to dogs as they went. Cass battled to remain calm rather than listening until Margaret said, "...and he was a search and rescue dog. A good one, I understand. But he went blind in one eye and that ended his career."

Cass's attention remained riveted to the light-gray-furred German shepherd lying quietly in the back corner of the cage.

"He hasn't adjusted to being here as we would like. I think we're rather dull to him after his exciting life." Margaret's voice was sympathetic.

Cass empathized with the dog's pain. She, too, was out of her comfort zone for reasons beyond her control.

"Now, this is McDuff. Everyone's favorite." A big dog with shaggy fur and wide brown eyes came to greet them.

Cass reached out to him without thinking. He smelled her hand, fluffy tail wagging.

"Now that you've met everyone I'll show you where the supplies are and tell you some of your duties. I have to admit you're the first resident to offer to help us with dog care and I'm very glad to have you. We don't have enough help."

Margaret showed Cass the room where food was stored, the grooming area and where cleaning tools could be found. She explained what Cass needed to do and on which days of the week.

"Also, we would like you to walk any dogs that don't currently have assignments. That's the list on the board over here." She walked to the wall where a clipboard hung. "Currently there are just three dogs. You're free to take them outside for a walk on the lead or a run in the outdoor pen."

Cass would turn them out in the pen. Leash walking was more than she was emotionally prepared for. Too personal, too risky. She might start caring.

"You think you'll be okay with the work?" Margaret checked her watch.

Cass nodded. This she could do. She would be active instead of sitting around with a dog in her lap or on the floor beside her. Surely she wouldn't get attached tending to all the dogs on a daily basis. Having one assigned to her was the danger. She could feed them, walk them, and clean their cages and meet her therapy requirements then move on. All she had to do was make up her mind to do what she had to do. For some people that type of work might be beneath them. But it was the perfect means for Cass to ease back into interacting with a dog without the temptation of completely committing.

Over the next hour she fed and watered the dogs. When it was time to enter the search and rescue dog's cage, she had to read his name on the sign because she'd missed it when Margaret had said it earlier. She hesitated. Hero didn't scare her, instead he reminded her too much of herself. He remained in that corner as if he wanted to shut the world out. Was that what she was doing?

"Hey, fellow, it's nice to meet you. I understand we've been in the same business. I'm sorry to hear about your eye. That's tough." She moved to fill his food bowl. He watched her closely as she worked. Cass filled his water bowl from a bucket. He came up on his haunches as if he might be thirsty. "Come and get it. I won't hurt you."

"He mostly speaks German."

Cass heart clinched. Just like Rufus.

"I should have told you that." Margaret stood outside the cage. "But I'm sure he appreciates your soothing voice. I've been watching. You're good with the dogs."

"I've been around them all my life." Cass unlocked the cage.

"It shows. It's time for you to go." Margaret held the gate to the cage open. "I don't want to wear you out on your first day. I'll see you tomorrow."

"Okay. I need to put some things away before I go." Cass walked back toward the storeroom.

"Can you see yourself out?" Margaret called, heading the other way.

Cass placed the bucket she carried on the floor. "I can."

"Good. You did well today, Cass." Margaret gave her a smile and left.

Hopefully each day would get easier.

Three days later Cass was on the minibus to the village with five other residents. She looked out the window at the beautiful and fascinating countryside. She'd seen much of the world and, even covered in patches of snow, this place appealed to her. Her doctors had been wise to send her here.

Going to the canine therapy center still didn't fill her with excitement but it wasn't as difficult as it had been on the first day. She'd managed to interact with the dogs while remaining emotionally removed from them. She was pleased to see that Dougal was growing stronger each day. His odd appearance with some weight on him was beginning to make him look cute. The only dog that did disturb her was Hero. He still remained standoffish. Cass was trying not to let it bother her, yet it did.

Today she wasn't going to think about dogs or therapy or even the past. Instead she was going to enjoy her trip to the village. She didn't know what to expect of Cluchlochry, but she was enchanted from the moment she stepped off the bus. It looked like a scene from a Victorian Christmas card. Wreaths of fresh greenery with bows were on every building door and window. The main road was just large enough for two small narrow vehicles to pass. Her large American SUV would never be able to make it.

The sun was shining this morning, promising a warmer day than usual, and she was glad she'd left Lyle's scarf and hat behind, not wanting to have to carry them.

In the center of the village just feet from where she'd stepped off the bus was the cobblestoned village square. She followed the crowd to a building she'd overheard was called the community center. There were a number of tents set up outside, but Cass found the majority of the stalls inside. The individual areas each had their own holiday decorations. It was like entering a winter wonderland. Excitement filled her at the thought of some retail therapy. She wasn't much of a "girly-girl" where most things were concerned, but she did love a shopping trip. The van had come in early enough that the crowd was still comfortably small. Visiting the stalls should be fun.

She planned to buy boots and socks today as Lyle had suggested that first night. However, she would wait until later to shop for them to avoid carrying them around any longer than necessary. After she was finished at the Christmas market she would ask someone where to do shoe shopping. For now, she was going to see what the market had to offer.

The first stall she came to held handmade wooden figurines. Behind the table sat an older, grizzled man with the air of an outdoorsman. He glanced up for a moment then went back to whittling.

Cass picked up an angel and admired the workmanship. The texture was smooth and there was attention to detail. The face had the kind of expression befitting an angel. It was old-world craftsmanship at its best. Her mother would love any of the items on display. She would return to buy something for her mother before she headed back to the castle. Hoping she would make it home before Christmas, she planned on being prepared to celebrate with her family.

When they'd heard she was injured they had wanted to come to her in Germany. She had convinced them not to, assuring them she was going to be fine. Once she'd been sent to therapy she had persuaded them she would be home sooner if she concentrated on getting better. What she hadn't said was that she needed time to recover emotionally so she wouldn't fall apart in front of them, as she had with Lyle.

Cass paused at every stall, fearing that if she didn't she might miss something. At this rate she wouldn't see all the market today and would still climb back on the bus with an armload of purchases. However, she needed to get some local money to buy things. She went outside to the street and searched for an ATM sign. Soon she had some pounds in her pocket. Conscious of smiling for the first time in a long while she went to the nearest stall.

This one offered handmade Christmas-tree ornaments. Cass was enthralled. Each one unique, they were made out of natural things like nuts, twigs, and pine cones. They would be perfect on a tree. Once again she resisted the impulse to buy and moved on to the next display.

There she found leather goods of quality craftsmanship. She continued walking, merely looking at some stalls and handling items at others. Coming to town had been a good decision, even though she had initially intended only to buy new walking boots and socks. Nevertheless she was having a nice day. Even the bustle of the growing crowd made her feel more alive. She had needed this kind of therapy.

Spying a sign with the words "Aileen's Knitting" on it, she made her way over. It was past time to return Lyle's hat and scarf but Cass wanted to get her own before she did so. And some gloves.

The stall had two tables and a number of hat racks filled with hats and scarfs of every color. Cass went to one of the tables and ran her hand over a few of the items of outerwear, even trying on a couple. She studied herself in a mirror hung on a stand to see how she looked. The pale pink and gray striped scarf and matching solid pink hat she especially liked.

A plump middle-aged woman sat behind the table next to a small heater. Her needles clicked as she spoke. "That looks lovely on you."

Her Scottish brogue was so thick Cass had to concentrate to understand her. "Thank you. Your work is beautiful. And so soft." Cass pulled the cap off and picked up another in the same color but with a rosette on the side. She studied it.

At that moment a familiar masculine shoulder pushed a door open just behind the woman. Lyle entered, carrying a box. He turned and the door closed. She must have caught his eye because he looked at her with surprise. A smile curved his lips that made her middle flutter. "Well, hi, there. I see you took my suggestion about coming to the market."

Her face warmed. This was their first encounter since they had kissed. Surely if she acted like it hadn't happened, he would as well. "Yeah, I'm doing some shopping therapy, like the doctor ordered."

Lyle looked over the box at her. "I wouldn't say I ordered it, but I'm glad you came."

She nodded toward the box. "I see you're moonlighting. You don't have enough jobs already?"

He chuckled as he rested the corner of the box

on the edge of the table, continuing to hold it. "It's more like helping my mother out. Muscles and all that."

Cass knew those muscles well. She had felt those strong arms around her and the firmness of his chest when she'd pressed her face against it. She glanced at Lyle's mother, who watched them with pronounced interest, her knitting momentarily forgotten.

Lyle's head turned as if following Cass's line of sight. "Mum, this is Cass Bellow. She's one of our residents at the castle. Cass, my mother, Aileen Sinclair."

Cass was unsure how to respond. Lyle's mother was looking between the two of them as if she suspected something Cass was refusing to admit to herself. A second too late to sound natural, Cass finally managed to get out, "It's nice to meet you. Your work really is lovely. I wish I had your talent."

The door opened again and a tall man who was undoubtedly an older version of Lyle joined them with a box in his hands. "Aileen, where do you want this?

"Over in the corner will be fine." Lyle's mother pointed to the one opposite hers. "I don't want it near the heater."

The man put the box down as instructed and turned to Cass. Something about his bearing made Cass want to stand at attention and pass inspection yet he looked in poor health. His was gaunt, far too thin for his height. There wasn't a sparkle in his eyes like Lyle's. His skin had a grayish tint to it. Lyle's father was sick.

"Sir, this is Cass Bellow. My father, retired Colonel Gregor Sinclair."

Still resisting the urge to salute, she settled for, "Hello, sir."

"Hello, young lady." The older man offered his hand. Cass put hers inside his. He still had a firm grip, but his fingers felt fragile in hers.

She looked at Lyle's parents. "It's nice to meet you both."

"You're not from around here, I can tell," Lyle's father said.

Cass chortled. "Is it that obvious? No, I'm from America. Montana currently."

Lyle's father nodded. "I worked with many Americans while I was in the military. Good sorts. I expect that Lyle will be working with some as well when he returns to active duty."

Her look swung to Lyle. Was he going to join the army again? He seemed to love working at the clinic.

Before she could ask, he took the hat from her hand. "This will look nice on you."

She unwrapped the scarf from her neck. "I think so too. I'd like to get both of them, and the gloves as well. They're too nice to pass up. Plus I need to return yours."

"You do?" Lyle's mother gave him a questioning look.

"Cass didn't have a chance to prepare for our Scottish weather before she was transferred here." Lyle turned to put his box on top of the other one as if discouraging more of his mother's questions.

Cass pulled out her cash, counted out the correct amount indicated on a sign next to the mirror, then handed it across the table.

"Thank you, Mrs. Sinclair. Maybe one day I'll learn to knit and make something half as lovely as your work."

"If you'd like to learn I could show you. Lyle could bring you to the house some day for lunch." Lyle's mother looked from Cass to her son, a small smile on her lips.

Was Aileen's maternal intuition working overtime? Cass shook her head. "Oh, no, I didn't mean to imply you should teach me."

"Nonsense. I'd love to give you a lesson. And at this time of the year knitting is about all I'm doing anyway, with the Christmas market going until the season is over." The clicking of the needles started again.

Cass didn't know what to think about Aileen's invitation but she said the polite thing. "Thank you."

"Would you like a bag for those?" Mrs. Sinclair asked, a nod of her head indicating the knitted items Cass held.

Cass glanced down. "No, I think I'll wear them." She stuffed the gloves in her pocket, looped the scarf around her neck again and pulled the hat snugly over her head. "It was nice to meet you Colonel and Mrs. Sinclair." Giving Lyle a swift look as she turned to leave, she added, "Bye." Hesitating a second, she turned to look at Lyle. "Would you mind giving me directions to where I can buy some boots?"

"Why don't I show you instead?" he offered.

"I don't want to put you out. I'm sure your mother needs your help." Cass didn't need him thinking she was using that as a ploy to spend more time with him.

"I'm good for now." Aileen waved a hand. "While you're gone, Lyle, why don't you stop by McKinney's Pub and get Cass one of their pies?" She looked directly at Cass. "Best meat pies you'll find anywhere."

Lyle stepped around the table and came to stand beside Cass. His hand touched her back briefly and was gone. He called over his shoulder to his mother, "I'll do it."

They worked their way around the people coming and going as they walked in the direction of the door. A couple of times Lyle put a gentle hand in the small of her back while guiding her through the crowd.

"That hat and scarf color is very flattering on you," he said. "Reminds me of when you blush. Your cheeks turn that shade." He grinned as their gazes met. "Like right now."

The compliment gave her a luscious warm throughout her body like a hot drink heating her from the inside out.

They exited the building and turned left down the street. As they continued walking toward the other end of the village green they approached a monument. It consisted of a tall narrow shaft encircled by steps. On top was a small statue.

"What's this?" Cass stopped and studied it.

"It's a Mercat Cross. They have been used in Scotland since the eleven-hundreds to distinguish the right by the monarch to hold a market or fair. They were symbols of authority. There're aren't many of them left now. We're rather proud of ours."

"That's interesting." She liked learning historical facts about places she went.

"They're not only places for merchants to meet but places where state and civic proclamations would be made. Even to this day in Edinburgh the town crier will still make proclamations on occasions."

She looked up to where the statue stood on top. "I would love to hear one sometime."

"Maybe you will one day."

Cass doubted that. She wouldn't be here long enough for that to happen.

They moved on in comfortable silence until they made their way through the crowd and out into the open again.

"So how have your last few days of working with the dogs gone?"

Cass glanced over at him. "Don't you already know? I figured you've been checking up on me."

Lyle chuckled. "I have, but I'd like to hear from you."

She appreciated his honestly. "It's going better than I expected. I admit it was tough to get started, but I'm getting used to the dogs and them to me."

"I'm glad to hear that." He did sound pleased, as if her happiness really mattered to him.

She couldn't say she was happy yet, but she'd moved the needle that direction. "You're not really surprised, are you?"

"Not really. Canine therapy has proved very effective. Even on those who are resistant." He gave her a knowing look.

"Is that your way of saying I told you so?" Somehow she didn't mind if he did. This was the best she had felt since before the accident. Her thoughts weren't so dark anymore.

Lyle stopped in front of a shop built of brown timber. The upper half of the door had four window panes. A Christmas wreath hung low beneath the glass. Attached above the door was a swag of greenery entwined with red ribbon. On either side of the door were display windows filled with boots, coats and other outdoor wear. All of it was arranged to create the impression of presents under a Christmas tree.

Lyle opened the door for her. "The shoes are at the back on the right."

Cass followed him down a narrow aisle lined with high shelves stuffed with items. The dim lighting added to the alluring atmosphere. The place smelled of wood oil and pine. Cass inhaled, taking it deep into her lungs. It reminded her of Lyle. She was enchanted with the shop. In fact, she was charmed by everything about the Heatherglen area, including Lyle. What was happening to her?

They arrived at the back of the shop. There in one corner was a small wooden bench along with boxes of boots piled on the floor.

Lyle stretched to his full height and looked over the shelves. "Apparently Mr. Stewart isn't around. We'll have a look at these and he should be back soon. He must have stepped out for lunch. I have experience with this so we'll just help ourselves."

Cass lowered her chin, eyeing him dubiously. "You've been a shoe salesman?"

He gave her an indignant look. "I worked here when I came home on school breaks."

"Oh. So you *are* a jack-of-all-trades."

He stepped toward the boxes. "I wouldn't exactly say that, but I can handle reading shoeboxes. What's your size?"

"Eight and a half, US." She sat on the bench.

Lyle nodded and studied them a moment. Moving a couple, he pulled one out. "I hope I made the European to American conversion correctly. Give these a try and we'll see."

She took the box from him and opened it. Removing her shoes, Cass pulled the new boot on her right foot. She stood and wiggled her toes. "Nicely done. Feels good but I would really rather have them in black."

"I aim to please. Let me see what I can find." Lyle shifted around a few boxes. With a bright smile on his handsome face, he handed her a box.

Cass sat on the bench again and started trying on the second boot.

"What's your favorite color?" Lyle asked, his back to her as he straightened boxes.

"Why?"

"You need some good socks." He studied her with visible curiosity.

She continued trying on her new boots. "Blue."

He moved down the wall and seconds later handed her a pair of thick socks. "These'll keep your feet warm and wick the moisture away. I promise you'll like them."

Cass removed the boots and her socks then pulled on the new ones. "I can already tell the difference." She flexed her foot then slipped her foot into the boot. Nice. Quickly she pulled on the other boot and laced them both up.

Standing, she walked back and forth a couple of times, testing the feel of the footwear. "You know, if you ever decide to give up medicine you could have a future as a personal shopper."

Lyle gave a regal bow. "Thank you. I have to say with complete confidence that's the first time anyone has suggested that to me."

They both laughed.

When was the last time she'd laughed like this? How had she not noticed it slipping away?

She liked Lyle's relaxed view of life. With his job and military background she marveled he wasn't uptight and domineering. Instead he seemed to accept life as it came and made the most of it whenever he could. Cass needed more of that in her world.

Lyle had a way of making her smile, and she also needed more of that right now. However, she must not start depending on him to make her feel better. She had to depend on herself. She had to regain her strength. Be strong.

If she opened up to him any further, leaving him

would be a new trauma, one she knew she couldn't handle. Her job certainly didn't lend itself to an easygoing and emotional personality. Even when she was at home her focus had been on working with Rufus to keep them both sharp. Had the men in her life been right? Did she live too closed off? Had been concentrating on her job and Rufus more than she should have?

"You want to keep those on?" He picked up the box.

"I believe I will. Start breaking them in." Cass picked up her other shoes and placed them in the box while Lyle held it. She met his gaze. "By the way, what's your favorite color?"

"Green." His eyes didn't waver. "I'm particularly fond of the shade of green of your eyes."

Her breath caught. "Are you flirting with me?"

"What if I am?" He took the box and set it on the bench. "I've been thinking about that kiss."

A tingle ran through her. "You shouldn't."

"What? Think about it or think about doing it again?"

"Both, " she squeaked.

"Why?" His voice turned gravelly, went soft. Lyle stepped toward her.

Because she was damaged. Because she was scared. Because she couldn't handle caring about anything or anyone again. "Because I'm leaving soon."

"Cass, we can share an interest in each other without it becoming a lifelong commitment. I'd like to get to know you better. Couldn't we be friends? Enjoy each other's company while you're here?"

Put that way, it sounded reasonable. Lyle moved so close that his heat warmed her. Why was it so hard to breathe? She simmered with anticipation. His hands came to rest at her waist as his mouth lowered to hers.

She didn't want his kiss. That wasn't true. Until that moment she'd had no idea how desperately she did want Lyle's lips on hers. Her breath caught as his mouth made a light brush over hers. He pulled away. Cass ran her tongue over her bottom lip, tasting him.

Lyle groaned and pulled her tight against his chest. His lips firmly settled over hers. Cass grabbed his shoulders to steady herself. Slowly she went up on her toes, her desire drawing her nearer to him. Sweet heat curled and twisted through her center and seeped into her every cell. She'd found her cozy fire in a winter storm.

The sound of the door opening brought both their heads up. Their gazes locked with each other's.

"Hello? Is someone here?" a man called.

"It's Lyle, Mr. Stewart. I'm in the boot section."

"Please don't do that again," Cass whispered, and stepped as far away as the small space would allow. She couldn't deal with the feelings swarming in her. This wasn't what she needed or wanted. She needed to figure out her life, not complicate it.

Now that she'd really been kissed by Lyle, she wanted more. *No!* And she couldn't handle the feelings his kiss had kindled in her. This was too much at the wrong time. Panic welled in her. She shook her head. Letting something grow between them would only turn into disaster. She didn't want to hurt Lyle, and she couldn't endure another heartache.

He studied her for a moment, then picked up the box, placing it under his arm as if nothing earthshaking had happened. "Let's go and pay for these then get one of those pies."

That suited her just fine. She could pretend nothing had changed as well as he did. Head held high, she followed him two aisles over to a wooden counter. A middle-aged man with white tuffs of hair, rosy cheeks and a white beard stood behind it. He could pass for a Santa Claus.

"Well, hello. How're you, Lyle?" Mr. Stewart gave them both a wide smile.

The man's accent was just as thick as Lyle's mother's.

"Fine, thanks, Mr. Stewart. We've been helping ourselves to some boots. I was just going to write you a note and leave the money."

"Give me a second to set this down." The older

man placed a brown bag on the counter. "I went to get a meat pie before they were all gone. I look forward to Mrs. McKinney's pies all year."

"I hope you left some for Cass and me. We're on our way there next." Lyle leaned toward the bag and inhaled deeply. "Mrs. McKinney makes the best."

While the men were talking, Cass managed to get her purchase paid for. She and Lyle exited the shop. The sun was shining but clouds were gathering.

"It looks like it'll snow again tonight," Lyle commented. "We need to go this way." He indicated to the left. "McKinney's Pub is down this way."

Cass shook her head. "I'm not really hungry. I think I'll just look around some more then go back to the castle. I appreciate your help with my boots."

Lyle said nothing until she looked at him. "Cass, I didn't mean to make things uncomfortable between us."

"You didn't."

He searched her face for a long moment. "Then you won't mind joining me for lunch. You don't want me to have to eat alone."

She pursed her lips. "Somewhere in there I think there's a touch of emotional blackmail."

He quirked a brow, his grin devious. "Could be. Live dangerously and join me."

She was doing that by just being around him. Her body still hummed with awareness, but she did owe him. He'd been nothing but kind. More than once Lyle had gone far beyond what was necessary. Helping her with her new boots was just one of the small things. Still feeling unsteady after their kiss, she was afraid that remaining in Lyle's presence might further break her tightly strung nerves. It was risky to her well-being for her to say yes. "If you're going to insist."

A winning smile lit up his face. "I am. You know how I hate to eat alone. This way."

They didn't walk far before they came to a building with an elaborate sign stating that it was McKinney's Pub above the door. "Here we are."

Cass turned the doorknob and pushed the door open, to find a room with a dark timber-beamed ceiling, stone-flagged floor and a handful of wooden tables and chairs unoccupied. Men were standing at the bar with drinks and talking. She glanced back at Lyle to see him duck to enter.

"Why don't you go see if you can find us a table near the fire while I place our order?"

"Okay."

"Before you go, would you prefer beef or pork?" Lyle asked.

"I don't know. You make the call." She didn't often let others decide anything for her. Being with Lyle was definitely having an odd effect on her.

For some reason she trusted him not to let her down.

"Okay. One more thing, hot drink or something cold?"

"Hot, definitely hot." She shivered. "I can't even imagine drinking something cold." Cass reached into her pocket. "Here's money for mine."

Lyle looked offended. "Put that away. I'll get this."

"I don't expect you to buy my lunch." She couldn't continue being indebted to him. "You're always doing something for me."

"You can return the favor sometime. Now, go and find us a seat." He started toward the bar.

"You don't need my help carrying the food?"

He shook his head. "I can handle it. You find us a place to sit before they're all taken."

"All right." Cass made her way to an empty table to one side of the roaring fire in the fireplace. She turned a chair toward the flames and sat down, stretching out her hands to the warmth. A couple of minutes later she looked around to see where Lyle was.

She quickly found him among the people at the bar. With his height and broad shoulders he stood out among the others. His hair was mussed but it matched his easygoing personality. Lyle was every bit as appealing to look at as he was to talk to. She was getting in deeper and deeper the longer she was with him. As hard as she tried to push away, the greater the pull he had on her.

Soon, carrying two drinks with steam wafting from them, Lyle joined her. He placed them on the table. "You got us a perfect table. How did you manage that?"

Cass shrugged and picked up her mug. "Lucky, I guess."

Lyle picked his mug up as well. "This is hot punch. I think you'll like it."

She took a sip. "Mmm…"

"I like it when you make that sound," he said, just for her ears. "You did it a while ago when I kissed you."

"I did not!"

Lyle gave her a wicked smile that said, Do *you* want to bet?

Heat that had nothing to do with the punch surged through her. "You shouldn't say things like that to me."

"What, the truth?"

Much to her relief, they were interrupted by a young woman placing two plates on the table.

Lyle said politely, "Thank you." The woman gave him a shy look and hurried away.

It appeared Lyle sent most women into a tailspin by just being nice. Cass had imagined he only had that effect on her.

She watched as Lyle used a napkin to pick up

the perfect brown half-moon pastry. He closed his eyes and took a bite. His eyelids dropped as an expression of pure bliss washed over his face. He slowly chewed. Something low within Cass tightened. She shook off the vision of Lyle naked in bed, wearing that same expression. How could just two kisses cause such an idea to pop into her head?

Instead of concentrating on her traitor of a mind, she followed Lyle's lead and picked up her pie. She took a small bite of the flaky pastry. It melted on her tongue as the taste of tangy beef hit her taste buds. She closed her eyes and enjoyed the moment. Did she have the same look on her face as Lyle? She opened hers to find him watching her closely, an intense flame of desire in his eyes. Oh, yeah, she had.

His voice turned husky as he said, "You should look like that all the time."

"How's that?" Cass dared to ask, unable to take her gaze off him.

"Angelic, as if you had found nirvana."

Emotion that had nothing to do eating meat pie and everything to do with the fire in Lyle's eyes flashed through her. This caring and comforting man wanted her. That knowledge was empowering.

"Hello, Lyle." a woman's soft voice said from behind Cass.

The pleasure lighting Lyle's face went out,

leaving a blank look with a hint of surprise. The woman was important to Lyle. Cass turned to see her. She had vivid blue eyes and was heavily pregnant. A sick feeling filled her stomach. Who was the woman to Lyle?

The last person Lyle had expected to see was Freya. He hadn't seen her for some time. Through his mother and father, he'd learned that she had married and moved to Fort William. He was truly glad for her, but that didn't make the surprise of seeing her again any less nerve rattling.

He laid his food down and stood. "Freya."

"It's nice to see you, Lyle." She sounded hesitant, as if she was afraid of his reaction. "How are you?"

"Well. And you?"

Her hand went to rest on her protruding middle. "I'm doing fine."

Lyle felt a sharp, piercing pain. They had talked about and planned on now many children they would have. There had been so many dreams they'd shared. He mentally shook his head. Those were long gone. Their relationship had been doomed the minute he'd boarded the train for training camp. He knew that now, but back then he'd been too caught up in pleasing his father by joining the army and the image of his fiancée waiting on his glorious return to see reality. Knowing his own mind and what he wanted out of life hadn't entered the equation. Much less fighting for it.

Freya glanced at Cass, who was observing them with interest. Was Cass thinking the child was his? "Freya." He nodded toward Cass. "This is Cass Bellow. Freya is an old friend."

"Hello," Freya said with a small smile as the two women studied each other.

A man not much taller than Freya but with huge shoulders joined them. He studied Lyle then Cass before giving Freya a questioning look, his brows making a V at his nose.

Freya cleared her throat. "This is Angus, my husband."

Lyle extend his hand. "Lyle Sinclair." It took a second before the man's eyes widened in recognition, then narrowed.

Angus shook Lyle's hand briefly, then put his arm across Freya's shoulders in a statement of ownership. To her he said, "Your parents are waiting."

Freya gave Lyle a sad, apologetic look. "It was nice to see you, Lyle."

"You too, Freya." He watched them walk away. That had certainly been interesting. Why had the meeting left him feeling so disconcerted? He'd got over Freya years ago, yet it still shook him to see her again. At one time they had been so close. Now there was a fence between them so high that they would never be able to climb it. Her husband's actions and facial expression made him question how controlling and overly jealous he might be. Was Freya truly happy?

"I think it's time for me to get back to the castle." Cass stood. "I promised Flora I would help with some of the decorations today instead of formal therapy."

Lyle blinked. How had he forgotten Cass was there? She must think him an idiot. "But we haven't finished our meal."

She gave him a curious look. "I have. Thank you for the pie. I should go."

"I'll walk you to the minibus." He needed to answer the questions hanging between them.

Cass waved for him to sit down. "No, you finish your lunch. I can find my way. I'll see you back at the castle."

Before he could order his thoughts, she was gone.

What was Cass thinking? Imagining? Had she seen what had once been between him and Freya?

Chapter 6

Back at the castle Cass debated whether or not to return Lyle's coat and other belongings that evening or wait until she saw him during work hours. Surely he needed his clothes. Yet her growing curiosity about the history between him and Freya made her cautious about seeking him out. It really wasn't her business, and yet she couldn't dismiss the distinct impression that something between them had caused Lyle great pain. Or was the baby the issue?

She knew Lyle well enough to know he would take responsibility for a child he'd fathered. Having a family of his own would be a serious matter to him. So was the baby his?

As hard as Cass had tried to maintain her emotional distance from Lyle, she cared about him. He had made it impossible for her to remain uninterested. Not only did she find him attractive, he had also proved he was a good man. So here she was, caring about him, concerned for him.

The feeling he needed someone to talk to also nagged at her. She owed him. Maybe she could help.

With her new socks and boots on and wearing her own jacket, which she'd found a few days ago laid out on her bed, she bundled Lyle's coat, socks, scarf and hat in her arms and made her way out of the castle. It would soon be dark, so she had tucked her flashlight safely in her pocket for the return trip.

At the gate leading into his yard she stopped. Was she being too forward by coming to his home like this? What would he think about her just showing up? Still, the need to see him, be there for him if he needed to talk, neutralized her apprehension. Her outlook on life had improved so much since he'd let her spill her problems to him. Maybe tonight he needed someone to listen to his troubles. She owed him and cared about him enough that she should at least be here for him. They were friends.

Pausing in the act of knocking on the door, she had the uneasy feeling her "honorable" thoughts about Lyle needing her were just an excuse to see him again. He had friends, colleagues, even his parents to confide in, so what had possessed her to think he required her?

As if of its own accord her fist hit the door. Breath held, she listened for movement inside, half wishing Lyle wasn't home, half hoping he was. All of this was so against her nature. She'd always known her own mind. Why was she doubting herself now? Why had she started acting like a silly schoolgirl around Lyle?

She had stepped off the porch to leave when the door opened. Her heart beat faster as she straightened her back.

"Cass?" He sounded both startled and pleased.

Did he think she was seeking his interest by showing up like this? Was she? "I, uh, wanted to return your things now I have my jacket back and a new scarf and hat." She thrust them into his hands before turning away.

"Would you like to come in for some coffee?" He asked, sounding hopeful.

She looked at him, even less sure about being there. But hadn't she been eager for Lyle to invite her in? "Could we make that tea?"

He chuckled. "Of course. Come in."

Inside, Lyle helped her off with her coat. As he did so, his hands rested on her shoulders for a moment. She missed the heaviness of them the second they were gone. She had the impression he wanted to keep an appropriate distance between them. Wasn't that what she'd all but told him she wanted? Especially after their kiss in the shop. Or did she want that?

"Come and join me in the kitchen," Lyle suggested as he moved through the door opposite the living room.

"Let me take my boots off first. They're pretty muddy." Cass sat on the small bench underneath the coat rack and removed them, then followed him.

Lyle was already at the stove with the kettle in his hand when she entered. He placed it on the element and leaned against the counter. "I see you're wearing your new socks again."

"Yes. They're the best I've ever worn. I plan to buy a few more pairs before I leave for home." Cass settled into one of the wooden chairs at the small round table in the middle of the room.

"Flora tells me that if you continue making the progress you have been, it'll be sooner rather than later." He opened a tin filled with biscuits and placed it on the table before returning to the cabinets.

She reached for a biscuit. "I'm pretty determined to get through this as quickly as possible."

Lyle glanced over his shoulder, studying her for a moment. What was he thinking? He returned to removing mugs from an upper cabinet and added tea bags to them. "I noticed that."

Did it bother him that she so was eager to leave the clinic? Cass looked around. "I like your kitchen."

"Thanks." He put a bowl of sugar and small pitcher of milk on the table. The kettle switched itself off as the water was boiling. Lyle poured the steaming water into the mugs before setting one in front of her and the other at the place beside her, rather than across from her. He took a seat.

She liked him being close enough to touch. Maybe she had imagined he was trying to keep distance between them.

Lyle pushed the tin in her direction. "Have another if you wish. It's interesting you like my kitchen. These old cottage kitchens have charm but they're often difficult to modernize. I've been led to believe women like to have the latest and greatest to work with."

Cass added sugar and milk to her tea. "That sounds like you're speaking from personal experience."

"Yeah. Freya always wanted one of those new brick houses with all the glass."

A zip ran along Cass's nerves. He had made it that easy for her to ask about Freya. Still, she hesitated to pry. Would he be upset if she did? Cass watched him. Lyle studied his tea. "Would that be the Freya I met today?"

"That's the one." A pensive look remained on his face. "I think I owe you an explanation."

"Why?"

"Because I was kissing you and then a pregnant woman who I'm sure you figured out shared a past with me shows up. It didn't make me look good."

"You didn't—don't—owe me an explanation." No matter how much she wanted to hear one.

"Maybe not, but I'd like to give you one anyway. The baby isn't mine. I haven't seen Freya in over a year. She was my girlfriend when we were teenagers. I asked her to be my wife the night before I left for basic training."

"Now I understand the look on her husband's face." It had been jealousy.

Lyle nodded. "Yeah, I'm not his favorite person, I imagine. But he has nothing to worry about. It's been over for a long time."

"What happened?" Cass hissed in dismay. "I shouldn't have asked that. It's not my business."

He finally met her look. "It doesn't matter. I don't want to have any secrets from you."

What was he saying? That sounded too much like he wanted a relationship more intimate than friendship. Their kisses had certainly been a step beyond mere friends.

"I received the classic 'Dear John' letter. By the

time I was able to come home months later she was already married."

Cass placed her hand over his hand resting on the table. She had been right. He did need to talk. "I'm sorry that happened to you. You deserved better."

He turned over his hand and held hers. "It was a rotten feeling at the time but far better than marrying the wrong person."

She couldn't disagree with him, but it must have been a horribly painful experience. To feel so helpless. She knew that all feeling too well. In too many areas of her life.

"It took me some time, but I realized that we would never have made it. Ours was a young immature love and an engagement based on me leaving, not on something lasting. I promised myself that the next time I asked a woman to marry me, we would both be mature enough to know what we were doing, and that we understood what real love is." He let go of her hand.

"Enough of this serious talk. Here I am dragging up my long-gone past while your tea is getting cold."

Cass took a sip from her mug. "I knew something big had gone on between the two of you. I just wasn't sure what. Her husband made a point of making it clear where she belonged."

"I noticed that as well. I hope she's happy. My

mother said this is her second child." He bit into a cookie.

"I must admit I was curious. In fact, half of the reason I came tonight was that I thought you might need to talk. You helped me by listening so I thought I could return the favor."

He gave her a thoughtful look then grinned. "I see. And here I was thinking you wanted to spend more time with me."

Just like that Lyle had changed the atmosphere. He knew how to ease a tense situation.

She returned his smile. "Please don't let anyone tell you that you lack an ego."

His grin turned suggestive, causing her middle to quiver. "I'm not sure that was a compliment, but I'm going to choose to take it that way."

Cass huffed in humor. "Does anything keep you down long?"

"I try to keep a positive outlook where I can. I learned long ago that life was easier that way. How do you see the glass? Half full or half empty?"

She winced in her mind. Most of her life she would have said half full but right now she wasn't sure she could. "Can I get back to you on that?"

Lyle watched her far too closely for comfort. "Sure. I just want you to know that I'm here for you."

"Thanks. I know I showed up at the castle with a chip on my shoulder. I'm trying to do better."

"From all I've heard, you are."

Cass pushed away from the table. "I should be going."

"Do you have to? Stay awhile and I'll walk you back later." His face was hopeful.

She ought to leave. Hadn't she already stepped over the line by coming here? Yet she did want to remain longer. "I guess I could."

"Great. Would you like to watch TV, play chess or maybe do a puzzle?"

She blinked and laughed. "Wow, you know how to show a woman a wild time."

He carried their mugs to the sink. "What can I say? Most of my excitement comes from accidents. I'm not planning one to impress you."

"I'll be more than happy to settle for a puzzle. I haven't done one of those in a long time." That seemed like a safe enough activity.

"During the winter months I keep one going all the time. It's in the living room. Go on in and see what you can do. I'll be in after I finish here." He turned to the sink.

Cass did as he suggested. A fire was burning. She found the table with the puzzle laid out on it behind the sofa. It had to have been there the other night but she had been so out of it she hadn't noticed. The puzzle was a picture of a lioness and her cub. A difficult one at best. She sat in the chair, adjusting the lamp over the table to shine it where she wanted it.

Lyle entered to find Cass sitting in his chair at his puzzle table. Something about the sight seemed right. She looked like she belonged, fit in his world.

Her head remained lowered. The glow of the fire reflected off her hair. He longed to brush his hand across it. Test its softness. Pulling another chair close, he joined her.

"So this is how you spend your evenings?" She picked a piece up and tried it. It didn't fit. She put it down and went for another.

"Not every evening." He wished Cass would put as much energy into getting to know him as she was into working on the puzzle. Was he really that desperate for a woman? No, it was more about the sensations Cass stirred in him. Sensations that had lain dormant for a long time. The same ones he'd been afraid to show for so long.

"I would think a hot young doctor would be too busy with the ladies at the pub to spend time doing puzzles." She put a piece in and made a tiny sound of joy, and it sparked something in him.

What would it be like to kiss her again? That thought was all it took to set his blood humming. How would she react if he tried to kiss her right now? Would she push him away or tug him closer, like she had at the shop? He had to stop these runaway thoughts.

Focus on the puzzle, he told himself. Concentrate on finding that one missing piece. Maybe if he did that, he'd forget the sweet smell of Cass's hair moving just inches from him, or the breathiness of her voice when she spoke or the soft touch of her hand as it brushed his when they both tried to fit a piece into the same space.

Minutes ticked by, the longing in him growing, groaning with the seconds. To stop himself from reaching for Cass, Lyle stood and went to the fireplace, using the need to put another log on the fire as an excuse. With his back to the warmth, he watched her. She truly was striking. Every fiber of his being was on alert for the least hint of encouragement.

Cass looked up. "Hey, are you going to leave all of this to me? This is such a great picture."

"I like the one I'm seeing." His gaze met hers and held.

Cass's head dipped to the side as if she was making a decision. Moments ticked by as they watched each other.

Lyle cleared his throat. "Cass, I've been thinking of little else but kissing you again. If you don't want that to happen then it might be better if you go."

She blinked. "Go?"

Lyle chuckled softly as he stepped toward her. "Or stay? That's up to you." When Lyle reached her, he lifted a strand of her hair and let it drift through his fingers. He didn't miss the hitch in her breath.

Taking her by the shoulders, he brought her to her feet and against him. The chair turned over with a bang but neither of them gave it any notice. His lips found hers. They were as soft and pliable and welcoming as he remembered.

There was no uncertainty on Cass's part this time. Her arms circled his neck, pulling his head closer as he took the kiss deeper. She moaned low, wiggling against him and sending his desire into orbit. Her mouth opened without his request and her tongue eagerly met his in a sensual dance.

With his desire for her increasing by the second, he buried his fingers in her hair. Cass gripped his shoulders as his mouth left hers to leave kisses along her jaw and up to her ear. She did a super-sexy wriggle against his taut length when he planted a kiss behind her ear.

Cass cupped the side of his head and guided his mouth back to hers, then kissed him deeply. His body throbbed in appreciation. Cass ran her hand over his chest and down to his beltline. There she pulled his sweater up and his shirt out of his pants. Seconds later his skin rippled with the pleasure of her hand moving over it.

Lyle had to touch her, all of her. He lifted Cass to the back of the sofa and stepped between her legs. Finding the edge of her sweater, he stripped it from her and let it drop to the floor. He kissed her temple. "I've dreamed of doing this for so long."

"You have?" Her whispered words held a note of wonder.

He looked into her eyes. "I have."

The smile that lit her eyes and curved her mouth was suggestive and stimulating, promising delights to come. Excitement set his blood on fire.

Cass reached for his sweater and started to remove it. He stepped back just enough to whip it off. As she balanced on the sofa back, her hands went to the bottom button of his shirt. She unfastened each one with astonishing speed, pushing the material to either side, exposing his chest.

When she licked her lips, he was almost undone. Only with self-control that he wasn't aware he possessed did he manage not to flip her over on the cushions of the sofa and have his way. But Cass deserved better than that. She was someone who merited the best he could offer, and he vowed she would receive it. He cared too much about her for their joining to be anything less.

Lyle watched her face as her index finger traveled across his chest, around his nipples, then followed the line of hair disappearing beneath his pants. She let that naughty finger dip inside his waistband and tugged him to her. Her eyes were wide, questioning.

He found her lips again. When she pushed his shirt off his shoulders, he finished removing it without his mouth leaving hers. More than once he'd seen the fire in Cass. Her intensity for life was momentarily banked but he hadn't been prepared for this profound craving to explore her passion. He wanted, needed, to see more of her, touch more of her, to experience all of Cass.

Pulling her shirt up, he ran his hand over the smoothness of her back until he found the edge of her bra and followed it around to her breast. His hand covered it. She stilled. Her breathing had turned into panting. Satisfaction filled him when just the brush of his thumb made her nipple harden, pushing against the material of the bra. He quickly found the back clasp and released the barrier. Pushing it away, he caressed her skin until he found her breasts once more. Cupping one, he judged its weight. Perfect.

Cass leaned back slightly against his arm. Her eyelids were half-closed and her lips swollen from his kisses. She was gorgeous. Stunning. Her lips parted. Heat shot through him. He pushed her shirt out of the way and covered her nipple with his mouth. Cass moaned. Her fingers ran through his hair as she held him close.

He twirled his tongue, teasing her nipple until

it stood high. Cass made a crooning sound. When it turned to a coo, Lyle's heart sored. Pleased with himself, he moved to the other breast. As he achieved the same results his desire matched hers. Holding her securely around the waist with one arm, he leaned her back to view the full landscape. Cass lying out before him was beautiful scenery to behold. Eyes satisfied, his mouth feasted on her full breasts until she forcibly pulled his lips to hers.

As her flesh meshed with his, the aching in his body became raw pain. He pulled away, helping her to sit up straight. He steadied her with his hands on her waist. "Cass, are you sure you want to do this? Do you want to go upstairs? You decide."

To his alarm and disappointment, she pulled her shirt down over the mesmerizing view. Just as he let go of her waist so she could move away she said in a soft sexy voice, "I've always wanted to see your bedroom."

Lyle grinned. "Always, is it? I like the idea of that." He offered his hand, palm up. "Then let me give you a tour."

Cass floated more than walked up the narrow stairs behind Lyle. His firm hand clasping hers reassured her of his desire. She didn't want that to ever wane.

Even so, this impulsive decision to share Lyle's bed was reckless and far out of character. Yet this newfound freedom was intensely exciting. Anticipation tingled along every nerve. Lyle's touch, his smell, the flames of desire in his eyes all drew her to him. Being with him made her feel wonderful. Made her forget her losses. Dream of the gains. She wanted these precious moments and as long as he was willing to create them, she would take all he offered.

Tomorrow she would worry about the repercussions.

Right now, she was going to enjoy feeling, being alive as never before and leave her fear and hurt outside in the cold.

Lyle's bare back was wide, solid and strong. He was everything she needed in life right now. Was she using him? Maybe, but she would see to it he received as good as he gave. Because of him she had remembered how to give and felt whole for the first time in weeks.

At the top of the stairs he turned right down a small hallway and entered a dark room. Not letting go of her hand, he continued to lead her across the floor. Her socked feet sank into a plush rug seconds before a click heralded light. A lamp sat on a small wooden table beside a large impressive bed. The dark headboard almost reached the ceiling while the matching footboard rose a few feet above the mattress. A quilt in browns and tans covered it.

Lyle turned to her. "Are you still sure you want this?"

Cass cherished his thoughtfulness. She cupped one of his cheeks. "Oh, yes." Going up on her toes, she kissed him.

That was all the invitation he seemed to require. Pulling her tight against him, Lyle tumbled with her to the bed. She winced.

Lyle said a harsh word under his breath. Raising himself so that he could see her, he asked. "Did I hurt you? I'm so sorry." He made a move to leave her.

She pulled him back. "Just a little tender. But I'm all right. How about kissing me?"

Lyle smiled. "With pleasure." His lips found hers.

As he kissed her his hands explored and caressed her waist and hips before lightly trailing between her legs. By the time they pulled apart, her center beat like a drum keeping rhythm with their heavy breathing.

Lyle rolled to his side, supported his head in his hand, and studied her. His other hand went to the hem of her shirt and beneath it. She shivered when his fingers found skin and skimmed along it. His heated gaze met hers. "Shh… I want to see all of you."

She looked away. "I have scars from the accident…"

Lyle's lips found hers briefly. "Even those. They're part of who you are now. The amazing person you are."

Cass had never thought of them like that. Her fear had been that they would be one more turn-off for men. She tried to relax as Lyle pushed her shirt and bra up, exposing her breasts. When he wanted to remove her shirt, she lifted off the bed enough for him to do so.

"More beautiful than I imagined."

She studied him in wonder. He'd been thinking about her, imagining her without clothes? The revelation was like a balm to her battered emotions.

Lyle gave her a gentle kiss before moving to one breast, then the other. "So sweet." He rotated her so he could see the injury on her arm then gently kissed the area. "I'm so sorry you were hurt."

Moments later his hand moved to the button of her pants and undid it. It took him no time to find the aching need at her center and slide a finger inside. She squirmed. Instead of giving her the relief she yearned for, his caress heightened her burning need.

"Lyle…" she crooned. Her gaze met his.

He kissed her deeply and continued his ministrations. Stopping, he tugged at her pants. Cass lifted her hips, assisting him in the process before kicking them to the floor. Lyle ran his hand along her right thigh. He paused over the puckered skin, then leaned toward it.

She shifted away. "Don't. It's so ugly."

"Shh… Nothing about you is ugly."

Lyle lightly kissed the area then his mouth moved to hers as his nimble finger entered her again. As it teased, his tongue mimicked the erotic dance.

Cass forgot everything but the sensation Lyle was creating in her. Cass's body tightened as the longing built, pleading for release. When she reached the limits of her endurance her body took over as if leaving her behind. She closed her eyes, flexed her back and tightened her legs around his hand, slipping into the land of wonder and delight that Lyle had built just for her.

Lyle's kisses gentled. He gave her one quick peck before he left her. Cass opened her eyelids just enough to see him shuck his pants in one swift movement. He stood strong and proud. Her breath caught in her throat at the beauty before her. She had caused this reaction in him. With that knowledge came a sense of amazement and power. Lyle obviously wanted her as much as she did him. He opened the drawer on the bedside table and removed a package, tore it open and rolled the condom on. Stepping to the bed, he looked down at her.

Cass opened her arms. Lyle came to her and she

pulled him close. Her legs opened and he entered her slowly. She accepted all of him, but just barely. He eased out of her snug core, then plunged in again. Taking his head in both hands, Cass brought his mouth to hers. She loved kissing him. Loved how he made her feel—happy and healthy once again. Lyle increased his pace. The friction grew, building on itself. That growling need she'd known before returned with a vengeance.

Her eyes widened as she broke off their kiss and stared into Lyle's blazing ones. "Oh."

There was a lift to the corners of his mouth as she went over the edge of pleasure again.

Returning to herself, she saw the tension in Lyle's face that made his cheekbones more pronounced. His eyes were still locked with hers, but his attention was elsewhere. He thrust into her, faster and stronger. Throwing his head back, he let go a throaty groan as he found his release.

Cass's eyes slowly closed as Lyle shifted to her side, still breathing heavily. He intertwined his fingers with hers. Like their lives had become.

Could she let them remain so?

Lyle returned to bed to find Cass napping under the covers with her head on his pillow. Her scent would linger there when she was gone. Fulfillment filled his chest, made his heart light. Cass had come willingly and given without reservation.

He eased in next to her and pulled her close. She was warm and sleek along his side. After murmuring something unintelligible she settled like a kitten beside him. He brushed her hair from her face. Her lashes rested in a dark semi-circle long her cheek.

With Cass he'd found the most pleasure he'd ever experienced. He'd had relationships since Freya but only Cass had managed to capture his attention so fully that he thought of her more often than his job. No matter what he was doing, she slipped into his mind. Even after she'd left the pub this afternoon, he had been more concerned about her reaction than his own to seeing Freya.

Cass shifted against him. He looked down to find her watching him. "Hey."

A shadow of uncertainty filled her eyes. "Hi. I didn't mean to fall asleep on you."

"I'm not complaining." He hoped it would happen often. His body was already coming to life. Leaning down, he kissed her.

Cass stopped him from taking it deeper and further with a hand to his chest. "I'd better go. I don't want to miss the head count at the clinic."

Lyle wanted her to stay but he wouldn't make her. Still, he had to protest at her leaving. "They don't do a head count, do they?"

She smirked. "So asks the man running the show."

"I'm not a dictator."

Cass sat up, bringing the sheet along to cover her. To his disappointment. Was she still self-conscious about her scars? "I know that. In fact, next to my father you're the nicest man I know."

Lyle's chest tightened. Having felt his father's disappointment most of his adult life, to hear Cass say that touched him. He felt valued. He put his hand behind her neck and brought her lips to his. "Thank you. I think that might be one of the nicest compliments I've ever received."

"You're welcome. Now I'd better get going."

By slipping off the bed and snatching up her clothes, she gave him no time to argue. "Bathroom?"

Lyle gave a fleeting thought to outright asking her to stay. He didn't. Apparently she needed distance to think about what had just happened between them. Maybe he wanted that as well. He pointed. "Door in the hall."

When he heard the door close, he got up, dressed and went downstairs. Cass didn't even come into the living room where he was. Instead she went straight to her boots. It was as if she was running. Was she regretting what had happened?

She was in the process of pulling on her jacket when he placed his hands on her shoulders. "Cass."

"Yes?"

"What's going on inside that head of yours?"

She didn't look up.

Suppressing a sigh of frustration, he said, "I think we've come far enough in our relationship that we can trust each other. Why the speedy exit? At this rate you're starting to put a dent in my self-confidence."

That brought her head up. "Oh, no. It has nothing to do with you. It has everything to do with me. I don't want the staff gossiping about us. But let me assure you your ego is well deserved."

He wanted to thump his chest but he settled for a big smile. "That's good to hear. I'll walk you back to the castle." He helped her on with her jacket then pulled on his coat.

Outside the cottage Lyle took her hand. He was relieved Cass didn't try to pull free, half-afraid she would.

At the side door of the castle, she held him back when he would have gone in. "It might be a good idea for us to say goodnight here. Do you really want the staff to know the despicable things you've been doing to a resident?"

Lyle chuckled. "Despicable? What about the wicked things you did to me?"

"Wicked?" She sounded appalled.

"I like the wicked you. But I agree. We should keep this between us. There's no reason we should be the talk of the clinic, or the village for that matter." She already had enough troubling her. He didn't want her worrying about gossip.

Cass reached for the doorknob.

"You're forgetting something." Lyle brought her to him and kissed her soundly. They broke apart and he searched her face. "Sometime soon I plan to have you to myself all night."

Cass's eyes widened, as her mouth opened and closed before she shut the door between them.

Gratification filled him. She was not as unaffected by what had taken place between them as she acted.

Chapter 7

Two days later Cass sat in the castle lounge in front of the roaring fire snuggled into one of the wing-backed chairs. She was attempting to read a book she'd found in the library about the history of Cluchlochry. What she was really doing was thinking about Lyle. She had only spoken to him briefly a couple of times since they had been together. He acted as if he was abiding by her implied suggestion they make their time in bed together a one-time occurrence. Even though she had intentionally given that impression, she missed kissing him or being held in his arms. It was driving her crazy not seeing him. But she would be leaving soon. Could her heart stand for her to take it further?

Was he waiting for her to come to him? Could she let herself do that? Would she be able not to? Indecision roiled in her.

It was a relief to have the distraction when Melissa pushed a young man in a wheelchair into the room and over beside her. At least now she had something to take her mind off Lyle.

The young man, dressed in a T-shirt and sweatpants, looked older than she guessed was the reality. He was gaunt. Dark rings beneath his eyes emphasized his lost look. One of his hands had a tremor.

"Hi, Cass. Have you met Andy Wallace?" Melissa asked as she parked the man near the fire. A small brown and white cocker spaniel jogged along beside him, coming to lie at his feet.

"No, I haven't. Hi, Andy." A week ago, could she have sounded that friendly? Being at the castle had changed her...or had it been Lyle? The thought both worried and thrilled her.

Andy nodded, then looked down at his clasped hands in his lap.

Wasn't he the patient who had been admitted the same day as she had been? In all the time she'd been there she hadn't seen him. "I've heard of you. Nice to meet you."

Melissa locked the brake on the wheelchair. She

patted him on the shoulder. "I need to check on another patient then I'll be back to take you to therapy. I won't be long."

She gave Cass a quick smile and was gone.

Andy's eyes flickered to Cass with a look of uncertainty before they jerked away.

She leaned down and patted the dog. Not long ago she wouldn't have done that. "I do know Molasses. I work at the canine therapy center every afternoon so I get to take care of Molasses when she isn't with you. She's a good dog."

"Maybe when I start walking I can do that as well. The doctors keep telling me I'll walk again but I'm not sure that'll ever happen."

"Getting well takes time. I'm sure you'll get there." Who did she think she was to give encouragement when she'd been little more than a walking package of ugly emotions with a bad leg and arm a couple of weeks ago? This morning she'd even caught herself smiling when she thought of Lyle. Her leg was getting stronger and her arm was extending further. She smiled. Lyle had kissed her injuries. She had made more progress than she could have believed possible when she had arrived. For once she'd started thinking there was a future.

Andy said nothing more as he stared into the fire.

There wouldn't be much conversation unless she helped keep it going. She sensed he needed it.

Wasn't that what Lyle had seen in her? The need to talk about the unseen trauma that physical therapy had no effect on? Could she help do for Andy what Lyle had done for her? Giving him an ear, just listen to him?

She raised the book in her hand. "I've been reading about the history of Cluchlochry. This is an amazing area."

He grunted.

A response. Somewhat.

"We don't have anything like this where I'm from." She waved a hand indicating the castle. "It's a special place."

"I used to spend a lot of time here," he muttered.

Cass had to lean forward to hear him. There was moisture pooling in his eyes.

"You've been to Heatherglen Castle before?"

"Yes. I grew up in Cluchlochry." His voice had grown stronger.

"It must have been a fun place for little boys. There are plenty of places to hide. Big spaces to run." The castle and grounds would be a wonderful place to spend a childhood. Would Lyle's kids one day do that? The thought of him having children with another woman caused a dull ache around her heart.

Andy's eyes took on a shadowed look. "Nick and I used to play hide and seek here all the time. I never could find him." He didn't say anything more, returning to staring at the fire. "He's gone now."

"Gone?" she prompted.

"Died in Afghanistan."

Cass sucked in a breath.

"Nick was my best friend," he mumbled.

She wasn't sure who he was talking about, but the name sounded familiar. Waiting, she hoped he'd answer her questions without her saying more.

"It should have been me who died. He should have got out of the army. Should have come home. Not gone back. I told him not to," he said, less to her and more to himself.

Cass's heart went out to him. She cringed, too well acquainted with loss. Of emotions so enormous and distressing they were difficult to live with. Hers had many fronts. Rufus being gone. What to do with her life now. Could she have a real lasting relationship with a man? Now to live with the scars. All of those were bundled into a massive ball of insecurity. She could understand the forlorn man beside her too well. That added to her discomfort. "Heatherglen was Nick's home?"

Andy gave her an odd look as if he was confused by her confusion. "Nick was Charles's older brother. Dr. Charles Ross-Wylde, the Laird."

"Yes, I've met the Laird. I know who you're talking about now. I'm sorry to hear about your friend. Losing someone you care about is hard."

"Have you lost someone?"

This was not the direction Cass had anticipated their conversation going. If she had she wouldn't have started it. Over the last few days thoughts of Lyle had managed to overtake all those ugly, sad feelings that had weighed heavy on her and she liked it that way. The pain had dulled. Maybe, just maybe, if she could share some of her pain with Andy, he wouldn't feel so alone, maybe believe that life could get better.

To her surprise, she had begun to believe that. It had slipped up on her but, yes, she did. "I have. It wasn't a person but the next thing to it. He was my partner and friend. Rufus, my dog."

Andy gave her a long searching look. "What happened?"

Cass wasn't sure she could go into the details but she'd opened the door so Andy deserved the truth. Her eyes clouded over. "We were a search and rescue team. We had just saved a child when there was a ground tremor and the wall of the building started to fall. Rufus barked, warning me. The wall fell on him. Hit me in the leg and arm." She could say this next part. Had to say it. "He saved my life and lost his."

Andy gave her a compassionate look. "I'm sorry about your dog."

Moisture filled Cass's eyes, making Andy a foggy blur. "I miss him every day. I'm not sure if I can or want to return to my job without him. It may be just too hard. But search and rescue is all I know."

Lyle walked to the lounge door when he heard Cass's voice. He halted inside the door, just in time to hear her confession about Rufus. He listened for more. She hadn't told him the entire story. No wonder she had been so devastated by what had happened to her. The loss of the dog was some of it but her fears and agony went deeper. Her world had been turned upside down. She was unsure what direction to take. The change in her life must be terrifying for her. She'd experienced a major loss of not only her dog but life as she had known it. He knew her well enough to know that, for her, losing her job was like losing her identity.

Yet she had shared her grief and feelings with another hurting person. That had to have been difficult for her. He should feel hurt that she had confided the deeper meaning of the loss of Rufus with Andy and not him, but what Lyle had just heard told him what a large heart Cass had for people.

Andy had refused to come out of his room for days. Lyle had finally convinced him to come down. On top of not wanting to interact with others, Andy refused to talk about his accident and about losing Nick. Lyle would be eternally grateful to Cass for getting him to open up, to take a metaphorical step forward.

Cass and Andy were so adsorbed in their conversation they didn't see or hear him. He shouldn't stand here eavesdropping but he couldn't move either. Thankfully that was taken out of his hands when Melissa brushed past him.

"Hi, Lyle. How're you today?" She kept going until she reached Andy.

Cass's head whipped around so that she looked directly at him. Surprise, concern and happiness ran over her features in rapid progression.

Lyle was glad to see her as well, but he was still disturbed by what he had heard and what it meant in her life. He had made less of it in his mind than he should have. He now understood why Cass acted the way she did about the dog they'd found, the sadness about her when she'd first arrived, even her not wanting to get too involved with him. Her emotions must be in turmoil. She had been and was suffering far more than he'd given her credit for.

He stepped forward as Melissa announced as she took off the brake on the chair, "They're waiting for you in therapy, Andy. We must go."

Andy gave Cass a nod.

She offered him a wry smile. "See you soon, Andy."

Melissa rolled him back, turned him and they headed out the door.

Cass's eyes rose to meet Lyle's. "You heard?"

Lyle nodded. He didn't even try to question why she hadn't shared with him how losing Rufus had affected her. Now wasn't the time to analyze that. There might never be one. She didn't owe him anything. One hot evening together didn't mean they could or should bare their souls to one another. That was the way she seemed to want it. Didn't he as well?

Pushing herself to her feet, she said, "I'd better go."

He took a couple of steps forward, his voice going low. "I've missed you, Cass. I was coming to look for you when I heard your voice."

"Did you want something?"

"I'd like a kiss." He looked around, "But I won't do that here."

Cass rewarded him with a blush. She might be acting as if she was immune to him but she wasn't, not even a little bit.

"I'll wait until later. But I will kiss you." He stressed the last sentence.

She grinned at him. "Is that a promise, Doctor?"

Lyle's heart soared. He liked that much better than her sad look. "It is. I do have something to ask you, though. My mother rang and would like me to bring you around to Harlow House for dinner this evening. She wants to keep her promise to teach you to knit."

Cass looked away as if she was unsure. "That's not necessary."

He waited until she met his gaze again. "My mother will be disappointed if you don't come."

Cass looked down as if her shoes required her attention. "I'm just not sure that's a good idea."

"Why not? You have been invited." Lyle watched her closely. It shouldn't matter so much that she agree.

"I don't want to give her any ideas about us, with me leaving so soon."

"If that's now you feel…" He turned to go.

She reached out and grabbed his forearm. "Wait."

Lyle didn't realize until that second just how much he'd missed Cass's touch. He placed his hand over hers.

Cass's eyelids fluttered as she gave him a wary look. "I guess I could go. I'd never want to hurt your mother's feelings."

He made a *tsk*ing sound. "And here I was hoping you wanted to spend time with me. I'll meet you in the foyer at five."

She nodded.

Lyle ran his thumb across the top of her hand. "By the way, Cass, you're beautiful both inside and out. You really helped Andy out today. He needs someone to confide in, someone who understands where he's coming from. You're a special person, Cass Bellow."

Her eyes softened. Lyle had to leave before he kissed her right then and there.

A few hours later Lyle strolled into the foyer, expecting to see Cass waiting near the door. Instead he found her with a staff member and a couple of other residents, tying large red bows on the banister. The greenery had been draped the week before.

"It's really starting to look like Christmas in here." His attention was directly on Cass.

Everyone turned to him.

"Thank you," the staff member said. "I have some excellent help."

"I have one more bow to tie and I'll be ready," Cass called.

There was a happy note in her voice. That had been missing when she'd first arrived and he rather liked hearing it. Had he had anything to do with putting it there? He really hoped so. "We have time."

She moved up a step with only a slight hesitation. Soon she would be coming down those stairs as part of her graduation and be leaving him. The thought brought a wince deep within him. Did he want her to stay? Could he ask her to? He refused to do a long-distance relationship again. From experience he'd learned those didn't work. Cass's life was going all over the world, helping people, and his was staying here and doing the same. It would never work. It would be better for both of them to let go sooner than later.

Another few minutes went by before Cass came down the steps slowly, holding tightly to the rail, but she was doing it on her own. She approached him.

"You have made progress. It won't be long before you'll be going up and coming down the grand staircase instead of using the lift."

She smiled and his world brightened. "I have to admit that a few weeks ago I looked at it as if it was Mount Everest. I was halfway up before I knew it."

"You've worked hard. You should be proud of yourself." Lyle was.

"Thanks." Cass picked up her coat off a chair and slipped into it. Buttoning it, she quickly wrapped the scarf around her neck and pulled on her hat.

"Ready?"

"I am." She headed toward the front door.

Lyle followed. When they were out of hearing of the others he asked, "I thought you didn't want anyone to know about our…uh, friendship? You didn't seem to mind the others knowing you were going out with me."

Over her shoulder she said, "I told them you were testing my endurance by going for a walk with me."

"Ah, I see." He had a sour taste in his mouth. When she had suggested the other night that they keep their relationship between themselves it'd seemed the wise thing to do. Now he wanted people to know that Cass was his and he hers. Or was it really that way? "We do need to walk to my place and then take the car from there."

"Your parents live far?" She started around the castle toward the path to his cottage.

"No, but further than *you* would even wish to walk."

They were soon out of sight of the castle and Lyle took her hand. His heart thumped an extra beat when she didn't pull away. After they reached the seclusion of the large trees, he pulled her behind one and into his arms.

"I've waited too long to do this." His lips found hers.

Unsure what Cass's reaction would be, he was elated when she stepped into him and joined him in a kiss that should have melted the snow beneath their feet. They stayed like that until the wind blew and a pile of snow dropped off a branch, landing on their shoulders. They giggled like school kids then started toward his place again.

Once there, Lyle led her to the detached garage to where he kept his car. Inside it, he reached over and cupped her cheek. "I have missed you. I wished there was time to take you inside and have my way with you, but my mother is expecting us."

Cass smiled. "We all like to keep our parents happy."

He groaned. "That we do." He'd spent the better part of his life trying to do just that and was still managing to disappoint his father. If he returned to the army, he would be choosing his father's happiness over his own.

Cass looked over at Lyle as he backed out of the garage. It had been so long since she had been alone with him that she'd feared she might rush into his arms when she did have him to herself. The moment she had looked up from tying the bow to the spindle and her gaze had locked with his, her heart had galloped like a horse making the last quarter-mile.

What had he been thinking? Had he been as excited to see her? She'd left things between them as if their time together had been nothing but a nice evening. She'd been fooling herself. Being with Lyle had been more than that. She couldn't say that to him earlier in the lounge, so she was glad to have the invitation to his parents'. They would have a chance to talk. More than that, to touch.

She'd only agreed to help decorate the foyer

because it gave her nervous energy an outlet. If she hadn't, she would have been pacing the floor when he arrived. It had to have been high school since she'd last been this wired up about seeing a guy. Her attraction to Lyle had tipped over into need in such a short time.

That horse had broken into an even faster gallop the second Lyle had pulled her out of sight of the castle and kissed her. She'd been back where she belonged. When the snow had fallen on them she had laughed like she hadn't laughed in far too long. Instead of having second thoughts about becoming involved with Lyle, she was running headlong into doing so. Especially by going to his parents' house.

After Lyle had driven onto the main road, he took her hand and held it as often as the narrow winding roads would allow. He drove through the village and out the other side. Soon he turned into a lane that led to a stately house that was a larger version of Lyle's cottage.

Lyle's mother greeted her by pulling her into a hug. Cass instantly missed her own mother, who she hoped to see soon. She glanced at Lyle. That would mean she would be leaving him. At that moment, she decided she would make the most of the time she had with him. She wanted this happiness to last as long as possible. The difference between misery and joy had been made clear over the last couple of weeks and she would take all the cheer in life she could grab for as long as she could have it. Right now, that meant being with Lyle.

When Mrs. Sinclair finished embracing Cass, she moved on to Lyle with the same vigor, as if she hadn't seen him in years. Done, she escorted them into a living area where the TV was on. Lyle's father didn't stand as they entered.

Mr. Sinclair did offer his hand. "Hello again, young lady."

Lyle would age well based on his father's looks, despite the older man's illness. Some other woman would get to watch that. Cass wasn't going to think of that now. "Hello. Thanks for having me."

"Glad to. Hello, son." He and Lyle shook hands.

Something about the action bothered Cass. Shouldn't they have hugged? A second of coolness seemed to surround them.

"Cass and I are going to the kitchen to have our knitting lesson," Mrs. Sinclair announced, and turned to Cass. "Unless you have changed your mind?"

"Oh, no, I would love to learn."

"Then come with me. Lyle, you watch the match with your dad while we have our lesson." Mrs. Sinclair waved a hand at him as she moved toward a door off the room.

Cass glanced at Lyle who was already settling into a chair. Maybe Cass had just been imagining things. Lyle acted as if spending time with his father wasn't a problem.

She found the more she was around Lyle's parents the more she liked them. His mother was what every mother should be—warm and open. His father was harder to get to know with his gruff voice and iron exterior, but Cass suspected he loved his wife and son deeply, and they him.

Cass followed Mrs. Sinclair into the kitchen. It, like the rest of the house, was in perfect order. The counter tops were spotless and the floor gleamed.

"Why don't we sit by the fire? We'll be warm there."

A large range sat against one wall with two rocking chairs in front of it. Beside one of the chairs was a basket full of yarn with large needles stuck in it.

Cass took the chair that didn't have the basket next to it, reasoning that it was Mrs. Sinclair's.

Lyle's mother settled into the other. "We're going to start with something simple. Just learn to knit. I think it will be all that you want to do in the first lesson. Now I'm going to show you how to start then I'm going to let you do it."

Cass eagerly sat on the edge of her seat, watching every move Mrs. Sinclair made. "That sounds fine. I know nothing about knitting."

Mrs. Sinclair's mouth formed a smile much like

Lyle's. "Today you'll learn. Here are some needles and you pick out a skein of wool."

"They're all so lovely." Cass decided on a blue that reminded her of the color of Lyle's eyes. When she was gone at least she would have that to remember him by.

Lyle's mother picked up some needles and pulled out a length of wool. "The first thing you want to do is make a small loop and slide it onto one of the needles."

Mrs. Sinclair was already in her element. Cass watched intently.

"Now you bring this up around here, the tip of the needle through here and the wool around like this." The wool worked perfectly onto the needle. "Now I want you to try with your needles and wool."

Cass did as she had been shown until it was time to move the wool up and around the needle.

"Not quite, dear." Mrs. Sinclair's voice was patient. Did Lyle get that from her as well? "Let me show you." She brought the wool around and got Cass started correctly once again.

Cass had made ten rows and was proud of her accomplishment when Lyle's voice came from behind her. "It looks like you're making progress."

Cass held up what she had done. "Look, I'm actually knitting."

He smiled as if he was proud of her as well.

"She's a really good student," Mrs. Sinclair offered.

"Cass is good at anything she puts her mind to," Lyle said.

A warmth that had nothing to do with the fire spread through her. Looking over her shoulder again, Cass saw Lyle gazing at her with a twinkle in his eye. Was he thinking about their time together in bed? She gave him a shy smile then glanced at his mother to find her watching them closely. Did she see the attraction between them?

"I hate to break this up, but Dad and I were wondering how long it would be until dinner?"

Mrs. Sinclair put her work into her basket and stood. "Lyle Sinclair, you know as well as anyone that in this house we eat promptly at six. We have all your life. Gregor wouldn't have it any other way."

"Yes, once in the army always in the army." Lyle said it as fact, but there was a note of bitterness there as well.

She gave her son a direct look. "I'll have you know I don't worry about you starving when you eat Mrs. Renwick's food all the time."

Lyle's mood lightened. "I do have to be careful not to overdo it there."

Cass placed her work in the basket as well. "What can I do to help?"

"We're just having a chicken pie tonight. It's

already in the oven so there's not much to do except set the table."

"Lyle and I can take care of that, can't we?" Cass looked at him.

An amazed look came to his face, but he nodded. "Yes, we can."

Over the next few minutes she and Lyle gathered what was needed. A couple of times he brushed past her, making her tingle all over. When she asked him for a fork he handed it across the table in a manner that let him trail his fingers over her palm, which started her center throbbing. She'd had no idea that setting the table could be such an erotic activity. Her eyes met his. She didn't see a flicker of desire there, but a fire burning.

His mother cleared her throat, bringing them back to where they were. Cass dropped the fork with a clang onto a plate.

Lyle, the devil, grinned and picked it up. He put it in its place. "All done, Mum."

His mother smiled. "Thank you." She turned back to the counter to where a large bowl sat. "Oh, my goodness, we all need to give the pudding a stir. I don't want to forget it."

"Pudding a stir?" Cass gave the bowl a dubious look. "Exactly what're we doing?"

"Stirring the Christmas pudding," Mrs. Sinclair stated, as if it was a great occasion.

"I don't know what a Christmas pudding is."

Cass looked into the bowl from which she had removed the cloth.

"I think they call it a fruit cake in America." Lyle moved up beside Cass.

"I have heard of them but never seen one or eaten one." Cass still studied the mixture.

"You'll have to join us for some in a few weeks." Lyle's mother pulled out a large wooden spoon from a drawer.

Cass felt more than saw Lyle tense beside her. Did it matter to him that she would be gone soon? It did her. She wanted as much time with him as possible before she left. "I'm not sure that I'll be here that long."

"Well, if you're here then you must come for a slice." Mrs. Sinclair didn't miss a beat. "You need to stir three times and then make a wish."

Lyle's mother handed her the spoon.

Wish? What should she wish for? To hurry home? For a new partner? She wasn't sure she was ready for that. She glanced at Lyle. To have him in her life always? What did she want most? Happiness. She glanced at Lyle. She felt that right now. But could it last?

It took more effort than she'd anticipated to stir the thick mixture but she managed to make the three turns. She made her wish.

"So what did you ask for?" Lyle took the spoon and started to stir.

"I can't tell you that. It won't come true." And she wanted it to come true no matter how improbable and unrealistic it was.

His mother stepped away. Lyle whispered, "Was it about me?"

Cass whispered back, "Such an ego."

"Lyle, if you'll carry the pie to the table and Cass brings the beans, I think we'll be ready." Mrs. Sinclair pulled a round golden-brown-crusted pie out of the oven. It smelled heavenly. She set it on the counter.

Lyle then picked it up and moved it to the table. His mother handed her the bowl with beans in it.

"Gregor," Mrs. Sinclair called. "Come to the table."

Lyle's father joined them, but it took him a while. He moved slowly.

Over the next hour they enjoyed good food and lively conversation. Cass looked around the cozy room. At Lyle. This was what she would like to have in her life. Lyle smiled at her. This was happiness.

"So what do you do in America?" Lyle's father asked her.

Her heart sank at the reminder. This wasn't her home. "I work in search and rescue." Did she still, though?

Gregor nodded. "Interesting work."

"It can be." She didn't really want to talk about it. "I understand you're retired military?"

He sat straighter, if that was possible. "I am. All the men in my family have made a career in the armed forces." He gave Lyle, who had turned stony-faced, a pointed look. "I'm hoping Lyle will decide to go active again soon."

She looked at Lyle, who was pushing food around on his plate. Had she said something wrong?

"Dad, let's not get into that now."

For the first time since Cass had arrived Mrs. Sinclair had no smile on her face. An uncomfortable feeling settled around them, completely wiping out the ease of earlier.

She had said something wrong!

Lyle's request went unnoticed by Mr. Sinclair. "You need to do it soon or time will run out for promotions."

"Isn't Lyle needed here? You should have seen him in action the other night. He had two patients to see about and then me. I understand that he's the only emergency medical care around here. That's a big burden for anyone. I think there are different ways of fighting for people. You did it by being in the military and Lyle does it by caring for people when they are hurt. In my book you're both heroes."

The others looked at her, speechless. Not even

Mr. Sinclair said a thing. Lyle gave her a tender look of wonderment and appreciation.

Mrs. Sinclair pushed back from the table. "I'll get those biscuits I bought at the market the other day for dessert."

An hour later Lyle was driving them back to his cottage.

"I hope I didn't say anything wrong at dinner," Cass said in a small voice. "I didn't mean to."

Lyle couldn't believe that Cass had even asked that. After her speech to his father Lyle's chest had puffed out like a bird preening for a new mate. Few managed to put his father in his place and Cass had done it effortlessly and had complimented his father at the same time. Lyle looked at her like she was a queen. "You were wonderful. The subject is an age-old sticky issue between my father and me."

"How's that?" Her attention was focused on him.

"You could tell that I'm a disappointment to him. He's sick. Dying, in fact."

Cass squeezed the hand he already held. "I'm sorry."

"I am, too. If I re-enlisted he'd be so happy. I could give him that before he died. Right now, I'm letting the family name down."

"You are not! He can't believe that. You help people. Look how much you have helped me."

Lyle raised a brow and gave her a suggestive look. "I don't help all the residents in the same way as I have you."

Her lips turned up in a smirk and she poked him in the shoulder with a finger. "And you had better not."

He was even feeling better about himself after that statement. It was the first time Cass had indicated that she felt any ownership of him, that he was important to her on a level outside bed. He liked the idea of her being jealous. She was definitely good for his ego.

Lyle pulled into his garage and turned off the engine. Twisting toward Cass he brought her to him. She looked at him expectantly. "I thought you were perfect tonight. Thank you for the vote of confidence. It means a lot. Especially coming from you."

Cass gave him a tender smile as his lips slowly lowered to hers. They were as soft as he remembered. A second later, her hands gripped his coat and pulled him closer. She returned his kiss. He lifted her onto his lap. It wasn't until she winced that he remembered her injuries.

He let go of her and she slid back into the passenger seat. "I'm sorry again. I keep forgetting you've been hurt. That hero certificate you said I deserved should be revoked."

"I'm fine. When I make certain moves my leg lets me know it doesn't like it."

"Necking in a two-seater car would be one of those times." What was wrong with him? He forgot everything but touching Cass when she was near. He climbed out of the car and hurried around to help her out. "I'm really sorry."

She wrapped her finger around his coat lapels and pulled him to her again. "Why don't you shut up and kiss me, then take me inside?"

He brought her into his arms with a smile on his lips. "I can do that."

Chapter 8

Four mornings later Cass was still in his bed when he woke up. Lyle liked it that way. Too much. She had stayed the night after they had gone to his parents'. They had agreed to eating dinner at his place the next evening.

As he'd held her in his arms after they had made love, he'd asked, "Will you stay the night?"

She'd leaned up to look at him. "I will if you understand that this can only be a short-term thing between us. As soon as I am given a clean bill of health, I'm going home. I can't handle anything serious in my life right now. I've just gotten to where I can get out of bed without dreading it."

Lyle had wiggled his brows. "That wouldn't be because you've been in bed with me, would it?"

She'd brushed a hand low over him and his body had twitched in reaction. "You might say that. I just need things to remain easy and fun between us. I've been on emotional overload for so long. I don't think I could handle more."

"I can do slow and easy. In fact, I'd like to practice now." He'd rolled Cass on her side and brushed a feather-light finger over her hip. Lyle had been rewarded with a shiver from Cass.

The next two nights they had eaten at the castle and then walked hand in hand to his place. Lyle had tried not to question Cass's decisions. Instead, he enjoyed having her in his life. No one at the castle had asked him where she was at night and he'd offered no explanation. All he knew was that life was better than it had ever been.

What they didn't do was talk about when she was leaving. Yet both knew it was coming. Too fast for him. Did Cass feel the same way? He didn't want to ruin what they had by asking.

On Saturday morning, they were lying in bed and Cass's hand was causally rubbing back and forth over his chest when she asked, "Hey, have you ever thought about making this place more festive? Everyone else is busy decorating for Christmas but you have nothing up."

"Are you thinking I should have a tree in my bedroom?"

Her hand gave him a light swat. Which he liked more than resented. "Of course not. I was thinking of you putting one up in your living room. It looks like Scrooge lives here."

"You can hurt my feelings, you know? I'd just planned to enjoy what's up at the castle. I've never really gone in for that sort of stuff, and I go to Mum and Dad's on Christmas Day." He pushed her hair back, letting his fingers run through it. "But maybe if I had somebody to help me, I could put a few things up. Would you be willing to help?"

Cass twisted around, looking him in the face while giving him a tantalizing view of the curve of her breast and hip. She seemed to give no thought to having scars anymore. "I thought you would never ask."

Lyle chuckled.

She grinned. "So do you have any ornaments or anything to put on a tree?"

"No. I hadn't had any need for them."

"Then we'll go to the Christmas market and get some. I saw some really pretty ones made out of natural stuff in one of the stalls."

Later Cass sat at the kitchen table, having a cup of coffee, while he scrambled eggs and prepared toast. She looked up and smiled. Lyle liked this Cass much better than the one who had first arrived at the castle. He would miss her when she was gone. "I really appreciate you talking to Andy. I've been worried about him."

"Unfortunately, I think we have a lot in common." There was a dejected note in her words.

"You might be right about that." He really couldn't break patient confidentiality. "I wish you hadn't kept all that happened to you from me, but I understand why you did. I'm so sorry."

She gave him a look of appreciation then went back to her coffee. Cass would talk more when she was ready. He finished the eggs, put the toast on a plate and carried it all to the table.

"I can help you." Cass reached for the plate.

"I told you that I wanted to cook for you. If we're going to get a tree and ornaments today you need to keep up your strength." He winked. "I might have other plans for you as well."

He was rewarded with an attractive blush. She never stopped amazing him. Cass was as tough as stone on the outside but could blush like a young woman after her first kiss. He loved the two sides of her. Love! Was he falling in love with Cass?

She spooned out scrambled eggs and took a piece of toast. "So can we go to the market as soon as we're through eating?"

"Are we in that much of a hurry?"

Cass gave him an insistent look. "We have a

lot to do if we're going to get this place looking festive today."

"We have to do it all today?" He gave a theatrical groan.

She put her fists on her hips and gave him a huffy look. "We do. I won't be here much longer, and I want to enjoy it for as long as I can."

That statement stabbed Lyle with reality, but he refused to let on that her leaving would upset him. She wanted casual and he would try to give her that. He chuckled. "Where did all this newfound Christmas spirit come from?"

Cass looked directly into his eyes. "From being around you. Thank you for bringing me back from that dark place."

His heart swelled. This was what it was like to be appreciated, valued for who he was as a person. He'd not felt that in some time. He needed it. Cass had given him a real gift. "You're welcome." He kissed her, keeping it tender, wanting her to sense his gratitude, then he pulled away, "You're right, I do need some cheer."

Soon after they'd finished breakfast, they left for the village. Few people were around. The sky was dark and it was starting to spit. It would snow again before the end of the day. Cass led the way to the stall with the ornaments she had seen. There, the owner greeted Lyle, whom he had known all his life.

Lyle told Cass, "Get whatever you think I need."

She grinned. "You shouldn't have said that." Cass went about picking out ornaments and putting them into a pile on the corner of the table.

Lyle paid the man, who was grinning from ear to ear as they walked off.

"Shouldn't we stop and say hi to your mother?" Cass looped her hand in the crook of his elbow.

"Yes. She would be hurt to know you came here and didn't say hello." Lyle led her down another aisle to his mother's stall.

His mother saw them and stopped knitting to greet them. "What're you two doing here?"

Cass gave this mother a self-satisfied smile and held up the bag she carried. "We came to get some ornaments for Lyle's tree."

His mother gave him a pointed look then asked with a sarcastic note, "Lyle's going to have a tree?"

He'd not had a tree or decorated his cottage since his return home. Freya had always made a big deal out of Christmas but he had never cared one way or the other. It wasn't worth the effort as far as he was concerned. But if Cass wanted him to have a tree, he would have a tree with all the trimmings.

"He is," Cass said proudly.

His mother looked from him to her and back again. Her smile had broadened.

"We're on our way to get one right now but we

wanted to come by and say hi to you." The cheerful words seemed to bubble out of her.

"Gregor," his mother called.

Lyle turned to see his father shuffling toward
them. He looked more tired than usual, older.

"Hello, son. I'm glad I got to see you. I spoke
to Colonel McWright a minute ago. He said you
haven't been by to talk to him about re-enlisting."

That was the last conversation Lyle wanted to
have with him. "I've been busy at the clinic. I'll
try to get by sometime this week."

"You need to do so. He'll be retiring soon and
won't have the influence he has now. If you want
that position you need to be talking to him."

The smile on Cass's face faded to an expression of curiosity and concern. Lyle wanted that
smile to return. His hand went to Cass's elbow.
"I'll take care of it. It's good to see you. Cass and
I are putting up a tree so we need to go and pick
out one before they're all gone." He started them
toward the door.

"Nice to see you, Colonel and Mrs. Sinclair."
Cass waved.

"Bye, Mum. Dad," Lyle called as they walked
away.

Cass pulled to a halt when they were out of
sight of his parents. "Are you really returning to
active duty?"

"No. Maybe. I don't know. Look, we have a fun

day planned and I don't want to talk about that. Let's concentrate on putting up a tree."

Cass studied him a moment then smiled brightly. "Works for me."

He would miss that smile when she returned to America. A stab of pain shot through him. This wasn't supposed to happen. He didn't, wouldn't, do long distance. It didn't work. He'd learned that the hard way. Yet he couldn't stop himself from holding onto what time he had left with her.

Cass came to another sudden stop at a stall selling Christmas-tree skirts. She fingered a navy one with silver stars sewn closer to the trunk of the tree and sloping mounds of white depicting snowy mountains. Was she thinking of the night he had found her sitting on the rock wall? Lyle smiled. Even then he had been captivated by her.

"Get it, if you want it." He pulled out his wallet.

"I wasn't asking you to buy it." She gave him a concerned look.

He gave her an indulgent smile. "I know that, but every good tree needs a skirt."

A few minutes later they left. Cass carried their purchases with a happy look on her face.

On their way back to his cottage they stopped at a place on the outskirts of the village to buy a tree. He had to remind Cass that his ceilings weren't that high when she admired a ten-foot tree. With an exaggerated expression of disappointment, she located a six-foot tree that he still hoped would fit through his doors. Cass's happiness with her choice made him keep his concerns to himself.

They made one more stop at a shop and bought a tree stand and lights. They spent the remainder of the day putting up the Christmas tree and decorating it. Done, they switched off the main lights and sat by the fire with a hot cup of tea.

Cass laid her head on his shoulder. "What kinds of family Christmas traditions does your family have?"

"You already know about the Christmas pudding. One year when I was off on the other side of the world Mum posted one to me. I hate to admit I was pretty lonely that year."

Cass said softly, "It was the year you got the letter."

For once the mention of what had happened to him didn't include pain. "It was. I sliced the pudding and shared it with the patients in my unit and we had a right fine celebration."

Lyle looked at Cass. To his amazement she had tears in her eyes. "What's all this about?"

She took his hand and tenderly rubbed it. "I just hate to think of you away by yourself at Christmas."

"Aw, honey, I'm home now. My Christmases are happy. This one will be especially so with this tree." What he didn't say was that he wished she would be there as well. He wouldn't think about that; instead he would enjoy what he had at this moment. She would be leaving soon. They had an agreement. Still the need to keep her there pulled at him.

A heavy knock at the front door broke the moment. Lyle opened it to find one of the local police officers standing there.

"Lyle, a five-year-old girl has gone missing. She wandered off from the market. We need your help to search."

"Missing?" The low sound of Cass's voice held a looming note of fear.

He forced himself to concentrate on what the policeman was saying. Cass he would soothe later. "How long has she been gone?"

"Two and a half hours." The policeman was wasting no time in giving answers.

His next question made him sick to ask but it was necessary. "Do you believe someone has taken her?"

The man's lips thinned. "Right now, no, but we're ruling out no possibilities."

"What do I need to do?"

"We've made a grid of the area." He handed him a map. "We need you to look here." He pointed to a square.

Cass came to stand in front of Lyle. "Do you

have a piece of the child's clothing?" she asked in a determined voice. "I can help."

"You are?"

"This is Cass Bellow. She's trained in search and rescue," Lyle offered.

Cass let him say no more. "Time's of the essence. Do you have something or not?"

The officer glanced at Lyle. He nodded. "I can get something."

"Then we'll meet you at the market cross in twenty minutes." She made that announcement, turned and started putting on her coat.

"We'll see you then," Lyle said.

The officer looked unsure, but nodded and left.

Lyle closed the door and asked Cass, "What're you thinking?"

"One of the dogs at the center has past search and rescue training. I've been working with him. He knows me. He might be able to help." She wrapped her scarf around her neck.

Lyle had to admire her. Working with a dog on a search had to take all her fortitude. For her to even volunteer said something about what kind of person she was. "You sure you can handle that?"

"Don't really have a choice. A child is missing." She jerked her hat down around her ears and opened the door.

"Hey, wait for me." Lyle snatched up his scarf and hat and hurried after her.

Chapter 9

"*Komm!*" Cass commanded Hero out of his pen at the canine center. She had made friends with him over the past couple of weeks so she had no trouble encouraging him to come to her. As he exited the cage she clipped on the leash. "*Fuss.*" Hero walked beside her to Lyle's car.

He opened the door and Cass said, "*Komm,*" and Hero jumped into the backseat.

Less than a minute later they were on their way into Cluchlochry.

Cass clutched her hands in her lap. It hadn't been long since she'd had an assignment and worked with a dog, yet it seemed like years. She was a bundle of nerves. What if she broke down?

What if they couldn't find the girl? What if…? All that fear and sadness that had held her heart in a vise had returned. If Rufus was here she'd have no doubts about locating the girl but she didn't know Hero well or his abilities. Still, she had to try.

Lyle drove faster than the speed limit, but every minute mattered. Hero sat calmly in the backseat of the car. Lyle pulled into a parking space close to the market cross. With the market over for the day, there were plenty available.

The policeman who had come to Lyle's cottage was waiting. As soon as they joined him, he handed Lyle a small orange jacket. "I understand she was wearing this earlier today."

"So she has no coat on?" Lyle asked, concern lacing his words.

Cass shivered as much from the cold as from her fear for the little girl.

The officer's face was grim as he said, "From what her parents tell me, she's wearing a jumper, jeans and boots. We don't know if she still has gloves on or a hat, or anything like that."

"Then we need to worry about exposure as well." Cass's words were flat and to the point.

"I'll get a thermal blanket and my medical bag out of the car." Lyle wasted no time in doing so.

"May I see the jacket?" Cass reached out her hand.

The policeman handed it to her and she knelt so that Hero could get a good sniff of the clothing.

Lyle returned with a satchel on his hip, the strap across his chest. He looked at her. "Ready?"

"Yes. You have a blanket?"

He patted the satchel and clicked on a large torch.

She gave the command to find. *"Voran."*

Hero started off across the village square with his nose close to the ground. Cass followed and Lyle was close behind.

Hero led them down a side street and out into a lane. Cass remained encouraged because he acted as if he had located a scent.

Her hand stayed on the leash as they continued walking at a brisk pace. Well outside the village Hero headed off the road and onto a path.

"It looks like he's taking us to the ruins," Lyle said, walking close beside her.

Her leg began to burn as the gradient grew steeper. She would push through it; she had no choice. When she faltered, Lyle supported her with a hand on her forearm. "Let me take the lead. I know this path."

"Okay. I'll let Hero go off leash." She unclipped the dog and he moved ahead of them.

Lyle took her hand and they worked their way up the path. It became more difficult to maneuver the closer to the Heatherglen Keep ruins they climbed.

Occasionally Hero would stop and look back at

them. He acted impatient for them to join him. He didn't have the same trouble with the steep terrain. Soon Cass's leg went from aching to really hurting but she wouldn't let on. She was the expert in this work. A little girl's life depended on her.

Now that the sun had gone down it was pitch black. There was no natural light from the moon. Making matters worse was the fact that clouds were rolling in. It would snow tonight.

When—if—they found the girl she could very well be hypothermic. She would need medical attention immediately. Could they find her soon enough?

Cass stumbled and Lyle caught her before she went down.

"Do you need to stop?" His concerned look touched her heart.

She shook her head. "No. We have to find her."

For a second he looked as if he were going to argue. "I don't need two patients."

"I'll keep that in mind." Cass trudged forward.

Lyle pursed his lips and nodded, then joined her.

Not soon enough for Cass they made it to the ruins. In the daylight she had no doubt the area was interesting but in the dark it had an eerie feel to it. Hero sniffed around, making a circle. Finally he stood beside a couple of huge stones and barked.

"Have you found something?" Cass said to the

dog as she made her way toward him, with Lyle shining the flashlight that direction. *"Setzen."*

The dog sat.

She and Lyle were looking into a hole.

"This was the dungeon at one time," Lyle murmured.

"Looks about as much fun now. Do you see anything?" Cass searched while being careful not to lean over too far.

Lyle went down on this belly. He directed the light straight down.

"There she is," Cass cried. A small body lay curled on the ground, not moving.

She stepped closer and Lyle said, "Cass, careful! Don't fall in."

"How're we going to get her out?" Cass was already looking for things they could use.

"We'll call for help." Lyle pulled out his phone. "Damn, I don't have a signal. One of us will have to go for help. But right now we're going to have to see to her. Minutes could mean the difference between life and death."

"We're going to have to get down to her somehow." Cass paused, panic filling her. The girl just couldn't die.

"I'll climb down." Lyle was already in the process of removing his bag.

"It looks too slick to do that. You'll have to lower me. I'm the lighter of the two of us. We can use the strap on your bag. It might not be long enough, but it'll get me close enough to drop the rest of the way."

"What about your leg? It might not hold up under that kind of pressure." Everything in Lyle's voice said that he wasn't going to agree to her plan.

Cass faced him. "That's just a chance I'll have to take. You know the path back better than me. The girl needs help now. I'm not going to argue about it anymore."

The determination in her voice must have got through to Lyle because he started unclipping the strap from his bag. With it removed, he pushed the extender so that the strap was as long as possible. "You ready?"

Cass took an end of the strap, wrapping it around her hand. "I am."

They both moved to the side of the hole. Lyle shined the light into the hole.

"There's still no movement." Cass's chest tightened. They had to get to her soon. Was she gone already?

Lyle dropped the flashlight into the hole giving them some light to work with. He then wrapped the strap around his hand just as Cass had done. She lay on her belly and crawled backward, going feet first into the hole. Lyle went to his knees, holding her under her arms as she slipped over the side.

"Feel for footholds." His voice was tight from the effort of holding her.

She did as Lyle instructed and located one. It was near the foot of her injured leg. She couldn't let the pain that shot through her slow her progress. She had to keep moving. When she was completely over the side she hung onto the strap as Lyle lowered her. She went further into the dark abyss. Thinking she had gone as far as possible, there was a sudden jerk and she was lowered further. Lyle must be on his stomach with his arms extended. She could only imagine the strain holding her was putting on his shoulder muscles. Guessing she was only a few feet from the ground, Cass let go.

She fell, hitting the ground. Pain that made her clench her jaw rocketed through her leg. She rolled onto her hip. "Huh."

"Cass?" Lyle's fear-filled voice came from above her.

"I'm fine. Harder landing than I anticipated." Cass picked up the flashlight and crawled over to the girl. She still hadn't moved. Worry leaped in Cass. Was she already gone? No, she wouldn't believe that.

Placing two fingers to the girl's neck, Cass found a pulse, but it was weak. The child's skin was icy to the touch. Hypothermia had set in. Pulling off her jacket, she wrapped it around the girl.

Cass removed her hat and scarf and put them on the girl as well.

"Cass, move far to one side so I can throw the bag down. I want vitals before I leave."

"Ready." A few seconds later Lyle's bag landed with a flop a couple of feet from her.

"Check her temperature and let me know what it is. Also, can you tell if anything is broken?" Lyle was giving her more orders than she could carry out at once. He was in full doctor mode.

Cass pulled the bag to her. Searching through it, she found the thermometer. Cass positioned the flashlight so that it shone on the girl. Thankfully Lyle had a battery-powered tympanic thermometer that Cass could just push into the girl's ear. Removing the girl's clothing would only make things worse. At least she wasn't wet.

Hero barked.

"Bleib!" Cass yelled and the dog stopped barking. *"Braver hund."* She called up to Lyle's shadow as she spread out the thermal blanket. "Temp is ninety degrees Fahrenheit—that's 32 degrees Celsius. Pulse is weak. Skin pale and cold to touch. Her breathing is shallow. I'm wrapping her in a blanket now."

"Can you do a BP?" There was an anxiousness to his voice.

"I'd rather not remove the warmth I've already given her."

"Aye. There's no question she has hypothermia."

Cass lay down on the thermal blanket and pulled the girl to her then wrapped the shiny, crinkly material around them. Maybe her body heat would help some.

Lyle's voice rang out again. "There are two heat packs in the bag. Squeeze them and put them under her arms. Don't put them against her skin."

She already knew that from her own training, but Lyle could only be frustrated by not being in the hole and the one taking care of the patient. He was a hands-on type of doctor.

"I'm leaving to call for help. Please don't take any chances. Stay put. I'll be back as soon as I can."

"Hurry."

"I will. Cass? I want your promise you won't do anything foolish." Lyle's worry laced every word.

Cass's heart swelled. He was such a good man. "Hero will be here. We'll be waiting for you."

"I'm counting on that."

Lyle hated to leave Cass but he had no choice. He had to go for help. They needed more than his to-go medical bag to save the girl's life. She needed hospital care. Right away.

Without his flashlight the walk down the rocky narrow path was slow, frustrating and dangerous. The fact that it had started sleeting only added to the difficulty. Despite that he had to keep moving. Not just for the girl's sake but for Cass's as well.

Lyle stopped often to see if he had a cellphone signal. Everything in him pulled at him to return to Cass. As brave as she was, she still must be frightened in that black hole with a child close to death. Lyle worked his way down the hillside. He had no idea how far he would have to go before he found a signal but it couldn't be soon enough for him.

The weather was taking a turn for the worse. To complicate the conditions, the ground was slick, the path narrow and the rocks numerous. Could the situation get more dangerous?

His heart jumped when the phone connected and started ringing. Finally. The police officer answered. Lyle told him where they were and that they had found the girl. He then gave him instructions to call the hospital in Fort William and have the ambulance sent. Also, to call the clinic for the medical van. They would meet the ambulance. Every second counted. The girl might not make it if she didn't get to the hospital right away.

Lyle wasted no more words and started climbing up the hill once again. More than once he slipped as the sleet grew harder. Before he reached the ruins the sirens of help could be heard, filling the air. On flat land again at the top, he ran to the hole. Hero was still obediently sitting beside it.

"Cass!" There was no answer. "Cass?" Still

nothing. Fear washed through him. What had happened to her? Had a rock fallen and hit her? All kinds of horrible scenarios played like a movie through his head. He couldn't lose Cass. He yelled louder. "Cass!"

"I'm here." Her voice wasn't strong, but it was there.

Relief flooded him as if a dam had broken.

She turned on the flashlight and pointed it toward him. "I hope help is on the way. I know now why the dungeon was the least favorite place in a castle."

Lyle chuckled. "Help is on the way. Has there been any movement out of the girl?"

"No. But let me take her temp."

He waited impatiently for her report.

"It's ninety-one Fahrenheit—a little under thirty-three Celsius."

"That's progress." He would take that. "How're you doing?"

"I'd rather be cuddled up next to you."

Lyle's heart melted. He wished that too. He was in love with Cass, he realized. "Honey, I promise you I'll make that happen just as soon as I can."

"Promise?"

"You have my word on it." When he got his arms around Cass again he might never let her go.

The sounds of people hurrying up behind him drew his attention. "Over here." A group of six people headed his way. "They're down here. In this hole."

"They?" one of the rescue men asked.

"Yes. A friend of mine, a woman who works in search and rescue. I lowered her down." Guilt pricked him. He should have gone. "We'll need a rope. I'll go down."

"You're staying put. We'll need your skills up here when we get them up." Les McArthur, the leader of the group and a man Lyle had known all his life, said, and pointed to a spot near the dog. "You stand there out of the way. What's the name of the woman in the hole?"

Lyle didn't like the idea of not being the one in charge but he did as he was told, knowing his friend was right. Still, that didn't calm his nerves. "Cass."

One of the men dropped a bag on the ground and unzipped it. He pulled a rope ladder out. Securing it to a large slab of stone, once part of the keep, he dropped it into the hole.

Les walked to the edge. "Cass, it's Les McArthur. We're coming down. Rope ladder first."

"Okay."

Lyle watched as Les went over the side. Behind him was a man with a foldup stretcher strapped to his back. Soon a bright light shone from the hole. Apparently Les had a portable light in the pack on his back.

"We're going to need ropes down here," someone called from inside the hole.

Another man pulled ropes out of a bag.

Lyle shifted from side to side, not just to keep warm but in his need to do something active. "Can I help?"

"No, this will go a lot faster if you let us do our part. Then you can do yours," one of the men said. "They're going to be fine."

Cass had better be. The girl as well.

The men threw the ropes in. A few minutes later Les called up, "Ready."

Everything in Lyle wanted to go down into that hole to Cass. Instead he stood watching all that was happening with his hands fisted at his sides and shoulders braced against the sleet-filled wind that was blowing harder by the minute.

Slowly the men started hauling the rope up. Soon the stretcher with the girl on it was being laid on the ground. At her feet was his medical bag. Cass had made sure he would have what he needed. She impressed him more every day.

"Let me check her pulse. I need to tell the hospital what to prepare for." Lyle went down on his knees beside the stretcher. He wasn't going to stand on the sidelines any longer.

The child was wrapped up in the thermal blanket. On her head was Cass's hat and around her neck was her scarf. Lyle pulled a section of the blanket back. And there was her coat. Cass had nothing to protect her from the elements.

With two fingers, he checked the child's pulse. He found it, but it wasn't easy to locate. The girl needed to leave for the hospital now. As much as he hated it, he had to trust that Les would take care of Cass. His next call after the ambulance would be to Charles and Flora. They'd also see to Cass. But he wouldn't be satisfied until he had her in his arms again.

He quickly stood, putting his bag under his arm. Giving the hole that Cass hadn't emerged from a longing look he said, "Let's get her down the hill. There's no time to waste."

Cass's body shook violently. She was so cold. Where was she? In a damp, dark, freezing hole.

No, that wasn't right. She had been cold, down to her bones. Now she was in a soft place, huddled in warmth. Her eyes flickered open. It was dark outside and a fire burned in the fireplace. She could see the flames reflecting off the wall. That was the only light in the room. Her room at the castle.

She turned her head to find Lyle asleep in a chair too small for him next to her bed. He was close enough to reach out and touch. His hair was tousled, as if he had run his fingers through it more than once. He snored softly. He must be exhausted.

The last thing she had a clear memory of at the ruins was the men securing the girl to the stretcher. She'd been so cold that all she'd been able to think about was sleeping. One of the men had given her a blanket but that hadn't stopped the cold from seeping deeper. She vaguely remembered her teeth chattering as she'd stumbled down the hill with the help of one of the rescuers.

Lyle hadn't been there when she'd come out of the hole. She'd known he wouldn't be. He would be with the girl, as he should have been. Still, that didn't mean she hadn't missed having his arms around her or his heat. It would have been preferable to those of a stranger, no matter how nice they were.

At the bottom of the hill a police car had been waiting. She'd climbed into the rear seat and the officer had turned the heat up high. Despite that, she had been bitterly cold and in a daze when she'd arrived at the castle. Charles and Flora had been waiting for her in the foyer.

"Lyle called us. Gave us strict orders to give you a full examination," Charles had said, pushing a wheelchair over to her.

Cass had been glad to see it, despite saying, "I don't think all that's necessary."

"Lyle does. And based on what he told us, you earned our attention. Thanks for what you did," Flora had added.

"Hero?" Cass had mumbled as Charles had pushed her and Flora had walked beside her.

"Esme is seeing to him. One of the police officers took him to the center. I understand he's going to get an extra helping of food. Esme said she could use a person with your skills at the center."

Cass had gone in and out of awareness while Charles had been examining her. When he'd finished, Flora had taken her turn, flexing and contracting her arm and leg. "We need to increase your therapy a bit for a few days, but I don't see why you can't be discharged on time."

Cass looked at Lyle. Discharged. At one time, all she'd wanted to do was to get home. That day would be here soon. Flora hadn't given her a specific date yet, but it was coming. Her leg and arm were much better. Despite all her efforts not to become involved, it had happened. It would be hard to leave Lyle. But she must.

She'd arrived with her emotions in a jumble and they weren't in any better shape now. In fact, her feelings for Lyle had only added to the issues. He deserved better than a woman who was so messed up. How did she even know the feelings she had for him were real? Maybe she was just reacting to her need to have someone care about her in a weak moment. That wasn't fair to him.

It didn't matter. After all, they had agreed only to a good time while she was here. Lyle hadn't said anything about wanting more. She'd made it clear she didn't. So what was she worrying about? She would leave as planned. He understood that. She would be home for Christmas.

But what if Lyle asked her to stay? Would she?

She couldn't. Heavens, she didn't know what she wanted. Taking a chance on them being together would be like jumping off a ledge. They didn't really know each other. What if it was just sexual attraction? It was best for Lyle to think of what they'd had as a nice friendship and let him move on.

It would be better for her as well. She'd learned last night that doing search and rescue was too emotionally hard for her. If that little girl had died, she would have as well. So what would she do now to make a living? Where would she end up living? There were too many unknowns.

Cass shifted. That was enough to wake Lyle. "Hey."

He sat straighter in the chair. Wrinkles filled his forehead as he studied her. "How're you feeling?"

"Better." She looked toward the window. "It's not morning?"

"No, it's still early. Do you need anything?" He leaned toward her, studying her.

"A hot bath."

"That I can handle." Lyle got to his feet.

Cass was confident he could handle almost anything.

"Let's get you into the bath. While you're there I'll go down and brew you some tea."

She grinned. "There it is again. The cure-all, but it does sound wonderful."

He started toward the bathroom. "I can tell your smart mouth isn't frozen any longer."

She giggled.

"You stay put and I'll be back for you," Lyle ordered.

"I can walk."

"Maybe so, but I'd like to carry you."

She would enjoy that. Seconds later water began running into the bath. The sounds of Lyle opening and closing cabinet doors soon followed. In a few minutes he returned to her.

"I know you've been sitting here thinking how you could walk in there by yourself but it's not going to happen." His accent became more pronounced when he was trying to make a point.

"You don't know me well enough to know what I'm thinking."

He put his palms on the bed and leaned in close enough that his nose almost touched hers. "Then deny it."

She met his gaze with a smirk. "I do. I was actually thinking how much I'd enjoy being in your arms."

Lyle's look turned to one of bewilderment as he continued to stare at her. It quickly changed to one of pleasure that included a smile spreading across his face. "Then we have a plan."

Cass pushed the covers back. Lyle placed an arm around her waist and under her legs then lifted her against his chest. The overlarge T-shirt she wore slipped up, exposing her thigh. Lyle's hand was warm and sure on her skin. She looped her arm around his shoulders and enjoyed the ride.

He sat her on the side of the tub. "Let me check the water temp before you get in."

Cass waited, watching him trail his fingers through the water. She like the tender attention from Lyle. It made her feel cherished. When had another man come close to giving her that feeling before? Never.

Jim had come the nearest, but he hadn't understood her, her job—and especially not her relationship with her dog. His idea of caring had been to tell her she should quit doing something so dangerous. He'd never appreciated what drove her. If it had been him there tonight instead of Lyle, Jim would have never trusted her enough to care for the patient while he was gone. Jim hadn't seen her as a partner, a strong person. Lyle did.

She respected him for that. Felt Lyle returned that respect. He had searched for a missing child without questioning her judgement of using a half-blind dog, then had lowered her into the hole on her directive, and cared for the girl when she'd been pulled out. Now he was looking after her. Was there anything he couldn't do?

"How's the girl doing?"

"She'll recover with a good story to tell. I understand her family went hiking up there last week. She'd lost her doll and was convinced that it was in the ruins. She went looking for it."

"I didn't see a doll." Surely she would have noticed one.

"I didn't either, so I had a new one sent to her." He said it as if it was no big deal.

"Lyle Sinclair, you're a really nice guy." She meant every word. Too nice for her to screw up his life.

"This is ready, if you are." He reached for the hem of her T-shirt and pulled it over her head.

Cass watched him but he didn't let his gaze drop below her face. He was being such a gentleman. Scooping up her feet, he placed them in the water. Cass slipped into the bath with a sigh of contentment. It rose to just below her breasts. She glanced at Lyle. His focus had fallen lower now.

"Hey." She took his hand. His gaze met hers. A flame of awareness burned in his eyes. "It feels really wonderful in here." She closed her eyes and lay back, giving him the full view.

Lyle groaned. "I'm going down for the tea. I'll be back in a few minutes."

Cass smiled, then said in her best seductive voice, "I'd much rather have you warm me up."

"I'm the administrator of this clinic. I can't be climbing into the bath with a patient." He didn't sound convinced.

"Lock the door, put out the *Do Not Disturb* sign. Live a little. Take a walk on the wild side. You know you want to." She tugged on his hand. "Mmm…it sure is nice." Cass opened her eyelids to slits. She could see the small upward curl of Lyle's lips. He was weakening. "At least kiss me."

Lyle leaned over her, his lips finding hers. She wrapped her arms around his neck and gently pulled him into the tub. Water sloshed everywhere but she didn't care and apparently neither did Lyle. She continued to kiss him as he settled around her and brought her against him, taking the kiss deeper. When they broke apart Cass pulled at his long-sleeved shirt until her hands could wander freely over his back.

"Cass, you'll be my undoing. And the end of my job if I'm not careful." He kissed the sweet spot behind her ear.

She started working on the opening of his pants.

"How am I supposed to get out of your room without being seen in soaking wet clothes?" He sounded more perplexed than angry.

She wanted him that way. Her hand brushed across his hard manhood. "You have other things to worry about right now. I'll show you a secret passage out."

"Secret, uh?"

"First things first." She gave him an open-mouthed kiss while pushing his pants over his hips.

A few days later, Lyle sat on the couch in his cottage with his arm around Cass and her cuddled under his arm and her head on his shoulder. All the lights were off except for those on the tree. It was the prettiest Christmas tree he'd ever seen. Or maybe it was because he was sharing it with Cass. Yet he sensed something was bothering her.

She had walked home with him after work but had been more quiet than usual. Normally she told him about her day or something a dog had done during her therapy. Today had been different. They had prepared dinner of soup and sandwiches, working together like a long-married couple who knew the next move of the other. Still she'd said nothing.

Was it worry over her leaving? He'd certainly spent more time thinking about it than he found comfortable. Flora had said nothing specific about planning to discharge Cass, but he and Cass both knew the time was near. He would find out before they went to bed what was going on in that busy mind of hers.

Lyle smiled to himself. He had really come out of his respectable world with Cass's stunt of pulling him into the bath. She had added excitement to his life.

Cass had helped wring out his clothes with a grin on her face. They'd laid them to dry near the fire and climbed into her bed. Just before dawn he'd pulled the damp clothing on so he could go home and put on some dry ones. He'd shrugged into his coat, grateful it wasn't wet. Cass gave him a goodbye kiss that had been hot enough to make them both steam. He had slipped out of her room and down a back staircase, with the jubilant thought that he wouldn't be seen. The second he had put his hand on the doorknob, Charles had pulled the door open. Lyle could only imagine the dumbfounded look on his face at that moment. Charles often came in early, but Lyle hadn't realized he used the side door.

"Hey. Aren't you going the wrong way?" Charles looked beyond him as if searching for something going on.

"I was sitting up with Cass." And other things. Very nice things.

Charles's forehead wrinkled with concern. "I checked her out last night. She seemed fine. Was something wrong?"

"No, I just wanted to make sure she was okay." Lyle made to step to past him. All he wanted was to get home and change his clothes.

A look of understanding came to Charles's face along with a grin. He gave Lyle a pointed look. "And is she?'

"She is."

Charles continued to block the opening. "Glad to hear it. Cass is a really special person. I heard what happened and how she jumped in to help."

Lyle couldn't agree more. Cass was very special. "She is special."

"Freya did you wrong. Not every girl will." Charles's words were said softly but matter-of-factly. "Maybe it's time to give someone else a chance."

Lyle had been thinking the same thing. "You're one to be talking."

"Just because I'm a bachelor it doesn't mean you should be one. Just think about it." Charles slapped Lyle on the shoulder as he went by. "Are you wet?"

Apparently his fingers had touched Lyle's shirt. "I fell in the bath."

He heard the roll of Charles's laughter as he hurried out the door.

Cass shifted beside him now. "What're you thinking about?"

He gave her shoulders a squeeze. "I was just

thinking about Charles catching me leaving the other morning."

Cass smiled against him. "So he knows about us?"

"Yes. But he would anyway. The Laird knows everything that's going on in his domain."

"Do you mind?" She turned to look up at him.

"Mind? Why would I? You're wonderful, smart, beautiful, fun to be around. Why should I mind? I'm honored."

She shifted to face him and gave him a gentle kiss. "Thank you. That was a nice thing to say."

"I meant every word."

Lyle did. He wanted more moments like this with Cass. If the truth be known, he wanted her forever. Yet he wanted to do it right this time. Make no mistake. For him there could be no long-distance relationship. He didn't want to feel pressured to ask her to stay, because they would soon be separated. But could he let her go without letting her know he cared?

Cass moved away from Lyle, then turned to face him. They had to talk. She'd put it off while they'd walked to his place, through dinner, and now she had to tell him. It shouldn't be this hard—after all they had an agreement. She'd made it clear where she stood. So why was she having such a difficult time bringing up the subject?

"What's wrong, Cass? Tell me."

She clasped her hands in her lap. "I can't hide anything from you. You always read me so well. Flora said this afternoon she plans to discharge me in three days. I can start making travel arrangements. I'll be home for Christmas."

Lyle studied her a moment before he said, "I knew the time was coming. We both did."

"Yes, we did."

He had sounded resigned, while she was a ball of growing sadness. It should be easier than this.

There was a pause as if Lyle was considering what he was going to say. "If I asked you to stay, would you?"

Cass slowly shook her head. "It's a nice thought, but not realistic."

"What about it isn't realistic?"

Her chest tightened. "My life is a mess. I don't even know what I want to do for a job now. My emotions are everywhere. I fear I've used you because you were nice to me and I had no one else to turn to. I can't make a life-changing decision like staying here with you based on that. It might not end well and you deserve better."

"We can figure it all out together." His words were said softly, beseechingly.

"Lyle, I've enjoyed every minute. Well, almost every one of them." She made an attempt at humor, but his serious look didn't change. "But I have to figure out my life on my own, otherwise it would never work."

"It seems to me it's been working great up until now." He sounded mystified that she might not think the same.

"I'm just so confused. My feelings are so jumbled up right now. I have a poor history of keeping relationships alive. I'd never want to do to you what Freya did. You're a wonderful man who shouldn't be treated that way. I can't take the chance that you become like the other men in my life, and I disappoint you. I couldn't stand to see that look on your face."

Lyle watched her for a moment. There was grief in his eyes. "Do you really believe all that rubbish? After all we have shared?"

"We're good together in bed, but that was never supposed to last forever. We talked about this when we started out." She waved a hand between them. "We had an agreement. You can't change the rules now."

"The hell I can't. Why can't you call this what it is? A relationship. I care about you. I think you feel the same about me."

"And let's just say that I do, then what? I still live in America. I may return to a job that takes me all over the world. Anytime, day or night. Or what if I decide to do something else and it's still the States? Do you think we have a chance at a long-distance romance? How did that work out for you last time?"

He flinched. "There will be no long-distance relationship between us."

"So you plan to move to America to be with me?"

His face fell. "We can work something out."

She hated what she was doing to him. That she was pushing him away. "What I'm hearing is that you want me to give up everything and come here to you."

"Put that way, it sounds unfair. Still, I think we have something real here. Something that doesn't come along often in a lifetime. Come on, Cass, stop hiding behind your fear. It's easy to keep a wall up, it's harder to let go, start again. Stop being dishonest with yourself."

"Dishonest! Like you are with your father? Have you ever made it clear to him that you don't want to return to the army? Even tried to make it clear he can accept that or not, but it won't change things? That you want him to be happy, but not at the cost of your own happiness?"

Lyle looked at her as if she had slapped him. "It's complicated."

"And my issues aren't? I'm sorry. I shouldn't have said that. You and your father's issues are none of my business. But what I do know is that if you return to active duty for someone other than yourself you will be miserable. Do you really think that's what your father wants for you?"

Lyle stood. "You're right, my issue with my father isn't any of your business. It has nothing to do with us."

"I'm not sure that's true. Here you are, asking me to stay with you, yet you might be going off to who knows where with the army. What am I supposed to do? Sit here waiting for you? I thought that was the kind of relationship you didn't want. It seems to me that we both need to make some major decisions in our lives before we involve someone else in them."

The ferocity seemed to go out of him like air from an air-bag. "All I want to do is make his last days happy ones."

"I know. But is re-enlisting the right way to do that? Or would the truth be better? You deserve to be happy as well. If you make him happy, you won't be. I know for a fact you're valuable to the clinic and this area. That you're happy with the work you do now. You're thinking of making a decision, a life-altering one, based on emotion. That's not a good way to do things. I can't do that. My decisions have to be based on more than hot sex with a handsome doc. I need to think. Need to regroup." She hated to hurt him but one of them had to think rationally. "I think it's best we leave this as a nice interlude."

"Interlude," he growled with eyes blazing—and not in the way she would have liked. "An interlude. I see."

What did he see? Lyle made the word sound nasty, ugly. "That's what we said it would be."

"If that's the way you feel then I wish you the best. Since this *interlude* appears to be over, I should escort you back to the clinic." He walked into the hall and took her coat off the hook.

Cass didn't see Lyle again until three days later when she was getting into the taxi that would take her to Fort William to start her trip home. She'd cried into her pillow each night since their breakup as loneliness consumed her, then worked hard not to show her sorrow during the day. Still, she felt she had done the right thing, for both of them.

She looked longingly at Lyle. Her heart thumped in her chest. If he asked her to stay again, would she? She needn't have worried. He remained near the front door, watching her without a smile or raising a hand in farewell.

Cass closed the car door. As she rode away, she swiped at her cheek. Unable to resist one last look, she turned to see the steps empty. Lyle had gone back inside.

If the last three days had been awful, leaving Lyle was truly horrible. What would the next week or month, or her life be like when she was thousands of miles away from him? She couldn't count the number of times she'd told herself, "Stay strong."

What she had planned not to do she had done. She'd let herself take the chance of caring again. She had fallen for Lyle.

Chapter 10

Lyle had let Cass's words fester. He was hurt that she could so easily dismiss what he held as precious. He now understood the meaning of "It cuts like a knife." Cass's words that night had done just that. Over time he had examined them. She was right.

He had been unfair. She'd come to Heatherglen hurt and traumatized. Only a few weeks later he was making demands on her. Had he completely forgotten everything but his own needs? Cass *should* be upset with him. They both had issues to deal with before they could commit.

Lyle didn't plan to give up. He'd give her until

January then he'd go after her. Surely they could find a compromise between their lives? He loved her, and he believed she loved him. There was no way he'd misread all those touches, looks and how they felt when they came together. He couldn't be that wrong.

The woman he wanted to share his life with would not only love him but support him. Cass had proved to know him better than he knew himself. She understood who he was. More than that, she complemented him. She had strength, confidence, and the largest heart of anyone he knew.

Cass was the one for him. Of that he had no doubt.

He needed to be worthy of her. Part of being that was breaking away from his father's expectations. He had only considered his father's wishes when he'd first joined the army. No matter how sick his father was now, it was time for Lyle to concentrate on his own desires. He'd lived under his father's demands for too long. Through the clinic Lyle was providing quality and necessary care for people who needed it. He was proud of that service. It didn't matter if his father felt the same way or not.

It was past time to have a frank discussion with his father. Really talk. Not dance around the issue but make it clear the direction he intended his life to go. It was with that intention Lyle drove to his parents' house that evening.

His mother opened the door. She looked surprised and pleased to see him. She glanced around him. "Is Cass with you?"

Lyle's chest tightened at the reality that she was actually thousands of miles away. He reminded himself that he would soon be going after her. "No, she was discharged and has gone home. She asked me to say goodbye to you." Cass had. Just before she'd told him the same at the castle door and had gone inside.

His mother placed a comforting hand on his arm. "I'm sorry. I could tell you really liked her."

Lyle did. More than that, he loved her. "I hope she'll come back."

"If she is as smart as I think she is, she will." His mother gave him a quick hug.

Lyle gave her a wry smile. "Is Dad home? I wanted to talk to him for a few minutes."

"He's inside, watching TV."

Lyle took a step and stopped. "How's he feeling today?"

Her look turned to one of slight concern. "He's having a good day."

"I'm glad." Lyle started toward the living room again.

"Would you like to stay for dinner?" his mother asked.

"I'll let you know in a few minutes after I've

spoken to Dad." Lyle didn't look at his mother. He was sure her mouth was drawn with concern.

Lyle walked into the living room with his shoulders squared in determination. His father was watching TV. "Hi, Dad."

"Hello. This is an unexpected visit."

Lyle took a seat on the sofa instead of the closer chair so that the two of them faced each other. "Dad, I need to discuss something with you."

He turned off the TV. "Are you here to tell me you've signed up for active duty?" His delight showed clearly on his face.

"About that. Dad, I'm not going to go on active duty by choice ever again."

That joy on his father's face quickly turned to disappointment.

"I have a good job here. I'm needed and I believe I'm respected. Army life isn't for me. It never really was. I did it for you. That's not how I want to live my life. I need to do what I love and that's medicine here, at the clinic. I'm sorry if I'm disappointing you. I've known this for a long time and I've only led you to believe that I might one day go on active duty again to make you happy, and for that I apologize."

His father's look had darkened as Lyle spoke. He leaned forward and put his elbows on his knees and clasped his hands together. His expression didn't waver. Lyle knew that one well from his childhood days when he was in trouble. "I can't say that I am pleased with your decision. It's in our family's blood to be career soldiers. I brought you up to think that way as well."

"You did. But I love private medicine more. I want to serve in another way."

His father settled back, looking both old and tired. "I see that now. I guess I didn't want to before. I grew up with my father stressing that our family fought for people by serving in the armed forces. I was given no choice, my father wasn't given one either. But we were both happy with our lots in life. It was our duty to protect. It was all I knew. All I knew to hand down to you. I never thought you would want to go another way, Lyle. I have to admit your young lady's impassioned speech did make me think, though."

Cass had done that. Lyle's ego still got a boost whenever he thought of her words.

"I heard the talk around the village about that girl going missing and what you and Cass did to save her," his father continued. "Since then others have stopped me and told me how much they appreciate you being here and the importance of the clinic. I'm proud when I hear it. I'm sorry that you're not going to return to the army but I do love you, son."

Lyle went across to his father and gave him a hug. Afterwards he called, "Mum, I'll be staying for dinner."

* * *

Cass had never known misery like the kind she'd endured on the way to the airport. Everything in her screamed to return to Lyle. But he hadn't even waved goodbye. Had she hurt him that much? She felt sick inside.

The tears had flowed the entire trip to Fort William and then on to Aberdeen. More than once the taxi driver had looked in his rearview mirror with apprehension, but he'd said nothing.

She'd done everything she'd told herself not to. She'd let herself care. About him. The people at Heatherglen. Even Andy and that funny-looking dog, Dougal. Hero. Her emotions had been in a muddle when she had arrived at the clinic, and they weren't any better now that she'd left.

She'd known fear from when she'd almost lost her brother. She'd experienced deep loss from losing Rufus. And now Lyle was gone. This time was harder. She couldn't even breathe, the pain was so strong. Worse, she had chosen this. She wrung her hands.

She couldn't turn back. All she'd said to Lyle was true. She needed to have her act together before she made an emotional commitment to anyone, especially to him. Her parents were expecting her. It was Christmas, and they were worried about her. She had to see them first.

What her future would look like still needed to

be decided. Search and rescue was no longer for her. So what would she do now? There was also her house to think about. When she had her life in order, she'd see if Lyle still felt the same. He deserved someone who knew what she wanted and had her head on straight. Only then would she return to Lyle and discuss any future they might have.

The flight home wasn't much better emotionally than her ride to the airport. She'd only found relief in the few hours she had slept. Her parents were there to meet her. They quickly enveloped her in tight hugs. She needed those more than anything at the moment. They insisted that she go to their house for dinner and stay the night. Cass didn't resist. Right now she wanted their circle of security. With them she could just be, not think. She needed time to regroup.

Her parents' home was decorated for Christmas. Cass should have expected that. The minute she looked at their tree, her eyes filled with tears. It was all light, tinsel and glitter. It made her appreciate the simple, natural tree that stood in Lyle's living room. More than that, she wanted Lyle.

Her brother and his family came for supper the next day. With two young children, the meal was lively. Cass was glad to see them but she was so exhausted, both mentally and physically, that she excused herself early. Despite all the tears she'd shed during the day, she still wanted a good cry.

She hurried to her childhood bedroom and closed the door. Minutes later she was in the shower, letting those banked tears flow.

By the time there was a knock on the door she was in bed. "It's Mom. Can I come in?"

"Yes."

Her mother entered, carrying a mug. "I brought you some tea. I thought it was too late for coffee."

That was enough to have Cass's eyes swimming once more. She'd never cried this much in her entire life. Never been this distraught. The idea she might never have a chance to share time with Lyle again had her emotionally splintered. She had to get control of herself. Showing her emotions like this wasn't her. But, then, much about her over the last few weeks was different. Like pulling Lyle into the tub. That had been so much fun, for a number of reasons.

Her mother set the tea on the bedside table then perched on the edge of Cass's bed. "I had no idea you hated tea so much, or is something else going on? What're you not telling us? Are you still in pain?"

Cass hated the fear she heard in her mother's voice. "I told you everything about my injury. I promise I'm much better. It's my heart that's broken. And I think I'm the one who broke it." She poured out her sorrow and what had happened while she'd been at Heatherglen.

Her mother held her while she cried. When she settled down her mother said, "So what're your plans now, honey?"

"I don't know. Tomorrow morning I'm going to call about my job. I'm going to resign from it. That work isn't for me anymore."

Her mother patted her leg. "Your dad will be pleased to hear that. We've worried about you being in all those far-flung places by yourself for too long."

Cass hadn't been by herself. Rufus had been with her. Now she had no one. "I've been thinking that I might enjoy training rescue dogs instead."

"That sounds like something you'd be good at. And what about that amazing doctor of yours?"

Hers? She hoped despite how she had left things between her and Lyle that he would at least speak to her when she saw him again. "Mom, he asked me to stay. I was afraid to make such a big decision when I was so messed up over being hurt, Rufus dying and not being closer to home. I didn't know what I wanted my future to look like then. I hurt him badly. I'm not sure he'll ever want me again."

"So, do you know how you feel now?" Her mother held her hand.

"I knew the minute I left the clinic. I wouldn't let myself turn around, though. I needed to come home. To see you and Daddy." Cass looked directly at her mother. "I love him."

"Then I suggest you go back and tell him."

Cass murmured, "I don't know if he wants me anymore. He didn't even say goodbye."

"Honey, if all you've told me is true, I wouldn't worry about that. He wants you. I'd suggest you take care of business here as soon as possible then go tell him how you feel and see what happens."

"I don't know…"

She mother stood. "Our family knows better than most how easily something can be almost taken away. Grab every chance at happiness and have no regrets."

The one thing Cass had been with Lyle was happy—and at Heatherglen, too. "What about Christmas?"

Her mother shrugged. "We'll celebrate it early. Or late." Then she grinned. "Or come to Scotland."

"Oh, Mom." Cass wrapped her arms around her mother. "I love you."

Over the next few days Cass resigned from her job, packed her bags and closed up her house. She was on her way to find that happiness she wanted. And that started with Lyle.

Christmas had never really mattered to Lyle. Cass had managed to make it exciting for a while, but that had gone with her. He'd spent the last week going through the motions. To say he wasn't in a festive mood would be an understatement.

He was actually heading into the worst Christmas of his life. It was going to top the year Freya had left him, and the one when his father wouldn't speak to him because he'd said he was going inactive so he could take the job helping Charles get the clinic started.

Losing Cass was like losing an arm or a leg. He had to relearn how to function without her. Every day he forced himself to do what was necessary. People were starting to notice. The few times he had seen his parents his mother had watched him with worry and hugged him a little tighter than normal. Even Charles had made a smart remark about Lyle not looking as cheerful dry as he had wet. Lyle had snarled and stalked way.

No, Christmas couldn't go by fast enough for him. He was living for the new year. Surely he and Cass could sort something out? Find a way they could be together? If he had to leave Heatherglen and follow her all over the world, then so be it.

Now he was doing his duty as the doctor on call at the Christmas-tree lighting in the village square. He remained on the outside of the crowd around the huge tree. It was dark except for the interior lights of the businesses that surrounded the square.

As soon as he was no longer needed he would slip away to his cottage, even though he found no solace there. His home held too many memories of Cass. Their tree still stood in the living room.

More than once he'd thought of taking it down but he couldn't bring himself to do it despite the fact it was a daily reminder of Cass.

Lyle stuffed his hands in his coat pockets and focused on Charles giving his Laird of Heatherglen annual Christmas speech. It was the only time Lyle smiled because he was well aware of how much Charles disliked being in the spotlight.

A movement in front of him and to the right caught Lyle's attention. *Cass?* He shook his head. For him she was like the ghost of Heatherglen. More than once he had walked around a corner and thought he'd glimpsed her. Or walked by the lounge and heard her voice. Each time he'd had to calm his rapid heartbeat as disappointment had set in. He had to remind himself she was in America.

He had laid out a plan, one he would adhere to. She would have the space and time she needed to think, and process what she wanted. Lyle was determined to give her that, even if it killed him. In January he would go after her. From there they would figure out what their future together would look like.

The person continued toward him. Lyle narrowed his eyes in the hope of seeing better. Despite his efforts not to let his heart race or hold his breath in anticipation, it didn't work. Still, in the dim light he couldn't make out any facial features.

It was a woman. She came nearer. Her walk was

so much like Cass's. She held herself just as Cass did. Was his mind playing tricks on him?

Finally, she stepped close enough that he could see a scarf around her neck and a hat on her head like the one Cass had bought from his mother. Lyle remained still, sure she was a figment of his imagination.

It wasn't until she said, "Hello, Lyle," that he let himself believe and breathe. His heart raced as if he were running. It was Cass! She'd come back. Was really here. Unable to move, he stood there in disbelief.

She closed the distance between them. "Lyle?"

He put one foot in front of the other and grabbed her, pulling her against his chest. Lifting her off the ground, he was rewarded with a sigh from her as her arms tightly circled his neck. Sometime later, Lyle let her slide down his body and he stepped back. The last thing he want to do was scare her off. "Cass, is it really you?"

"Yes."

"Are you okay? Is your leg okay?" He gave her a searching look.

"I'm fine." There was a smile in her voice. "I just forgot something."

"Forgot something?" Now he sounded like an idiot. His hands shook in his eagerness to touch her. He shoved them in his pockets.

"Yes. You."

"Me?"

She watched him closely with a look of uncertainty. "Yeah, you. I was wondering if we could have that conversation about compromise you suggested."

"I'd like that. A *lot*." He pulled her to him again and kissed her with all the pent-up emotion he'd had to hold in check. It was a long and deep kiss.

The roar of the crowd broke them apart. They gave each other a startled look, then grinned. The cheer had been for the Christmas tree being lit.

Lyle looked at her beautiful, much-loved face. "I'm finished here. Where're you staying?"

"I was going to stay somewhere in the village, unless I had a better offer." Cass grinned.

"You have one now. Where are your bags?" Lyle looked around.

"At the airport, I hope. Long story that I don't want to talk about now."

Smiling, he took her hand and hurried her to where his car was parked. They needed to get away before people started talking to them. He held Cass's hand as much as the drive to his cottage would allow, afraid if he lost contact she would disappear.

As he helped her out of the car, he pulled her to him again, inhaling deeply and filling his head with her scent. "You have no idea how I've missed you."

* * *

A flutter like birds taking off filled Cass's middle. She looked at Lyle's handsome face. The one she had missed so much. "I'm glad."

"Glad?" Lyle sounded incredulous.

"Yes, I was afraid you wouldn't talk to me." She watched him for a reaction.

"Are you kidding? I'm in love with you, Cass. Nothing will ever change that."

"In love with me?" So this was what it felt like to have everything she'd ever dreamed of.

"What did you think I meant when I asked you to stay here with me?"

She lifted a shoulder in a shrug and let it fall. "I don't know. I had so much stuff going on in my head I wasn't sure what you meant."

His hands went to her shoulders. "Cass, I wouldn't have asked you to stay with me unless I meant forever."

"I should've known that. I should've heard you out. I was scared. Of myself and what you wanted."

"Come inside. We'll discuss this out of the cold. I want you to be warm and comfortable when I explain how much I love and want you." He gave her a quick kiss before he took her hand then pushed the car door closed.

Inside his cottage, Lyle helped her hang up her outer clothing. She took off her shoes, walked to the doorway of the living room and stopped. Their tree was still there.

"Is something wrong?" Lyle said from behind her.

She turned and smiled. "No, everything is perfect. I missed you and your cottage."

"I hope it was me more." There was still an unsure look in his eyes.

Cass went up on her toes and kissed him. "It was you. Almost all you."

When they separated, he called over his shoulder as he walked to the kitchen, "I'll make us some tea. We need to talk."

She liked the sound of that. They did. She needed to apologize and tell him how she felt. It was time to stop worrying about woulda, coulda, shoulda and try living. When she was around Lyle she wanted to live. She was happy. Blissfully so.

A few minutes later he offered her a mug of tea. Instead of sitting beside her, Lyle chose the chair. Cass couldn't help but pout. Maybe he was still mad at her.

"I'm sitting over here because I can't trust myself when I sit next to you. We need to talk."

Cass's heart jumped. "I know what you mean."

That brought a smile to his lips before he said, "I know I wasn't fair to you. I was so self-absorbed that I wasn't thinking about what was best for you. You were here to recover from a horrible experi-

ence, and I should've given you more room, not
asked you for more than you could give. Before
you left you said some things I needed to hear. I
have to admit it made me angry but that didn't
mean that I didn't need to hear them. Or that I
didn't love you. I talked to my father. Told him in
clear and concise language that I wouldn't be returning to active duty."

Cass hissed in a breath. "How did that go?"

"He didn't like it, but he accepted it. Even told
me that he's proud of the work I'm doing at the
clinic."

That had to have been a tough conversation for
both men. She had to admire Lyle for doing it.

Lyle continued, "At least it's a positive start. I
don't think he'll ever get over it but, then, I can't
live my life for him. I've got to live it for me."

"You're right. That's a hard lesson I've had to
learn over the last few days as well. I knew the
moment I looked out the rear window of the car
for you as I was going down the drive that I was
leaving behind the best thing in my life. That you
held the key to my happiness. I was afraid that if I
took what you offered, somewhere down the road
it might be taken from me. I couldn't stand the
thought of that happening. What I soon learned
was that trying to live without you was far worse.
I love you, Lyle."

That was all it took for Lyle to come to her. He

wrapped his arms around her and gave her the sweetest kiss that held a promise that he loved her too.

After they broke apart, Lyle said, "If you don't want to live here, we can live in America, or anywhere else for that matter, as long as we are together. I can practice medicine anywhere."

"Oh, no, I would never take you away from Heatherglen. Cluchlochry. You belong here. Are needed here. I've been thinking about something Flora said. She mentioned Esme could use me at the canine therapy center. I think I would like to train dogs."

"That sounds like a wonderful idea." Lyle hugged her.

"You think you could stand to have me around all the time?" She studied his face.

He chuckled. "I can't think of anything better."

"I love you, Lyle."

"I love you, Cass."

Sometime later they were lying in Lyle's large bed in each other's arms. Cass had found the place where she belonged, where she was completely happy. "You know, there's something to the Christmas pudding thing."

"How's that?" Lyle's hand caressed her bare back over her shoulders.

"I asked to be happy." She cupped his cheek. "And I am. Blissfully so."

He gave her a quick kiss. "And I wished for you to stay longer."

"Why?"

"Because I need a date for the Christmas ball!"

* * * * *

Annie O'Neil spent most of her childhood with her leg draped over the family rocking chair and a book in her hand. Novels, baking and writing too much teenage angst poetry ate up most of her youth. Now Annie splits her time between corralling her husband into helping her with their cows, baking, reading, barrel racing (not really!) and spending some very happy hours at her computer writing.

Books by Annie O'Neil

Harlequin Medical Romance

Miracles in the Making

Risking Her Heart on the Single Dad

Pups that Make Miracles

Making Christmas Special Again

Single Dad Docs

Tempted by Her Single Dad Boss

Hope Children's Hospital

The Army Doc's Christmas Angel

Hot Greek Doc

One Night with Dr. Nikolaides

Her Knight Under the Mistletoe
Reunited with Her Parisian Surgeon
The Doctor's Marriage for a Month
A Return, a Reunion, a Wedding

Visit the Author Profile page
at Harlequin.com for more titles.

MAKING CHRISTMAS SPECIAL AGAIN

Annie O'Neil

This one goes out to my ladies who create!
Thank you so much, Annie C, Karin and Susan
for, once again, being epically fabulous. xx

Chapter 1

Hell's teeth, it was cold.

For once the all-consuming distraction of lungs vs arctic winds hurtling in from the Highlands was welcome. Physical pain outweighed Max Kirkpatrick's rage just long enough to remember that for every problem there was a solution. This time, though...

Trust the festive season to send him another blunt reminder that, no matter how hard he tried, the universe simply wasn't going to let him put some good back into the world.

He'd genuinely thought he'd done it this time. He really had.

His eyes travelled the length of the scrubby inner-city hospital then scanned the former vacant plot. There'd been snow on and off for weeks and yet there were still patients wandering around with pets and still more in the greenhouse, fostering their plants as if they were their own flesh and blood.

He traced his finger along a frost-singed rose. The parents of a little boy who'd lost his struggle with cancer had planted it three years earlier when Max had only just started Plants to Paws. The lad had loved coming out here to play with the family mongrel. Golden moments, his parents had called them. Golden moments. They still came and tended it as if their son were still with them. In a way, he supposed, he was.

This week.

Max's disbelief that someone was going to destroy the garden shunted through him afresh. Gone were the piles of rubbish, the burnt-out car, the thick layers of tagging on the side of the Clydebank Hospital walls. In their place were raised vegetable patches, benches with the names of loved ones on shining brass plaques dappled about the small wildflower meadow and, of course, the greenhouse and extra-large garden shed he'd built with a handful of other doctors. They'd recently installed a wood stove for added comfort. That would go, too. Along with the bow-laden wreath someone had hung on the door, despite his protestations that it was too early.

He crouched down to pop a couple of stones back onto the rock garden one of the Clyde's long-term leukaemia patients had helped build. Her first ever garden, she'd crowed. She'd be gutted when she found out it was going to be demolished, all to help some fat-cat property developer.

As he nestled another rock back into place, a young Border collie ran up to him with the tell-tale wriggle of a happy dog. She rolled onto her back for a tummy rub. He took a quick glance around and couldn't place her with anyone within sight.

He gave her soft white belly a rub. "Hey, there, little one. You're a pretty girl. Now, who do you belong to?"

"Some would say they don't *belong* to anyone."

The female voice slipped down his spine like warm honey. Low and husky, it was the type of voice that could talk a man into anything if he didn't watch himself. Good job he'd put the emotional armour on years back.

Max was about to say he was very familiar with the way canine-human relationships worked, thank you very much, when a pair of very expensive boots appeared on the woodchip path. Expensive boots attached to a public school accent. Still Scottish, but he would put money on the fact their schools had had a mixer dance. The military school his stepfather had deposited him in strongly encouraged shoulder rubbing with the "power makers', as the school head had liked to call them.

"Deal breakers' would've been a better moniker if today's news was anything to go by. He still couldn't wrap his head round the hospital reneging on their word. Sure, they needed the money, but obliterating Plants to Paws to let a developer build a car park?

Bam! There went three years of hard work. Not to mention the slice of peace that came from knowing he'd finally made good on a years' old vow to do what he hadn't done for his mother: offer a refuge from a life that wasn't as kind as it should have been. All for a bit of money they'd never see on the wards. Hello, cement trucks, sayonara Plants to Paws.

The puppy nuzzled against his hand.

"What's her name?" He had yet to look up.

"Skye," the voice said.

She sounded like a Christmas ornament. Angel? Whatever. Too damned nice was what she sounded.

Her leather boots moved in a bit closer. Italian? They looked handmade.

"I think you'll find her "love me tender" routine is an act. Skye's always got an ulterior motive and, from the look of things, you're playing right into her paws."

He didn't even want to know what that meant.

"Is she a working collie or one of those therapy dogs?" They'd been trying to introduce the therapy dogs into the hospital but, as ever, stretched resources meant the lovable fur balls weren't seen much on the wards.

"Working. Though she's still in training. Precocious. Just like her mother."

Damn. This woman's voice was like butter. Better. Butter and honey mixed together. If he was to add a shot of whisky and heat it up it'd be the perfect drink on a day like this.

"What type of training?" he asked, to stop his brain from going places it shouldn't.

"Search and rescue."

That got his attention. He had been expecting agility. Maybe sheep herding. A voice like that usually came attached to some land. Land managed by someone else. As he tilted his head up, the sun got in his eyes and all he could make out was a halo of blonde hair atop a stretch of legs and a cashmere winter coat that definitely wasn't from the kind of stores he shopped in.

Miss Boots squatted down to his level and the second their eyes met he stood straight back up.

Piercing blue eyes. A tousle of short curls the colour of summer wheat. A face so beautiful it looked as though it had been sculpted out of marble. For every bit of wrong she elicited in his gut, there was an equal measure of good.

"Are you a patient?" It was the only thing he could think to ask, though he knew the answer would be—

"No." She put her leather-gloved hand out to shake his. "Esme Ross-Wylde."

He kept his facial features on their usual setting: neutral. Though society papers weren't his thing, even *he'd* heard of the Ross-Wyldes. Scottish landed gentry of the highest order. The Ross-Wylde estate came with about five thousand acres, if memory served. A couple of hours north of Glasgow. Before his mum had married The Dictator, as Max liked to think of his stepfather, she'd taken him there for one of their famous Christmas carnivals. Huge old house. A castle actually. Expansive grounds. Extensive stables. Skating rink. Toffee apples and gingerbread men. It'd been the last Christmas he hadn't been made to "earn his keep".

"So." He clapped his hands together and looked around the sparsely populated garden. "Have you brought Skye along to meet someone?"

She unleashed a smile that could've easily lit him up from the inside out. Good thing she'd met him on a bad day. On a good one? He might have had to break some rules.

"I was looking for you." She held up a familiar-looking scarf.

"How'd you get that?" He knew he sounded terse, but with his luck she was the developer. If she was trying to sprinkle some sugar in advance of telling him when the wrecking ball would swing, she may as well get on with it.

Esme was unfazed by his cranky response. She tipped her head towards the garden shed as she handed him his scarf. "A member of your fan club gave me this to give Skye a go at 'search'."

He glanced over at the shed and, sure enough, there were a couple of patients from the oncology ward waving at him. Cheeky so-and-sos. They'd been trying to blow some oxygen onto the all but dead embers of his social life ever since they'd found out the nurses not so discreetly called him The Monk. He rolled his eyes and returned his attention to Esme Ross-Wylde. "I presume that means you're here for the 'rescue' part?"

She shrugged nonchalantly. "If you're interested."

Skye's tail started waving double time.

If he wasn't mistaken, the corners of her rather inviting lips were twitching with the hint of a smile.

Something about this whole scenario felt like flirting. He didn't do flirting. He did A and E medicine in Glasgow's most financially deprived hospital. Then he slept, woke up and did it all over again. Sometimes he came out here and dug over a veg patch. There definitely wasn't time for flirting.

When he said nothing she asked, "How do you fancy keeping Plants to Paws the way it is?"

His eyes snapped to hers, and something flashed hard and bright in his chest that had nothing to do with gratitude. It ricocheted straight past his belt buckle and all the way up again. By the look on her face, she was feeling exactly the same thing he was. An unwelcome animal attraction.

Oh, hell. If life had taught him anything, it was the old adage that if something seemed too good to be true, it usually was.

The Dictator had taught him that everything came with a price. Best to rip off the plaster and get it over with. "What's the catch?"

"Charming." Esme quirked a brow. "Is this how you win all the girls over?"

"It works for some." Dr Kirkpatrick's shrug was flippantly sexy.

"Not this girl." Her hip jutted out as if to emphasise the point she really shouldn't be making. That she fancied him something rotten and her body was most definitely flirting without her permission.

"Suit yourself." His full lips twitched into a frown. Something told her it was for the same reason her mouth followed suit. They'd both been burnt somewhere along the line and if she was right, those burns had been slow to heal. If at all.

She sniffed to communicate she would suit herself, thank you very much, but the butterflies in her belly and the glint in his eye told her Max Kirkpatrick knew the ball was very much in his court.

He wasn't at all what she'd expected when she'd heard about an A and E doctor who'd set up a multi-purpose garden where patients could grow carrots and play with their pets. For some reason she thought he'd be older. Like…granddad old. And not half as sexy as the man arcing rather dubious eyebrows at her.

She called Skye to her and gave her head a little scrub. Here was someone she could rely on. Even as puppies, dogs were completely honest. Constant. Loyal.

Men? Not so much. Something she'd learned the hard way after her entire life had been splashed across the tabloids as a naive twenty-year-old who'd been taken for a fool. These days the Esme Ross-Wylde people met was friendly, businesslike and, despite the inevitable tabloid update on her charitable activities, able to keep her private life exactly that. Private. Which was a good thing because the rate of knots at which she was mentally undressing him would've won a gold medal.

"Are you going to tell me what the catch is or

are you going to make me beg for it?" His frown deepened. As if he was fighting exactly the same onslaught of images she was. Sexy ones that most definitely shouldn't be drowning out any form of common sense.

Normally sponsoring a struggling charity was incredibly straightforward.

Normally she didn't feel as though her entire body was being lit up like a Christmas tree. Flickering and shimmering in a way she hadn't thought possible after years of protecting her broken heart. All of which was tying her insides in knots because feeling like a lusty teenager was not a safe way to feel. And yet…she couldn't tear her eyes away.

C'mon, Esme. You know the drill. Find a charity. Offer a lifeline in the form of a Christmas ball. Donate a couple of service dogs after two weeks of training up at Heatherglen. Job done.

She forced herself to answer. "From what I hear, you might need my help."

The doctor crossed his arms and squared his six-foot-something form so that she could see nothing else but him. Classic macho male pose. Designed to intimidate.

Although…she wasn't really getting that vibe from Dr Kirkpatrick. It was more protective than aggressive. There was something about the ramrod-straight set of his spine that suggested he'd done some time in the forces. Her brother had had the same solid presence. Unlike everyone else, who was bundled up to the eyeballs, Max Kirkpatrick wore a light fleece top bearing the hospital logo over a set of navy scrubs and nothing else. A normal human would've been freezing.

A normal human wouldn't be messing with her no-men-for-Esme rule. This guy? Mmm... Dark chestnut-brown hair. A bit curly and wild. The type that was begging her fingers to scruff it up a bit more. Espresso brown eyes. The fathomless variety that gleamed with hints of gold when the sun caught them. Everything about him screamed tall, dark and mysterious. And she liked a mystery.

No!

She did not like mysteries. She liked steady and reliable. Although...steady and reliable hadn't really floated her boat the last few times her brother had presented her with "suitable dating material'.

Dr Kirkpatrick broke the silence first. "Any chance you're going to explain this rather timely offer to rescue me?"

Ah. She'd forgotten that part. An oversight she was going to blame on Skye for unearthing the softer side of this impenetrable mountain of man gloom towering over her. Sometimes being short was a real pain.

"I run the Heatherglen Foundation. I founded it

after my brother—an army man—and his service dog were killed in a conflict zone."

A muscle twitched in his jaw. She'd definitely been right about the military.

She continued with more confidence, "I am particularly interested in helping charities that use animals as therapy and who, more to the point, are in danger of closing. It's relatively straightforward. I select the charity, and in a few weeks the foundation will be hosting a Christmas ball, where the bulk of the funds raised will be donated to said charity, and ongoing support from the Heatherglen Foundation will also be provided."

"Sounds great. Have a good time!" Max said in a "count me out' tone.

"But—it'll save Plants to Paws." Didn't he want his charity to survive? "The ball's just before Christmas. It truly is a magical event."

He rolled his eyes. "So...what? Is this your stab at being Scotland's very own Mrs Claus?"

"There's no need to be narky about it. I'm trying to help." She didn't like Christmastime either. Her brother had been killed on Christmas Eve and ever since then her favourite time of year had been shrouded in painful memories, but it didn't mean she took it out on others. Quite the opposite, in fact. The Christmas ball was her attempt to recapture the love she had for the festive season. Ten years and counting and it still had yet to take.

He opened his hands out wide. "How would you feel if the one thing you'd poured three years of hard graft into was going to be paved over for a pay by the minute car park? At *Christmas*."

"I'd do everything in my power to save it."

"Trust a stranger I've never met to save a charity she'll most likely never make use of? I don't think so."

She was hardly going to tell him to search the internet because, depending on which site he hit, he could definitely get the wrong impression. She took a deep breath and started over. "The donors are personally selected by me. People who believe in giving back to communities that have treated them well." The look he threw her spoke volumes. He wasn't biting. She spluttered, "Think of it as your first Christmas present."

"I don't trust things that come in pretty wrapping."

The way he looked at her made it crystal clear he wasn't talking about ribbons and sparkly paper. He was talking about her.

Now, *that* was irritating.

She wasn't some little airhead who bolstered her ego by doing seasonal acts of charity.

He shoved up his sleeve to check his watch. "I've got patients to see and bad news to dispense, so if you don't mind...?"

"I *do*, actually. I mind very much."

He rolled his finger with a "get on with it' spin.

What was with the attitude? Founders who believed in their charities tended to drop it. Not this guy. Either he'd been royally screwed around at some point or was just plain old chippy. Even worse, somehow, in a handful of seconds, Max Kirkpatrick had slipped directly under her thick winter coat, beneath her cashmere sweater and burrowed right under her skin, making this interaction feel shockingly personal.

The Heatherglen Foundation wasn't a platform for her to prance about Scotland, giving away her family's money. It was the one good thing that had come out of the most painful chapters in her life. As quickly as she'd been unnerved by his attitude, she'd had enough. She wasn't going to beg this man to take her money. He didn't want it? He couldn't have it.

She wiped her hands together as if ridding them of something distasteful. "I came here with a genuine offer of help and a list of donors as long as my arm. If you're not interested in stopping Gavin Henshall from paving Plants to Paws over, I'll be on my way."

He blinked. Twice.

Ooh. Had she found a chink in the strong, silent man's armour?

"I suspect it'll take more than a few thousand to keep Henshall at bay."

He was right. She told him how much the last charity she'd sponsored had received.

He blinked again. "Can we skip straight to the what do I need to do to get the money part?"

Blunt. But it was a damn sight better than being dismissed as a bit of society fluff.

Her frown must've deepened because he suddenly folded into a courtly bow before unleashing an unexpectedly lavish charm offensive. "I do humbly ask your forgiveness. Etiquette school clearly failed me. I didn't mean to be rude, Miss Ross-Wylde. Or is it Mrs?"

"Ms," Esme snipped.

His eyes narrowed. Probably the same way hers had when he'd stiffened at the mention of Gavin Henshall.

He'd found her chink. She'd found his. Normally this would be her cue to run for the hills. But something about him made her want to know what made him tick. *Sugar.* Why couldn't Max Kirkpatrick have looked like a troll or been long since married to his childhood sweetheart? She checked his ring finger.

Empty.

Her heart soared so fast she barely knew what to do with herself.

Explain the details. Accept his refusal—because he will *refuse—then leave. Problem solved.*

She crossed her arms, aiming for nonchalant,

not entirely sure if she'd hit her mark. "I've just been up to speak to the hospital administrator, who has agreed to stall the sale until the new year. If the Christmas ball goes to plan, the hospital is happy to leave Plants to Paws as is."

"In perpetuity?" Max obviously had his own set of conditions.

"Precisely. The only thing—"

He huffed out a laugh. "I knew there was a catch."

She let her eyebrows take the same haughty position his had earlier. "The only thing, Dr Kirkpatrick, is that I require the head of each charity to select two patients whom you think might benefit from a service dog."

"Oh. You require it, do you?"

She ignored him and soldiered on. "We can offer the patient two weeks of one-to-one training at the canine therapy centre, all expenses included, and a follow-up care package if they have financial difficulties."

His expression didn't change, but she could see he was actively considering her offer.

"What sorts of things do your dogs do, apart from search and rescue?" Max asked.

She smiled. She might have trouble bragging about herself, but she could big up her dogs until the cows came home. "We have service dogs specially trained to work with epileptics, diabetics, people with cancer, people with mobility problems. I imagine you see the full gamut of patients in A and E. I'll forward you a full list of the services we can provide. We also have emotional support dogs, who work with people suffering from PTSD or anxiety."

He nodded. "Would I have to play any part in this?"

Normally he would, but no way was she inviting Max Kirkpatrick to Heatherglen. He was setting off way too many alarm bells. Before guilt could set in, she reminded herself that she made the rules. She could also bend them.

"Apart from attend the ball to receive a big fat cheque?" She shook her head. "Not necessary. We're an all bells and whistles facility, so..." The lie came a bit too easily. She always invited the charity founder to join the patients and their families up at Heatherglen, but two weeks in close proximity with Max Kirkpatrick at this time of year, when the castle was romantically bedecked for the festive season? Not. Going. To. Happen.

Her mouth continued talking while her brain scrambled to catch up. "We run the training sessions at our canine therapy training centre. There's also a medical rehabilitation clinic my brother runs in the main building. I have a week-long slot from December fifteenth up until the twenty-third of December, when we hold the ball. I understand the timing could be awkward with Christmas and family obligations, but as the developer is so keen to get construction under way, I thought we'd best get cracking. The patients could take the dogs home over the holidays then return for a second week of training sometime in January. If that suits."

She watched his face go through a rapid-fire range of emotions. All of which he erased before she could nail any of them down.

"I'm fine with that," he said evenly. "As long as we make a few of my guidelines clear."

Esme couldn't help it. She laughed. "Excuse me, Dr Kirkpatrick. If I'm not mistaken, I'm the one helping you here and as such—"

"As such," he cut in, "I don't want you steamrolling my charity into something it isn't."

"And what makes you think I plan on doing that?"

"Bitter experience."

The second the words were out of his mouth Max regretted them. Hearing Gavin Henshall's name had a way of catapulting him straight back into the scrawny fourteen-year-old kid who'd mown lawns, taken out rubbish and thrown himself at all the rest of the chores his stepfather had set him as if his life had depended on it, only to discover he'd changed the goalposts. Again.

Military academy, apprenticeships over the

summer holidays, boot camp. No matter what he'd done or how hard he'd worked, he had never been permitted into the house to shield his mum from the emotionally abusive relationship she'd unwittingly married into.

Not that he blamed her. They'd both fallen for Gavin's smooth lines. He'd promised her love, respect, a house with a big garden on the right side of town. A proper education for her "shockingly bright boy', the son he'd always hoped to have.

How the hell Gavin had convincingly passed off the lies still astounded him. The only plus side of the cancer that had taken his mother's life was that it had freed her, at long last, from Gavin. It was more than he'd been able to do.

He shook his head and forced himself to focus on the here and now.

Esme Ross-Wylde didn't strike him as a steamroller socialite. The type of do-gooder who blithely floated round the city flinging gold coins for the "have nots' to do her bidding. Sour memories teased at his throat. Money brought power and no one had made that clearer to him than Gavin. *"You earn your keep? You're in. You don't? You'll have to learn how to make a real man of yourself."*

"What's your role in all of this?" Max had already been hit by one bombshell today. This one—the Henshall H-bomb—was making it harder to harness any charm. If he was going to tell everyone who cared about Plants to Paws it was going to survive, he needed to trust it was a genuine offer. Trusting a woman who could clearly cut and run from any scenario that didn't suit her was a tall order.

"Apart from being Mrs Claus, you mean?" She pursed her lips in a way that suggested he'd definitely hit a sore spot then said, "As well as running the foundation, I'm a vet and an animal behaviour specialist. I also pick up poo, in case that's what you're really asking."

It was all he could do not to laugh. Brilliant. Esme Double-Barrelled-Fancy-Boots picked up poo. It was a skilful way to tell him there was a vital, active brain behind the porcelain doll good looks. A woman who wanted to be mistress of her own destiny as much as he'd worked to be master of his.

"That it?" He knew he was winding her up, but…his flirting skills were rusty. Rusted and covered in a thick layer of dust if he was being honest.

Her smile came naturally, clearly more relaxed when talking about her work. "The vet clinic is the only one in our area and the therapy centre's busy pretty much round the clock. The service dogs are trained to aid patients with specific tasks they are unable to do themselves. Like press an alert button for someone having an epileptic seizure, for example. Much like a dog who works on a bomb squad or for drug detection, they are not for the general public to cuddle and coo over."

"That's the therapy dog's job?" Max liked hearing the pride in her voice as she explained.

"A therapy dog's main role is to relieve stress and, hopefully, bring joy—but often on a bigger scale. Retirement homes, hospital wards, disaster areas. An emotional support dog tends to provide companionship and stress relief for an individual. People with autism, anyone suffering from PTSD. Social anxiety. That sort of thing."

Max nodded. The smiles on the faces of patients when they were reunited with their pets out here in the garden spoke volumes. Pets brought joy. Too bad people couldn't be counted on to do the same.

She continued, "We're obviously highly selective, but find that dogs who come from animal rescue centres are particularly good for emotional support, learning and PTSD. The bigger dogs are wonderful with ex-soldiers who might need a service and emotional support dog all in one big furry package."

He gave a brisk nod at that one. A few guys from his platoon could probably do with a four-legged friend. He still didn't know how he'd managed four tours in the Middle East without as much as a scratch. Physically, anyway. Emotionally? That was a whole mess he'd probably never untangle. "And your brother? The one with the medical clinic?" Max crossed his arms again. "How much of a say does he have in who I choose?"

A flicker of amusement lit up her blue eyes.

One that said, *You think I let my big brother push me around?*

"My brother's a neurologist, but his clinic is predominantly for rehabilitation. The foundation has pretty much always been my baby, so..." There was a flicker of something he couldn't identify as she paused for breath. Something she was leaving out. When she noticed him watching her she quickly continued, "You'll see for yourself when you come up to Heatherglen—" She stopped herself short.

"I was under the impression I wasn't invited." He wasn't hurt by it. Had been relieved, in fact, but...he had to admit he was curious. And he wasn't thinking about the castle.

Her cheeks were shot through with streaks of red. "Normally the head of the charity comes up, but I just assumed with the dates I have available being so close to Christmas... I just— I didn't think it would be feasible for you to come along and observe, so..." The rest of the sentence, if there had been any, died on her lips.

Max pulled up the zip on his fleece and glanced across at the hospital where an ambulance was pulling in. His break was coming to an end and this was already getting more complicated than it should be. No point in watching the poor woman squirm. She obviously had a big heart and he shouldn't play hard to get. The future of Plants to

Paws was on the line. "Don't worry about it. My dance card's been full for a while."

"I see." She tucked a stray curl behind her ear.

Max's thumb involuntarily skidded across his fingertips wondering if her hair felt as soft as it looked. He forced his voice into fact-finding mode. "So where would the patients stay? If we go ahead with this."

"At Heatherglen." Esme reluctantly met his eye. "The castle has been partly remodelled as a residential clinic and we've refurbished the old stables as a training centre and kennels."

"No more hunts, then?"

Her brows dived together as her eyes finally met his frankly. "You've been to Heatherglen?"

"Not for a long time." He felt her eyes stay on him as he knelt down to give Skye another cuddle. The last thing he was going to tell her was that that long-ago day at Heatherglen was one of his handful of good memories from his childhood. Guilting her into an invitation she didn't want to give wasn't his style. Especially if it meant the ultimate outcome was helping patients with the added bonus of sticking one to Gavin Henshall. The money he'd give to see the look on Gavin's face when he found out he wouldn't get his precious car park.

"So…" Esme's voice trickled down his spine again. "Does this mean you're considering my offer?

He stood up and looked her square in the eye. "If it means saving this place, let's do it. How do I get in touch with you?"

Esme shook her head. She might need her ears checked. Did Max Kirkpatrick just say he wanted to touch her?

An image pinged into her mind. Ice skating by moonlight. Her mittened hand in his bigger, stronger hand. The two of them skating away beneath the starlit sky until he pulled her to him and... She screwed her eyes shut and forced the image back where it had come from.

"Email? Phone?" he prompted.

Oh. Right. That kind of contact. She handed him a card. "From here it's pretty easy. We'll do two video calls with you and the patients once you've picked them."

"For what purpose?"

"It's how we introduce the dogs to the patients before training at Heatherglen gets under way. It gives me a good feel for who they are before they arrive. If you could take part in the calls, that would be greatly appreciated."

"Why do you need me?"

Esme bridled. If he was going to persist in questioning every single thing she said and did, she was right to keep him away from Heatherglen. "If a couple of video conferences and formal wear is too much of a sacrifice to secure two free, incredibly talented service dogs for patients who would normally have to wait years to receive one... I completely understand." She gave him her most nonchalant smile, hoping it disguised just how intense she was finding all of this. The penetrating looks. The pointed questions. The downright yumminess of him. The last time someone had had this visceral effect on her... *Oof...* She shuddered as she felt Max's dark eyes continue to bore into her.

"Why do I need formal wear for a conference call?"

"It's for the Christmas ball. You're req—" She stopped herself from saying *required*. She didn't like being bossed around and had the very clear impression he didn't either. "It's really useful if the founder of the charity comes along and speaks with the donors."

"Schmooze, you mean." A flash of a smile appeared. "You might want to reconsider that. It's not really my forte."

"So I noticed," she said dryly.

He laughed and once again that strangely comfortable feeling she got from banter with him made the day seem a bit less cold.

"I can pick any patients I want?" He asked.

"Doctor's choice." She nodded. "The harder the better."

Her eyes dropped to just below his waist.

Oh, good grief.

Work. She should think of work. Work was not sexy. Complicated patients to match to hard-working service dogs. Also not sexy. Big brothers. They definitely weren't sexy. Work, complicated patients and big brothers. Okay. Her heart rate began to decelerate. She liked bringing in clients Charles knew nothing about. He was far too serious for his own good and this was her annual chance to pop a little spontaneity into his life. And her own.

She followed his gaze as it drifted across to the hospital, his mind obviously spinning with options.

She got the feeling he was going to test her. Good. Maybe *this* would be the year that signing over the proceeds from the charity ball gave her back that magical feeling she'd lost all those years ago when her brother had been killed in action, she'd married a hustler and just about everything else in her life had imploded.

"You're not going to bend on the Christmas ball thing, are you?" A smile teased at the corners of his mouth.

"Nope!" She grinned. "And let me know if you don't have a tuxedo. You'll need one for the ball." She gave him what she hoped was a neutral top-to-toe scan. "You'd probably fit into one of my brother's if you don't have one. I'm sure we could stuff socks in the shoulders if you don't fill it out."

What was she on? He'd make a fig leaf look

good. Which was an image she really shouldn't let float around her head quite as gaily as it was.

"If I go formal, I wear a kilt, thank you very much."

A kilt! Yum. She had a weakness for a Scotsman in formal kilted attire. Her brain instantly started undressing and redressing him. What she saw she liked very much. Too much. Was it too late to uninvite him to the ball as well?

Yes. Yes, it was. Besides, as much as seeing Max Kirkpatrick in a kilt could very well tip her into the danger zone of dating outside her brother's "pre-approved' choices…she needed him. The donors loved hearing about the charities from the founder.

"A kilt will do very nicely," she said primly.

He gave her a sharp sidelong glance as if he'd been following her complicated train of thought, then took a step back and said, rather formally for someone who'd just been flinging about witty banter, "In which case, Ms Ross-Wylde, I'd be delighted to accept your offer to participate in two phone calls and the ball."

It was a pointed comment. One that made it clear he'd understood loud and clear she hadn't asked him up to Heatherglen. A wash of disappointment swept through Esme so hard and fast she barely managed to keep her smile pinned in place as she rejigged her vision of what the next few weeks held in store. Training patients. Absolutely normal. The hectic build-up to Christmas. Ditto. The Christmas carnival being set up out at the front of the castle that would, once again, be a good opportunity to practise with the dogs and their handlers.

It was ridiculous of her to have imagined for as much as a second that she might finally make good on that fantasy to skate by moonlight, hand in hand, with someone who genuinely liked her for herself. Let alone share a starlit kiss.

"Delightful." Brisk efficiency was the only way she'd get out of this garden with a modicum of her dignity intact. She called Skye to her side. "We'll expect them on the fifteenth and you on the twenty-third in Glasgow."

She turned and gave a wave over her shoulder so he wouldn't see the smile drop from her lips.

Stupid, stupid girl. The last time she'd let her heart rule her actions she'd ended up humiliated and alone. She'd been a fool for letting herself think that Max Kirkpatrick could be the one who would bring that sparkle of joy back into Christmas.

Chapter 2

Max wasn't sure who was more nervous. Him or the twelve-year-old kid squirming like a wriggly octopus on the wheelchair beside him. His eyes flicked to the chair behind them. Euan's mum was there. Carly. Timid as ever. Gnawing on a non-existent fingernail, her eyes darting around the office he'd managed to commandeer for the video call.

The poor woman. She didn't look as though she'd had a good night's sleep in years. The same as his mum back in the pre-dictator days. Getting Carly here today had been a feat and a half. How on earth she was going to get two weeks off work was beyond him.

"You ready for this?" Max asked. He wasn't. He was no stranger to sleepless nights, but he definitely wasn't used to erotic dreams. Or a guilty conscience. There was a hell of a lot more information he should've told Esme that would've explained his spiky behaviour when she'd appeared at Plants to Paws last week, but having jammed himself into an emotion-proof vest quite a few years back, sharing didn't come easily. Sharing meant being closer to someone. Opening up his heart. There was no point in doing that because he'd learnt more than most that opening up your heart and trusting a person meant someone else got to kick the door shut.

It had happened with Gavin. And with his fiancée. Now very much an ex-fiancée. And out on the battlefields of Afghanistan where lives had been lost because he'd trusted his commanding officer and not his gut.

He gave Euan and Carly as reassuring a smile as he could. They were living breathing reminders that if everything Max had been through hadn't come to pass, Plants to Paws wouldn't exist and Euan wouldn't be getting this once-in-a-lifetime chance to get his life back on track. Not the world's best silver lining, but… *"Start small, aim high."* One of his mum's better sayings. *"Forgive him, Max…"* being one of the worst. There was no chance Gavin Henshall deserved his forgiveness. Not after everything he'd done.

Euan's mum fretted at the hem of her supermarket uniform. "Could you run us through what the call's going to involve again, please?"

"Absolutely. It'll be similar to the one Fenella's going to have tomorrow."

"She's the poor woman with epilepsy?"

Max nodded. Fenella had first came into A and E on a stretcher after a horrific car accident. Since then the forty-one-year-old had come in with cuts and bumps after experiencing severe epileptic seizures resulting from the head trauma she'd suffered. The poor woman was nearly housebound with fear. A service dog could change her life.

"She'll be getting a dog specifically trained for her requirements."

"And Euan's dog will be trained to help with his…situation?" Carly asked.

Bless her. She never could bring herself to say PTSD.

"My crazy brain, Mum. My *crazy* brain!" Euan pulled a wild face and waggled his hands.

The poor woman looked away. She blamed herself for what her son was going through, as parents so often did, when, in reality, the attack on Euan had simply been very, very bad luck. The kind of bad luck that could change his life for ever.

Max looked Euan square in the eye. "Esme

knows what happened and will find a dog that can be there for you. It'll make being at home on your own more relaxing." He glanced at Esme's email again, trying not to picture her lips pushing out into a perfect moue as she concentrated. He cleared his throat and continued. "She mentions having a chat with the headmaster at your school. Some therapy dogs are permitted, so…if you need it, he might be coming along to school with you."

Euan's antsy behaviour suddenly stilled. The poor kid. The past couple of times he'd shown up in A and E had been for black eyes and cuts from fights at school. Despite the best efforts of the headmaster, it definitely wasn't Euan's safe place.

His story set the bar for cruel cases of mistaken identity. He'd been walking home from school about eighteen months ago when a local gang had mistaken him for someone else and had near enough pulverised the life out of the poor blighter.

Even in the war zones he'd been in, Max struggled to remember a kid who'd met the wrong end of a fist to such ill effect. He was a poster boy for PTSD. He bunked off school regularly. He had frequent panic attacks. His nightmares woke everyone in the flats around them, the screams were so piercing.

Carly was a single mum and worked shift hours so couldn't be there for him when he needed it most. He was a scared kid with no one to back him up and the only way he knew how to deal with all that fear was rage. With waiting lists longer than Max's arm, Euan needed someone beyond the psychiatric profession on his side. Someone to give him a bit of confidence. A reason to see the bright side of life. Someone with the unerring loyalty of a dog.

Max glanced up at the clock. "Right. It'll be a short call. Enough time to meet the dog, find out his or her name."

"I hope it's a boy. A huge bulldog!" Euan's eyes gleamed with possibility.

"There's only one way to find out." Max pressed the button and waited for Esme to answer.

Seeing Max Kirkpatrick's face appear on her screen brought back a whole raft of emotions Esme thought she had dismissed a week ago. So she'd thought he was hot. So what? Lots of people were hot. Like…um…movie stars. And models. And ex-soldiers with dangerously sexy hair working in inner-city A and Es who were doing their damnedest to keep their hearts off their sleeves.

But now that she was seeing him again?

Heart hammering. An entire swarm of butterflies careering round her tummy. A flock of birds might as well have been circling her head. She tore her eyes away and did her best to focus on the young lad sitting next to Mr Extra-Gorgeous with a cherry on top.

The boy he'd selected, Euan Thurrock, really pulled at her heartstrings. Skinny. Buzz cut. Looked ready for a fight, but it was so easy to tell there was a scared little boy hiding beneath all of that bravura. She couldn't imagine having to live in the same neighbourhood where he'd nearly lost his life. When the proverbial rubbish had hit the fan when she'd lived in Glasgow, she'd had a five-thousand-acre estate to hide in. Euan had to confront his biggest fears on a daily basis. She wasn't entirely sure she ever had.

She glanced at Max then looked back at Euan. "So, are you ready to meet Ajax?"

Euan punched the air. "Ajax sounds awesome. Like an attack dog. Is he a Rottweiler? A Doberman Pincer?"

Esme smiled. "None of the above, I'm afraid." She whistled the dog over and watched Euan's face melt with affection when the golden Lab popped his furry face up to the screen. "Euan, meet Ajax."

Despite having done "the big reveal' hundreds of times, Esme felt the familiar sheen of tears glaze her eyes. It wasn't just the dog's adorable face as it tried to make sense of what it was seeing on the screen, and this dog was particularly adorable. Dark brown eyes, black nose, fluffy golden fur and ears that quirked inquisitively at any unfamiliar sounds. It was Euan's face that caught her heart and squeezed a few extra beats out of it.

Seeing this tough kid's eyes light up to see something that represented hope would've turned anyone into a puddle. It was an expression that said he believed someone was finally, unequivocally on his side.

She gave Ajax a treat then asked him to sit beside her. "So, Euan, d'you mind introducing me to your mum? She's the adult coming to stay with you, right?"

Euan's mum gave a nervous wave as Max and Euan pulled their chairs apart to make room for her to scoot forward. "This is Carly," Max said, his voice a bit thick with emotion if she wasn't mistaken. "She's all booked up to join Euan next week."

"Actually…" Carly put her hand to her mouth then dropped it "… I've got a wee problem on that front."

Max's eyes went wide with concern. "Is everything all right?"

She shook her head. "My bosses have pretty much said if I leave at this time of year, I can expect not to have a job when I get back."

Esme was shocked. She always covered costs and rarely had problems with employers. "Would you like me to make a call?"

Carly shook her head again. She looked as timorous as she was sure Euan felt. "I don't want to make a fuss. I'm afraid the job's a bit more important than the dog."

Esme bit down on the inside of her cheek. If only she'd had the training centre in Glasgow, as she'd planned all those years ago.

If only the world was populated by nice, honest men who didn't spend their new bride's trust fund on nightclubs instead of training centres.

Before she had a chance to say anything, Max jumped in. "I'll go."

The look of sheer gratitude Euan threw him near enough tore Esme's heart out of her chest. When Euan got himself together enough to give Max a fist bump, neither of them managed to meet the other's eye.

Esme's chin began to wobble. She cupped her hands over her mouth.

Max straightened up, looked back at the video screen and what felt like straight into Esme's soul. "If that's all right? Wouldn't want to mess around your well-laid plans."

There was an edge to his voice, but it was a protective one. An edge that spoke of a fierce protectiveness that wasn't going to let Euan experience one more disappointment.

If Esme hadn't fancied Max before, she...well, she was really going to have to command her heartstrings into place. No fawning, or drooling, or looking with dopey-eyed fondness at a man who so clearly wanted to be warm, kind and open but, for whatever reason, couldn't.

One week ago, her instinct had been to keep him as far away as possible.

In the last five seconds her entire nervous system had done a one eighty. Take away the rugged good looks, the hands she would've paid money to see hold a puppy and that chestnut hair just begging her fingers to play with it—and underneath it all was a solid, reliable and trustworthy man.

Which was perfect. So long as he stayed at the end of a video call. Which was no longer happening.

Right! So. She started a mental to-do list with just one very important item: do not fall head over heels in love with Max Kirkpatrick.

This was her most vulnerable time of year and, as such, she had to be on her guard.

"So!" She scribbled some nonsense onto a pad no one could see then gave Max a bright smile. "Just a few little rules and regs to cover."

"I would expect nothing less," he said with a… oh, my…rather sexy smile. The type that said he could see right through her and back again.

Rule number one was going to be tough.

Esme gave what she hoped was a briskly efficient nod and ran through a few things, including what clothes to bring, what sort of weather to expect and asking about any dietary requirements.

Max looked at Euan. "I think just about anything beyond a sausage roll will be a new one on this lad."

Euan jabbed him in the ribs. "I'm not that bad. I've heard of…um…sushi." He abruptly leant in and whispered something to Max.

Max answered quietly then gave the lad's head a slightly awkward scrub. "Maybe we can scratch the sushi." The two of them threw each other a shy grin.

If there was any time to wish for some Christmas magic, now was it. Esme had a feeling it wasn't just Euan who needed a bit of TLC from a service dog. Max looked as though he had a wound or two himself that could do with being salved.

Esme glanced down at the stray pup one of their physios had found who was curled up at her feet. Dougal. Maybe she could convince Max to give him a forever home? Dougal was cuddly and responsive enough that he'd easily be a therapy dog, but…

When she looked back up at the screen Max was all business. Times. Schedules. Anything else they needed to bring. She answered his questions as efficiently as possible, all the while telling her hammering heart that she could do this. She could survive a week with Max Kirkpatrick. Besides, the second her brother Charles laid eyes on him she knew he wouldn't pass the big brother approval check list. Not that Charles was officially in charge of who she dated but having a second opinion after her disastrous elopement had seemed pretty wise, all things considered.

She followed Max's hand as it stuffed a few of his wayward curls back into submission.

What Charles didn't know...

As they signed off, Esme looked out the window towards the castle, merrily twinkling away in the early evening gloaming. It looked like something out of a fairy-tale. It was far too easy to imagine that long dreamed-of kiss under the starlight with all of the glittery warmth still swirling round her chest. Glittery warmth brought to life by one dark-haired, reluctant hero.

Good grief.

What had she just agreed to?

"How long's it going to take, Doc?"

Max gave his back-seat passenger a quick glance. "As long as it takes, Euan."

About eight days with any luck. Then he wouldn't have to go through the hoop-jumping Esme had no doubt set up for him. Attending Euan's training classes. Ensuring Fenella, his other "volunteer', was all right as her elderly mother couldn't come along either, owing to previous commitments. Day in. Day out. Dining together. Training together. "Fun time." Whatever the hell that was. Together.

Bonding.

He didn't bond. He assessed, treated, then moved on. Precisely why he'd opted to work in A and E after hanging up his camos. Move 'em in, move 'em out. Zero time to bond.

Bonding made you start Plants to Paws, mate. You're going to have to own it one day.

Unbidden, an image of Esme introducing the dogs via the video call to Euan and Fenella popped into his head. He was pretty sure he was the only one who'd caught the little surreptitious swipes she'd made at her cheeks when the patients' eyes had first lit on the pooches. He was positive he was the only one in the room who'd itched to reach out and wipe them away.

"D'you think Ajax is going to be allowed in the castle?"

"How would I know? Do I look like I was raised in a castle?"

Euan snorted then asked, "Hey, Doc, I was supposed to do a maths quiz today. Epic thanks for getting me out of school, mate!"

Max glanced into the rear-view mirror of his clunky old four-by-four and meet the lad's eyes. "I'm not your mate and this isn't a jolly, pal. There will be homework tonight. Of that you can be sure."

"Why're you so tetchy?" Euan countered in a tone that suggested he was well used to cranky adults.

"I'm not tetchy." Max's knuckles whitened against the steering wheel.

"Actually," Fenella gently cut in, "you are a bit tetchy."

Max harrumphed. Whatever. So he was a bit out of sorts. Spending a week with a fairy dog-mother who, via numerous phone and video calls, had managed to do all sorts of things to the steel walls he'd built round his psyche wasn't exactly something he'd been looking forward to.

Not to mention the annoyingly inviting visions that kept popping into his head of Esme in a ski suit. Esme in a onesie sprawled in front of a roaring fire. Esme in nothing at all.

He pulled off the multi-lane motorway that led north from Glasgow. The fastest option. "We'll go the scenic route," he growled.

Esme checked her watch. Again.

"The more you look, the longer he'll be," her colleague Margaret teased, then gave Esme's shoulder a little pat. "Don't worry. Lover boy will be here soon."

Esme gave a dismissive click of her tongue. Good thing they were friends as well as co-workers.

"He's *not* lover boy! And I'm definitely *not*

worried." Esme flounced away from the window. Worry wasn't her problem. Lust was. And the last person she was going to tell was Margaret— a woman on a single-track mission to get Esme to date someone "interesting'. Just because Margaret was now madly in love, it didn't mean Esme had to be as well.

"What's he like? Your sexy doc? And don't trot out the line about how you can't say until Charles meets him because we both know what the men he approves of are like." She feigned an enormous yawn to show just how interesting she thought his choices were.

Esme laughed. Her brother did have a tendency towards introducing her to men who…well… lacked lustre, but she'd told him she wanted a man who didn't have a single surprising thing about him. He'd taken her at her word. Not that he played cupid all that often, but when he did? Suffice it to say there had yet to be a love match.

"Ez? C'mon. Details, please."

"I told you. He's a Glaswegian A and E doctor." With gorgeously curly brown hair and the darkest, most fathomless brown eyes she'd ever seen. He'd been a bit stubbly when they'd had their last video call. She could just imagine his cheek rasping against hers when he— No! No, she could not.

Margaret grabbed a gingerbread man from the tray Mrs Renwick, Heatherglen's long-term cook, had given the therapy centre staff and held it in front of her face. "Won't you tell your dear friend Mags something more interesting about the big handsome doctor?"

"Who said anything about him being handsome?"

Margaret just about killed herself laughing. "You didn't have to. The way your cheeks go bright pink each time you come off a video call with him tells me everything I need to know." She began to chant in a sing-song voice, "Esme needs some mistletoe!"

Esme picked up another gingerbread man and stuffed it into her friend's open mouth.

"Do not."

Margaret tugged on her staff hoodie. When her head reappeared she grinned. "Suit yourself." She pulled on a gilet over her hoodie. "I'll see for myself in a few seconds." She flicked her thumb towards the window. "Lover boy's here!" Before Esme could protest—again—Margaret was on her way out the door, saying she'd get the dogs ready.

Esme tried to ignore the tiny tremor in her hand as she took a distracted bite of the gingerbread man, her eyes glued to the battered four by four that would give their new vet Aksel's bashed-up staff vehicle a run for its money. His arrival had been a godsend at the busy veterinary clinic. Running it and the canine therapy centre was a Herculean task and Aksel tackled everything Esme put his way with a fabulous mix of pragmatism and care. Mind you. Aksel was so loved up these days they could've issued him a wheelbarrow and a workload for ten men and he would've accepted with a smile.

Her thoughts landed in a no-go zone. It was a bit too easy to picture Max gazing at her in the same adoring way Aksel lit up whenever Flora, the rehab centre's physio, appeared.

The last time Esme had looked at someone like that she'd lost her heart and hundreds of thousands of pounds of her family's money. Not to mention her dignity, sense of self-worth and, yes, she might as well admit it, since the divorce papers had been finalised, nearly nine years ago now, she'd found it hard to believe she was worthy of love. All the compliments Harding, her ex-husband, had lavished on her had turned out to be lies. Lies she'd vowed never to fall for again.

Her tummy flipped when she caught a glimpse of Max behind the wheel.

She bit the head off the gingerbread man.

The next week was going to be a test of sheer willpower.

Via the Clyde's administrator, she'd learnt that Max had done several tours in the Middle East. Two more than her big brother, Nick had done. As a surgeon in conflict zones he would've seen enough horror to make that difficult-to-read face of his even more practised—giving away no more than he was comfortable with, which, in her case, was just about nothing.

She'd get there in the end. She always did. She loved teasing apart the complicated webs of her clients' personalities. Not that she ever bothered turning the mirror on herself. She knew what her problems were. Trust. Trust. And trust.

The car slowed as it climbed up the hill towards the castle. She craned her neck to watch as the passengers rolled down their windows and took a look. Max was the only one not to stick his head out of the window. As ridiculous as it was, she was a bit put out. Heatherglen Castle was more than a pile of rocks thrown together to impressive effect. It was her home.

The huge stone structure was framed by a crisp blue sky, the dozen or so chimneys puffing away with fires as the weather had turned so cold. Though some of the rooms were enormous, she and her brother had done their absolute best to make the castle feel as cosy and inviting as possible for the residents. Residents like Max who—because they were running at capacity—would be sleeping in her and Charles's private wing. Just. Down. The. Corridor. When they'd put Euan's mum there it hadn't been a problem. When the thirty-something mum had turned into Mr Tall

Dark and Utterly Off Limits, Esme's stomach had swirled with far too much delight.

Silly stomach. Just because a good-looking man is on the grounds, it's no reason to behave like a goofy lust-struck teen.

The car pulled up outside the clinic.

Right! Time to get to work.

Hamish, Mrs Renwick's grandson, tucked a stack of files under his arm as she walked into the reception area then pointed at her jumper. "You going to leave any of those for us?"

She flashed him a guilty smile when she saw the crumbs. "Of course, silly billy. I was just doing a quality control test."

"Of Nan's biscuits?" He didn't bother to disguise his disbelief that she could say such an outrageous thing.

Her guilty smile turned sheepish. They all knew Mrs Renwick's biscuits were insanely delicious.

"Can you take this plate back to the pooches, please, Hamish?" She handed him a platter of dog-bone-shaped biscuits made to a special dog-friendly recipe. "Make sure Dougal gets one. He adores them!"

"Aye aye, boss." Hamish gave her a jaunty salute and headed back to the kennels. He was openly enjoying his work experience at the clinic. She hoped he followed up his dream of becoming a vet one day.

She hurriedly wiped the gingerbread crumbs off her jumper and tuned into the loud laugh of a boy as the door opened and banged shut. Euan. A woman's delighted giggle followed up the boy's. *That would be Fenella.* Good to hear everyone was in such a good mood.

Before she could come out from behind the reception desk the door to the clinic flew open, slammed against the doorstop and whacked back again, only to meet a human doorstop. She shivered against the blast of cold air and looked across in time to catch the divot between Max Kirkpatrick's eyebrows furrow in apology. "The door caught a draught." He scanned the large reception area in slow motion. There were the usual accoutrements of a veterinary clinic. Dog food displays. A wall full of indestructible toys. Educational posters.

As Max's eyes narrowed and the divot between his eyebrows deepened, she suddenly saw what he saw. An insane riot of Christmas decorations covering absolutely everything. Hamish may have gone a bit OTT with the tinsel and glittery snowflakes. "You certainly like your Christmas decor," he said dryly.

"Not your cup of tea?"

"Not so much."

She gave a nonchalant shrug. Drowning in tinsel wasn't everyone's idea of Yuletide joy. She was more of a warm twinkly lights and a few well-placed baubles girl herself but ever since Nick had been killed on Christmas Eve and the news of his death had reached them on Christmas Day thirteen long years ago, she'd struggled to recapture the love she'd always had for the festive season.

She glanced behind him. "Where're your patients?"

"Outside." He flicked his thumb over his shoulders, those dark eyes of his not leaving hers for as much as a millisecond. "They're having a snowball fight."

"Brilliant!" She clapped her hands. "Some say it's good for the soul."

"Some say it's good for getting pneumonia." His eyes left hers and landed on her jumper. It featured three polar bears ice skating along a river up to the North Pole. "Nice jumper." His eyes were not on her belly button.

"Thanks." She tilted her head, forcing his eyes back up to meet hers. "I bought it in town if you want one."

"It isn't my usual colour palette."

She snorted. The man was dressed in top to toe navy blue.

"At least you're honest."

"Some say to a fault." He dropped her a wink that, judging from his follow-up expression, he hadn't planned to drop.

Esme looked straight into his eyes and just as they had that first time they'd met, they released a hot, sweet glittery heat that swept through her bloodstream with a not-too-subtle message. Max Kirkpatrick floated her boat. She gave herself a little shake. This wasn't a dating session, it was the beginning of a series of rigorous training sessions for the dogs and the new residents. And yet…

She forced her cheeky grin into a look of pure innocence. "Any chance you're open to being converted? To the Christmas thing?"

A shadow tamped out the glints of fun in his dark eyes. "I'd say about as likely as one of Santa's reindeer swooping down and taking me for a ride."

No wiggle room in that response.

She rolled her shoulders beneath the thick wool of her jumper. Rough against smooth. Would she feel the same sensation if Max were to slip his hands…? *Stop that!*

She wove her fingers together and adopted a pious expression as she began the lie she told herself every year. "I happen to love Christmas and all of the ancillary—" her voice dropped an octave *"—accoutrements."*

They both looked surprised at her foray into "bedroom voice'. No one more so than Esme. The last thing Christmas was was sexy. Hot chocolate, cosy fires and Christmas trees, definitely. Sultry voices and shoulder wriggles in silly Christmas jumpers? Not even close.

The fact she even looked forward to the holiday was little short of a miracle.

Ever since Nick's commanding officer had shown up at their front door on Christmas Day all those years ago, Esme had been trying to convince herself it was still the best day of the year. Impossible when they'd been told the rebel forces had taken advantage of the holiday to set intricately built tripwire bombs across the village where Nick had been stationed. Even tougher when they'd found out the only reason Nick had been out and about had been to deliver presents to a bunch of young soldiers who'd been finding it tough to be so far away from home.

Ever since that day Christmas had been like participating in a dreary panto. Each of them going through the motions, pretending they were happy, when all they wanted to do was weep for the golden boy they'd lost. Not that "they' were much of a they any more. Esme's doomed romance had taken up the first year after Nick's death.

Her mother had reshaped her grief into a near pathological need to enjoy life. Parties, swanning around the globe, scandalous affairs that had quickly led to the end of her parents' long and happy marriage. Her father had passed away three years after Nick had and their mother was now married to a Greek shipping magnate, so it was just Esme and Charles now, neither one of them doing all that well at re-injecting joy into Christmas.

No doubt as a former soldier, Max had his own particular days he didn't like. Unlike her, he didn't seem all that interested in trying to tap into any tendrils of Christmas cheer lurking somewhere in his heart. For the past thirteen years it had been like a mission for her. Which maybe defeated the purpose—pounding a square peg into a round hole—but there was something about Christmas that sang to her and she wanted to find that music again.

From a very early age she had believed that Christmas was magical. The decorations, the frenzied build-up, the secrets. More than any of those, though, she'd always loved the *giving*. Much more than the receiving. Seeing the joy on someone's face when they opened an unexpected present, or a child who had their first proper spin round the ice rink at the Christmas carnival, or someone's eyes widening as the first snowflake of the season landed on their mittened palm…she loved it. She just wished that the joy of the season touched her heart the way it used to.

All of which reminded her… She lifted up the tray of biscuits resting on the counter. "Are you so anti-Christmas that you'd refuse a homemade gingerbread man?"

Max rolled his eyes at her as if she were the lost cause.

Well, to each his own. At least he knew his mind. Honesty was clearly his policy and he stuck to it even if it did make him look like a Scrooge. She could respect that. A slow grin crept back onto her lips. Even Scrooge saw the light in the end.

Chapter 3

Two seconds.

Two measly seconds was all it took for Max to start working on an exit plan. Impossible, given his idiotic instinct to volunteer as Euan's guardian, but how the hell was he meant to survive? Esme was a walking, talking Christmas minx. One who, without as much as a how do you do, had him dropping winks and staring at her boobs. Classy. He really suited the whole "landed gentry' surroundings. Not.

If he didn't watch himself he'd have her over his shoulder, out the door and high-tailing it around Heatherglen on a quest for mistletoe. He'd bet her lips tasted like peppermint. Or whatever it was Christmas was meant to taste of.

Sugar and spice and all sorts of things that were wickedly nice.

He stuffed his hands in his pockets. He shouldn't be thinking about what anybody's lips tasted of. He should be thinking about Euan and Fenella and their dogs and the time he'd no longer have to spend with them in A and E because of this excellent opportunity to turn their lives around. A much more practical line of thought.

A woman wearing a gilet with her name and the therapy centre's logo stitched onto it pushed through the swinging doors that led to the kennels. Margaret. She was thirty-something. Dark-haired. Rosy-cheeked, from the cold most likely. Her eyes pinged from Esme to Max then back again. Margaret smirked. Esme glared.

If he was any good at reading women's signals and, like his flirting skills, they were rusty, Max would've bet cold hard cash Esme had told her that he was a crusty old man. Esme had obviously lied. Not that he slathered himself in youth potion or hunky man juice or anything, but he was relatively confident he was a step up from the abominable snowman's granddad.

Perhaps the exchange of meaningful looks between the women meant Esme was staking a claim on him.

He quickly pulled the plug on that idea. Esme was a beautiful woman and an heiress. She doubtless had queues of men ready to slip a ring on her finger.

Something instinctive told him the socialite scene wasn't her gig. Anyone who announced she picked up poo wasn't someone who fancied being a pretty bauble for some man to parade around on his arm. Maybe that was why her clinic was hidden away up here in the Highlands. Down in Glasgow or Edinburgh she could be at the doorstep of so many more people who would benefit from her therapy dogs. He had something teasing at his memory he couldn't quite bring to mind. Something he'd skidded over on the internet when he had been researching her work here at Heatherglen. A romance gone bad, perhaps? Whatever. Not his business.

As if she'd been reading his mind and wanted the thoughts to stop, Esme cleared her throat.

"Margaret," Esme said pointedly, "may I introduce you to the man behind Plants to Paws, Max Kirkpatrick?"

"Hello, Max," Margaret said, a merry twinkle in her bright blue eyes. "It's *very* nice to meet you. Esme simply hasn't been able to stop talking—"

Before Margaret could elaborate, Esme cut in with a very polite, stagey voice, making great use of her enunciation skills. "Margaret, don't you think it would be lovely if we got the dogs ready to meet the new residents? Max here was just on his way to get them."

Margaret's eyes pinged between the pair of them before she answered in the same stagey, highly enunciated voice, "Why, yes, Esme, I think it *would* be lovely."

"Great!" Esme gave a decisive nod. Margaret didn't move. Esme tilted her head towards the kennels.

Margaret threw an apologetic look in Max's direction. "We normally wait for the residents to be in the room before we bring the dogs in."

He took that as his cue to leave. Which was just as well, because it was all he could do to keep a straight face. Not that he was certain the women were having a non-verbal *he's mine* fight over him, but…it certainly felt that way. It'd been a hell of a long time since anyone had played tug of war for his attentions. No offence to Margaret, but if he were remotely interested in having his heart shredded to smithereens again, he knew which way the pendulum would swing. Not that falling for Esme was an option.

He'd adored his ex. Had loved her to within an inch of his life. She'd been all for his plan to save up money to buy his mum a house. Had supported his extra tours of duty. The overtime. The delayed returns. He'd thought she was amazing. Right up until he'd discovered her largesse was easier to bear because she'd been having a full-on affair with her boss. Not that she'd offered him the ring back or anything, but the fewer reminders of what it was like to have his emotions in someone else's power the better.

After he'd managed to brush most of the snow out of Fenella's hair and Euan's hood, they went back to the reception area, where Esme was wearing a very professional, very controlled smile.

They made a quick exchange of names, handshakes and the obligatory offering of gingerbread men. Both Euan and Fenella were so excited they could barely stand still.

"Have you had a chance to settle into your rooms yet?"

Fenella and Euan exchanged quick looks before Fenella answered for the pair of them. "We've not seen the barracks yet, no."

Esme's eyes shot to Max's.

Oops. He should've warned her he might've been teasing them on the ride up. There may also have been a mention of dungeons and castle keeps.

She twisted her lips into a little moue before that cheeky grin surfaced again. She'd rumbled him. "I think Dr Kirkpatrick may have been preparing you for a Christmas surprise." She nodded towards the castle. "Your rooms are in there."

Euan threw Max an incredulous look. "You mean we're staying in the castle?"

"Looks like it." Max gave the back of his neck a swift rub. It was nice to be giving good news for once.

Euan put his hand up for a fist bump. "Result, Doc!"

Max met his fist bump and then, to make sure the kid still knew his place, pulled him into a loose headlock and gave his head a light knuckle-dusting. Euan seemed to like it. Poor guy. He didn't have a dad to rough and tumble with. Someone to have his back when he needed it. Snap. At least Max had had the military. Brothers in arms and all that.

When he looked up, he caught Esme looking at him and Euan with that soft smile of hers. One that rammed an arrow straight into his heart. It wasn't often a woman saw his soft side. Then again, it wasn't often she stuck around long enough to find out he had one. After things had gone so apocalyptically wrong with his fiancée, he had decided he wasn't built for relationships, so didn't see the point in letting a woman know he had a heart thumping in his chest. Anyway, moving on…

Esme suggested Fenella and Euan pick a toy and a couple of bags of treats each from the display rack before they met their dogs.

Euan looked at her with disbelief. "You mean…

we just take them?" He threw an anxious look at Max.

"I told him everything was gold plated here." Max said, as neutrally as he could. There was no chance in the universe these two could afford some of the high-end collars and doggie coats on display so he'd wanted them to know things were for looking at but not for coveting. A valuable lesson his stepdad had made a point of impressing on him right from the start. He wanted cool trainers? He'd have to earn them. No time for a job and military academy? Well, then, looked as though he'd have to do without.

Euan's eyes were practically glittering with possibilities. Max's hand went back to his wallet. He'd pay if necessary. Just the once. It was, after all, Christmas.

"They may not look like it, but these are tools that will help you work with your dog. So, while you're here, these are free," Esme explained, without the slightest air of a have giving to the have-nots.

Max's respect for her went up another notch.

"Don't worry about stocking up on treats for ever. We'll be sending along food and treat parcels once a month to keep you going for at least the first year as we're well aware you weren't prepared for this sort of expense. If it's too much at the end of that, we'll set up a support programme. For now, though, help yourselves. Think of this as an all-inclusive Christmas pressie."

Fenella laughed. "Don't say that to Doc Kirkpatrick. He hates Christmas." She put on a voice to mimic Max's. "Nothing comes for free in this world."

Euan guffawed and gave Max a light arm punch. "Yeah. I tried to get him to wear some reindeer antlers on the way up and he near enough decked me."

"Is that so?" Esme's eyebrows shot up.

"Well…not literally but, yeah." Euan gave a very serious nod. "Doc Kirkpatrick and Christmas are not BFFs."

"Any particular reason?" Esme kept her tone light, but she clearly wanted to know. He couldn't blame her.

"Nope." No one needed to know just how miserable a time of year Christmas was for him.

"He's always working double shifts at the Clyde." Euan explained.

There was a reason for that. Double shifts didn't let the demons in. Euan was trying to give him an out. There was hope for the kid.

"All work and no play," Fenella teased, "makes Doc Kirkpatrick a…" She ran out of steam. "Well, you're not exactly dull, are you?"

Max could practically see the wheels turning behind Esme's sparkling blue eyes. As if she was already gearing up to change his Scrooge-like ways. Was there a challenge the woman didn't like?

"As none of this is relevant to service dogs, shall we get cracking?"

Esme narrowed her eyes as if she was staring straight at the chip on his shoulder. Oh, hell. She wasn't actually going to try to wheedle some Christmas cheer out of him, was she? To his surprise, she gave him a nod that indicated she knew exactly what he was talking about. That she understood pain and loss and everything that came along with it but she, unlike him, was trying to muddle through to the light at the end of the tunnel.

It was the type of look that made him wonder if his approach—no light, no tunnel—was a bit too blunt. He was the first to look away.

"Right, then." Esme clapped her hands together and pointed to the displays. "Why don't you two get a lead each and some treats? The dogs already have specialist collars that we'd like you to use. They've tried and approved of pretty much all of the treats on the wall, so take your pick."

Max noticed Esme sending him a curious look after another round of victory air punches from Euan. He moved in closer, lowered his voice, his eyes flicking to Euan as he spoke. "The kid's had a rough ride. That's why I didn't tell him about staying at the castle. I like to keep expectations low. Makes anything good that happens a welcome change."

"Ha!" Esme laughed. "That's my policy when it comes to men!"

"Good policy," Max said darkly. He didn't like the thought of her with other men. He also didn't like that he didn't like it. He shouldn't care and he did. Which was precisely why keeping Esme at arm's length—further if possible—was the only way he'd get through this. Basic training had been easier.

Esme shot him a look so full of hurt he knew she'd taken it the wrong way. Before he could fix it, Margaret bounced through the double doors and cheerfully interjected, "You ready, boss?"

Esme gave herself a little shake as if it would flick the pain away. "Absolutely. It's time for Fenella and Euan to meet their dogs in real life."

As she turned to go there was only one thought in his mind: This was a woman he would never allow to walk away. Which was why letting her think he was a bastard was for the best.

Now that Esme had properly humiliated herself in front of Max, she was as grateful to be around the dogs as she was hoping Euan and Fenella would be. Normally this was her favourite part—introducing the dogs to their new companions. This time, though, she was still stinging from Max's glowering response to her dating comment.

What had he been trying to say? That she'd always disappoint? That she'd never be enough? Hurt became anger. How dared he? He didn't know her. Another Harding MacMillan. She scowled. At least he didn't seem to want anything from her.

Against her better judgement, she glanced at him. He looked away.

Oh, yes. She'd read the comment right. He had no time for her except when it suited him. At least his affection for Fenella and Euan seemed genuine.

She snorted. Honest like a dog. She loved dogs, and dogs were trainable so—

No. Don't even go there.

"Any chance we're going to get this show on the road?"

Humph! Impatient like a dog.

"If you'll follow me," Esme snipped. Margaret went to fetch the dogs as Esme showed Euan and Fenella into a large room that was a bit like a sports hall. Big, airy, more than enough room for a large group of dogs to be trained and, of course, for their new owners to learn how to handle them.

"Now, a word of warning—mostly to Max rather than the two of you," Esme began. "No offence."

He put his hands up. None taken. Of course. He was ex-military. He could take it. Then again, the look on his face when Euan had fist bumped him. It was as if he'd won the lottery. There was definitely a big old softie lurking under that tough-guy exterior of his. Probably just as well it didn't extend to her.

She forced herself into work mode.

"Right! In a wee while we'll give Max a dog too, so he can experience the same training as you are. First things first, though...your dogs are precisely that. *Your* dogs. They need to bond with you and only you."

She scanned the small group again, her confidence growing as her professionalism came back into play.

"The most important thing to remember when you meet your dog is that you are their new best friend and you are going to establish a bond that, up until this point, they've only had with their trainer. Margaret and I are the main handlers, but we tend to raise a lot of the puppies down in the village so that they grow up in a home environment. They've been well socialised. What that means is you are going to have to make extra-sure that the praise they seek is yours. That the only treats they receive are from you. That the cuddles they want are from you. So this means, no matter how much you want to spread the love with Max..."

Her eyes flicked to his and she instantly wished they hadn't. *Spread the love?* Was she mad? No. She needed to make her own point now that he'd made his.

"You can't. No treats. No cuddles. Nothing."

There. Line drawn.

* * *

If Esme was trying to make a point, Max heard it. Loud and clear. Any chemistry he might've felt humming between the two of them had run its course. Fair enough. He'd been a jerk. She wasn't one to beg. Good for her. Too bad he hadn't had that same ability back when he'd kept hoping his stepdad would finally realise he was a good kid, or that he had been hallucinating when his fiancée had told him there was someone else. Someone worth loving. He felt a scowl form. Being here was reopening a whole ream of memories he'd hoped to never revisit.

He made himself tune back into what Esme was saying.

"Are you ready for me to bring the dogs in?"

Euan and Fenella were so excited he thought their heads would pop off if they nodded any more vigorously. Even he had to admit it was pretty damn sweet. When Margaret brought the dogs in, it was all he could do to keep the tears at bay. And that was saying something.

Margaret dropped the lead to the biggest of the two dogs and said, "Go, Nora. Go to Fenella!"

Fenella dropped to her knees and immediately embraced the large, creamy-haired goldendoodle. "You're absolutely gorgeous, aren't you lovely? Look, Max! Isn't she gorgeous? No, I mean don't look. She's all mine!" Then she burst into giggles and dug into her pocket to give Nora a treat. Nora took it then licked Fenella's face.

There it was. A forever bond made in a second.

Euan was equally over the moon. Max had thought the lad would've tried to put on more of a cavalier attitude. Pretend he kind of liked the dog. But when the big old bandy-legged golden Lab bounded over to him and offered a paw? Instant love.

Max gave his jaw a rub then shoved his hand through his hair, willing the scrubbing on his scalp to keep the bottleneck of feelings exactly where it should be. Suppressed. Churning away in his gut. Wherever. Anywhere but on display.

"It's pretty amazing, isn't it?" Esme had appeared by his side without him noticing. Little magical Christmas nymph that she was. She probably had elf dust or something like that in the small treat pouches she had hanging off her belt. "I always cry."

He looked down at her and, sure enough, she was wiping away a couple of tears. One glistening liquid diamond from each eye.

"How do you do it?"

Her eyebrows furrowed together. "Match them up, you mean?"

He nodded.

"That's relatively easy. Well, you obviously have to have the dog trained up for the right job.

Then I read the profiles that you send and…" She gave an unreadable shrug. "I just get a feeling."

Against his better judgement, he laughed. "Female intuition?"

Her eyes dropped to half-mast and moved from him to the dogs. "No. Past experience, a wealth of knowledge and a finely tuned instinct for my dogs and the types of people they'd suit."

Well, that told him.

They silently watched Fenella and Euan play with their new dogs as Margaret showed them, in turn, how to get the dogs to sit, shake paws, high five. No doubt they'd get to the "serious stuff" in a bit. For now, it was bonding time.

Damn. He hated to admit it but these two were experiencing exactly what he had hoped would happen when his mum had told him there was a new man in both of their lives. She'd organised a picnic in Glasgow's Botanic Gardens. Proof, if he'd needed any, that this was no casual boyfriend and that he definitely wasn't from their neighbourhood.

Max had brought along a football and a chest bursting with hope that this time he and his mum might've found "their guy', as she'd liked to put it. She'd never brought men home. Said it wasn't right as she wasn't just seeing someone for herself. It was for both of them. She'd get Max the dad he deserved after she'd made such a poor choice the first time round.

A fresh wash of guilt poured through him. He should've told Esme he knew the developer. He'd tried to convince himself it didn't matter because he would've fought whoever was trying to crush Plants to Paws. But there was a part of him that wanted to crush Gavin Henshall, too. No. Even that was wrong. Not crush, just…

"Forgive him, Max."

He looked across at Euan, whose dog was lolling on his lap, his tongue hanging out of his mouth, his eyes glued to Euan's. He wanted that.

Bonding. He'd been desperate for it with Gavin.

And he was never going to get it.

Without his having noticed, Esme appeared beside him, her eyes solidly on Euan and Fenella.

"I know," she said softly. "That's why I do this. Pure love with absolutely nothing expected in return."

He chanced a glance in her direction and when their eyes met? He saw it. The clear-eyed gaze of someone who understood exactly what it felt like not to be enough. And at that instant he fell a little bit in love with Esme Ross-Wylde, though every part of him knew there was no chance of a happy ending. Not for guys like him. Not with girls like her.

Esme shot him that impish grin of hers. "Right, then, pal. It's your turn."

"My turn?"

"Yup. We've got a dog for you to do some training with, so you don't feel left out. He can stay in your room with you, just like the others' will, or he can stay here in the kennels. On his own. Crying himself to sleep at night."

"Yeah, I don't think so."

Esme said nothing.

"I live in a flat. I work all the time. I don't have a life that's got room for a dog."

He decided not to remind himself that he'd made the life that didn't have room for dogs, or other humans for that matter.

"No one's asking you to fall in love with him," Esme said neutrally. Her eyes told a different story. She was daring him not to.

"Do what you must," Max said.

"Nice attitude, mate."

His stepfather's voice rang loud and clear in his head. One of the many things he hadn't been able to shake from his past. The low rumbling voice. The biting quips that never failed to make him feel lower than the mud on Gavin's shoe. *Time to earn your keep, mate. Pull up your socks, mate. Off to military school, mate. Maybe they'll know what to do with you.* As if he were a lost cause before Gavin had even tried to like him, let alone love him.

Euan's laugh pulled him back into the room. He followed his eyeline, then heard Fenella get the giggles as they all watched Margaret jog in with the scruffiest puppy he'd ever seen. The little puppy was wearing miniature red velvet reindeer antlers and a jumper covered in snowflakes. He could've scooped the little mess of fur and quirky ears up in one hand and barely felt the difference. If he was into scooping up puppies and going all doe-eyed, that was.

Esme's grin split into that superstar smile of hers. "Max? I'd like you to meet Dougal. Your very own fur buddy for the next fortnight."

"Ha-ha, very funny. Pair the big lunk with the tiny mongrel."

Esme feigned dismay. She picked the puppy up and nuzzled him, holding his face to hers, both of their eyes all wide and innocent. "How on earth could you say no to this poor orphaned pup? All alone at Christmas with no one to love him?"

Hell. He knew what that felt like too. Esme was really punching each and every one of his buttons today and he wasn't even on the patient roster. He felt Euan's eyes on him and made the mistake of letting some of the hope in the lad's eyes transfer to his own heart.

"Hand him over." He held the puppy up so they were eye to eye. "It's you and me, pal. What do you think of that?" Dougal licked him on the nose and barked.

Chapter 4

"All right if I hang out with Euan and Fenella until we set off?"

"Go for it," Esme chirped a bit too enthusiastically, trying to resist the urge to touch Max's arm, his hand, his anything really because each time they so much as brushed a pinkie finger…fireworks. For her anyway. Twenty-four hours in and, despite her best efforts, that same heated attraction that had lit her up from the inside out the first time she'd laid eyes on him refused to be tamped down. If anything…it was worse.

She watched from a distance as Fenella and Euan showed Max the tricks they'd just learned

in the clinic. They "shot' their dogs to get them to
play dead. He laughed appreciatively. Then they
"shot' him, after which he picked Euan up and
tried to carry him away, only to have Euan's dog
cut in and "save' him as they'd done in one of
the practice sessions. If she hadn't known better,
she would've thought he was a father trying to do
his very best by his son. Did he want children of
his own? Marriage? Though he came across as
gruff and spiky with her, Fenella and Euan clearly
adored him. They must think he was heaven sent.
They probably thought a lot of things. None of
which probably included being scooped up in his
arms, flung onto a four-poster bed and having their
wicked way with him.

Nope. She hadn't thought of that once.

He glanced over and caught her eye. The gold
sparks that lit up his brown eyes whenever he let
himself relax became shadowed.

Well, then. At least she knew who, of the two
of them, wasn't fizzing with frissons.

"Shall we get going?" She rubbed her hands together then pointed towards the path they would
be taking.

Max passed on the instructions to Euan and
Fenella then walked over to her as if she were an
obligation to fulfil.

Esme's heart sank a little. She didn't want to
be an obligation. She wanted to be... Her breath

formed into a little cloud as she huffed out a frustrated lungful of air. She wanted to be loved, that's what she wanted. What she didn't want was to have it be unreciprocated, so she needed to nip this whole *light my fire* vibe in the bud.

"The place hasn't changed much since I was here last," Max observed.

"Oh, yes!" She clipped Dougal's lead onto his collar and tried to match Max's long-legged stride. "I thought you'd mentioned you'd been to Heatherglen."

He nodded soberly. "Twenty-three years ago."

"And how many days?" She joked.

"Seven." There wasn't a trace of humour in his voice.

"Sounds like quite a memory."

"It was. Is. My mum brought me here."

About a thousand questions poured into her heart as he scanned the brightly decorated stalls surrounding the ice rink at the centre of the Christmas carnival. His eyes took on that faraway look she often saw in her brother when he was thinking of Nick or their father. It was almost as if she could see the memories shifting past his eyes. First the good ones…then the harsh reminder that there would never be more.

She'd been so gutted when Nick had been killed she'd entirely lost sight of who she was. Her father had become a workaholic. Charles had poured himself into med school as if his life had depended on it. Her mum had filled the empty hours with parties and, eventually, other men. She'd never felt more lonely.

She had became two people. A diligent student determined to become the very best vet she could be and a dedicated party girl who'd thought getting lost in the mayhem of yet another mad night out on the town was the only way to stem the grief she felt. Harding MacMillan, the leader of Glasgow's most elite pack of party people, had sensed her weakness, her desperation to feel loved. She'd stepped straight into his web of lies and deceit, willing it to fill the dark void of loss in her heart.

"Are the stables the only thing that you've revamped?"

Neutral territory. Phew.

"Apart from some of the medical elements we've added to the castle, you're exactly right." Esme pulled a knitted hat out of her pocket and put it on. "My parents were big fans of tradition so Charles and I tried to keep everything as it was. As you can see, the skating rink's a bit bigger, but…" she held her hands out as they approached the entryway to the carnival "…it's still toffee apples, chainsaw sculptures and mulled wine for all!"

Euan ran over, with Ajax in tow. "Are we going in?"

Esme smiled at his undisguised enthusiasm. If

Max had been anything like this as a kid, no wonder the memories had stuck. "We're going to save the Christmas carnival for another time, if that's all right. We'll definitely have a go as we need to help you operate in crowds and tricky situations together. We'll also head into town one day. Maybe take you to the Christmas market. And there's always the Living Nativity to think about. Who thinks Max would make an excellent Joseph?" Esme shot him a playful smirk. Her first in the past twenty-four hours.

He shot a "yeah, right' look back at her and there it was…that buzz of connection that crackled between them like electricity. If a right place and a right time for a kiss presented itself…

This way danger lay.

Esme nodded at the dogs. "Are you two all right with them? Happy with the training so far?"

A chorus of "Yes' and enthusiastic "More than' filled the wintry air. Esme and Margaret had already done a lot of one-to-one work with them. Esme focused on the drills Fenella's seizure dog knew whilst Margaret had been tasked with showing Euan all the tricks of the trade his dog could help him with when he was feeling panicky or depressed.

The grin on Euan's face near enough hit ear to ear. "I love him!" He dropped down low so he was eye to eye with the golden Labrador he had been assigned. "Ajax and I are going to rule the world!"

Esme laughed good-naturedly. "How about we see how the two of you do on a woodland walk first? Plenty of distractions out there. Squirrels, hares, deer. Maybe reindeer."

Ajax gave Euan's face a lick and when he raised a paw to shake hands with the boy, he laughed without an ounce of the self-consciousness he'd arrived with. Now, *that* was satisfying.

"Do I have to keep my dog on a lead?" Fenella asked.

Esme nodded. "Everything we're going to be doing for the next week ensures you are developing a relationship with your dog."

"Do you think Ajax would like cake?" Euan's gaze travelled over to a parade of food stalls at the Christmas carnival. "I love cake."

Esme laughed. "Cake is definitely not on their menu. Think of Ajax as an athlete. You want him to be in top health, right?" Euan nodded solemnly and blocked Ajax's view of the cake stall. It was easy to see he would let no harm come to his new furry friend.

Esme pointed to a path leading off into the woods. "I thought we could go down to the pond for now. Another big lure for Labs and goldendoodles. Even in the winter. But remember! You're in charge. Let's see how well you two can do at making sure they resist all of the temptations along the way."

She held out a lead to Max. At the end of the lead was Dougal wearing yet another Christmas jumper. "Happy to tag along with me and Wylie as back-up?"

Wylie was a huge old St Bernard who leant in protectively towards Esme's leg. When Max didn't immediately take the lead, a thought struck her. "Are you all right with dogs? I can't believe I didn't ask. With Plants to Paws I just assumed."

"No, it's not that."

"What is it?"

Max tilted his head towards Wylie. "Loyalty. Hard to find it these days."

The click and cinch of eye contact that followed hit Esme hard and fast.

From the shift in his stature she knew in her very core that Max felt it, too.

When she finally spoke, she barely recognised her own voice. "Should we get a move on? I think Fenella's got an appointment with one of the physios in an hour or so."

Esme set off at a crisp pace, reminding herself with each step that Max wasn't here to find a new girlfriend. He was here to make sure his charity didn't get paved over. Eyes on the prize. Just like her ex had had his eyes on her family money. Suddenly, the air felt a little bit chillier.

* * *

"What sort of behaviour do they have to exhibit to be a service dog?" Max's attempt to start up some casual chitchat wasn't exactly stellar but it would definitely beat the ice-queen vibes coming from Esme.

Esme briefly considered the two dogs walking beside them. "Probably the same traits it takes to be a good soldier. Commitment. Hard work. Intelligence." She glanced at him. "You were in the services, weren't you?"

He nodded. She'd obviously done her research. "Army. Twelve years."

"As a medic or a soldier?"

"Started as a soldier but worked my way into the Royal Army Medical Corps." He hadn't been able to stand waiting for someone else to help when one of his fellow soldiers had been injured. Mashing your hand on top of a wound rarely helped. Telling them you were there for them counted for something. Listening to their final goodbyes. As a nineteen-year-old soldier with his own emotional scars, Max had wanted something practical he could do. Medicine had rescued him from the deep morass of helplessness he'd felt ever since the Dictator had entered his and his mum's lives.

"You must've seen a lot of awful things," Esme said.

He nodded and scrubbed at the back of his neck.

They all had. At least he'd been able to walk off the plane when they'd landed back in Scotland.

"Have you chatted with Andy at all?"

Max had heard Euan introducing his dog to him the first night. "The chap in the wheelchair?"

Esme nodded.

"Euan and he seemed to have struck up a friendship and I didn't want to interfere. He has that ex-military look about him."

"Army. He was one of my brother's best friends."

"Charles?"

"No. Nick." An air of sadness cloaked her words. She shot him a sad smile. "You aren't really friends with the internet, are you?"

He shook his head. "Not really. For twelve years I lived and breathed the military and since then I've been deeply involved in the A and E unit. The internet fuels gossip. I don't like gossip."

She huffed out a disbelieving laugh. "That would make you a rare breed."

Shards of pain lanced through those pure blue eyes of hers and if he were the sort of man who knew how to make them go away, he would've. It was a cruel reminder that the only thing he'd learnt over the years was how to push people away.

"Nick was my older brother. Much older. He was in a canine dog squad in the army and one day… Christmas Eve, actually…things didn't go so well."

All the little pieces he'd been trying to put to-gether fell into place. The castle as a rehab cen-tre. The rescued mutts. The repurposed search and rescue dogs. Those intense looks she sometimes had when she held a dog close. All of this was for their brother.

"He must've been an amazing man."

"He was my hero."

The depth of emotion in her voice punched him right in the solar plexus, loosening up the muscles that held his own story deeply embedded in his heart. He wanted her to know she wasn't alone. That he understood pain and loss. His mum had been his best friend up until when his stepdad had entered their lives. A man whose method of put-ting a relatively wayward kid back on track was to ship him out to a military academy instead of let-ting him live in their new home, as promised. How the same man had verbally subdued his jolly, full-of-life mother into being little more than a timo-rous mouse, frightened to say or do anything that might embarrass her social-climber husband. As the dark thoughts accumulated, Dougal nosed his thigh. He gave the dog's head a scrub. The pooch definitely had a sensitive side. That was for sure.

As if the move had also jostled Esme, she gave herself a little shake, popped on a smile and asked, "What made you choose the Clydebank Hospital? Pretty rough area of town."

"It's where I grew up."

"Oh. Um…are your parents still there?"

"Nah." He cleared his throat because it still choked him up to say the words. "My mum passed. Three years ago now."

There was no point in mentioning his father. Step or otherwise. Neither had treated his mum the way she'd deserved.

Cancer had stolen his chance to give her the house he had bought for her. It'd taken him twelve years of service to buy it outright. He'd meant it to be a refuge from the Dictator and his constant micromanagement. As far as Max knew, he'd never laid a hand on her, but guys like that knew how to bruise and hurt in other ways. Gavin had been chipping away at his mother's self-worth for years. He hadn't wanted a wife. He'd wanted someone to feel small so he could feel big. It was a miracle she'd had any confidence left at all in the end. Or the generosity in her heart to forgive a man he didn't think he ever could forgive.

At least her battle with cancer had been swift. A cruel mercy. The day she'd died, Max had put the house on the market. He'd thought of making it a shelter, but he simply hadn't had the funding to keep one up and running. He'd used the money to establish Plants to Paws instead. His mum had loved gardening. It had been the one place she'd known her husband couldn't fault her.

He needed to bring up his relationship to Gavin before a single penny came his way from Esme, but for now he was enjoying the thoughtful silence she'd chosen in lieu of asking, *And your dad?* Like her therapy dogs, she seemed to know when to push and when to back off. If he wasn't careful he'd be pouring out all his secrets but he knew more than most that putting his heart in someone else's hands was always a bad idea. So he followed Esme's earlier lead and sidestepped the real stuff.

"Where'd you find this cheeky chappie?" He pointed at Dougal.

"A couple of our staffers found him. Cass and Lyle. Someone had abandoned the poor wee thing." She gave the dog a goofy grin and he barked his approbation. "Up until a few days ago he was staying with our physio, Flora, but she's moving in with Aksel—the new vet—and they already have an assistance dog for his daughter, so…" Esme looked up to the wintry sky as if for inspiration.

"Because he's so young and such a little scruffball we weren't sure he'd be up for much training, but he seems pretty adaptable. Aksel caught him trying to purr next to a cat the other day." She laughed, her features softening as she unclipped his lead and gave him a bit of a cuddle. "Poor Dougal. He deserves someone who will love him exactly the way he is. A little broken. A lot in need of love."

Something told Max she was describing herself. She sure as hell was describing him. Though he could hardly believe the words as they came out of his mouth, he said them anyway. "Want to talk about it?"

"About Dougal?" Esme knew he'd been asking about her, but she was hardly going to pour her heart out to a man who had more control over her emotions than she cared to admit. "Nothing to say really. His past is a mystery." Her eyes flicked towards Max. *A bit like you.* Adopting what she hoped was a fun, interested look, she asked, "So what's your kilt like? I'm not familiar with the Kirkpatrick tartan."

"Probably because it's Lowland. I'm guessing the Ross-Wylde tartan is—forgive the pun—cut from a different cloth."

It was as it happened. Highlander through and through. But that didn't mean he could tar her with a brush of superiority. "I don't use my name to get things I haven't earned."

His eyes widened. There had definitely been bite to her bark and Max wasn't a man to stand around getting attacked. "You certainly seem happy to use it when it comes to flinging your money about."

Everything in her stilled.

"Don't say that."

Max's spine realigned into ramrod position. "Sore point?"

"Something like that."

She saw him reeling through the possibilities of what could make the poor little rich girl so touchy about money. When she failed to explain he asked, "Is this why you fund the charities through the ball instead of donating it all yourself? Gives you a bit of emotional clearance so you don't have to feel responsible for anyone and they don't have to come crawling to you for more?"

He was hitting close to the bone. Too close. And he wasn't bothering to sugar-coat it.

She flicked her hair out of her eyes and tucked it back underneath her hat.

"How I run the foundation is nothing for you to worry about, Max. It's a charity event, not a Princess Charming Ball." Instead of stropping off, which she should have done, she lashed out, "And don't think for a minute I need to find a male version of Cinderella to make me happy."

"No?" countered Max, the space between them diminishing as the heated intensity between them increased. "What do you need to make you happy?"

Her heart was pounding so hard she could barely hear her own thoughts let alone the sounds around them.

Someone like you?

"Max!" Euan was running towards them. "Come fast! It's Fenella!"

Max took off with the practised speed of an athlete. Esme scooped up Dougal's lead and, as best she could, ran behind, silently adding, *Make self immune to grumpy but sexy Scottish doctors* to her list of things to do.

When Max reached the clearing, he could hardly believe what he was seeing.

Fenella's dog, Nora, was nudging herself under Fenella's head as she came to the end of a seizure.

"She was fitting, Doc." Euan said, breathless and a bit pale from fright. "I stuck my glove in her mouth so she wouldn't bite her tongue or anything, but she spat it out. Too mucky, I guess."

"It's all right, pal." Max dropped to his knees and did a quick check of Fenella's vitals. "You've done the right thing in finding me. From the look of things, Nora here knows what she's doing."

"Absolutely." Euan looked awestruck. "I know we saw her in the practice hall, but this was the real thing. It was like she knew it was going to happen." He looked up as Esme jogged into the clearing. "Did you know Nora makes herself into a cushion?"

Esme gave Nora a quick pet and a treat as Fenella slowly came to. "Absolutely. That's what she's trained to do."

Max helped Fenella sit up. "You all right there, hun?"

The post-ictal phase was always a bit tricky. The person who'd had the seizure could feel perfectly fine or often exhibit signs similar to those of a stroke. Headaches, slurred speech, nausea and fatigue. In rare cases, some epileptics could suffer from post-ictal psychosis and suffer from paranoia or extreme fear. Usually the anomaly occurred in people who weren't taking their medication.

"Yes, I…" Fenella looked a bit confused and then, when her eyes lit on Nora, it was as if everything pinged into place. "I felt a bit woozy and the next thing I knew, this one was being my pillow." She ran her hand through the dog's fur and automatically reached to her pocket to get her a treat. "Good girl. You're a clever girlie, aren't you?"

"She was!" Euan jumped in. "Out of, like, absolutely nowhere you fainted. But you weren't fainting. You were having a seizure, I guess, and it was like Nora knew exactly what to do. She broke your fall. Then she stuck herself under your head while you were fitting. No offence, but it was really cool."

Max glanced across at Esme. She looked concerned for Fenella but pleased her new service dog had fallen straight into her new role. She was actively avoiding eye contact with him. Served him right. He'd been an ass. Sticking his nose where it didn't belong. He should tell her about Gavin. It would break just about every rule in his play-your-cards-close-to-your-chest handbook, but he felt he owed it to her to even the emotional playing field. He got it. Sometimes things were personal. Luckily for his emotional armour, taking caring of Fenella took precedence.

"Did you take your AEDs?" Max asked. Anti-epileptic drugs helped but weren't a failsafe, especially if they weren't taken regularly or weren't the right dosage. Having seen her in his A and E several times for sprains and cuts sustained while she'd been fitting, he knew she had struggled for years to find the right balance of medication.

"Yes." She looked away, rubbing her elbow.

It didn't sound like a one hundred percent yes, but he wasn't going to embarrass her in front of everyone if there was a story behind her not taking it. Or, as was often the case, she might need to change meds. They weren't a one-pill-fits-all type of medicine.

"Did you hurt yourself?"

"No more than usual." She held up a lightly scraped hand then qualified her answer. "I probably would've cracked my head on a stone or something if it hadn't been for Nora." She wrapped her arm round the dog and nuzzled her face into the fluffy goldendoodle's coat. After a few moments,

Max quietly asked, "What do you think set this one off?"

Fenella shot him a sheepish look. "Lack of sleep most likely. I've been so excited the past few days, I've hardly slept a wink."

He nodded. "Perhaps it'd be best if we all head back to…um…"

"The castle?" filled in Esme, with the ease of someone who'd grown up in one.

Had it been more burden than blessing?

Esme glanced at her watch. "Max mentioned you have an appointment with Flora, our physio. Shall we head back, get you a cup of tea and some quiet time before then?"

Fenella nodded, grunting a little as she sat up properly. Max reached out to steady her. Poor woman. Had to be tough being taken by surprise by seizures just when you thought you were having the time of your life.

"Are you two still all right having your dogs with you in your rooms? We can take them back to the kennels for the afternoon if you need a break."

They both asked if they could have their dogs stay with them. Esme grinned a naughty little sister grin.

Which did beg the question, "Is that not *de rigueur*?" Max asked, sotto voce. "Having the dogs in the clinic?"

"Oh, it is," she answered breezily. "It just annoys my brother. Speaking of him, if he has time later on, Fenella, it might be a good idea for you to meet Charles and talk through your medications."

"It's just the one right now. I'm sure it's fine." Fenella looked uncomfortable about the suggestion, which instantly put Max's protective streak into high gear.

"Does he know much about epilepsy?" Max asked. A bit too defensively from the look of Esme's own bristly demeanour.

"He's a neurologist, so he's pretty good at understanding why brains work the way they do. I'm not criticising any of the medical treatment you've received at the Clydebank, Fenella. They obviously have specialists there who are helping you and Max, here, of course. I'm just covering our bases as you are our guest. We want to make sure you receive all the treatment you need. If there's anything we can do—"

"Don't worry." Max helped Fenella get back to her feet. "Easy does it, lassie. Why don't we take this step by step and get this woman some rest first?"

He tried to block out the sharp looks Esme kept sending him, but the odd one or two pierced straight through to his conscience. Now he definitely owed her an apology. What had got into him? Accusing her of flinging gold coins at people for her own amusement. Dismissing her sensible offer of a fresh set of eyes on Fenella's case.

If she knew even half of the reasons why he swung from one end of the emotional spectrum to the other she'd...hell, he didn't know. Send him packing most likely. It seemed to be the remit.

His stepfather had lured him in with all the bells and whistles that had appealed to a twelve-year-old kid from the wrong side of the tracks. Tickets to premier league football matches, nights out at the scary films his mother couldn't bear, slap-up meals at the finest burger joints in town. It had been kid heaven. Until it hadn't been. And had set him up for a lifetime of keeping people at arm's length until they proved they were the real deal.

Ironically, it had been Gavin's constant demands that he "earn his keep' that had pushed him so hard in the military. Had made him the top-rate soldier and surgeon he knew he'd been. Gavin hadn't thought he had what it took? He'd vowed to show him.

He would have as well if he hadn't had a conscience. Or carried around those little-kid hopes and dreams that one day he'd be good enough. Worth loving. He supposed it had been that same little boy's belief in love that had made him blind to his fiancée's affair. Being so oblivious had made him feel every bit as weak as he'd felt when Gavin had shipped him off to military academy, instead of taking him to their new home, as he'd promised.

A few more proofs that truth and justice rarely reigned—dodgy commanding officers, innocents rigged up with IEDs, the cruelty of poverty had closed the book on the matter. Being wary of whatever met his eye was his modus operandi. Being suspicious of whatever touched his heart was critical. It hadn't exactly made him A-list boyfriend material. A handful of one-night stands he wished he hadn't had had been the clincher. So life as the Monk had begun. Which, of course, immediately made him think of all the people who were relying on him back at the Clyde to save Plants to Paws.

His conscience gave him a sharp kick in the posterior. His emotional baggage shouldn't be a factor. Normally it wasn't. Not with the chaos he encountered in A and E every day. And yet…here it was, front and centre. His hypersensitivity did beg the question, did he want Esme to think well of him?

He stuffed his hand through his hair. No need to ponder that one. It was an unequivocal *yes*. Which meant the next week was going to hoist this festive season up amongst the worst ever.

You could try being nice.

"Go on, then," he said when Esme shot him another *look*. "Give your brother a call."

And there it was. The first chink in his "don't

ask for help' armour. If you don't ask, you don't
need. And if you don't need, you're never disappointed. It was a little pact he'd made with himself
when the Dictator had asked him to put a value on
himself the very first Christmas they'd spent together. Turned out the pair of them had disagreed.

It hadn't been a very nice Christmas.

When Esme's smile of thanks hit him on full
beam, he began to wonder if his pact had flaws.

Chapter 5

Esme carefully placed the enormous tabby back into Mrs Elsinore's arms. "It might be an idea to cut back on Theo's treats. The extra weight could be contributing to his arthritis."

Mrs Elsinore looked horrified. "But, dear, we have a routine." She talked Esme through morning treat, morning breakfast, elevenses treat, lunchtime and so on.

"No need to veer from the routine, it's more a question of reducing—" Something, or rather *someone* caught her eye just beyond the exam-room window. A six-foot someone tugging a hat over that touch-me-now hair of his. Was it time for the afternoon walk already? Not that she hadn't been counting down the seconds or anything, but the last few patients in the vet clinic had mercifully managed to steer her thoughts away from Max. Not any more!

"What was it you were saying about routine, dear?"

"Yes. Right. Routine." Her gaze involuntarily drifted back out the window. Max was laughing at something Margaret had said. Margaret looked so relaxed and at ease with him. The total opposite of how *she'd* been. By turns uptight, weirdly flirty, downright snippy.

He glanced over towards the window and caught her eye. He raised his hand in a half-wave but turned the instant Margaret said something. Something *hilarious* from the look of things.

Ruddy Margaret.

Wait. *What?* She loved Margaret. Margaret was her friend. Her friend who had a boyfriend and was no threat at all. Not that she was feeling competitive. It wasn't as if she wanted to date him. Or press her hand to his chest to feel his heart beat. Or find out if his lips were as kissably delicious as they looked.

"Esme, dear…shall I carry on as normal, then?"

"No. I mean…cutting back a wee bit on Theo's treats would be advisable." Esme gave her face a quick scrub with her hands. "Apologies. I'm a bit distracted today. New residents…"

Mrs Elsinore looked out the window and smiled. "With residents like that I think I'd be distracted, too."

Esme blushed instantly. "What? Him? Oh, no… he's not…"

"Don't deny it, dearie," Mrs Elsinore tutted. "He is. Now, if you tell me what else you want me to do with Theo that'll free you up to go on out there and be distracted a bit more up close and personal."

Esme pretended she hadn't heard that part.

A few dietary tips and one prescription for glucosamine tablets later and Esme was pulling on her staff puffer jacket and heading out to where residents and their dogs met for the afternoon walk.

Margaret waved her over when she saw her. "Big favour."

"Sure." Especially if it involved being nowhere near Max. He was currently at the far end of the barns with Hamish and Dougal. Max didn't look as pleased as Hamish was about Dougal's new Christmas jumper.

"Woohoo! Esme." Margaret waved her hand. "Eyes over here, please."

"I wasn't—"

"Yes, you were. Which brings me to my favour. Do you mind taking Max for the next couple of hours?"

"What?"

"He's brilliant, but Euan keeps deferring to him for everything and we need to take a walk where Euan's sole focus is Ajax, not Captain Gorgeous."

"He's not—"

"Esme." Margaret stopped her cold. "He totally is and there's absolutely nothing wrong with fancying him."

There was. There were a thousand reasons and probably another thousand right behind those.

"Hey." Margaret forced her friend to look at her. "Not everyone's Harding MacMillan. Go on a walk with the man. What's the worst that could happen?"

She was about to launch into an extensive list of all of the bad things that could happen, even though Margaret knew the whole sordid story. Before she had a chance, Margaret had called Max over, explained the situation then told them where the group would be going so Max and Esme could go elsewhere.

When Margaret walked off and left the two of them standing there Max huffed out a laugh. "Feels a bit like a set-up, doesn't it?"

"If you're not interested in taking a walk with me, I'm more than happy to take the dogs on my own."

"Hey, easy there. I wasn't suggesting anything

of the sort, I was just saying—" What was he saying? That being alone with her made his brain go all sorts of crazy? That sleeping down the corridor from her meant not sleeping at all? That he wanted her?

It was that simple.

All he had to do now was find a way to get his body to fall in line with his brain, which was telling him to step away from the beautiful woman and everything would be fine.

Esme tightened her lips then pointed towards a path. "If we go that way towards the old castle ruins we should stay clear of them. I'm perfectly happy to go on my own, though."

"No. I wasn't saying anything like that."

"Well, what were you saying?"

"I was just saying your colleague has a way of making everything sound like a date whenever she matches the two of us up."

Esme rolled her eyes then grudgingly laughed. "Margaret has a way of doing that. She sees herself as my personal matchmaker."

He didn't push for details, opting to let silence do the work. If she wanted to talk about her love life, she would. If she didn't, she wouldn't. As plain as that.

After about ten minutes of briskly paced walking, Esme threw up her hands. "It isn't that I don't find you attractive, all right?"

Despite himself, Max laughed. She'd obviously been having a conversation all by herself. Again, he decided not to push for details. Lord knew, the more he was pushed, the less he wanted to say.

"I don't date clients."

"Who said anything about dating?"

Esme glared at him. "You did. The thing about Margaret making everything sound like a date?"

Max rubbed the back of his neck. This was one of those complicated conversations he had no way of winning. Did he want to take her out? Not particularly. He didn't do dating. Was he attracted to her? Absolutely. More than he had been to anyone, to be honest. There was something about Esme's combination of vulnerability and fiery strength that spoke to him. A kindred spirit who may have started off in life on a different path but, like it or not, they were on the same one now.

"You're right. This is a professional relationship. Nothing more."

"Good," Esme said, sounding absolutely miserable. "I'm glad we've cleared that up."

All of a sudden, they heard someone calling out, a loud piercing scream. It sounded like a name.

Esme scooped up Dougal and took off at a run. Max did the same, with Wylie loping along in his wake. The screams stopped abruptly. Esme pointed towards a gated field. "A lot of villagers use this field as a shortcut to get up to the ruins. Maybe someone's dog was hit. Let's tie up the dogs here. I'll ring Aksel to come and collect them and bring the four-by-four in case we need to take anyone back to the vet or the clinic."

All the tension tightening her features over the "dating incident' had re-formed into exacting focus. This was not a woman fazed by crisis. Once the dogs were secured and Esme had made the call, they ran across the field, Esme leading the way. When they got to the far end, Max's doctor brain kicked into high gear. A woman was curled around a grey lurcher absolutely covered in blood. She was moaning and crying her dog's name over and over. When she looked up at them, they could see she was also covered in blood. She sobbed, "Help! Teasel's been cut!"

"Janet, it's all right. We're here now." Esme dropped to her knees beside them. "Are you hurt?"

"I'm not sure. I had to jump over the fence after him and I think I twisted my ankle."

Esme shot a glance up at Max. "If I take the dog, can you look after Janet? She works down at the pub and has had this wee thing for…what is it, Janet four and a bit years now?"

"Five!" wailed Janet. "We were out for his birthday walkies."

"Well, then, we'll have to make sure we look after him with extra-special care, won't we? Why don't you sit up and we can take a look?"

Max could see what Esme was doing. Putting both of the patients at ease. Her voice was calm and steady. Her energy completely soothing. Animals read humans much better than people did and Esme had an impressive ability to match her energy accordingly.

"Sure thing." He took his fleece off. "Here, use this for Teasel."

Janet clung even more tightly to her dog as Esme reached out to take him. "I'm afraid to let go. He was chasing a deer. I tried to get him to stop."

That explained the screaming.

"When he leapt over the fence, the barbed wire snagged him." She sobbed again. "It's ripped a huge wound from his chest to his belly." She tried to pull herself up to standing, still reluctant to let go of the dog. Max reached out and caught her as she stumbled. Esme deftly grabbed hold of the dog and cradled him in Max's jacket.

"All right, darlin'." Max eased her back to the snow-covered ground. Not ideal, but until he knew what was wrong it'd have to do. They also weren't so far away from the castle that he couldn't carry her if necessary. She was a wee snip of a thing compared to some of the muscled soldiers he'd hoisted fireman style for over a kilometre.

Esme pulled off her puffer jacket. "Here. Use this for Janet. She's had a shock." The dog whimpered and Janet jumped up towards him.

"Hey," Esme soothed. "Teasel's whimpering is a good thing. It means his windpipe is intact."

Janet fell back to the ground using both her hands to clutch her ankle. "I think I sprained it or something."

Max saw blood around her ankle, swiftly rucked up her waterproofs and carried out a quick examination. She didn't have a compound fracture or any obvious cuts so that was something, but she'd need X-rays to rule out any fractures. He felt further up along Janet's leg and was satisfied that her ankle had received the brunt of the fall and nowhere else. "You don't happen to have X-ray facilities in the clinic, do you?"

"Yes."

"Brilliant." He checked Janet's pulse and suggested they keep her off her leg until he could do a proper examination. "Looks like you got your own set of cuts as well. We'll check on the status of your tetanus jabs and get these cuts cleaned up. I don't think you'll need stitches, but—"

Janet pulled her wrist out of his hand. "I'm not leaving Teasel! What if he's nicked an artery— what if—?" Janet became consumed with tears as she considered the very worst outcome.

"Hey." He pulled her to his side as Esme carried out her own examination. The last thing one doctor needed was another doctor's patient jumping in at what could be a delicate moment. From the look on Esme's face, it was grim.

Max cocked his ear at the sound of a vehicle.

"That'll be Aksel." Esme didn't look up as she wrapped the dog tightly in his coat. "He's going to be up with the dogs—can you guide him in, please? The less movement for this little guy, the better."

"Absolutely."

Esme could hardly believe it had barely been a couple of hours since the mere idea of going on a walk with Max had filled her with horror. Now? She would happily have him along—day or night. Not that she was always encountering incidents like this harrowing one, but if she ever had to face the eye of a storm with someone, it was Max Kirkpatrick.

His military cool and first-class medical knowledge were exactly what you would want in a crisis. He'd even showed his soft side when Janet had dissolved into tears. Dug a clean handkerchief out of his pocket and everything. The man might see himself as solid mass of impenetrable man mountain, but her gut instinct had been right. He had a heart the size of Scotland.

"How's he coming along, Esme?" Janet asked through a speaker in the viewing room.

Esme tied off the delicate stitch then looked

up. "Only a few more stitches to go and then he can have a proper rest." It was a highly edited way of describing what had been a difficult surgery. Teasel had had to be anaesthetised while she'd assessed the extent of the tissue damage. She'd had to debride some of the most heavily damaged areas right next to the wound and multiple layers of tissue had needed suturing but, luckily, they'd avoided having to put any drains in.

Despite Esme's insistence that Teasel would be receiving the very best of care, Janet had point blank refused to leave her dog. The best she'd agreed to was sitting in the large windowed room just outside the surgical area in the veterinary clinic, with Max in attendance. It wasn't standard practice, but...as the accident had happened on Heatherglen land, Esme felt an added responsibility to both patients.

With Janet and Max looking on, Esme had poured her concentration into the surgery as she'd painstakingly stitched Teasel's shockingly long wound back together. The barbed wire had done a real number on him, from his throat to his belly. He had miraculously managed to escape nicking his jugular vein. If he had, the nurses wouldn't be prepping a recovery kennel for him.

The nurse who was working with Esme turned off the microphone and asked, "Shall I ask Max to try and get her to go up to Heatherglen now?"

Esme shook her head. She wasn't going to admit it, but having Max there was strangely soothing. She didn't want to have to worry about Janet while she was working on Teasel and with Max there, she didn't even feel an ounce of concern. "It's not like it happens every day and she's been through such a shock. Teasel's her baby. I can understand her not wanting to leave him." Dogs were family in her book. You didn't abandon family when they needed you most. Having a mother who'd abandoned ship at her lowest ebb had taught her that the hard way. Having a brother who'd been there to pick up the pieces had confirmed it.

She glanced up and caught Max's gaze. A warm heat swirled round her belly with such intensity it was as if he'd slipped his hands under her scrubs. This was not the time to be distracted. Even so, she hadn't been able to help taking the odd glimpse at him. He had either been readjusting Janet's position so that her foot was elevated, giving her a proper blood-pressure test with a pump Lyla had run down with from the clinic along with some ice packs, or running her through a ream of questions all designed to keep Janet's eyes off the rather gruesome injury.

Max was a picture of calm, quick thinking, level-headedness in what could have been a difficult situation. Mercifully Janet's injuries hadn't been serious. She had a few cuts of her own, which Max had cleaned and put antibacterial cream on before lightly dressing them. He'd also called her GP and checked on her anti-tetanus status. She'd need a booster.

Half an hour later, when Teasel was resting in his kennel and Janet had been assured for the hundredth time that he'd be asleep for the next few hours and that they'd call straight away if there was any news, she finally agreed to let Max take her in for X-rays.

Esme had only just finished up at the surgery when she saw his vehicle leaving the castle grounds heading into town—to the GP's surgery and on to Janet's, no doubt.

She looked down and realised both of her hands were pressed tightly against her pounding heart. If she didn't watch herself…

Margaret came out of the front door of the clinic and locked the door behind her. "Fancy a drink down in the village?"

"No," Esme said a bit more dreamily than she'd intended. "I'm all right here."

Margaret followed her gaze as Max's four-by-four wended its way down the long drive. "Oh, you are in trouble!"

Yes, Esme agreed silently. Yes, she was.

Charles stopped Esme as she was about to enter the kitchen.

His big-brother expression turned serious. "The snow's just started, it's pitch black and it's icy."

"Thanks for the weather report, Charles."

He gave her a don't-be-daft look. "I'm trying to tell you it's not safe to go out driving."

Easily falling into her role as kid sister, she shot back, "I happen to be an excellent driver, thank you very much."

"Where are you going all dressed up like that?"

His eyes dropped to her flirty, swishy, feminine skirt. She never wore skirts. It was usually scrubs, workout clothes or pyjama bottoms at this time of the evening, unless she was meeting Margaret in the village for a glass of wine or, on very rare occasions, heading to Fort William or Glasgow for a dinner date. Yawn-fest more like. She silently vowed never to take her brother up on another suitable suitor again.

Though her features remained stoically neutral as he waited for an answer, she could feel tiny tendrils of heat creep into her cheeks. "I'm just on my way to see Mrs Renwick. Everything else is in the wash."

"Yeah, right."

"Why are you so grumpy?"

"I'm not grumpy."

He was. He was very grumpy. Which was annoying as he'd been in an absolutely brilliant mood when he'd come back from his medical conference a couple of months ago. It'd made a nice change from Dr Too Serious for His Own Good. Maybe he should go to another one. It would keep his prying eyes away from the fact she just might have accidentally on purpose put on something slightly more feminine in case she accidentally on purpose ran into a certain Max Kirkpatrick.

Since he'd come back a couple of hours earlier it was as if they were slowly circling one another, neither one willing to make the first move. Not that she even knew what kind of move was going to be made. If they were simply going to be friends, fine. She just wanted an end to this silly friction that existed between them. Working together today had helped, but when he hadn't bothered to find her after he'd come back from town, she'd gone into another one of her insane spirals of insecurity.

Was she good enough? Wasn't she? Was it time to simply grow up and not treat every single man who showed a flicker of interest in her as a potential pariah? Maybe in this case work was work and pleasure was a figment of her imagination.

Either way, she wanted the tension to end. She respected him and there was absolutely no reason why they couldn't be friends. She gave her brother a supercilious sniff then swished through the swinging kitchen doors before Charles could say anything else.

Esme was immediately drawn to the platters of Christmas biscuits covering the long kitchen counters, then sent her most winning look at Mrs Renwick. "Yum. How many may I take?"

Mrs Renwick gave Esme her loving equivalent of a glare and placed yet another tray of perfect Christmas biscuits on the marble countertop. "One. The rest are for the baskets I'm making up for the Christmas market."

"Which ones are these again?" Esme reached out to take one of the little pink cloud-like treats, only to have her hand lightly slapped away.

"You know perfectly well they're peppermint divinity, Esme. Heaven knows, you've eaten enough of them each and every Christmas." Esme dodged another tray of hot biscuits. "Off you go. I'm busy here. Scoot."

"Why can't I stay here with you?"

"Because you must have far better things to do than watch me mass-produce my Christmas biscuits."

True, but…also…false. Nothing was holding her interest. Ever since Max had returned and *not* hunted her down, she'd felt listless. She took a biscuit and watched Mrs Renwick at work.

After a few minutes of being stared at, her honorary aunt gave an exasperated sigh. "Esme Ross-Wylde, you are underfoot. Why don't you go to the lounge and talk to some of the residents?"

"Ha! No thank you."

Mrs Renwick gave her a sidelong glance. "You like seeing the residents."

"That's true." She took another biscuit. She did like spending time with them. Honestly, she did, it was just that *he* was out there and as he'd avoided her when he'd come back he obviously didn't want to talk to her. Then again, what if he thought *she* was avoiding *him*?

This was ridiculous. What was she? Twelve? There was no way she was going to get through the rest of the week unless they resolved the whole tension thing. But how?

It wasn't as if she was going to saunter up to him and say, *Hey, Max! Just so you know—I've got loads of trust and confidence issues thanks to my ex-husband. We got married when I was nineteen. I know...young, right? Anyway, I was grieving after my brother's death at the time, and the rest of the family were dealing with Nick's death in their own ways...you know how it is.*

One thing led to another—we eloped, he stole half of my trust fund and set up a nightclub, but made it seem like I was reneging on my promise to set up a canine therapy centre I'd told the universe I was going to establish in honour of Nick's death. Yeah. I know! Not very nice. It makes a girl paranoid. So, anyway...the thing is... I'm really attracted to you and it freaks me out. So sorry if I'm being weird. Friends?

Yeah, that definitely wasn't going to happen.

Maybe she should bring a thank-you present for everything he'd done today. She scanned the kitchen. "Is there anything I could take out to the residents as a night-time nibble?"

Mrs Renwick picked up a gloriously over-the-top chocolate cake. "Here. Take this and leave me in peace."

"Perfect." She leant in and gave Mrs Renwick a kiss. "Thank you, Christmas Fairy!"

When she left the kitchen the first person she laid eyes on was Max. He was at the doorway to the media room, staring intently at something. She poked her head in to see what was so interesting.

"Wow."

Euan and Andy were playing some sort of scuba-diving treasure-hunt game, their two dogs curled up beside their armchairs. It looked as though the forty-something soldier and the twelve-year-old had been friends for life. Playing. Cheering one another on. It was all quiet and modulated, but…there was a kinship there. Two broken souls finding a safe place to be happy.

Sensing her rather than looking at her, Max said, "This definitely falls into the category of things I thought I'd never see."

"You're not wrong," Esme agreed. "I never thought I'd see Andy this interactive again."

Max shot the pair a nervous look. "Should I get Euan out of there?"

"No. Not at all, it's just…" She rested her head against the doorframe and watched the ex-soldier offer gentle instructions to Euan as he navigated the game. A splashing sound came out of the speaker and they both flinched. Then fist bumped each other. "They've both found someone who understands what they're going through."

Max nodded, his eyes still on the pair. "They've each got PTSD for fairly different reasons, though."

Esme's heart softened. This definitely wasn't virgin territory for him. "I guess you know a fair few soldiers who came back from their tours seeing the world through a different lens."

He scrubbed his hand along his jaw before answering. "Everyone comes back from a conflict zone seeing the world differently."

Not an insight exactly, but…she supposed she'd seen Glasgow as her "conflict zone' after everything had gone wrong with Harding. It made hiding out up here too easy. Maybe it was time to see about that satellite clinic she kept promising herself she'd open one day.

They watched for a few moments as the game progressed. There was a third unused console sitting on a footstool. Esme pointed at it.

"You not playing?"

"Nah." He shook his head, loosening those

loose curls on top of his forehead again. "I'm no good at fantasy."

Oh, she would've bet actual money that he was very good at fulfilling fantasies.

Esme! Stop it. Your mind is very, very naughty. Especially when she was within a ten-foot radius of Mr Tall, Dark and Scrumptious here.

She shifted her weight to her other hip and balanced the cake on her left hand.

"After seeing you in action today, I would've thought you'd be good at anything you set your mind to."

Uh-oh. That had come out more flirtatiously than she'd anticipated. Mostly because her eyes were on the same level as that yummy-looking mouth of his.

Her tooth caught her lower lip as she felt Max's dark eyes glint then take a leisurely inspection of her. Nice and slow from her hair, to her eyes, to her lips, to her…

"You always walk around your castle with a chocolate cake?"

"Yes." She gave him a goody-goody smile. "It's my evening ritual. It's required actually."

"Oh?" That increasingly familiar little hitch of his eyebrow let her know he was back in flirt mode.

"Yes, that's right. Cake-bearing duties are obligatory for poor, beleaguered Highland spinsters who rely on their big brother's largesse for a roof over their heads."

He snorted. Rightly so.

She had inherited plenty of money when her father had died. The trust fund thing had been awful, but her father had been clever enough not to give his children access to vast lump sums. Charles had inherited the castle in line with tradition, but it wasn't exactly as if he was pushing her out the front door. Quite the opposite, in fact. Both of them loved it here, but they would've traded it all if they could have had their brother back. It was one of the reasons Charles had suggested they turn it into a clinic. A way for them to work together, honour their brother, and make their home a place to heal.

Max's eyes dropped to the cake again. "Are you planning on sharing any of that, or are you just going to walk round and show people what they aren't getting?"

The atmosphere between them went taut. Max wasn't talking about cake. Margaret's words coquettishly danced to the fore: *"What's the worst that could happen?"*

She was safe here. This was her home. She wasn't going to elope and give him all the PIN numbers to her bank accounts. Apart from that, Max Kirkpatrick simply didn't seem the type of man who would have any dealings with lies and deceit.

A mad urge to go with her gut instinct seized her. She swooped her finger into the thick icing then stuck the whorl of buttercream into her mouth, making a show of enjoying the rich icing as it melted on her tongue. "Mmm…"

"Looks good." Max's voice was as rough as his stubble. Not that she'd touched it. Yet. When she finished the icing she reached out to touch his cheek. He grabbed her wrist and swept her finger through the chocolate buttercream for a second time. "Uh-uh." He said. "My turn."

Esme's insides turned as hot as lava as he pulled her finger towards his mouth. *Oh, mercy.* He was going to— *Oh*…he did… He drew her finger into his mouth. It was hot and wet, and his tongue was making short work of that icing, but his eyes had not as much as blinked. This had to be one of the sexiest things that had ever happened to her and they were both completely clothed. She dreaded to think what would happen if they were naked.

No, she didn't. And that was a problem. She didn't dread it at all.

Just then Wylie bumbled over and gave her a nudge.

Max let go of her wrist.

"Your bodyguard?"

"Something like that." Gulp. "Want a proper slice?" She raised the cake.

"No." He shook his head, his voice still thick

with whatever it was that had just happened between them. "Not hungry."

"Neither am I."

"Give it to the lads."

"Okay."

And just like that Esme walked into the media room, handed the video-game players the cake and two forks then walked straight back out again.

"Want to see my Christmas tree?" she asked Max.

"Is that a euphemism?"

"No. But it can be if you'd like it to be."

Much to her astonishment, Max followed her as she silently led him towards the small sitting room in her and Charles's private wing. This, she was beginning to realise, was going to be a very different Christmas indeed.

Chapter 6

"This door have a lock?"

Max knew they were in the private wing, but private also included Esme's older brother and the last thing he wanted was to get a black eye as a result of what he was about to do.

"No." Esme swallowed. "But my bedroom does."

"So does mine."

"Mine has mistletoe."

"I don't need a reason to kiss you." He smiled at her shocked expression. Finally! He'd called a spade a spade and put that humming buzzy friction crackling between them out in the open. He wanted her. She wanted him. The only question was where. "Is Dougal in your room or mine?"

"He's in mine with Wylie. I think they're brand-new BFFs." She held out her hand. "Let's go to yours."

He took her hand but didn't move anywhere. Instead he pulled her to him and did what he'd wanted to do since that first moment he'd laid eyes on her. Cupped that perfect chin of hers between his thumb and forefinger, tipped it up and kissed her. She was every bit as sweet, hot and delicious as he'd imagined.

When she parted her lips and their kisses deepened, he felt things happening inside him he definitely didn't want her big brother to see.

"My room," he rumbled. "Now."

She didn't need telling twice.

Moments later they were in the room, locking the door and tearing each other's clothes off. Kissing as if their lives depended on it. His top first. Her jumper next…a bit of a stall as he relished the sensation of touching that creamy, freckly, décolletage of hers. His hands skimmed over the very nice lace of her bra and he was rewarded with a moan as her nipples turned into tight nibs under his touch.

Her skin was every bit as soft as he'd imagined. Staying steady and in control was almost impossible. In true "everything's magic at Heatherglen' style, someone had already been in and lit the fire in his room so enjoying the bit-by-bit exposure of Esme by firelight was little short of heaven.

"Let's slow it down," he said when Esme started fiddling with his belt buckle.

She instantly froze beneath his hands. "What? Why?"

He smiled at her aggrieved expression. "I was just saying we have plenty of time—twelve days before Christmas."

"It's seven, actually." He could see her begin to withdraw emotionally. "So...you don't want to do this?"

"Quite the opposite, darlin'. I've wanted you from the moment I laid eyes on you." He dropped kisses on her forehead, her nose, her lips then said, "The way I see it, once we start, there's no turning back. So we either agree that this is something that won't affect our "day jobs" while we're here or we walk away now."

Esme actually whimpered. Which was just about the sweetest thing he'd ever heard. "I don't want to walk away..."

"There's a lot you don't know about me." A lot he didn't want her to know. He'd been trying to leave the angry guy from the past behind for a long time now and he thought he'd finally done it, but...this whole business with Plants to Paws had dug up a bunch of unresolved feelings. Something about Esme made him want to wrap them up once and for all.

"Well…" Esme traced the pad of her fingertip along the stubble above his upper lip "…there's definitely a lot you don't know about me." Her eyes provocatively flicked to his. "But it doesn't seem to have stopped us from liking each other."

As her finger traced round his lips then dipped into his mouth, he couldn't resist drawing it in deeper and giving it another swirl as if it were still slathered in chocolate icing. When he let go of it, he said, "That's very true. Maybe we could call this getting-to-know-you time?"

"We could do that…"

He ran his thumb along the bare swoop of her waist to her hip and watched a smattering of goose pimples shift along her belly just as he'd thought they might. "Am I sensing there is another part to that sentence?"

Esme had a choice here. She could tell Max the truth. Tell him she was scared. Scared of being betrayed. Of being taken advantage of. Of not being enough.

She could also tell him she was so ready to rip the rest of his clothes off she could hardly see straight. An urge she hadn't felt in years.

And yet here she was, standing in his arms with nothing on but her bra and her skirt while he was still mostly clothed. Which was strangely sexy. No. Not strangely at all. Everything about Max Kirkpatrick was sexy. The touch of his hands. The warmth of his skin. The way his eyes looked at her like she was the most beautiful thing he'd ever seen.

Max deserved an honest answer. One that she could live with, too.

She flattened her hand against his chest, just itching to tease her fingers through the sparse whorls of dark hair around his nipples, but stopped herself. Teasing him when she hadn't yet said yes was little short of cruel. To both of them.

She waited until she could feel the beat of his heart beneath her palm. It was fast. He was as nervous as she was. And as excited. She could tell that easily enough by leaning into him. Cotton trousers didn't hide much in the way of male arousal. Before she shifted her hand down and felt it, she had to make a decision.

He wasn't Harding MacMillan. Or any of the exceedingly bland men she'd dated to avoid heartbreak since. Max Kirkpatrick was one of a kind. Something deep within her told her he wanted nothing from her apart from honesty and respect. All of which spoke to the very essence of who she was. The fundamental spirit of how she wanted to live her life. Courageously. Openly. Honestly. Would this be her chance to restore that bright flame of confidence, which she'd once felt, flickering in her heart again?

She tilted her head up for another kiss. He saw the questions in her eyes and knew it would be the deciding factor. The kiss he gave in response told her all she wanted to know. It was everything she'd ever wanted in a kiss and more. Soft then responsive. Inquisitive. Passionate. Hungry. Wanting absolutely nothing of her but that she enjoy his touch. Could she handle seven perfect days of Max and then watch him walk away?

When he shifted both his hands to her waist her goose pimples turned her insides to liquid gold. She pressed up against him so that her hips were just below his. "Yes," she said. "If we keep it low key with the staff, I'd be grateful, but other than that? Let's dispense with the seven swans aswimming."

Max didn't need any more encouragement. He swept his hands along her bottom, down to her thighs, and pulled her up so that her legs circled his hips so quickly she hardly had a chance to catch her breath. Didn't care if she did. She was already light-headed with her decision to give herself to this man. He was half untamed wild man, half cultured Casanova.

The light stubble on his cheeks brushed against her cheek as he carried her to his huge four-poster bed then laid her down on the thick linen bedding.

She almost purred in response. Rough with the smooth. That was life, wasn't it? That was Max.

"It's a very nice room." Max said, thinking she was cooing about the bedding.

"It's much nicer with you in it."

A rakish smile crept onto his lips. "Did you put me here by accident or design?"

"Neither," she said with an innocent smile. "Dr Sinclair does the room assignments. He thought you were going to be a thirty-something single mum. When he heard you were ex-military he said I'd be as safe as houses."

"Is that what he told you?" His eyes lit up with a dangerously scrumptious glint.

"That's what he assumed."

"Shall I show you what you can do with his assumptions?" Max began undoing his belt buckle.

"Yes, please."

What followed was by turns heartfelt, carnal and utterly luxurious.

Max had never experienced lovemaking like this before. It felt by turns entirely new and utterly familiar. As if he'd been waiting his whole life to find this. To find her. To hold Esme in his arms. Not that she lay still long enough for him to give her a cuddle. No, she was busy exploring his body as if she'd found Atlantis itself. He didn't mind being a stand-in for the mythical place. Not by a long shot.

She was busy tracing his abdomen at the moment. With her tongue. By the time she hit that divot between his ribcage and his hips, her blonde hair tickling the wake of where her hot, wet mouth had just been, he wanted nothing more than to turn the tables. It was his turn to pleasure her. Tease every tiny moan and groan of which she was capable out of her. Bring her to the climax he could already sense building inside her.

Before she could dip any lower, he pulled her into his arms and flipped her onto her back, her hair splayed out around her like a halo, her blue eyes glistening in the firelight. "Now it's your turn."

As she had earlier, she pressed her palm to his chest as if to bond their hearts. When she was satisfied that the beat of his own heart matched hers, he kissed her so hard and with such depth of emotion he could have disappeared into the kiss and never come back again. From the intensity of her response, she was feeling the same way.

After an utterly decadent spell of exploring her body he was barely containing his own heated tension. When she arched into the taut length of him it was all he could do not to thrust himself deep inside her and find his climax. It would come easily and quickly, as he suspected hers would as well.

But he didn't want that for Esme. He wanted slow, and intense and meaningful. Then maybe another round that was hot and fast. Yet another that was dirty and dangerous. And then they could spend the rest of the time they had left figuring out all the other ways the two of them made sense.

As if reading his mind, she smiled at him with such desire in her eyes he felt his heart seem to nearly double in size. Quadruple. Whatever. All he knew was that he cared about her. Knowing she felt the same way was worth its weight in gold. There was something vulnerable about her he wanted to protect. Something fiery in her, brave even, that he wanted to nurture. Though they had come from different worlds, he felt he knew her and that with each passing day there would be discoveries that would only make knowing her even more enriching than it already had been. So long as he didn't do anything stupid like fall in love—

"Stop thinking." Esme held his face between her hands. "I want you inside me."

This was the one time in his life he felt utterly obliged to do as the lady wished.

After a scramble for protection and an intensely pleasurable few moments ignoring Esme's cries for him to stop what he was doing with his fingers because she couldn't hold back much longer, Max was certain she wanted him as much as he wanted her. He positioned himself so that the thick tautness of his desire finally dipped between her legs. Her hips were urging him to enter her. He somehow managed to exhibit a bit more restraint than Esme, who was virtually glittering with frustrated desire under him. When at long last he finished teasing her, he pushed inside her. Both of them groaned with pleasure. If there'd been any doubt before, it was a certainty now. They were made for each other. Their bodies moved in a synchronicity he had never experienced before. An undulating cadence that built and strengthened and empowered.

He wanted to let loose. He wanted her to feel him completely inside her. He wanted to bring her to a climax she would never forget.

"Do it," she whispered. "Take me."

There was absolutely no hesitancy or fear in her voice. Only pure, undiluted desire.

He did as she bid.

When the moment of fulfilment came Esme cried out his name and Max actually saw stars. He almost laughed. If he told Esme she'd insist it was a Christmas star. He'd tell her sometime why it was such a complicated day for him. But for now he just wanted to hold his slightly breathless, incredibly beautiful, Christmas angel in his arms. That was more than enough Christmas magic for him.

Esme would've happily stayed snuggled all warm and cosy in Max's arms for the rest of the day. Longer if her tummy wasn't rumbling. Thank goodness he was still asleep and couldn't hear all of her mere mortal noises because last night…last night had been straight out of the heavenly bodies notebook. He was right. Once they'd had a taste of what intimacy was like between the pair of them? Catnip. Once hadn't been enough. Or twice. It was like discovering herself all over again. Discovering just how magical a connection between two people could be had been little short of revelatory. If not a tiny bit scary. He was perfect. And she was scared of perfect because she'd thought she'd had perfect once before and how wrong she'd been.

Even so, something told her she had to find a way to start trusting her instincts again. It had been over ten years since Harding had well and truly pulled the wool over her eyes. Surely she'd learnt her lesson by now. If what her gut was telling her was true, Max was the real deal. Complex. Loving. Generous, sharing, caring, sensual. She gave his hand, which she'd been using as a mini-pillow, a kiss. Yes, he was all that and more. The big, strong soldier was vividly on show every time he scooped her up and flipped her this way or that on the bed. But there was also a tender, unbelievably sensitive man whose hands could… Ooh… goosebumps.

When her phone alarm went off before the sun had even thought about coming up, she was tempted to throw it out the window, but duty called. Max's hand reached out to bat at the snooze button, but she swatted it away and turned the alarm off. "Uh-uh. Sorry, pal. I've got a long day of surgery ahead."

"Surgery?"

"Yup." She rolled over so she could face him, pulling a sheet up to her mouth in case she had morning breath.

"What are you doing?"

"Hiding my morning breath from you. Hey. Stop that! Don't. OMG, what if I kill you with morning breath?"

Max made a big stagey inhalation then grinned. "Delicious. Just like a candy cane. Now, out with it. What's with the surgery?"

She grinned, pleased that he was interested, and sat up, pulling a swirl of sheet around her as she did so. "Well! I have a knee surgery for a Great Dane."

"Sounds interesting."

"It will be. It's an ACL surgery. Almost identical to the ones they do for top athletes."

He arced an eyebrow. "Cruciate ligament on a giant breed. Definitely interesting. Can I tag along?"

Her eyebrows scrunched together. "Don't you want to be with Euan for his training?"

He gave his jaw a scrub. "They're going on some sort of outing today with Margaret. To a shopping centre, I think. I've noticed Euan tends to defer to me when he's nervous about something and seeing that he and I aren't going to be attached at the hip when we get back to Glasgow, I was wondering what you thought about the idea of letting him get on with things?"

Esme leant in and gave him a soft kiss. Margaret hadn't needed to farm him out for babysitting. He'd been well aware of what had been going on all along. "You're much sweeter in real life than you let on."

He growled and pounced on her until they were a kissing, cuddling, giggling tangle of legs, arms and duvet. When they flopped back onto the pillows with a contented sigh, Esme reluctantly climbed out of bed.

"Right! I'd better get across the hall before my brother sees me do the walk of shame."

Max jiggled his eyebrows. "Is this a frequent occurrence?

"Pah! Hardly." Like never. "Not even close. But he'd probably have a heart attack if he saw me tiptoeing out of a man's room. After last time—"

She clapped her hands to her mouth.

He traced a line from her throat to the little divot between her shoulder blades. "Want to talk about it?"

She didn't. But as she'd actively avoided talking about her past to every single man she'd ever dated before, perhaps it was time to see what happened if she was as open and honest as she wanted the men in her life to be.

"Later?"

"How about after work? I'll pick you up at yours." He winked. She blushed. It was settled.

She was going to have a date to discuss her evil ex-husband with her lover and it felt like the right thing to do.

She gave his hand another kiss. "Sounds good." She quickly pulled on her clothes for the run down the corridor.

"You're sure you're cool with me watching you in surgery today?"

"Why wouldn't I be? You watched yesterday."

"Yesterday I hadn't seen you naked."

"Good point." It wasn't very fun thinking of what lay ahead when all she wanted to concentrate on was the here and now, but… "Not to throw ice on this or anything, but I do live and work here. As you'll be leaving in a week, maybe we'd be best keeping it quiet?"

"Sounds sensible. Your wish is my command."

Oh! That was easy. There were a thousand ways he could've responded to her request to keep things quiet, but the way Max had taken on board what she'd said made her feel as though she'd really been listened to. Maybe this was what adult relationships were like. Honest. Straightforward. And super sexy.

Max pulled her in close so that she was standing between his legs as he sat on the edge of the bed. Mmm… He smelt of warm bedding and cloves and some sort of special man scent. *Yum.*

He pulled her in for a kiss then held her a few inches back and spoke in an exaggerated brogue. "All right, then, ma wee lassie. Just be warned, if anyone tries to swoop in and claim you, I'll tilt my lance for ye."

Swoon!

If she didn't watch herself, it would be very, very easy to fall for this man.

"Excellent. I shall get Wylie to do the same on my behalf." She was quite sure the St Bernard would know how to keep other women at bay. Slobber them to death most likely. "Speaking of that, I'd better let poor Dougal out. He and Wylie need a quick spin round the block before I head off to the clinic. Interested?"

He shook his head. "I've got a few phone calls to make to the Clyde and I'll have breakfast with Euan as I'll be abandoning him all day."

He pulled her in for a final kiss and when they finally came up for air she knew she'd have a big challenge ahead of her in regard to keeping this romance under the radar. Hiding the way she felt about him would be little short of impossible.

Chapter 7

Even with her entire body buzzing from the last twenty-four hours, Esme was not going to be kept from her morning cup of coffee. She was in the middle of frothing up some milk when Margaret walked into the staffroom with the daily schedule.

One look at Esme was all it took. "Ooh! I see why you blew me off last night."

Esme's plan to not tell anyone lasted about two seconds before she cracked. "It wasn't strictly planned but…" Her smile stretched from ear to ear.

"Finally." Margaret accepted the proffered latte and took a big slurp before giving Esme's arm a congratulatory pat. "I was going to have to reclassify you as a virgin if you hadn't got some action soon."

"Crickey." Esme play-sulked because she was too happy to actually sulk. "I didn't think I was that dire a case."

Margaret rolled her eyes. "Oh, believe me, Ez. You were definitely on the brink of being sent to a nunnery." She shot a surreptitious look out the door towards the main reception area. "So what is he? Short term or long term?"

Her gut said long term. Her head told her otherwise. "Short terms. Obviously."

"Why obviously? He's hot. And you look all loved up, so…if it works, why cut it short?"

"Cut what short?" Max appeared in the doorway. "Sorry, ladies. Was I interrupting something?"

"No!" they both shouted, then burst into giggles, which, of course, answered his question.

Esme choked out something about coffee, which Max accepted with a bemused grin. She busied herself making the coffee, praying he wasn't noticing Margaret's eyes ping-ponging between the pair of them as if she was expecting cartoon love hearts to blossom out of thin air and float round the staffroom. She wasn't *that* loved up.

Max took the cup of coffee from her and when their fingers brushed, she blushed.

Okay. Maybe she had a *crush* on him. Big time.

But that was normal when a girl had had such a lengthy hiatus from romance. A Christmas dalliance, she reminded herself when her eyes travelled across the room to the mistletoe hanging in the doorway.

Margaret took another big slurp of her coffee then asked, "Shall I run you through what I'm doing with Euan and Fenella today before I leave you two lovebirds to it?"

Max choked on his coffee. Esme's cheeks flamed.

"That would be lovely, Margaret." Esme had her public-school voice back on. "Please. Do tell us."

With an unapologetic grin, Margaret launched into a detailed explanation of the trip they'd be taking to the shopping mall, where Euan in particular would have a chance to deal with the loud noises. They'd work with how the dog could help in stressful situations. "It's getting so close to Christmas it's going to be very busy."

"Six days," Esme said, a bit too aware of the countdown to Christmas.

Max gave a little involuntary shudder. "You sure you're all right with the pair of them on their own? It might be a lot for Euan to take on board."

"He needs to get used to dealing with these things and if we ease him in with these baby steps, it'll be much more useful once you get back to Glasgow." She pulled her mobile out of her pocket.

"I've got one of these and know the staff at the shopping centre well, so if there are any problems I'll give you a tinkle. You two enjoy yourselves in surgery."

"Oh, we plan to," Max said, rubbing his hands together.

"I'll bet you do," Margaret said, then swished out of the room.

Esme shook her head. For heaven's sake! So, she'd had sex. No need to make a song and dance out of the whole thing. She glanced at the clock on the wall to gauge just how much time they had before her first dog came in for surgery.

Max looked at Esme as her smile widened. "What?"

A few hours in, Max had to admit that watching Esme at work was on a par with observing the finest surgeons at work in war zones. He'd never thought veterinarians were less skilled than human doctors, quite the opposite in fact, but he'd never really taken on board how much more complex it was because her patients couldn't explain where it hurt.

Didn't seem to matter to Esme. She appeared to have a sixth sense about them. And their owners. She was focused, exacting and utterly intent on bringing about the best results for her patient. After Max had popped on a set of the clinic's scrubs and a fleece, he parked himself in the corner as Esme kicked off the day with the promised cruciate ligament surgery for Arthur, a Great Dane who was virtually eye to eye with Esme when standing. Which wasn't long, because she liked to keep their distress to a minimum.

After Arthur's rather astonishing surgery, she neutered a cat and a dog, removed a large growth from a chocolate Labrador's spleen, sewing him up with the same exacting stitches she'd exhibited on Teasel, and plucked a rather painful-looking thorn from a bloodhound's paw without eliciting as much as a whimper of discomfort from the dog.

This, on top of an emergency extraction of a chicken bone stuck in a Chihuahua's throat, operating on a bulldog's cherry eye whilst singing "Rudolph the Red Nosed Reindeer', much to the delight of the vet nurses, and taking off the bandages and pronouncing good health to a ferret who had suffered a serious cut after getting stuck in a bit of guttering.

Unlike most of the human surgeons he'd met, she was also completely soppy. And not just with puppies. Any animal that entered her exam room or surgery brought that soft, dewy-eyed expression to her face as if she'd never before seen anything so utterly adorable. No wonder their patient roster was filled to bursting. All the pet owners absolutely adored her!

The bell tinkled above the main door to Reception just as Esme was dropping off a prescription for an arthritic lurcher. A woman wearing riding clothes, including her helmet, rushed in, carrying a heavy cardboard box. "Help! Please! Can you help!"

"Mrs McCann? What's happened?"

"It's Honeybear!" wailed the ashen faced woman.

Esme rushed over to her side to help her, her entire body stilling as she saw what was inside. "Max?" She threw him a quick look. "Could you do us a favour?"

He came over and looked inside. It was a small-ish dog—a beagle—who looked as though it had been hit by a car. He was alive, but bleeding from a bad cut on his right hip, and was panting in clear distress.

"Would you mind bringing Honeybear back to the surgical room? I'll be right behind you." He heard her ask the nursing staff to get the woman a cup of sweet tea and to see if they could call Aksel to come in a bit earlier than the afternoon shift they had him scheduled for. She also asked them to ring Arthur the Great Dane's owners and tell them he was doing just fine in Recovery and could be collected at the end of the day.

The second she was in surgery she was a picture of undeterred focus. Surgical cap, gown and mask on. Her instructions were crisp, thoughtful and modulated. Every single member of her team was made to feel like that…a member of a team. Which was every bit as sexy as Esme naked in his bed. He liked a confident woman. He liked Esme. More and more as the day progressed. All of which meant saying goodbye come Christmas Eve was going to be a wrench, but… He stuffed the thoughts away. No need to think about it now.

"You don't have to stand back if you don't want to." Esme smiled across at him. "Since you brought her in, you're part of the team. If you scrub in, you can come on over to the table and see how the real doctors do it!" She dropped him a wink. "All right, Honeybear, let's get you on the table, shall we?" Deftly she inserted an IV drip into the front paw one of her nurses had just shaved. They also fitted an oxygen mask to her small muzzle. "Lainey? Can we please get some samples?"

"What are those for?" Max asked from the scrub sink in the adjacent room. Nothing was going to stop him from being a part of this.

Esme worked as she spoke. "We need to see what the packed cell volume is, total solids, glucose and BUN."

"Same as for humans? The BUN levels?" Max asked.

"Exactly. Dogs need kidneys every bit as much as humans. If this little chap's kidneys can't remove urea from the blood, the same things happen to him as happen to a human."

She didn't need to spell it out. It was bad. The critical diagnostic test would indicate whether or not they needed to worry about liver damage, urinary tract obstruction or even gastrointestinal bleeding.

"The IV includes painkiller as well as fluids," Esme explained. "Apparently he was running alongside Mrs McCann when she was out for her daily ride on Hercules."

"And he is…?"

"Her shire horse. She likes to go for a bit of a hack through the woods up here on the estate but something spooked him and he kicked out. Unfortunately, Honeybear was caught, the poor wee thing. It's all right," she cooed at the dog, who was beginning to feel the effects of the sedative she'd just given him. "All right, darling." She grabbed a pair of scissors and a stack of swabs. "Let's see what's going on in here, shall we?"

Half an hour and a set of X-rays later, the prognosis was better than expected.

"What would your assessment be, Dr Kirkpatrick?"

Max had been so absorbed in the examination he answered instantly. "Initial observations are to keep an eye on the laceration on his right hip, presumably from the horseshoe. Perhaps the horse's hoof should be checked. There might be a loose nail in there judging by the jagged edge of the cut. I would give Honeybear a tetanus shot if they aren't up to date. His pelvic fracture will need external stabilisation. It doesn't appear to be displaced, but…" He glanced at the X-rays hanging on the wall again.

"If he were a patient in my ER, I would advise one or two days in hospital to stabilise. He'll need monitoring because of the damage and swelling. There's always the possibility that there's some internal bleeding we haven't caught yet." He wove his fingers together on top of his head as he leant in for a closer look. "The blunt trauma of the injury will cause significant bruising and swelling so any chance of haematomas or clotting will need to be reduced."

Esme nodded, only her bright blue eyes visible above her mask.

"So…you wouldn't put him down despite the catastrophic injuries?"

Max stood bolt upright. "No. You wouldn't do that to a human! Put them down just because of a bit of recovery time."

Soft little fans of crinkles appeared at the sides of Esme's eyes. "Very good, Doctor. A few more years of university and you'd make an excellent veterinarian here at the CTC if you ever decided to change over." The soft, approving look he knew was just for him sparkled with delight, then abruptly shifted back into professional mode as there were about four other staff members waiting for Honeybear's actual assessment.

"He'll definitely need a bit of time to recover from the shock before we do anything other than make sure this cut doesn't bleed any more. The only other thing is that once the swelling goes down, the pelvic fracture could require stabilising surgery rather than observed cage rest. Although… I agree. If we can avoid surgery, it'd be better for this little one. Possibly seven to ten days' cage rest would do the trick, which would mean…" Her eyes flicked across at a large digital clock and calendar. "It would mean, if all goes well, you just might be home in time for Christmas with your mum! It's what everyone wants, isn't it? To be home for Christmas with their loved ones?" Her eyes flicked to Max's just in time to catch his inevitable wince.

He felt awful. She wasn't to know his stepdad used to make Christmas the unhappiest time of year. From day one Max had never able to put a foot right in his stepdad's immaculate home. Or say the right thing. Or give the right presents. So much so the frequently made suggestions that he stay behind at the military academy to make sure he was on top of his studies had soon become the easiest option to keep his mum out of an ever-increasing line of verbal fire.

When she shot him an *Are you okay?* look, he excused himself. There was a side door out to a small covered porch just outside the surgical ward. He tugged on a gilet and went out into the wintry air and sucked in a deep breath. He cursed himself under his breath. He couldn't help feeling like that twelve-year-old boy who'd wanted nothing more than his stepfather's love. The eighteen-year-old boy intent on hating everything about him. The man who *bah-humbugged* his way through Christmas just to keep the dark memories at bay.

Time to grow up. Flinching and wincing and bracing himself against any and all things Christmas didn't change a damn thing. He looked in the window to the room leading to the operating theatre and saw Esme carefully carrying Honeybear in her arms, deftly shifting him into one of the fleece-lined kennels. His heart squeezed so tightly he could barely breathe, and he knew it wasn't the north wind that was making it so.

Perhaps he'd reached a crossroads. A point where he had to stop withdrawing from life, from relationships, friendships even for fear of messing them up. Sure, he'd taken a step into more intimate territory with Esme, but there was an automatic expiry date built into that. December the twenty-third—the night of the ball.

He barked out a laugh. Trust him to make sure he didn't have anything good to look forward to on Christmas Day.

He didn't have an immediate solution for the Christmas problem, but he knew it was time to change how he thought about relationships. Which meant moving on from that boy desperate for love. The young soldier intent on proving he was worth the wait, only to find out his efforts had been for naught. He wanted to open his heart to Esme. It wasn't right to keep her at arm's length, as he had everyone else in his adult life. What was the worst that could happen? His heart might break a little? Maybe this time the pain would be worth it.

He looked back at exactly the same moment as Esme crossed to the window, presumably to look for him. When she saw him her face lit up, her forehead lightly furrowed with concern. She put her hand up to the window. He reached out and pressed his to meet hers. When their eyes met? Magic.

Yes. She was worth the risk all right. Worth that and then some. Bring it on, Christmas. This A and E doc was ready to get his jingle on.

The last patient of the day was a very poorly Pomeranian called Snowy, who had stolen a mince pie off her owner's kitchen table. A quick injection to clear her stomach did the trick. Not very nice for poor old Snowy, but Max, much to Esme's amusement, had the giggles.

"This the sort of thing that tickles your funny bone?" she asked.

"No, sorry." He tried to wipe that adorable smirk from his face and couldn't. Which, of course, made her laugh.

Esme gave Snowy an apologetic cuddle. The poor wee thing could've died from eating the mince pie, which was toxic to dogs. It was no laughing matter. She gave Max his next "quiz' as he'd requested throughout the day. "Any idea what comes next for this little one?"

"An IV for fluids and mild food like rice or scrambled eggs for the next couple of days?"

Esme beamed. "Got it in one." She held the little fluffy dog up in front of her and asked it, "What on earth could be so funny about watching you get sick that made big old Dr Max have the giggles?"

All of which set Max off again. "It reminds me of weekends at the Clyde. I know I shouldn't laugh. It's not funny. But at this time of year there is always someone at an office party who manages to overdo it and in they come and out *it* comes and… well…" He crossed over to Esme's side and gave the fluffy pooch a tender little scrub on the head. "I'm glad there's a happy ending."

A warm swirl of happiness shifted round Esme's heart as she watched Max's features soften. It was similar to the look he got whenever Euan texted him to say he and Ajax had aced something. He'd sent Max a selfie about an hour earlier from the shopping centre, surrounded by crowds. Euan's smile was bigger than he'd ever seen it. Max had been so proud he'd looked fit to burst. She wondered if he'd look even more proud if he had children of his own one day. A wife.

She swallowed down the thoughts because even considering putting a ring back on her finger was absolutely ludicrous. Particularly given the fact she was going to bare her soul to him tonight and whatever this was between them might very quickly become past tense. She'd thought of countless reasons to change her mind and every bit as many to stay on course. The smile on Max's face was one of them.

"All right, then! I'll get one of the nurses to set Snowy up with a drip."

Half an hour later, after Esme had done a final round of checks on everyone, she and Max were the only ones left in the clinic. She pulled off her surgical cap, ran her hands through her hair and gave it a good old shake. "Phew! What a day!"

Max was looking at her with an odd expression on his face.

"What? Do I have something on my face?"

"Nope." He pulled her to him, hip to hip, her breasts brushing against that big man chest of his.

"Nothing but pure perfection." He dipped his head down and gave her the slowest, softest, most sensual kiss she could bear without her body turning to complete jelly. When he finally pulled back, which was too soon, he dipped his forehead to hers. "Mmm... I've been wanting to do that all day."

Esme's butterflies swiftly adorned themselves with feather boas and started dancing to sexy music. "Is there anything else you've been wanting to do all day?"

"There most definitely is, ma wee lassie." Max's voice swept through her like wildfire. If there had been blinds to draw on the big glass entryway to the veterinary clinic she would have drawn them immediately and torn off his scrubs in record time. "I think we should have pizza."

Er... It wasn't entirely what she was expecting to hear but, okay. "You're hungry?"

He circled his arms round her waist and leant back with a big grin on his face. "Yup. And you must be too after a big day like that. Impressive stuff, Dr Ross-Wylde."

Despite herself, she blushed. "We tend not to go by "Doctor" in the veterinary world."

"Well, you should. It's extraordinarily difficult to diagnose a patient who can't speak to you. I thought we played a bit of a guessing game in human diagnostics, but you take it to another level. Impressive."

She play-punched him in the arm. Getting compliments for doing what she loved most was great. Getting them from Max was some seriously divine icing on top. Speaking of which... "Fancy any more of that chocolate cake of Mrs Renwick's, if there's any left?"

She pressed close to him and felt his response to the naughty glint in her eye and the low purr of seduction in her voice. Who knew she could be a sex kitten? Who knew this would be the man to bring it out of her?

"Pizza first," he said, though she could feel his arousal though his scrubs.

She kissed one of his nipples through his top. Then the other. "Don't you want to take a hot shower first? Wash off the day and get ready for the rest of it?" She tried to slip her hands under his top to get better access to that scrummy chest of his. Windows be damned!

He held her out at arm's length. "Compromise?"

"Depends on the compromise." She wriggled in closer, unable to shut down the primitive need to feel the warmth of his body.

"You said you had something you wanted to share with me so I thought perhaps I should as well."

The part of her that had zero confidence in herself instantly wanted to shrink away but she forced herself to hold eye contact.

"Sounds a bit scary."

He gave a light shrug and a soft smile. "Not if you're eating pizza."

She almost laughed. When he put it that way…

He held open the door for her and tilted his head towards the castle. "I saw a wood-fired pizza van out by the Christmas carnival. Thought maybe we could get ourselves some and then tuck ourselves away somewhere warm to eat it."

An idea struck.

"I know *exactly* where we should go."

Max smiled and held out his hand towards the door. "Right, then, m'lady. Lead the way."

Chapter 8

"It was sweet of Euan to offer to look after Dougal while we came up here," Esme said as she climbed the stairs without as much as breaking a sweat.

"He's a good kid." Max took a peek out of a window he was passing. Three stories and counting. "This is an awful lot of stairs to climb for a pizza date." Max wasn't complaining. But he was bewildered. "Are you sure you've not put the dungeon at the top of the castle?"

"Ha! No. There *is* a dungeon in the old castle. A poor little girl was stuck in it the other week, but Cass and Lyle saved her."

"Who's going to save us if we get stuck up here?" Max joked.

"My big brother," she said brightly over her shoulder.

"Does he step in to save you from all your bad dates?"

The smile dropped from her face and she picked up her pace. "Just a couple more flights to go."

Well, that put him on ice. Or perhaps he'd just jumped the gun on the "something she wanted to talk about".

A couple of minutes later he and Esme were standing looking out over the whole of the Christmas carnival and beyond. It was a sparkling mass of light and laughter and…even he had to admit it…it was magical. They must've been a good four or five storeys up. Five, most likely as he could see the roofing of the rest of the castle alongside them. The room was small, octagonal and incredibly cosy. A deep cushioned bench seat had been built under the windows that ran around the room.

They were just about level with the star on the enormous Christmas tree at the centre of the carnival. To their right was the skating rink. Beyond that were the twinkling lights twisting through the maze with a miniature castle in the centre rising up as a goal for the happy carnival-goers. Snow was falling lightly. It was truly a winter wonderland.

"It's amazing, isn't it?" Esme whispered as she tucked herself onto the window seat. "I used to sneak up here as a kid with Nick and Charles and we'd watch everyone on the skating rink."

"Then you probably saw me one of those nights."

She shook her head, still trying to reconcile the big, strong man beside her and the young boy who had come here with his mum. "I wouldn't have thought something this Christmassy would have been your thing." She was teasing, not accusing, so he decided to just go for it.

He sat down beside her and took one of her hands in his, both their eyes still trained on the scene. "It was when I was twelve."

Esme gave his hand a squeeze. "Want to tell me about it?"

"Yes," he said, surprised at the raw emotion in his voice. "Yes, I do."

Esme listened, wide-eyed, as Max told his story. She knew he must've had a rough childhood, but the more she heard the more her heart ached for him.

"And you didn't mind being a latchkey kid?"

Max shook his head. "It was the only life I knew. Besides, we were happy, Mum and me."

"Even though she worked all those crazy shifts at the factory?"

"Yup. She was pretty strict about what I was and wasn't allowed to do and, lucky her, I was one of those dorky kids who always wanted to make her happy."

Esme swatted at the air between them. "I can in no way imagine that you were ever a dorky kid."

"Well…" he acquiesced. "Maybe in the privacy of my own home. I had my tough-kid image to look after on the mean streets of Glasgow after all."

"You weren't in a gang or anything like that?"

"No. But there were gangs and the last thing you could show was weakness. I was hardly going to brag to all the other kids that I knew how to roast a chicken and make Yorkshire puddings."

"Wow!" Esme's eye pinged open. "You can cook?"

"Had to if I wanted to eat. My mum used to leave me recipes. You must have a huge kitchen here. What can you make?"

She shot him a bashful look. "True confession? Mrs Renwick always did it so well and Mum wasn't all that interested, so I never really learnt." Before he could reply she said, "I suppose I could learn. I wonder how long it would take?"

Max laughed. "If you're planning on replacing your job with a pinafore, please don't. I like you just the way you are."

"Really?"

Max shot her an inquisitive look. "Of course. You're an amazing woman. Anyone who thinks otherwise can jog on to the land of no return as far as I'm concerned."

"Thank you. That means a lot."

She hadn't meant to sound as bone-achingly grateful as she did, but… Harding MacMillan hadn't liked her just the way she had been. He'd liked the bells and whistles and had merely tolerated her as a means to an end.

Max picked up another piece of pizza, his gaze drifting back out to the wintry scene.

"What was so magical about the time you were here with your mum?"

"It was our last proper Christmas together."

The sentence came out harsh and blunt.

"Did she—did something happen to her?"

"She got married."

"Isn't that normally a good thing?"

"It is if the man in question is after a twelve-year-old son."

"Oh, Max." Her heart squeezed so tight for him she could barely breathe. As a young boy who'd never known a father's love, it must've been complete torture. "Did he not even try?"

Max tossed the remains of his slice of pizza into the box and closed the lid. Thinking about his stepdad clearly wasn't good for his appetite.

"I used to call him the Dictator."

That didn't sound good. "And now?"

She saw something flicker in his eyes. A moment's hesitation as if he were debating whether or not to tell her something. "I call him Gavin Henshall."

Everything in her stilled.

So this was what he'd wanted to tell her. He was using her to get back at someone.

"Is that why you agreed to accept my help?" There was no chance he didn't hear the wobble in her voice.

He scrubbed a hand through his hair, looked out the window then back to her. "I should've told you that first day. It's been eating at me ever since."

"Why didn't you?" She forced the roar of blood in her ears into submission. She'd shared a bed with this man. If she was going to find out she'd been a pawn in something, she at least wanted to hear why.

"Because it was so personal. As you've probably noticed, sharing what's in here…" he thumped a fist against his chest "…doesn't come easily. Gavin changed my life and not in a good way. My mum's, too. But I didn't want you to think I was after revenge when what I really wanted was to save Plants to Paws."

Her hammering heart slowed its cadence. He was being honest. Looking her straight in the eye. If it was revenge he was after…well, he'd hardly be telling her now, would he? Before he'd seen as much as a penny. And then the proverbial penny dropped. He was telling her now because he didn't want her to find out later and with that revelation her heart opened far wider than she'd let it open in years. She knew how hard it was to separate rage and pain. She'd had her own fair share of teasing the two apart over the years and a castle to "hide' in to do it. Max had literally been on the front line and despite the incalculable amount of good he'd done, she could now see it was his past that was tearing at his heart.

"Well." Esme sniffed imperiously. "If he isn't a very nice man, I'm doubly glad we're keeping Plants to Paws as it is."

The relief in Max's eyes brought tears to her own.

"At the beginning, when he was courting my mum, he was all right. She'd made it very clear that we came as a package." He huffed out a laugh as his eyes travelled back out to the skating rink. "She used to date a man for at least six months before they were even allowed to meet me. Said she had to vet them to make sure they were top-grade father material. It made me think I was this special kid. Worth waiting for." His unhappy tone made it clear that special was the last thing he'd been made to feel.

Esme bristled on his behalf. "Every child should believe they're safe. Protected. Your mum sounds amazing. Not all single parents are so discerning."

"Not all single parents met slimeballs like him." There was no mistaking the bitterness in his voice now.

"Did he hurt you?"

He scrubbed his hands along his trousers as if

trying to get rid of a bad feeling. "No. But he used to… I think the term they use now is psychological abuse."

"To you?"

"Mostly to my mum. Which killed me. Because I was powerless to do anything."

"Why powerless?"

"He always had an answer or a comeback that I couldn't respond to. He was a master of manipulation. And he shipped me off to military academy as soon as he could."

"How awful."

He tilted his head to one side, as if weighing up whether her response was valid. When he lifted his eyes to meet hers his eyes burned with fury. "It was. But not for the reasons you'd think."

Esme pushed both pizza boxes away and wrapped her arms around her knees. She was desperate to throw them round Max but the last thing she thought he'd want was pity. He must have felt so helpless watching the person he loved most in the world fall prey to the man who had promised to look after her. Both of them. A Jekyll and Hyde from the sound of it. "What sort of things did he do?"

"Before they were married, he promised her a house on the nice side of town and a chance to be a stay-at-home mum. Host dinner parties, tend the garden, which she loved, that sort of thing."

"That doesn't sound too awful."

"It is when everything comes with conditions." His smile was grim. "She didn't get a choice of which house or where. Who she hosted at her parties. Which types of foods she could make. The clothes she could wear. The topics she could discuss when she was allowed to talk."

Ouch. Her own marriage had been a bit like that. Indulgent at first. Indulgent until there had been a ring on her finger. The fact Harding had managed to fool her seemed insane now but, in hindsight, they'd all been reeling from Nick's death and Harding had brought some focus to their lives. Something to look forward to. A wedding. Grandchildren. If only she'd known how devious his "courtship' had actually been.

Harding, who laid claim to some mysterious title, had insisted they go to the *right* balls and the *proper* restaurants and be seen with the *best* people. The types of people who tended to travel with paparazzi in tow. He might've even tipped them off, for all she knew. She'd been so naive, sad and lonely down there in Glasgow, away from her family and so desperate to feel loved she'd gone along with it all.

If Max's mum had felt that way… She wrapped her arms even tighter round herself. The poor woman. The only blessing was she hadn't had the tabloids smearing her misery all over the front pages.

"Are you cold?" Max started to take off his fleece.

"No, just…" *Just reliving some of the worst memories of her life, that was all.* "Please. Go on."

"Well, as I said, one of the first things he did to rip away any link to her old life was to pronounce me a bad seed in need of some proper schooling, so he sent me to a military academy."

"Bad seed? The chicken roasting, Yorkshire pudding making latchkey kid was a bad seed?"

He shrugged. "I could've hung out with a better crowd, but where we lived there weren't exactly choice pickings. It was all a bit rough and ready on our estate. In all honesty, military academy suited me. I got on pretty well there and I kept thinking that the better I did, the sooner I could come home and make sure Mum was all right. It was pre-mobile phone years for kids so I couldn't call home, wasn't sure if she got my letters. I was completely powerless."

"You said he didn't hit her, right?"

"No, but he may as well have for all the damage he did. *Not…*" he held up his hands "…that I would ever, ever condone hitting someone. Or putting them down. Just as vicious. Just as cruel. He was always picking on her. What she wore. How she set the table. Belittling her in front of guests when the whole time he was the one who was small and insignificant."

"Social climber?" she guessed.

His grim expression told her all she needed to know.

"I'm so sorry you both had to go through that. Did you get her out in the end?"

Much to her astonishment, Max's eyes glassed over. She let him wrestle with his emotions rather than pressing him to speak. She knew the courage it took to admit something hadn't gone the way you'd wanted it to. The core-deep fear she'd felt when she'd finally told her father what her ex-husband had done had been the scariest, most isolating sensation she'd ever experienced.

The love and unconditional response she'd received in return had set the bar high. Too high, some might say, but...waiting for someone who would love her that unconditionally was critical. She reached out and took one of Max's hands in both of hers. She pressed her cheek to the back of it then gave it a soft kiss. Was he that special someone?

"It's my worst regret." He sighed and balled his hands into fists. "I enlisted because I knew there wasn't a chance in hell he'd let me back into that house so I thought if I made enough money to buy her a house she could get out. Be free. Tend the garden any damn way she wanted to."

Ah...the garden. That's where Plants to Paws came from. Her own eyes filled with tears as she thought of just how much it must've destroyed him to learn that the charity garden was going to be paved over to make way for a car park. And by whom. She made a silent vow to double the guest list. Come what may, they were going to save Plants to Paws and ensure it was there for the patients at the Clyde for ever.

"So did you get the house?" Esme asked quietly.

He shook his head. "Cancer hit first and though I'd bought the house she was in a hospice and she passed away before I could even show it to her. At least I got to be with her then. My stepdad didn't handle the messy business of dying all that well so he wasn't around much." A sad smile teased at his features. "It was back to just the two of us in the end. She was so weak I bought her one of those miniature Japanese gardens. You know the little zen ones with stones and a bonsai tree and whatnot? She tended that thing as if her life depended on it."

"Oh, Max." There was nothing she could say to make any of it better. Her own experience with pain had taught her sometimes it was best not to say anything at all. Being there and listening was the best thing to do.

"After she died, I began to notice more and more patients wishing, above anything, that they could grow something. Keep something alive since they were powerless to do the same for themselves. So I sold the house to build Plants to Paws."

No longer able to hold back, she wrapped her

arms around him. "I'm so sorry you've been through that. Let me assure you we will do everything in our power to make this the best Christmas ball ever. Gavin Henshall be damned!" She threw a fist in the air, hoping to tease out a bit of relief from the sadness he'd been carrying all of these years. There was a change. The tiniest flicker of something she couldn't put her finger on shifted through his eyes as he pulled her to him for a kiss.

Max had never once considered the possibility that feeling vulnerable could also make him feel strong. Opening up to Esme in the way he had had paid emotional dividends he'd never considered. There'd been a moment—right when he admitted he'd known who Gavin Henshall was all along— when he'd thought he'd lost her, but she'd silenced whatever was going on in that head of hers and heard him out. For that alone, Esme would always have a special place in his heart.

"C'mere." Esme beckoned him over to the long wooden counter. "What shoe size are you?"

"Eleven." He couldn't help smiling at Esme's puckish face. After his big emotional purge she'd said she was more than happy to carry on talking but he'd had enough and suggested they do something she wanted to do. So here they were, preparing for an after-hours ice skate. He was bound to spend more time on his rear than his feet, but...

what the hell. Her eyes had glittered with excitement at the idea so there was zero chance he was going to say no.

She handed him the skates then pulled a pair off of the shelf for herself. "I can't believe we're doing this!" She clapped her hands and let out a quiet little "Woohoo!" She'd promised the security guards they'd be as quiet as dormice. The fact she was Esme Ross-Wylde and had arrived carrying a big plate of Mrs Renwick's Christmas biscuits had had a lot more to do with receiving their go-ahead than keeping the volume down.

The pair of them went out to the moonlit skating rink…completely free and clear of any marks from the evening's crowds. Perfect for a bit of midnight mischief.

"I haven't done this for years!"

"Why has it been so long?"

Max recognised the shadows of sadness instantly.

"I used to come out here with my brothers." She sighed and put a tidy bow on her second lace and clapped her hands to her knees. "I haven't really told you about Nick, have I?"

"No. But if it's too difficult to talk about…"

"It is, but… I think the two of you would've got along. He was army. Like you. Worked in the canine bomb disposal unit."

Max nodded. It was pretty easy to see where this was going.

"He was killed on Christmas Eve when I was eighteen and Charles was in the throes of med school."

"That's rough." And explained why she was so desperate for Christmas to be magical. She was trying to recapture a time that used to be. A memory of when life had been perfect. A bit like him, he supposed. Pretending Christmas wasn't happening never made the pain go away, so perhaps she had the right idea. Try and try again. One day it just might work.

"He was my hero. He was so much older than me, everything he did seemed amazing. When he died we all fell apart. Dad worked himself into an early grave. Charles buried himself in his medicine and I…"

Her voice caught as he saw tears form in her eyes. He put his arm around her and swept his hand along her cheek. "It's completely understandable if you were sad, darlin'. Losing someone you love is pure heartache."

Esme looked him straight in the eye. "I was more than sad. I lost the plot."

"I doubt that. Grief is a powerful emotion. Sometimes it is difficult to know how you're coming across to the world when everything seems so grey." The only thing that had saved him after his mum had passed was Plants to Paws. Knowing he was putting some good back into the world after channelling so much hate in Gavin's direction.

Esme took one of his hands in hers and said, "There's something I have to tell you."

He nodded for her to go ahead. She'd been amazing when he'd bared some of his darkest memories to her and she deserved his full attention.

"I met a man shortly after Nick was killed. He said all the right things, did all of the right things. He made me feel safe. Cared for in a world I wasn't so sure about any more. If Nick, my amazing strong, incredible brother, could be killed, what else could happen?"

A surge of protectiveness shot through him. "This man didn't hurt you, did he?"

She shook her head and covered her face with her hands. "It's more embarrassing now than anything."

"Hey." He crooked a finger under her chin and ran his thumb along her cheek. "Like I said, I like you just the way you are."

She gave his arm a squeeze. "I know. And that means a lot. In fact, it was your honesty with me that made me want to tell you my story. I owe it to you."

Esme was trembling as Max took her hands in his and said, "You don't owe me anything, love. Not one thing."

"That's exactly why I *want* to tell you. Because

you don't want anything from me. This man did." Before she chickened out, she took in a deep breath and told him everything. "I married him at the ripe age of nineteen. We eloped to Gretna Green, if you can believe it. Such a cliché!"

He gave a small shrug. "You were young, and clichés are clichés for a reason. It was meant to be romantic, right? An act of love."

Bless him. He was trying to find a silver lining. Little did he know this particular cloud was completely shrouded in darkness.

"It was romantic," she admitted miserably. "And then pretty quickly it wasn't. Mostly because there wasn't love. Not that I knew that yet. At his suggestion, I quit veterinary school and we—meaning I—rented a ridiculous penthouse in Glasgow. When we went home and told everyone, my family were actually pretty amazing. We'd all been so sad after Nick's death it was great to have a reason to celebrate. And Harding took his time before his true colours were revealed."

"Harding MacMillan? Isn't he the guy who's always on the covers of those socialite magazines?"

Esme looked at him in surprise. "You read those?"

"You'd be surprised what pops up as reading material in the staffroom on a night shift." He gave a self-deprecating laugh then admitted, "It's not my usual fare, but I recognise the name."

"If you'd been reading those same magazines eleven or twelve years ago you would've also recognised my name."

He shook his head. "They don't make much of a show in the Middle East conflict areas. Anyway, most of the stuff that's in those magazines is salacious gossip. Even if I had read it, I would've taken everything with a grain of salt."

She fretted at the knitted cap resting in her lap. Being betrayed in the way she had had opened up all the wounds she'd thought were healing after Nick's death. Turned out…they hadn't even begun to heal. The entire experience with Harding had only served to magnify the pain she'd felt at the loss. "Harding made me feel completely useless. And when, after it was all over, he sold his story to the tabloids with his own special spin, it made my life a living hell."

Max stiffened. "Why? What happened?"

"Not that he'd put it this way, but it turned out all of the wooing—fancy dinners, nights out on the town, weekends away—were all paid for with credit cards on the brink of being maxed out. He would fill one up then apply for another. Long story short, he married me because he wanted money. My family's money."

A bitter laugh caught in her throat as she remembered the day she'd found out how his family came to be "titled'. His father had bought the title years ago, along with one acre of woodland back when his business had been flourishing. He had since sold the same acre and title when the business had been failing. Not that Harding had bothered to tell anyone about the change of circumstances. If he hadn't been so deceitful about his family's lack of finances, she might've felt sorry for him, but Harding MacMillan had been one hundred per cent snake. A snake whose venom had no antidote.

She met Max's solid, kind gaze and shivered. Could this be the man she could finally put her trust in?

Max tucked a lock of her hair behind her ear then snuggled her hat back on her head. "Wouldn't want you catching cold," he explained, then continued after a moment's thought. "You know it's not your fault, right? He was preying on a vulnerable young woman. I'm surprised he's not in jail."

Her lips thinned. She would've pressed charges but…she'd given him her card. A joint account. It hadn't really been theft when it was a joint account. It would've boiled down to a case of him against her and Harding was very persuasive. It was how he'd convinced all the paparazzi to appear every time they'd gone to dinner or a club. She'd thought it was coincidence.

A sour taste filled her mouth as the worst of the memories returned.

"Because I wasn't at uni any more, I wanted to do something amazing for Nick. His service dog had meant the world to him and I'd heard about soldiers suffering from PTSD who needed their own service dogs so I decided to open a clinic to help them do that."

"Which you did."

She shook her head. "No. Remember, this was years ago, in Glasgow. I became obsessed with the idea. I was working crazy hours with a local organisation to learn how to train the dogs so Harding "volunteered" to take over setting up the clinic. Leasing the facility, kitting it out. That sort of thing. I was so wrapped up in the dogs and trying to drum up publicity for the service sog centre that I didn't bother checking up on him." She felt absolutely sick remembering it all. How the man could've done what he had, knowing it was in aid of her brother's memory.

"Did he get you a site?"

"Oh, he did that all right."

"You don't sound like you were very happy with it."

"I was at the time. It was all so romantic, and he had made such a show of wanting to take anything stressful out of my hands so that I could focus on the dogs and helping soldiers."

Max nodded. He'd fallen for a lot of stuff, too.

It had made him wary, but it had also taught him that anyone could fall for a conman.

"He said he didn't want me to see it until the grand opening. That he wanted to see the surprise in my eyes. Oh, he saw surprise all right. So did all the society magazines."

"I thought you said you'd invited the media."

"I had. He'd found my list, cancelled them all and replaced them with his people. So, there I was, ready to cut the ribbon, glass of champagne in my hand, the whole nine yards… Harding had hung this huge, ridiculous red velvet curtain in front of the building and when he pulled it open…" her voice caught at the memory but she continued as if she had just swallowed sour milk "…instead of my humble canine therapy centre there was a gaudy, glitzy nightclub called Wylde."

Max swore under his breath. That was a whole new breed of low.

"So, of course, once the legitimate papers got hold of the fact I'd opened a nightclub instead of the service dog centre, they dismissed me as just another airhead heiress who had more money than sense. It still makes me furious for not having seen through him before I put that stupid ring on my finger. Sure," she acquiesced, "it was a whirlwind romance. Maybe…three or four weeks? Insanity really, but I thought he loved me when all along it turned out it was my money he loved."

Much to her embarrassment, tears began to trickle down her cheeks. And then flow. She hadn't cried about this in years but telling Max was strangely cathartic. Cleansing even. She'd felt so small back then. Humiliated and worthless. But she'd changed. She'd finally made something of her life. Which was a lot more than she could say for Harding. If her mother's short emails were any sort of guide, Harding was still living with little beyond his charm to keep him afloat. A hollow life if there was one.

Max pulled out a clean cloth handkerchief and handed it to her. Her heart squeezed tight. He was such a gentleman. Why couldn't she have fallen for someone like him back then? She thought back to the story he'd just told her and realised he probably wouldn't have been in a chivalrous place back then. Perhaps, despite the pain, they'd each needed to go through these tribulations to become the people they were now. A bit wiser. A bit more wary.

"I presume your family took him to task," Max said after wiping away a couple of her stray tears.

She shook her head. "I didn't want them to. It would've compounded the whole poor little rich girl thing having my family swoop in to rescue me. Particularly given the fact that, at the time, Mum was showing up at one too many nightclubs herself."

"Did Harding actually think you would go for it? The nightclub, I mean?"

She shrugged. "My best guess is that he thought I was so under his spell I would go for it to make him happy. He thought the service dogs thing was a fad."

"Sounds like he didn't know you at all."

She gave him a sad smile. "We can definitely agree on that. The whole thing was so humiliating. Afterwards, once we'd split up and I'd come back here, it still took ages to shake everything off. The tabloids were paying people to get staff jobs here at Heatherglen. Undercover maids hoping to find me curled up in a weeping, sobbing ball in the corner of my gold-plated bedroom. That sort of thing. The last thing I wanted the world to see was me being pathetic, so I got myself back into veterinary school and set up the clinic properly. With no publicity."

Max laughed and gave his head a rueful shake. "That's my girl."

Despite the seriousness of the talk, Esme blushed. His girl? She liked the sound of that. Even if it was just a saying, there was something safe and comforting about talking with Max that she'd never felt with another man. It felt *real. Genuine.* As if there was nothing she could tell him that would make him think any less of her.

"I'm hoping he didn't get to any of your money in the end."

"Oh, he did. Not all of it obviously," she snorted and looked at the castle, glittering like a jewel in the crown. "The joint account we shared was actually my trust fund. I never really spent much from it. Unlike Harding, I wasn't really one to splash the cash about." She qualified the statement, so Max didn't get the wrong idea. "I'm not unaware that I have grown up with a privileged lifestyle. I mean, how many people get an ice rink and an entire Christmas carnival outside their castle at Christmas?"

Max laughed appreciatively. There was warmth in it. As if he didn't care if she was worth a billion or tuppence. It was her he liked, not the trimmings she came with.

She shook her head. "I still can't believe I fell for such a superficial poser."

"Everyone has someone who pulls the wool over their eyes." Max gave her back a soft rub and dropped a tender kiss on her forehead. "He really put you through the mill, didn't he?"

"Yup!" She stood up, using one of Max's strong shoulders as support to keep her balance on her blades, and gave him a proper smile. "But that was then and right now we've got a skating rink calling our names."

They spent the next hour having an absolute

ball, whirling and racing and falling down and kissing. It was every bit as fun as it had been when she'd sneaked out with her brothers to do exactly the same thing, minus the kissing part obviously.

That night when they made love it felt even more intimate than it had the night before. There was true sentiment behind the soft touches, the caresses, the deep, emotionally charged kisses they shared.

She was falling for him. Head over heels. The practical part of her knew she needed to put on the brakes and acknowledge that this was nothing more than a no-strings-attached fling. There was no way it could work in real life. His life was in Glasgow, hers was very much here at Heatherglen and, well, there was all the magic of Christmas that would melt away in the spring.

And yet…there was a tiny sliver of hope she hadn't felt in years. Hope that she might finally leave her scars from the past where they belonged. In the past. Hope that true love *was* real. That she deserved it. She stared at the lights twinkling on the tiny Christmas tree by the fireplace. Honestly? She wanted to believe in Christmas miracles. And Max was the man she wanted by her side when all of it came to pass.

Chapter 9

"Someone looks happy," Charles growled as he dug his spoon into a rather enormous, well-sugared bowl of Mrs Renwick's delicious porridge.

"Someone else looks like they woke up on the wrong side of the bed." Esme smiled benignly in return. She was in a gorgeous floaty love bubble. Four days in and her days with Max had morphed into a lovely little routine. Sometimes he spent time with her in the vet surgery and at others they worked on training with Euan and Fenella. Max usually had his meals with them, but he always, every single night, crawled under the covers with her. Not even a grumpy older brother whose mood had plummeted daily since he'd returned from his medical conference could burst the particularly lovely mood. "Would you pass the blueberries, please?"

"They're out of season," Charles snapped.

"So's your mood," Esme chirped, tacking on a "tra-la-la-la-la" to prove her point.

Charles grimaced, ate a spoonful of porridge, then pushed it away.

"What's up with you?"

"Nothing. Busy day, that's all."

She was about to retort that all their days were busy but it didn't mean they had to be miserable but she opted for the kinder, gentler version of her kid sister self. She, after all, had three more glorious days of naughty nights and flirty days ahead. Charles, on the flip side, showed no signs of even as much as casting the slightest glance at a woman, let alone falling in love again. "Anything I can do to help?"

"No. Thank you, though." He pushed up and away from the kitchen table then turned back. "I had a meeting with Fenella, by the way. I've put a call through to the Clydesbank to send up her records. She's agreed to let me take a second look at her meds."

"Oh! Great." Her gut instinct was to run out the door, find Max and tell him immediately, but the fact she and Max had agreed to keep their romance low key kept her in her chair, smiling dreamily up at her brother. "You're the best."

He narrowed his eyes. "Are you sure you're all right?"

"Never better." She took a huge spoonful of porridge so she couldn't answer any more questions. The truth of the matter was, no matter how much she told herself she shouldn't, she was falling in love.

Max was spending the day with Euan and Fenella as their training with the dogs intensified. He was being absolutely brilliant, ensuring they felt they were receiving proper support, asking questions for them when they were too shy to do so themselves. They were lucky to have a man like him in their corner. She was lucky to have a man like him in her bed! And utterly insane to let a man whose life was so solidly based elsewhere into her heart.

The morning at the veterinary clinic whooshed by and, as Aksel was now on hand to help, she was treating herself to an afternoon at the Christmas carnival where they were going to put Euan and Fenella's dogs through their paces.

She had just changed out of her scrubs into a cosy pair of leggings and a thigh-length jumper with a Christmas tree knitted into the pattern when she heard a knock on her office door.

"Come in."

Her heart skipped a beat when she saw it was Max. "Hello there, you. How's tricks?"

"You're looking festive as ever."

She skipped over to him and gave him a quick peck on the lips. "Mmm…chocolaty."

"Margaret just made us all hot chocolate before "The Big Adventure"."

Esme pulled a sad face. "I wanted to be the first one to make you hot chocolate! It's the one feather in my cooking cap."

"Not to worry. I'm sure I'll be up for another before I head back south."

Her sad face gained traction. "I can't believe it's all coming to an end so soon."

"I know." Max pulled her into a cosy hug. "It's not going to be nice, saying goodbye."

She pulled back so she could look him in the eye and asked the one question she'd vowed to herself she wouldn't. "Do we have to? Say goodbye?"

"I don't really see another way around it. Your life is here. My life's in Glasgow."

"You don't fancy practising somewhere up here?"

The second the question was out she regretted it. It wasn't fair to ask him to change his life because of what they'd both known would, at best, be a festive fling.

He swept her hair off her forehead as his own brow crinkled. "I think you know the answer to that, but let's talk about it tonight." He tilted his head towards the door. "We've got a very eager Fenella and Euan waiting out in Reception with their hounds, ready for the carnival."

Though he sounded the same and looked the same, Esme's stomach twisted with anxiety. She'd overstepped the mark. Pushed when she should've accepted the situation for what it was. Doing her best to mask her misplaced disappointment that he hadn't immediately suggested that they scrap all their sensible, practical plans so they could get on with the business of falling in love, she said, "Absolutely. Let's get on out there and enjoy some Christmas cheer, Heatherglen style!"

Max would've had to have been blind not to see the splinters of dismay pass through Esme's eyes when he put off answering her question. A dodge was a dodge and with her history, looking shifty was never a good thing. Of course he wanted to drop everything and stay in the magical world of Heatherglen—a place whose sole remit appeared to be making dreams come true. Whether it was to recover from PTSD, heal from a traumatic injury or meet that one faithful companion who would never lie, never cheat, never say one thing and mean another...

Damn. He was either going to have to grow a backbone and test the remaining elasticity in his heart or stick to his guns and go with their original plan: enjoy the here and now—then get back to real life.

Esme was bright enough as the group walked towards the Christmas carnival, each with a dog on a lead. Dougal, as ever, was lavishing love on whoever looked at him.

Esme threw Max the odd smile, but he couldn't see the light hitting her eyes like it normally did and it was killing him.

Of course he wanted whatever was blossoming between them to continue. More than anything he wanted to throw caution to the wind, pull her into his arms and tell her he loved her. Because he did. He knew it right down to the very last fibre in his body. He loved Esme Ross-Wylde heart and soul. So…what was the problem, then?

She'd been amazing when she'd heard his story. Didn't seem to give a monkey's that he'd come from a poor background. Or that he'd had a complicated, messy upbringing. Just as he loved her exactly the way she was, she seemed to care for him solely because of the man he was now.

So why was he holding back his feelings and, more importantly, his concerns when he knew honesty was the best policy with her? The only policy. The one way to know if Esme believed in him. Loved him even.

And then it hit him. Somewhere, deep inside

him, he still hated Gavin Henshall for all he'd done to his mother. Worse than that, he was still beating himself up for not finding a way to forgive the man as his mother had asked him to. Forgive him and move on. It had been her last request and he'd failed her. Failed himself. And if it weren't for Esme's timely intervention, he'd very likely be failing everyone at Plants to Paws as well.

Esme had had an awful time with her brother's death and her subsequent marriage. She'd harnessed her anguish and turned it into something good. He'd thought he'd done the same with Plants to Paws, but without Esme? He'd be back at the Clyde clearing out the greenhouse and telling everyone the bad news. Again and again in his life, money and power had trumped good intentions. Could it be that love and its ally, forgiveness, were more important than both?

The thought hit him with the force of a lightning bolt. Was he strong enough to accept that having to start over didn't necessarily equate to failure? That the journey was every bit as important, if not more so, than the outcome? That he might be hurt by love again but that it was completely worth the risk?

Unless the answer was a solid yes, he wouldn't be able to love Esme the way she deserved to be loved. With all of his heart. Because there'd always be a part of him wondering if he'd done enough to deserve her. Acknowledging that simple fact just about killed him. He watched as Esme led their motley crew towards a small log cabin where people could make gingerbread houses. After everyone entered, she looked back. "Aren't you coming?"

He shook his head. "I've got something to do. Can I meet you later?"

She gave a little nod, her features closing in on each other. Proof, if he'd needed it, that she knew something wasn't quite right.

"Are we okay?" she asked.

The anxiety in her voice near enough slashed his heart in two.

"We're okay," he said, because he couldn't say what he wanted to. That he loved her. That he was going to have to find a way to reach down into his past and pull out some of his darkest memories, confront them, and pray that he came out stronger.

Esme poured a pile of cereal into her bowl then sloshed some milk in. It looked revolting. And it was her favourite cereal.

Something weird was up with Max. They'd spent the night together, but he'd not brought up whether or not he wanted to see her any more after Christmas. Something about the intensity in the way he'd looked at her, touched her, had made her feel as though he was memorising her in preparation to say goodbye.

All of which had her in a particularly foul mood.

She stared at the cereal then at Wylie. "Want my cereal?"

He wagged his tail. She gave it to him.

She looked around the kitchen for something else to eat. Her eyes eventually landed on her gingerbread castle. Why make a house when you can build a castle? she'd thought. Fenella and Euan had thought it was hilarious. Max had given it a glance, her a smile and then told her he wouldn't be joining her in the veterinary clinic today as he'd volunteered to cover Lyle Sinclair's medic shift at the ice skating rink. Lyle wanted to tag along with Cass, who was due to rehearse for the Living Nativity down at the village. Fussing more like. Doting. Caring, adoring, lovesick man that he was.

She'd thought it was adorable about twenty-four hours earlier. Today? Not so much. She wrenched off the gingerbread turret and took a bite.

There was a light knock on the kitchen door. Max stuck his head into the room. "I was just going to make a call to the Clyde then head out to the skating rink. Everything all right?"

"Not particularly," she said, tacking on a petulant smile. He blinked his surprise.

Okay, fine. It wasn't a particularly mature way to respond, but she wanted Max to feel as bad as she did. She pulled a section of the wall off her gingerbread castle and chomped down on it.

Charles appeared behind Max, who let him through to the kitchen. "Good to see healthy eating is still the order of the day," he said in a remarkably similar strain of crankiness. "May I?" He nodded at the castle.

She shrugged. "Help yourself."

He did, and the castle collapsed.

Her expression must've been one of pure fury because both Charles and Max made their apologies and left. It wasn't the castle she was cross about. It was not having the guts to have it out with Max and find out what was going on with him. She'd thought they were good at being open with one another. Telling each other the truth. And here she was exactly where she didn't want to be. Feeling scared. Panicked she wasn't enough. Would never be enough for someone when all she wanted was to be enough for one man. For Max.

A horrible thought landed in her head. What if the only reason he was doing this was to make sure he got the money for Plants to Paws? Surely he knew her well enough to know she didn't offer lifelines like the Christmas ball with strings attached. The fact they seemed to adore each other's company was just an added bonus.

All of which meant she was being ridiculous. A

bit of insecurity went a long way in her case, and it was time to keep it in check.

Doom and gloom would get her nowhere. It was probably nothing. Max was a busy man, who was doing his best to be as present as he could be here as well as keep tabs on his very busy life back in Glasgow. A life he'd dropped to give two of his patients this amazing opportunity.

See? Proof, if she'd needed any, that she was being ridiculous. He'd made just about the sweetest love to her a girl could imagine only a handful of hours ago. No one could be that intimate, that loving and also be looking for an escape plan.

Right! She took one last bite of her gingerbread castle, wiped her hands then announced to Wylie that it was time to go out and make the world a better place. No point in spreading her ridiculous mood any further than this kitchen. She knelt down so she was eye to eye with her big, furry bear of a dog. "I'm being silly, aren't I, Wylie?" He rubbed his nose against hers. "He's *not* Harding. All this silly insecurity is nothing, right?" He licked her chin. "Well, that settles it. Just a blip on the old emotional barometer." She called him to heel and together they walked to the veterinary clinic. When she passed Max, who was on his way to the ice-skating rink with the reflective safety vest on, she waved and smiled. She'd apologise for being such a grump later. In bed. He threw her a confused wave in return but seemed happy that her mood had improved.

"See, Wylie? Nothing to worry about. Absolutely nothing at all."

With half an eye on the skating rink and half an eye on the veterinary clinic, Max's gut was churning with indecision. Should he tell her why he hadn't brought up their relationship last night or would it scare her off? Carrying around rage and fury over something he would never be able to change was not going to help anyone. Least of all him and Esme. He wanted to give this a shot. Be the man she deserved. Woo her properly. Take her out. Show her his favourite places in Glasgow. Discover her favourite walks up here. Hold hands at the movies. It'd be tough with his schedule at the Clyde but putting a few thousand commuter miles on his old four-by-four was worth it. Especially if he were to accept in advance that there was always the possibility it might not work out. Once the charity ball was over and he was back to work, they might discover their lives were simply too different for them to be a perfect match. It didn't mean their time together had been for nothing, but it did mean talking about the future at this juncture was a bit of a moot point. Live in a fairytale for ever? Sure. Why not? Commute two hours there and back every day to hold hands with his girl? Maybe yes. Maybe no.

He looked up as a few squeals erupted from the ice rink. A gaggle of girls had collapsed into a giggling heap of jewel-coloured winter jackets and scarves. They looked as though they didn't have a care in the world.

He wondered if Esme had ever had a chance to be that silly. The other night she'd told him that, as children, the local paper had always taken a picture of them going to church on a Sunday and had made note of the times they didn't. Never mind the fact they'd often been down in Glasgow, working for a soup kitchen. No wonder she cherished those stolen moments of fun on the ice rink with her brothers. No one to perform for.

For every ounce of him that had bones to pick with his own childhood, he wouldn't have traded it for hers. At least his most tumultuous years had only been under two people's radars. His mum's and his stepdad's. The press? It must've been awful. And incredibly impressive that she'd managed to turn it back round in her favour in the form of her annual Christmas ball.

It was tomorrow night. Maybe that's why she'd been so crisp this morning. It was a lot to organise. And the pressure had to be immense. They'd have to raise a lot of money if they wanted to put Gavin and his car park plans out of the picture.

He sensed someone approaching from behind him. "Well, here she is." He put his arm out and while Esme didn't snuggle close in to him her smile was sincere enough. She was all kitted out in her canine therapy centre winter gear and he was on duty so fair enough. She gave him a little hip bump. "Sorry about earlier."

He looked at her blankly. "What do you mean?"

"Oh, don't be silly. You know I snapped at you."

"I suspect your plate is rather full with the ball tomorrow."

"It is," she agreed, "but that wasn't what I was grumpy about."

"Want to talk about it?"

She scrunched up her nose. "Not really. I was being silly. Imagining things."

"About?"

"Absolutely nothing." She gave his hand a squeeze. "Just…sorry. I don't want there to be anything funny between us, seeing we haven't got much time left." It was all he could do not to pull her into his arms and tell her he was confronting his very worst demon so that maybe they wouldn't have to call it a day. That Christmas, for once, would be the herald of good things to come for both of them.

He followed her eyes as they travelled out to the skating rink. She was watching a middle-aged couple skating along hand in hand. "That's a first date."

"How do you know?"

"He's showing off for her." Her voice took on a dreamy quality. "And the way she's looking at him…it's like she's won the lottery."

Esme was right. The woman was beaming. More so when her beau pulled a bit ahead of her to do a bit of a jazzy move. Judging by his wind-milling arms, it wasn't going to plan. The woman pulled ahead to do her own move. She put her arms out ballerina style, gave a couple of strong strokes of her skate blades and lifted her back leg into a lift when all of the sudden the giggling teens and happy couple collided and became a sprawled mass of bodies in the centre of the rink.

Max was on the ice with his medical bag in seconds. His rubber-soled boots didn't have brilliant traction, but they got him where he needed to be.

Max could hear Esme instructing the rink monitors to clear the other skaters from the ice.

The teens were examining themselves for injuries.

The gentleman was sandwiched between them all as he had tried to fling himself protectively over his girlfriend. When he rolled off, he howled in agony. "My shoulder!"

Max shot a quick glance at his partner, who

looked a bit dazed but was pushing herself up to a seated position. "Can you let me have a look?"

The man stared at him blankly. "Only if you can make it stop."

Max made a quick examination. "You've popped your shoulder out, mate. I don't think your wrist is looking all that brilliant either."

"It's my shoulder that hurts most. Make it stop. Make. It. Stop." The man's breathing was coming in short, sharp huffs as he tried to grapple with the pain. He launched himself forward so that his forehead and shoulder rested on the ice bearing some of his body weight.

"It's not the easiest way to treat you, pal. What do you say we try to—? Oops. Okay. Stay as you are if that helps you to breathe."

Esme appeared beside him. "I've called an ambulance from the hospital up the road. They'll try to get here in twenty minutes or so."

"Brilliant. I should be able to get everyone triaged before they come. Relocate this chap's shoulder, at the very least."

"Anything I can do?"

Max did a quick scan of the group who were still sprawled on the ice. One teen was clutching her elbow. Another had her hand pressed to her forehead with a bit of blood appearing between her fingers. The woman who'd been trying to do a trick move was squeezing her knee into her chest.

He tilted his head towards his medical bag. "Do you mind popping on some gloves and pressing some gauze to that poor girl's forehead? I'll examine her in a second."

"On it."

Esme was swift and efficient. It was a shame vets weren't allowed to treat humans. Esme was every bit as confident with people as she was with animals. So much so he was happy to turn his full attention to the poor bloke and his shoulder, knowing she'd call him if something urgent was required.

"What's your name?"

"John."

"All right, John. It looks like you've dislocated your shoulder and possibly fractured your wrist in your valiant attempt to be a bodyguard for your friend here." Max shot a reassuring look in John's girlfriend's direction.

"That's my wife of over thirty years, I'll have you know!"

"Thirty years?" Max did a quick check on whether or not there was blood flow to John's arm. "What's your secret?"

"Exactly that," John huffed through his pain. "Not having any secrets. Never once told her a lie. Jeanie's my absolute best friend. What she sees is what she gets. Isn't that right, darlin'? Oh— Ow!"

"That's right, lovebird. Nothing but honesty."

Jeanie gingerly pressed herself up to her hands and knees and began to crawl over.

"Hold steady there, John. Just checking for any other breaks or fractures. It looks like it's mostly your shoulder, although that wrist is beginning to swell."

It was important he reduce the shoulder displacement quickly as that would no doubt swell as well. If that swelling were to cut off blood flow to the hand, it wouldn't be a very merry Christmas.

Jeanie crawled across to her husband. "Are you all right, love?"

He tried to sit up and howled in pain.

"I'll take that as a no." She shot Max an anxious look. "It's our wedding anniversary. I was trying to show him how spry and delightful I was still was, even though I'm all wrinkly and grey-haired now."

Max started talking John through the steps they'd need to take to alleviate the pain.

"You're as beautiful as you were the day I met you, darlin'."

"If you can just hold still now, John, I'm going to check your vitals before I administer any pain medication."

"Will it take long? We've got lunch reservations at the pub."

Max smiled. "I'm afraid you'd be best cancelling. I'll pop your shoulder back into place in the next couple of minutes, but you'll need X-rays to make sure there aren't any tears to the musculature and a stabilising sling at the very least."

Esme was back at his side. "What can I do?"

Max glanced at the ice rink as he slipped on the blood-pressure cuff. No one else was there but John and Jeanie.

Esme explained, "My elves helped me escort everyone off the ice. We've got them wrapped in blankets and waiting by the hot chocolate hut. I hope that's all right. I've also put a call in to Lyle. He's had similar medical training to you so can lend a hand if the ambulance gets caught up in traffic or anything."

She was an amazing woman in a crisis. No surprise, given how incredibly calm and methodical she was in her own surgery.

"Doc! You're killing me."

Max glanced down at the blood-pressure cuff that he'd been pumping up. "Sorry, mate. Good news. Your readings are strong. We can administer some morphine sulphate to see if that helps ease the pain. We've also got some nitrous oxide in this kit here if I'm not mistaken. Just need a couple of more checks before we administer anything."

"Please! Anything! No, Jeanie! Don't make me move."

Jeanie had been trying to get him to sit up but the only way he could bear the pain was to put pressure on his shoulder. It looked like he was kowtowing to them all. John's peculiar position meant getting pain medication straight into the shoulder would be impossible. "I'm going to have to inject into your gluteal muscles. Is that all right?"

"I don't care, just do it!"

"Oh, my poor big macho man. Leaping to my rescue like that." Jeannie looked at Esme with tears in her eyes. "Look what a hash I've made of showing off for him. Now his poor lily-white bum— Ooh, Doctor! Be quick about it or he'll get sunburn."

"I'll be fast." Exposing a man's derriere for any length of time on a sunny but very cold winter's day wasn't in anyone's best interest.

Esme was grinning. "Is this your first date?"

"Oh, no," said Jeannie as she stroked her husband's hair. "He's been my man for over thirty years now. We had our very first date here, in fact. On this very day thirty-five years ago. That's why we picked this date for our wedding day."

"I thought it was because you wanted a winter wedding," John said, the painkiller clearly beginning to take effect.

Jeannie batted away the comment with a smile. "It's because of our happy memories here. Of course, it's a bit different now. Why, back in the day…"

Esme kept them talking while Max got himself

into position to do the shoulder reduction. "It all sounds very romantic."

Max laid out a thick wool blanket on the ice. "Right, John, I'm just going to roll you over onto your back here."

After another round of agonised *No* and *Please Stop* and a couple of things not suitable for children, they got him there. Max slipped the face mask onto John that would allow him to breathe in some nitrous oxide. "When you want to take a breath with the nitrous oxide, you press this button here. A few deep breaths and it should help your nervous system relax a bit."

"What if it doesn't?"

Max shot a quick glance at Esme, who was waiting to hand him equipment from his medical kit. "There's stronger stuff, but if we can avoid it, it'd be best."

"You can do it, John," his wife encouraged him. "You'll not want to be on the strong stuff as we've got dinner with the Carmichaels on Christmas Eve, then there's the Boxing Day lunch with the bridge club. Don't forget we're hosting the Hogmanay drinks do—"

John turned to Max, "We might need that extra bit of painkiller if she carries on reminding me of all our social engagements!"

"John, you rascal. You know you love them. Just as much as you love me." She planted a kiss on his cheek as if it settled the matter. Which, apparently, it did as John was visibly more relaxed. "Right, then." Max rubbed his hands together. "Let's get this shoulder back where it belongs."

After manipulating the arm to a ninety-degree angle then gently levering his forearm to the side, he felt the shoulder shift back into place.

"There you are."

"That was it?" John looked at his arm, clearly expecting more.

"'Fraid so, pal. There are more dramatic ways, but this one hurts the least."

"Sounds like the voice of experience."

"Army rugby."

John nodded as if that explained everything. "Our lads play rugby. They've dislocated just about everything that moves!"

"Well, don't try too hard to catch up with them. From the sound of things, you've got a busy Christmas schedule. Want to stay fighting fit for the wife, don't you?"

The silver-haired gent laughed. "That I do, son. Thank you. You've rescued me from a world of pain." After putting his arm in a sling and some ice on his wrist, John allowed himself to be gently helped up and escorted off the ice.

After the ambulance had come, and they'd gone through everything with Lyle Sinclair for the record, the rink opened again. Esme crooked her hand into Max's elbow and grinned up at him. "Fancy a spin?"

"Maybe not today."

"Good answer," she said. "I was thinking we could head into town and see the Living Nativity. Cass is in it and a couple of the lads from the vet clinic."

"I'm not really sure the nativity is my thing." He backpedalled when her smile dropped. *This may not last for ever, but you have it in your power to be kind.* "But if you think it'll be fun, count me in."

Esme could hardly believe how transformed Cluchlochry looked. It was straight out of a fairytale. Glittering lights everywhere. Tasteful decor binding the different shopfronts and buildings together in a harmonious seasonal aesthetic. She didn't think she'd ever seen so many holly and evergreen swags looping from window ledge to window ledge. It was gorgeous.

"So where's this nativity?"

"Just across there on the market square. Oh!" Esme clapped her hands. "Look! Cass is Mary! She told me she was going to be the donkey."

"I would've thought you'd have volunteered Wylie to be the donkey." Max gave Esme's faithful canine companion a scrub on the head.

Esme smiled as Max moved Dougal's lead from one hand to the other so he could hold Esme's hand. He led them all across the square and found a place near the front where they could see the full tableau.

The Living Nativity was just that…a life-sized version of a nativity scene, with local villagers and their livestock standing in for the miniature versions of Jesus, Mary, Joseph, the three kings and, from the look of things, a candlestick maker—a woman Esme recognised from one of the shops who sold all sorts of products to do with bees.

Cass was glowing as Mary. As promised, Lyle had fashioned an old ladder, which wouldn't have looked out of place in a stable, into a perch for Cass so her leg wouldn't hurt. The tableau was only for an hour but even so…as she was still recovering from her injuries sustained during a search and rescue mission at the site of a massive explosion, there was no point in taking risks. Cass was so fiercely independent it was wonderful to see her allowing someone to help. Across the crowd from them Esme could see Flora and Aksel gently steering his daughter and her service dog to the front of the display so Mette could enjoy the new "cast'.

The whole scenario made Esme feel peaceful. Content in a way she'd never felt before.

Just a girl out with her man, looking at the Christmas delights.

See? She *had* been ridiculous this morning, thinking Max was hiding something from her.

Here they were, out in public, and he was more than happy to hold her hand as if they'd been a couple for ever. A warm, swirly, happy heat whirled though her when he popped a scratchy kiss onto her head. It was time to trust again. *Time to love.* She could hardly believe she was thinking it, let alone believing it.

She was in love with Max. Whether or not they could make anything of their relationship remained to be seen, but if this season was about anything it was about having faith. Faith and hope. Believing in the impossible.

"It's amazing, isn't it?" Esme looked up at Max.

"Absolutely. I've never seen anything like it. Do you see, they've even got a few wee early lambs over there?" Max pointed out the furry little beasts whose tails wriggled with delight when their mother was led into the small pen. "They've done a brilliant job."

"Apparently they need someone to stand in for one of the three kings on Christmas Eve. I'm already signed up to be Mary." Esme looked up at Max. "Do you fancy coming back up here after the ball?"

It was a loaded question and, from the look on his face, one Max clearly hadn't expected. She'd actually wanted to ask him up for the whole of Christmas but was so used to being cautious the

Christmas Eve invitation was about as brave as she could get.

"I'll have to check in with the hospital. See what sort of rosters they've put me on."

"Of course," Esme said brightly, quickly turning back towards the nativity. She didn't want Max to see the disappointment in her eyes.

"I did tell Andy I'd like to have a chat with him before I headed back to Glasgow."

"You mean Euan's new bestie? Those two seem inseparable."

"I know, a pair of odd bods, aren't they?"

She almost said you could say the same about the pair of them, but Max started rattling off a list of things he needed to do tonight before he packed up and headed back to Glasgow to dust off his kilt. Not quite the romantic gesture she'd been hoping for, but she'd been the one who'd insisted they bring Wylie and Dougal along to the Live Nativity, even though he'd suggested they leave them behind, so perhaps this was what real relationships were all about. Give and take. Compromise. Balance.

She twisted round so she was facing Max and gave his scarf a little tug. "Sounds good. Shall we head back see if we can rustle up some you and me time tonight?"

He gave her a decidedly wolfish wink. "Absolutely, my dear. Time's awasting."

Chapter 10

Margaret pulled the strings tight and tied off the corset. She looked over Esme's shoulder into the full-length mirror and beamed. "Oh, Esme. You look absolutely *amazing*. You're so lucky your family tartan brings out your blue eyes. Mine makes me look all pale and revolting."

Esme laughed. "It does not. You look beautiful. Green tartan and dark hair? A perfect combination. Besides—" she pointed out the obvious "—you're only wearing the sash and your parents won't be there. You could take it off if you want to. I won't tell if you won't."

Margaret grinned. "I just might do that." Margaret picked up a bit of gingerbread from the remains of Esme's gingerbread castle then sighed as she looked back at Esme. "You look like a blinking princess. Perfect, seeing as you're about to be in the arms of your Prince Alarmingly Charming."

"Don't be ridiculous." Esme swatted at the air between them then gave another little twist in front of the mirror. As silly as it was, for the first time in years she actually cared whether she looked beautiful or not. The setting for the ball had been specifically chosen to match the charity—the Kibble Palace at the Glasgow Botanical Gardens. She knew Max's mum had loved it there and had thought it would be the perfect place to tell Max she loved him. A spray of nervous energy gripped her chest as she silently walked herself through the plan. Host the ball. Give Max his cheque. Then, once all of the madness of the ball was over and done with, she'd say those three perfect words: *I love you.*

Plants to Paws would be saved, so he wouldn't 'need' her any more. His reaction would tell her in an instant whether or not he felt the same way about her as she did about him.

Tendrils of insecurity began to seep into place despite her very best tentions. Despite spending the night together, Max still hadn't brought up whether or not he thought the idea of seeing each other after he headed back to Glasgow was a good idea. He didn't strike her as the type of man who would ghost a girl, but… No.

She stared at her reflection and gave herself a stern frown. Max Kirkpatrick was a gentleman. It could be that he didn't want to see her any more, but there was no chance he'd just up and leave her. A man who kissed a woman the way he'd kissed her when he'd left Heatherglen that morning was a man who would be coming back for more.

Margaret barked a loud and very unladylike laugh. "What are you grinning at?"

"What? I'm not grinning." She was. She was definitely grinning.

"You look like the cat who got the cream. Mind you, I'm perfectly happy, but with a man like Max about to appear in a kilt? I'd be grinning like the Cheshire cat as well."

Esme tried to wipe the smile from her face but couldn't. "He is rather scrummy, isn't he?"

There was a familiar knock on her bedroom door and, as usual, Charles didn't bother waiting for a reply before sticking his head in.

"We could've been naked!" Esme chided.

"Hmm. Well, you aren't." Charles was clearly distracted. So much so she wondered if he would have even noticed if they'd been naked. "You lot ready to head down to Glasgow?"

"Come on. Let's see you in all your finery." Margaret beckoned Charles in. He gave a half-hearted turn in his dress kilt then jangled the keys. "All right, ladies? Your carriage awaits."

"Is it a pumpkin now or is that at the other end of the evening?" Margaret loved winding Charles up. It used to be because of a lifetime crush on him. Now it was just for fun. Being loved up with the local GP did that to a girl. Made her permanently happy. Esme was pretty sure being in love with a Glaswegian A and E doc did exactly the same thing to her.

They both grinned at him.

Charles rolled his eyes.

Poor Charles. Esme hoped he found someone to love, too. Even though hers was still in the baby-steps stage, meeting and falling in love with Max had already filled her with brand-new confidence. It wasn't a pushy, braggart's confidence. It was more…peaceful. Settled. As if love had finally made her whole.

"Where's Max?" Charles scanned the room. "I thought he'd be coming with us."

Esme put on her best casual voice. "He left late this morning. He said he had a couple of meetings in Glasgow so he drove Euan and Fenella back down. I'm sure he'll be there early. He said there was something he wanted to talk to me about, so…"

Charles shot her one of his intense, protective, big brother looks. "What kind of talk?"

Again…that clammy feeling she couldn't quite shake pushed to the fore. "It's probably nothing."

"Like a sparkly diamond engagement ring kind of nothing?" Margaret cackled, and wriggled her fingers dramatically.

"Don't be daft!" Esme shot Margaret a thanks-for-nothing glare. "He was here for Plants to Paws."

"Yeah, right. You keep telling yourself that," Margaret said dryly as she pulled her pashmina from the sofa and wrapped it round her shoulders. "What do you think of Max, Charles?"

"Why?" Charles's big brother mode flicked onto high alert. "What's he done?"

Esme glared at Margaret. She hadn't yet spelled things out to Charles. He was so protective. He still saw her as that messed-up nineteen-year-old, so she had wanted to be crystal clear what was happening with Max before she'd said anything.

She gave Charles an innocent smile. "Nothing beyond looking forward to presenting him with a big fat cheque for his charity tonight."

"I'll bet you're hoping to present a lot more than that," whispered Margaret.

Despite herself, Esme giggled. Charles barely noticed, thank goodness. Margaret started humming "The twelve days of Christmas', which made her giggle even more. That's more like it, Esme thought. Giggly, girly fun in advance of a beautiful Christmas ball. A big brother who was focusing on the right things. Fingers crossed, tonight would be the perfect evening before what could be the perfect Christmas.

"Forgive him."

Max heard his mother's voice as clearly as if she were sitting right there on the bench beside him. In his mind's eye he looked up towards the hospice room where she had spent her last days then readjusted the lavish Christmas wreath with a rueful smile. What a difference a week made. Never mind the castle, the top-rate medical and canine facilities and the Christmas carnival. The only thing—the only *one*—he was impressed with had blue eyes, blonde hair and had pushed at the elasticity of his heart and mind so hard and fast he had no choice but to decide if he was up to changing.

"I know you find it hard to believe, but he loved me in his own way."

Max's heart rate accelerated as an image of his stepfather closing the door on him when he'd returned from his first tour of duty popped into his mind.

"Always remember that the love we share is so much bigger than anything else. It has the power to heal. To lift. To inspire."

His mother's words had been the inspiration behind Plants to Paws. If all went well tonight, the place could virtually run itself from now on so he'd need something new to work on. And for the first time in a long time he looked deep inside himself to get answers.

He needed to forgive Gavin. *Wanted* to forgive him. Unless he let go of all that rage, he was not fit to love. Not properly. He closed his eyes tight and pictured the complexity of feelings he had about Gavin as a grenade. The hurt, the anger, the fear. For well over half his life he'd let Gavin define whether he was a success or a failure. And in Gavin's world success meant money. Power. Failure meant living in a run-down inner-city estate where, no matter how hard you worked or how kind you'd been, you were at the mercy of developers who thought nothing of paving over another man's hopes and dreams.

His mental grenade went incandescent with pent-up fury.

Then he mentally pulled the pin.

Two seconds later?

The sun came out from behind a cloud.

Yes, he was still Max Kirkpatrick. Still an A and E doctor in an inner-city hospital. A soldier who'd served his country. A doctor who'd saved many lives. He was also a man who was in love with a woman who deserved his whole heart. Would letting go of his past be as easy as willing it to be over? He sure as hell hoped so. It was time to get on with his life. Live the future he'd always dreamed of. A future he hoped with every fibre in his being included Esme.

* * *

An entire glitter bomb exploded in Esme's bloodstream when she finally saw Max enter the ballroom.

The man most definitely knew how to wear a kilt. Yum.

As she worked her way through the crowd, thick with Scotland's most generous donors, she was vividly aware that the only person who really mattered to her tonight was Max.

"Hey, you." She touched his arm.

When he turned and saw her, that heated buzz of electricity she now knew she didn't want to live without swept through her. It was time to change her life. Stop hiding out at Heatherglen and finally open the clinic in Glasgow she'd always dreamed of. Margaret and Aksel could run the Heatherglen site. She and Max could forge a life here. It'd be perfect.

Max leant in and kissed her cheek, the moment briefly closing out the rest of the world as she inhaled the scent that was so specific to him. The outdoors. A hit of citrus. Male inner strength.

With his cheek brushing against hers, he whispered, "You look beautiful."

She stepped back and gave a shy little twist in her dress. A nod to her family's tartan, the double skirts were in two shades of blue, the darker of the two rucked up so that the thick satin cornflower blue underskirt was visible as well. The under-bust corset was surprisingly comfortable now that she was used to it. It had been woven by a local woollen mill and showed off the family tartan to full effect. The appreciative look in Max's eyes meant wrestling into the ensemble had been worth the effort.

"Gorgeous, darlin'." He dropped her a wink. "Any chance you'll save a place for me on your dance card?"

They were hardly the words of a man who was about to tell her to take a hike so she crossed her fingers that he had decided they should see each other once the ball was over. Besides, it was Christmas. He couldn't possibly break her heart at Christmas, could he? She gave him a coquettish smile. "If you're lucky, I might even save you two."

Charles came up to them and said something about wanting to introduce Max to someone. She watched as they worked their way through the crowd, wondering...hoping... Charles would see everything in Max she saw. A passionate man committed to making the world a better place despite the way life had kept knocking him down. No matter how many times it had happened, he'd still got back up again.

There was a part of her that was still shy of marriage, but her heart was speaking loud and clear. A life with Max Kirkpatrick would make her a better person. A happier person. Living with fear, not trusting anyone to come too close, never feeling worthy enough to deserve being loved for herself and herself alone...it had depleted her.

With Max she felt like a newborn colt. Better even. Giddy, full of verve and willing to take on a thousand new challenges she would have never considered before she'd met him. A life that, perhaps, stretched beyond the gates of Heatherglen. Perhaps they should start tonight. Maybe, after they'd talked, she'd suggest they spend the night in Glasgow...give her a taste of all that lay ahead of them.

Max nodded and listened as Charles spoke.

"Do you understand what I'm trying to say?"

"Loud and clear." There had been no malice in Charles's words. One could argue it wasn't even personal. He'd explained how far Esme had come. How this was a vulnerable time of year for her. That she was more trusting than she should be. Though Charles hadn't spelled it out, Max understood what Esme's very protective older brother was saying with laser-sharp clarity.

Hurt my sister and you'll have me to answer to. Your best bet is to back off. Now.

Hurting Esme was the last thing on his mind. Being pulled to one side as he had been—being pointedly reminded he was here to receive charitable aid for Plants to Paws and nothing more—was like a sharp knife finding that sweet spot between his ribs. Or, more pointedly, a wrecking ball to his plan to finally open his heart to Esme and say yes, to everything. Yes to dating. Yes to love. Yes to trying to build a future together. He knew it wouldn't be perfect. Not right away anyway. He lived here, she lived at Heatherglen. Neither of them could just drop their lives. But he had shored up enough strength over the past week to admit to her he was flawed, and she hadn't slammed the door in his face. Quite the opposite, in fact.

He looked across to where Esme was talking with Charles and a group of donors. She really was a remarkable woman. She had made all this happen. And she did it every year. Every day if you counted the animal's lives she saved, the humans she empowered with service dogs. How a woman like her could've thought for a second she wasn't worthy of love…

Now was the time to make the call. Was he in or was he out?

He soaked in the beautiful surroundings, the waiters floating about the place with trays of luxurious canapés and delicate crystal flutes of champagne. Charles hadn't said as much—and certainly didn't strike him as the type to judge—but this wasn't Max's world. These were Scotland's movers and shakers. The power people. He was a grassroots man. A guy who rolled up his shirt-sleeves, grabbed a shovel and got stuck in. He gave a mirthless laugh. He was the guy who picked up the poop. Esme deserved someone who wanted more. Pushed harder. Thought bigger.

He was happy where he was. Serving Glasgow's not so finest. It was where he belonged. All of that boiled down to one thing. He would never be the man Esme deserved.

For the next hour or so, no matter how hard Esme tried to make good on that promise to dance with Max, she simply couldn't get anywhere near him. Again and again their eyes caught, but donors were virtually queuing up to talk to him about Plants to Paws. Those who couldn't get to him made a beeline for her. Told her what an inspired idea it was. Wondered if there were ways they could make similar gardens and pet visiting areas outside other hospitals. It made her feel so proud. All the charities she had championed were incredible, but this one had a special place in her heart. Before she'd as much as taken a sip of her champagne they'd surpassed their target. If things continued along these lines, Max would be able to set up ten Plants to Paws. It was truly inspiring.

Once again she sought him out in the crowd. She hoped this would be the proof he needed to finally realise just how valuable, strong and incredible a man he was. She hadn't been blind to his insecurities. To the little boy in him still trying to prove he was worth "investing in'. He didn't only deserve all the money that was pouring in, he deserved every ounce of love she had for him. He probably didn't even know how much he'd helped her. Being here, feeling so confident in front of the media and the donors, she realised Max had helped her reach a place where she was finally able to see Harding MacMillan for what he truly was: a small, conniving, opportunistic man. If he hadn't pulled the wool over her eyes he would've pulled them over someone else's. His actions were a reflection of who he was…not her. And that simple revelation made all the difference.

All too soon it was time for speeches. Esme managed to pull Max away from a group of well-wishers and asked if he was ready to head up to the podium.

"Absolutely, I just…"

There was something off. Something he wasn't telling her.

"Max? Is everything all right?"

"I need to tell you something."

"Miss Ross-Wylde?" The maître d' touched Esme's elbow and pointed towards the stage. "Everyone's glasses are being charged for the toasts."

"Of course." She turned back to Max, whose expression had shifted from agitated to resolute.

As if he'd made a decision and wasn't going to change his mind. "Do you mind if we talk after the speeches?"

Before he could answer she was being ushered up onto the podium.

Esme's speech of thanks to the donors was short but entirely heartfelt. "…in closing, without you this inner-city haven would have been paved over. A car park or a garden? You have spoken loud and clear. Thanks to your generosity, every single one of the Clyde's patients will now have a permanent lifeline to a beautiful garden where they can grow vegetables or flowers, play with their pets, or simply sit and watch the world go by as they go through their journey in hospital." As the audience applauded, she beckoned Max to step up to the podium. Plants to Paws existed because of him. He should be the one in the spotlight.

After making a few heartfelt comments of thanks, Max turned to Esme and raised his glass of champagne. "My biggest thanks, of course, go to this beautiful woman right here. Without her…" His Adam's apple dipped and lifted as he swallowed and started again. "Without her, a young lad's dream to put some good into the world would not have come true. In our time together she has shown me just how strong she is. Which is why I know she will continue to be a beacon of inspiration for all the people she will meet now that our time together has come to an end."

Esme felt as though she'd been hit by a truck. What was he talking about?

He continued, "I would like to propose a toast to a woman who I hope continues her incredible work. I know she will continue to bring change to people's lives. And I would like her to know that I will always remember her and the kindness she has shown Plants to Paws. The patients—"

A loud buzzing started in Esme's ears. *Always remember her?* Was this it? The last night she'd ever see him? She forced herself to tune back in again.

"...with her busy schedule I suspect our paths won't cross again, but she can rest assured that she will always be remembered."

Esme grabbed hold of the podium, the floor no longer feeling stable beneath her feet.

Max was breaking up with her. And though no one here knew it, except perhaps Margaret whose eyes were all but popping out of her head, he was humiliating her in public. Just as Harding had done.

"Ladies and gentlemen, if could you all please charge your glasses and join me in a toast to Esme Ross-Wylde..."

He lifted his glass, took a sip without losing eye contact, then leant in to whisper, "I'm so sorry."

Without waiting for a reply, he gave the crowd a quick wave then left the room.

It didn't make sense. None of it did.

Esme felt as though ice had filled her body. Once more she'd been played. Once more she'd misread a man from the moment she'd met him. Once again her heart was breaking. Only this time she knew she wouldn't be able to put it back together again.

Suddenly, urgently, all she wanted was to be back in her safe haven. Back at Heatherglen with her dogs and her big brother, where she was safe. If she never saw Max Kirkpatrick again it would be too soon.

Chapter 11

Even under heavy attack from enemy fire, Max's heart had never beat faster. He was leaving the woman who was more than likely the love of his life.

Though his flat was miles away, he walked through the Botanical Gardens and back to his neighbourhood to see if it would give him any perspective. A few freezing hours later he was none the wiser.

Defeat weighted his every footstep and when he finally got home, he fell into a restless sleep.

He woke up feeling exhausted and empty. He forced himself out of bed, into the shower then out the door to Plants to Paws. It was where this whole debacle had begun. It was where he'd lay it to rest with a few hours' hard labour.

When he eventually returned home, covered in earth from a few hours of digging and planting some fruit trees one of the patients had brought in, he glanced at the racks of newspapers outside a shop near his flat. There she was, right on the front page. The photographer had captured her perfectly. Beautiful. Capable. Strong.

And he'd just hurt her in the worst way imaginable. In a situation where she couldn't do anything other than paste on a smile and bury her pain.

The self-loathing he felt at that moment was powerful enough to consume him but something rose in him that said, no. Enough. Esme deserved more and he was the man to give her what she wanted. Love. Pure, unconditional, everlasting love.

He raced back through the conversation he'd had with Charles. Had Esme's brother ever told him to back off? No. Had he said he thought Max wasn't a worthy suitor? Quite the opposite. He'd said he respected him. Admired what he did.

Then how the hell had he heard what he had? That he wasn't worthy?

Because it was his biggest fear.

Well, he didn't want to let fear run his life any

more. It had for far too long and today it was going to end.

If Esme decided she didn't want him in her life any more after what he'd done he'd have to take it. But he wasn't going to just let her walk away without letting her know how he really felt.

He dug into his pocket for his car keys and a short while later hit the motorway for Heatherglen.

He loved Esme. More powerfully than he had loved any woman. If his life had taught him anything it was that standing by and doing nothing was the worst course of action. With grim determination he punched an address into his sat-nav and set off on the make-or-break journey.

Esme drew up a dose of anaesthetic and was just about to put it into the IV bag already hooked up to Boopsy the Labrador when Aksel put his hand on her arm to stop her.

Esme stared at the syringe then looked at Aksel. She could only see his eyes thanks to his surgical mask and cap, but he looked alarmed.

"What?" They urgently needed to put the young Lab under after an X-ray had revealed his lethargy and lack of appetite were due to a tennis ball being lodged at the top of his intestines. Proof, if she'd needed any, that having fun came with consequences.

"You've prepared the wrong dosage."

"No, I haven't."

The vet nurse who was with them winced, then showed Esme the dog's chart. "He's only twenty kilos, not forty."

Esme dropped the syringe as if it were on fire.

She'd let herself get so distracted by her emotions she had compromised the poor dog's life.

The roiling ball of fury she'd been wrestling with ever since the ball last night had nearly overshadowed her number one vow: to care for and protect the animals she treated with every ounce of her being.

The nurse picked up the syringe, disposed of the contaminated needle and waited for instructions.

The last thing she wanted to do was harm someone's beloved pet. It was the final surgery of the day. She'd managed to hold things together so far, but endangering a poor, innocent creature because she couldn't focus? Unacceptable. She looked Aksel square in the eye and did something she'd never done before. "Can you do the surgery? I think I need to sit this one out."

He agreed and mercifully didn't go through any ridiculous show of hugging her or asking if she was okay or if she wanted to talk about it. She never, ever wanted to talk about this again.

She tugged on her thickest parka as the snow was falling *yet again*. Normally she'd be thrilled. Snow on Christmas Eve! Today it was just *irri-*

tating. She glanced across at the Christmas carnival. It was all laughter and lights and couples holding hands and looking adoringly into one another's eyes.

She needed a walk with a dog. It was the only medicine that would get her to see straight. Especially as she had the Living Nativity to do tonight. Charles had said he'd ring to cancel for her, but she didn't want her big brother stepping in to fix things for her. She was a grown woman. A grown woman who should be able to deal with the fact she'd let a lying bastard into her heart yet again. From here on out? Total. Nun.

A few metres out from the clinic, Margaret ran out to meet her. "You taking Wylie for a walk?"

That had been the plan but if she admitted that, Margaret would want to come along and that would involve talking.

Wylie took hold of the lead dangling from Esme's hand and tugged it. Margaret knew that meant it was walkies time.

"I'm coming whether or not you want me to," Margaret said.

Esme huffed out a sigh.

Margaret gave her scarf another whirl round her neck and met Esme's speedy pace. "Just so you know, I'm as cross as you are."

Esme wheeled on her. "Cross? You think I'm *cross* with him?" Her fist slammed against her chest. "I trusted him. I opened up my heart to him. I *loved* him."

"Charles? Of course you love Charles."

Esme stopped cold. "What are you talking about?"

Margaret returned her perplexed expression with an equally confused look. "What are *you* talking about?"

"I'm talking about Max leaving the ball without as much as a thank you very much."

Margaret shot a nervous look at the castle. "Did Charles happen to tell you about the little talk he had with Max before the speeches?"

"No."

Margaret's features morphed into a full-on wince. "I thought you knew. That's why I didn't say anything."

"About what?"

Margaret scrunched her forehead, clearly debating whose loyalty to play to.

"Margaret! What did Charles do?

An hour later Charles zipped Esme's fleece up to her throat as if she were a five-year-old. She batted his hands away. If she didn't love him so much she would give him a punch in the nose. If she were that sort of woman. Which she most definitely was not.

He pulled the zip up anyway. "You're sure you want to do this?"

"Of course." She tugged herself free and pulled on the burlap dress the Marys had been wearing. "I promised the nativity committee I would do it. Unlike *some of us*, I do not let people down by telling them one thing then doing another!"

"I didn't realise you liked him in that way!"

"Even a blind person could see I loved him! Surely you were aware of it enough to give him that big brother talk of yours."

"Wait. You love him?" Charles looked dumbfounded.

"Yes," She'd never felt more certain of anything in her life. "I love him, and I want to date him and go on holidays with him and wear silly Christmas jumpers with him. For many years to come, if possible."

A clock chimed on the mantelpiece.

"Are you sure you want to be in the nativity? You're a bit high-strung. Do you think you'll be able to sit still?"

Esme glared at her brother. *Honestly.* "If Mary could ride a donkey to Bethlehem when she was nine months pregnant, I can do an hour in the market square. And then I'm going to get in the car and drive to Glasgow and tell Max I love him."

"You should ring him. It's snowing. The four-by-four hasn't been serviced in—"

"Uh-uh!" She cut him off. "This is something that has to be done face to face. A phone call isn't good enough. Besides, you're the reason I'm in this stupid mess."

"I didn't say anything!" Charles threw up his hands.

"According to Margaret, you told Max I was a fragile little piece of china that deserved the very best life had to offer!"

"Isn't that what a big brother is supposed to say to potential suitors?" Charles looked so bewildered it almost endearing. Almost.

"Don't you get it?"

"Obviously not." He threw up his hands and plopped down on the couch.

"You scared him off! If you tell someone like Max—a man who's been trying to do right by the people he loves—that he isn't good enough—"

"I never told him he wasn't good enough, I just said…" The penny dropped. He scrubbed his face with his hands. "I think I owe Max an apology."

"Good! Then you can come along to Glasgow and dig me out of any ditches if we hit any black ice." Before Charles could protest, she pinned on a bright smile. "Right! Let's get this show on the road."

The crowd round the nativity was especially big. The magic of Christmas Eve had wrapped everyone in its embrace. As it was snowing, it had been decided that rather than take up one of the villagers' very generous offers to let her toddler be the baby Jesus, Dougal was standing in instead as he had a built-in fur coat.

Wylie had on a pair of antlers and was lying with his head in Esme's lap as she knelt by the manger. Charles was one of the three kings. She eventually had to stop looking at him as his eyes were laced with such concern it was about to do her head in. Breaking down in front of the whole of Cluchlochry wasn't part of the plan.

About twenty minutes in, the crowd started murmuring and parting as if they were letting someone through. Her eyes widened as Mrs McCann's shire horse appeared. It was dressed up like a camel one of the three kings might've arrived on. Only…all the kings were there. Charles, Hamish from the clinic and Lyle. Wylie lifted his head and gave a friendly woof. Dougal jumped up in the manger and began wriggling in that happy way he had when he saw someone he knew.

When she looked up and saw who this unexpected arrival was, her heart leapt straight into her throat.

Max.

Her gorgeous, manly, wonderful Max. He was wearing his kilt, which had to be ruddy cold as it was beginning to snow. Big fat flakes fell on her face as she fruitlessly tried to blink away her tears.

He got off the horse and handed the reins to Mrs McCann, who gave him an utterly adoring smile.

What on earth was happening? The last place she'd thought he would've wanted to be was with her.

Wylie, sensing she'd been thrown completely off-kilter, pressed his big furry nose against her thigh.

"I think I owe you an apology," Max said when their eyes met.

Emotion stung at the back of her throat. "I think you might've got that the wrong way round."

His forehead furrowed. "No. I'm pretty sure it's me who needs to apologise for leaving you at the ball."

She shook her head. "And I'm relatively certain I know the reason why that happened."

She heard an uncomfortable cough come from the three kings' corner of the stable. *Charles.*

He stepped forward. "Perhaps you two would like some privacy?"

None of the villagers moved. Esme couldn't help it. She laughed. A real-life Christmas drama! She looked at Max whose face read pretty easily. Yes. Some privacy might be nice. Esme searched out one of the publicans from amongst the crowd. "All right if we nip inside by the fire for a wee bit?"

He nodded and a path was cleared.

Once inside the pub Esme pulled one of Max's big strong hands into hers. "I thought you had just left. I was terrified I'd never see you again."

Max's features softened. "That was definitely one of the plans."

"One of…?"

He tilred his head from side to side. "I had a few."

Esme's chest tightened. *Please, please, please, let one of his plans be with her.*

"The one I like best involves a lot of travel."

Her hands flew to her mouth to stem a host of follow-up questions.

"I went to the Clyde this afternoon and asked them if I could split my shifts between there and the hospital up the road from Heatherglen. I thought… I *hoped* you might be interested in seeing what we had between us might bring if we saw each other a bit more regularly."

Her heart skipped a beat. "What are you saying?"

"I'm saying I love you, Esme. I don't want to stop seeing you. One night away from you with all that insecurity and fear tearing at my heart and…" He folded his hands over his heart. "I don't want to live like that. I'm prepared to fight your brother for your honour if need be."

"Luckily that won't be necessary," Esme assured him, the smile on her face nearly stretching from ear to ear.

"You're the one I'm meant to be with. I will do everything in my power to convince you that I'm the man for you if you'll have me." He went down on one knee, holding both of her hands in his. "You are my heart, my soul and everything I could have imagined that would make me a better man. Please say you'll give me a second chance."

A different kind of tears welled in her eyes. Christmas was meant to be a time of giving. Of opening up one's heart to those you loved, and she loved Max. She'd let fear and her complicated past override what she knew to be true. That she and Max loved each other. She'd fled that ball like a frightened girl. She was a woman now. It was time to start acting like one. She leant forward and kissed Max with every ounce of passion she could muster.

When they started hearing applause coming from the pub windows they both laughed. "Looks like privacy is hard to come by here in Cluchlochry!" Max waved at the crowd, who cheered.

"Would you like to come back to Heatherglen for some hot chocolate? I think we probably need to talk a bit more."

Relief flooded Max's features. "I'd like nothing more."

When he rose and pulled her into his arms for another soft kiss, a chorus of "Ahh…" and a second round of applause cocooned them in the village's heartfelt delight. This, Esme thought as she pressed her hand to Max's chest to feel the cadence of his heartbeat, was where she belonged. With this man who would love her and stand by her side through thick and thin. "What a way to turn round one of the worst Christmas Eves ever," she whispered.

"Just wait until you see what I have in store for Christmas morning," he whispered back in a voice that left little to the imagination.

She slipped her mittened hand into his, rested her head against his shoulder and smiled. Christmas was back exactly to where she'd been hoping to find it. In her heart. She looked up at the sky and sent a special prayer to her family who were no longer with them, knowing that they would be over the moon for her. Letting go of the grief she'd carried all these years would take time but filling that void with love was the very best Christmas gift of all.

After three mugs of hot chocolate and hours of heartfelt conversation, Esme and Max were agreed. Honesty was not only the best policy; it was the *only* policy. Charles had generously volunteered to look after Dougal and Wylie for the night, but when Max and Esme awoke on Christmas morning, Esme sneaked into her brother's room to take them into the sitting room for a yuletide cuddle.

"I think Dougal looks good as a reindeer," Esme insisted as she adjusted the antlers headband she'd perched on top of his little puppy head.

"I think Dougal will do anything to bring a smile to your face." Max pulled her close to him and gave her a kiss. "Which makes two of us."

"Good!" Esme clapped her hands and pulled out a present from behind her back. "Now it's your turn."

Max opened the present and let out a huge laugh. "Seriously? This is what you want me to wear?" He held up the jumper. It was probably the most awful Christmas jumper he'd ever seen in his life. Pom-poms. Blinking reindeer nose. Sequins. Everything that would normally send him running for the hills.

"I had it made specially." Esme fluttered her eyelashes. "You wouldn't want to make me sad by not wearing it, would you?"

Max laughed. "Of course not, darlin'." He pulled it on and held out his arms. "Look good?"

Esme nodded. "Perfect." She pulled another package from under the tree.

"What's that?"

She giggled. "One for me! I knew Charles would never buy one so I got one for all of us."

"You goof."

"I know, I just… I love Christmas so much and after years of trying to pretend I was having a brilliant time, it finally it feels right."

"I hope that's because you are precisely where you belong." Max pulled her to him and gave her a deep kiss. "With me."

"Exactly." Esme grinned. "Now…" She unfurled her own jumper. "What do you think of this?"

"You've never looked more beautiful." Max said dryly.

"And you've never looked more handsome," she quipped. "Shall we take a look in the mirror?"

When they went over to the large gilt mirror hanging above the fireplace they both started giggling. "We look ridiculous," Esme said, barely able to control herself. "Ridiculous and perfect."

Max frowned at their reflection. "There's something missing."

"What?" Esme shot him a panicked look. "You don't have any more secrets up your sleeve, do you?"

Max ruffled her hair and gave her a soft kiss. "No. I am so sorry about everything that happened at the ball. The best-laid plans and all that. It was stupid of me to want to wait until Christmas Eve to tell you. I made a real hash of things, didn't I?"

"Nothing you didn't fix." Esme gave his hands

a reassuring squeeze. "Nothing you can't spend the rest of your days making up for," she said in a much saucier voice.

"In which case…perhaps you'd like to hear my proposal?"

Her cheeks instantly went pink. "Oh, Max, I love you so much, but you know how I feel about that."

"I do," he said, popping a kiss on his finger then transferring it to her nose. "And I respect it. Which is why I was thinking we might do something a little different."

"What kind of different?" She might not want to dive into a white frock anytime soon, but that certainly didn't mean she wanted to try anything too off piste. She was, after all, a traditional romantic at heart.

"This kind of different." He held up his pinkie finger and crooked it. "I want to be your pinkie promise forever man."

She giggled. "Is that even a thing?"

"It is if we make it a thing."

She stilled when she realised he was absolutely serious. "What do we have to say?"

He shrugged. "Nothing formal like wedding vows… Shall I go first?"

She nodded, too choked up with emotion to say anything back.

He crooked his pinkie with hers, looked straight

into her eyes and said, "Esme Ross-Wylde, I love you. You make the world a better place to live in. And one day I'd like to live in it with you by my side."

"One day?"

He laughed softly. "All the days if I'm being completely honest, but… I want to make sure what we have makes you the happiest woman on earth."

"It does." It was out before she could stop it.

"Good." Max dipped his head to kiss her, his lips brushing against hers as he finished. "Then let's take our time. Because all of mine is all of yours. Happy Christmas, love."

"Best. Christmas. Ever."

They sealed the promise with a kiss, knowing in each of their hearts that Christmas would for evermore be the happiest, most blessed day of the year.

Chapter 12

Two years later

"I can't believe it's snowing!"

"I can!" Margaret laughed. "Everything you've wished for since you and Max got engaged has come true. It's like that engagement ring of yours came with magical powers."

"Only the magical power of love," Esme teased. She held up the beautiful seasonal bouquet the florist had crafted for her. It was a bountiful mix of heather, holly berries and scarlet roses, dappled with fronds of spruce with miniature pinecones as seasonal flourishes. "Are you going to be the one to catch this?"

Margaret laughed. "You can count on it."

There was a knock on the door. Charles came in when Esme had made sure it wasn't Max trying to get a sneak peek at the bride.

"How's my wee sister doing on her wedding day?"

"Amazing." She smiled up at him then across to the pictures of her father and Nick. "I wish they could be here."

"They are." Charles gave her a warm smile then pointed to his heart then her own. "They're here with us."

"I still can't believe Mum came home."

"I know! Yet another Christmas miracle!" He laughed and crooked his arm. "Ready to go and meet your groom?"

"More than ever."

When Esme came through the small chapel doors and into the cosy church festooned with garlands, Max could hardly breathe. Two years together and she still took his breath away.

Behind her, bearing the rings, were Dougal and Wylie. Behind them were Margaret and a string of bridesmaids dressed in deep evergreen-coloured dresses. But he only had eyes for Esme. Her eyes glittered with anticipation as she walked past the packed congregation towards the altar. There'd be even more people at the reception. Testament to the respect Esme had garnered in her community and beyond. He could not have been more proud of her than he was at this moment.

When Charles handed Esme's hand to him with a stern but loving reminder to take care of his sister, Max answered solemnly. "I will take care of her until the end of time."

Esme gave his hand a squeeze and smiled up at him. "Are you ready for this?"

"More than ever."

"Do you think they'll let us skip ahead to the kissing the bride bit?" he whispered.

"Don't you worry." Esme's smile grew. "We've got a lifetime of kissing ahead of us."

"In that case…" Max and Esme turned to the minister and nodded. They were ready, hand in hand, to embark on the rest of their lives together, taking a special handful of Christmas magic along with them as they went.

* * * * *